Enid Blyton's

THE MAGIC FARAWAY TREE

MAMMOTH

First published by Newnes 1943
This edition published 1991 by Mammoth
an imprint of Reed International Books Ltd
Michelin House, 81 Fulham Road, London SW3 6RB
and Auckland, Melbourne, Singapore and Toronto

Reprinted 1992 (twice), 1993 (twice), 1994 (four times),
1995 (three times), 1996

ISBN 0 7497 0759 3

A CIP catalogue record for this title
is available from the British Library

Printed and bound in Great Britain
by Cox & Wyman Ltd, Reading, Berkshire

Enid Blyton's

THE MAGIC FARAWAY TREE

"Look!" Dick cried. "There's an enormous white cloud above and around us. Isn't it queer!"

Sure enough, a vast white cloud swam above them – but just near by was a hole right through the cloud!

"That's where we go, up that hole," said Jo. "See that branch that goes up the hole? Come on!"

They all went up the last and topmost branch of the Faraway Tree. It went up and up through the purple hole in the cloud. At the very end of the branch was a little ladder.

Jo climbed the ladder – and suddenly his head poked out into the Land of Topsy-Turvy!

Also by Enid Blyton in Mammoth

Amelia Jane Again!
Amelia Jane Gets into Trouble!
Amelia Jane is Naughty Again!
Naughty Amelia Jane!
Tales of Betsy-May
Billy-Bob Tales
Bimbo and Topsy
The Blue Story Book
The Green Story Book
The Red Story Book
The Yellow Story Book
The Book of Brownies
The Book of Fairies
Family at Red Roofs
The Folk of the Faraway Tree
The Magic Faraway Tree
The Enchanted Wood
The Hidey-Hole
Mr Meddle's Muddles
Mr Meddle's Mischief
Five Minute Tales
Ten Minute Tales
Fifteen Minute Tales
Twenty Minute Tales
Five O'Clock Tales
Six O'Clock Tales
Seven O'Clock Tales
Eight O'Clock Tales
The Adventures of Mr Pink-Whistle
Mr Pink-Whistle Interferes
The Put-Em-Rights
The Saucy Jane Family
The Seaside Family
Snowball the Pony
Those Dreadful Children
The Adventures of the Wishing-Chair
The Wishing-Chair Again

CONTENTS

I

DICK COMES TO STAY

Once upon a time there were three children, Jo, Bessie and Fanny. They lived with their mother and father in a little cottage deep in the country. The girls had to help their mother in the house, and Jo helped his father in the garden.

Now, one day their mother had a letter. She didn't very often have letters, so the children wondered what it was about.

"Listen!" she said. "This is something quite exciting for you. Your cousin Dick is coming to stay with us!"

"Ooh!" said all the children, pleased. Dick was about the same age as Jo. He was a merry boy, rather naughty, and it would be such fun to have him.

"He can sleep with me in my little bedroom!" said Jo. "Oh, Mother, what fun! When is he coming?"

"To-morrow," said Mother. "You girls can put up a little bed for him in Jo's room, and, Jo, you must make room for Dick's things in your cupboard. He is going to stay quite a long time, because his mother is ill and can't look after him."

The three children flew upstairs to get Jo's room ready for Dick as well.

"I say! What will Dick say when we tell him about the Enchanted Wood and the Faraway Tree?" cried Jo.

"And what will he say when we show him our friends there – Silky, and old Moon-Face, and the dear old deaf Saucepan Man, and everyone!" said Bessie.

"He *will* get a surprise!" said Fanny.

They got everything ready for their cousin. They put up a little camp-bed for him, and found some blankets. They put a cushion for a pillow. They made room in Jo's cupboard and chest of drawers for Dick's things. Then they looked out of the window. It looked on to a dark, thick wood, whose trees waved in the wind, not far from the bottom of the garden.

"The Enchanted Wood!" said Bessie softly. "What marvellous adventures we have had there. Maybe Dick will have some, too."

Dick arrived the next day. He came in the carrier's cart, with a small bag of clothes. He jumped down and hugged the children's mother.

"Hallo, Aunt Polly!" he said. "It's good of you to have me. Hallo, Jo! I say, aren't Bessie and Fanny big now? It's lovely to be with you all again."

The children took him up to his room. The girls unpacked his bag and put his things neatly away in the cupboard and the chest. They showed him the bed he was to sleep on.

"I expect I shall find it rather dull here after living in London," said Dick, putting his hair-brushes on the little dressing-table. "It seems so quiet. I shall miss the noise of buses and trams."

"You won't find it dull!" said Jo. "My word,

Dick, we've had more adventures since we've been here than ever we had when we lived in a big town."

"What sort of adventures?" asked Dick in surprise. "It seems such a quiet place that I shouldn't have thought there was even a small adventure to be found!"

The children took Dick to the window. "Look, Dick," said Jo. "Do you see that thick, dark wood over there, backing on to the lane at the bottom of our garden?"

"Yes," said Dick. "It seems quite ordinary to me, except that the leaves of the trees seem a darker green than usual."

"Well, listen, Dick—that's the *Enchanted Wood*!" said Bessie.

Dick's eyes opened wide. He stared at the wood. "You're making fun of me!" he said at last.

"No, we're not," said Fanny. "We mean what we say. Its name is the Enchanted Wood—and it *is* enchanted. And oh, Dick, in the middle of it is the most wonderful tree in the world!"

"What sort of tree?" asked Dick, feeling quite excited.

"It's a simply enormous tree," said Jo. "Its top goes right up to the clouds—and oh, Dick, at the top of it is always some strange land. You can go there by climbing up the top branch of the Faraway Tree, going up a little ladder through a hole in the big cloud that always lies on the top of the tree—and there you are in some peculiar land!"

"I don't think I believe you," said Dick. "You are making it all up."

"Dick! We'll take you there and show you what we mean," said Bessie. "It's all quite true. Oh, Dick, we've had such exciting adventures at the top of the Faraway Tree. We've been to the Rocking Land, and the Birthday Land."

"And the Land of Take-What-You-Want and the Land of the Snowman," said Fanny. "You just can't think how exciting it all is."

"And, Dick, all kinds of queer folk live in the trunk of the Faraway Tree," said Jo. "We've lots of good friends there. We'll take you to them one day. There's a dear little fairy called Silky, because she has such a mass of silky gold hair."

"And there's Moon-Face, with a big round face like the moon! He's a darling!" said Bessie.

"And there's funny old Mister Watzisname," said Fanny.

"What's his real name?" asked Dick in surprise.

"Nobody knows, not even himself," said Jo. "So everyone calls him Mister Watzisname. Oh, and there is the old Saucepan Man. He's always hung around with kettles and saucepans and things, and he's so deaf that he always hears everything wrong."

Dick's eyes began to shine. "Take me there," he begged. "Quick, take me! I can't wait to see all these exciting people."

"We can't go till Mother says she doesn't need us in the house," said Bessie. "But we *will* take you – of course we will."

"And, Dick, there's a slippery slip, a slide that goes right down the inside of the tree from the top to the bottom," said Fanny. "It belongs to Moon-Face. He lends people cushions to slide down on."

"I do want to go down that slide," said Dick, getting terribly impatient. "Why do you tell me all these things if you can't take me to see them now? I'll never be able to sleep to-night! Good gracious! My head feels in a whirl already to think of the Faraway Tree and Moon-Face and Silky and the slippery-slip."

"Dick, we'll take you as soon as ever we can," promised Jo. "There's no hurry. The Faraway

Tree is always there. We never, never know what land is going to be at the top. We have to be very careful sometimes because there might be a dangerous land—one that we couldn't get away from!"

A voice came from downstairs. "Children! Are you going to stay up all the day? I suppose you don't want any tea? What a pity—because I have made some scones for you and put out some strawberry jam!"

Four children raced down the stairs. Scones and strawberry jam! Gracious, they weren't going to miss those. Good old Mother—she was always thinking of some nice little treat for them.

"Jo, Father wants you to dig up some potatoes for him after tea," said Mother. "Dick can help you. And, Bessie and Fanny, I want you to finish my ironing for me, because I have to take some mended clothes to Mrs. Harris, and she lives such a long way away."

The children had been rather hoping to go out and take Dick to the Enchanted Wood. They looked disappointed. But they said nothing, because they knew that in a family everyone had to help when they could.

Mother saw their disappointed faces and smiled. "I suppose you want to take Dick to see those peculiar friends of yours," she said. "Well now, listen—if you are good children to-day, and do the jobs you have to do, I'll give you a whole day's holiday to-morrow! Then you may take your dinner and your tea and go to visit any friends you like. How would you like that?"

"Oh, Mother, thank you!" cried the children in delight.

"A whole day!" said Bessie. "Why, Dick, we can show you everything!"

"And maybe let you peep into whatever land is at the top of the Faraway Tree," whispered Fanny. "Oh, what fun!"

So they did their work well after tea and looked forward to the next day. Dick dug hard, and Jo was pleased with him. It was going to be fun to have a cousin with them, able to work and play and enjoy everything, too!

When they went to bed that night they left the doors of their rooms open so that they might call to one another.

"Sleep well, Dick!" called Bessie. "I hope it's fine to-morrow! What fun we shall have!"

"Good night, Bessie!" called back Dick. "I can't tell you how I'm longing for to-morrow. I know I shan't be able to sleep to-night!"

But he did—and so did all the others. When Mother came up at ten o'clock she peeped in at the children, and not one was awake.

Jo woke first next day. He sat up and looked out of the window. The sun streamed in, warm and bright. Jo's heart jumped for joy. He leaned over to Dick's bed and shook him.

"Wake up!" he said. "It's to-morrow now—and we're going to the Enchanted Wood!"

II

OFF TO THE ENCHANTED WOOD

The children ate their breakfast quickly. Mother told Bessie and Fanny to cut sandwiches for themselves and to take a small chocolate cake from the larder.

"You can take a packet of biscuits, too," she said, "and there are apples in that dish over there. If you are hungry when you come home to-night I will bake you some potatoes in the oven, and you can eat them in their skins with salt and butter."

"Oooh, Mother – we *shall* be hungry!" said Jo at once. "Hurry up with those sandwiches, Bessie and Fanny. We want to start off as soon as possible."

"Now don't be too late home, or I shall worry," said Mother. "Look after your cousin, Jo."

"Yes, I will," promised Jo.

At last everything was ready. Jo packed the food into a leather bag and slung it over his shoulder. Then the four of them set off to the Enchanted Wood.

It didn't take them long to get there. A narrow ditch was between the lane and the wood.

"You've got to jump over the ditch, Dick," said Jo. They all jumped over. Dick stood still when he was in the wood.

"What a strange noise the leaves of the trees make," he said. "It's as if they were talking to one another – telling secrets."

"Wisha, wisha, wisha, wisha," whispered the trees.

"They *are* talking secrets," said Bessie. "And do you know, Dick—if the trees have any message for us, we can hear it by pressing our left ears to the trunks of the trees! Then we *really* hear what they say."

"Wisha-wisha-wisha-wisha," said the trees.

"Come on," said Jo impatiently. "Let's go to the Faraway Tree."

They all went on—and soon came to the queer magic tree. Dick stared at it in the greatest astonishment.

"Why, it's simply ENORMOUS!" he said. "I've never seen such a big tree in my life. And you can't possibly see the top. Goodness gracious! What kind of tree is it? It's got oak leaves, and yet it doesn't really seem like an oak."

"It's a funny tree," said Bessie. "It may grow acorns and oak leaves for a little way—and then suddenly you notice that it's growing plums. Then another day it may grow apples or pears. You just never know. But it's all very exciting."

"How do you climb it?" asked Dick. "In the ordinary way?"

"Well, we will to-day," said Jo, "because we want to show you our friends who live inside the tree. But sometimes there's a rope that is let down the tree, and we can go up quickly with the help of that. Or sometimes Moon-Face lets down a cushion on the end of a rope and then pulls us up one by one."

He swung himself up into the tree, and the others followed. After a bit Dick gave a shout. "I say! It's most extraordinary! This tree is growing nuts now! Look!"

Sure enough it was. Dick picked some and cracked them. They were hazel nuts, ripe and sweet. Everyone had some and enjoyed them.

Now when they had all got very high up indeed, Dick was most surprised to see a little window in the trunk of the Faraway Tree.

"Goodness—does somebody live just here?" he called to the others. "Look—there's a window here. I'm going to peep in."

"You'd better not!" shouted Jo. "The Angry Pixie lives there, and he hates people peeping in."

But Dick felt so curious that he just *had* to peep in. The Angry Pixie was at home. He was filling his kettle with water, when he looked up and saw Dick's surprised face at his window. Nothing made the pixie so angry as to see people looking at him. He rushed to the window at once and flung it open.

"Peeping again!" he shouted. "It's too bad! All day and night people come peeping. Take that!"

He emptied the kettle of water all over poor Dick. Then he slammed his window and drew the curtains across. Jo, Bessie and Fanny couldn't help laughing.

"I told you not to peep in at the Angry Pixie," said Jo, wiping Dick with his hanky. "He's nearly always in a bad temper. Oh, and by the way, Dick,

I must warn you about something else. There's an old woman who lives high up in the tree who is always washing. She empties the water down the tree, and it comes slish-sloshing down. You'll have to look out for that or you'll get wet."

Dick looked up the tree as if he half expected the water to come tumbling down at once.

"Come on," said Bessie. "We'll come to where the Owl lives soon. He's a friend of Silky's, and sometimes brings us notes from her."

The owl was fast asleep. He usually only woke up at night-time. Dick peered in at his window and saw the big owl asleep on a bed. He couldn't help laughing.

"I *am* enjoying all this," he said to Fanny. "It's quite an adventure."

The children climbed higher, and came to a broad branch. "There's a dear little yellow door, with a knocker and a bell!" cried Dick in surprise, staring at the door set neatly in the trunk of the tree. "Who lives there?"

"Our friend Silky," said Jo. "Ring the bell and she'll open the door."

Dick rang the little bell and heard it go ting-a-ling inside. Footsteps pattered to the door. It opened, and a pretty little elf looked out. Her hair hung round her face like a golden mist.

"Hallo, Silky!" cried Jo. "We've come to see you—and we've brought our cousin, Dick, who has come to live with us. He's having a lovely time exploring the Faraway Tree."

"How do you do, Dick?" said Silky, holding out

her small hand. Dick shook hands shyly. He thought Silky was the loveliest creature he had ever seen.

"I'll come with you if you are going to visit Moon-Face," said Silky. "I want to borrow some jam from him. I'll take some Pop Biscuits with me, and we'll have them in Moon-Face's house."

"Whatever are Pop Biscuits?" asked Dick, in surprise.

"Wait and see!" said Jo with a grin.

They all went up the tree again. Soon they heard a funny noise. "That's old Mister Watzisname snoring," said Jo. "Look—there he is!"

Sure enough, there he was, sitting in a comfortable chair, his hands folded over his big tummy, and his mouth wide open.

"How I'd love to pop something into his open mouth!" said Dick at once.

"Yes, that's what everybody feels," said Jo. "Moon-Face and Silky once popped some acorns in—didn't you, Silky? And Watzisname was very angry. He threw Moon-Face up through the hole in the cloud, and landed him into the strange country there."

"Where's the old Saucepan Man?" asked Bessie. "He is usually with his friend, Mister Watzisname."

"I expect he has gone to see Moon-Face," said Silky. "Come on. We'll soon be there."

As they went up the tree, Silky suddenly stopped. "Listen," she said. They all listened. They heard a curious noise—"slishy-sloshy-slishy-sloshy"—coming nearer and nearer.

"It's Dame Washalot's dirty water coming!" yelled Jo. "Get under a branch, everyone."

Dick wasn't as quick as the others. They all hid under big boughs—but poor old Dick wasn't quite under his when the water came pouring down the tree. It tumbled on to his head and went down his neck. Dick was very angry. The others were sorry, but they thought it was very funny, too.

"Next time I climb this tree I'll wear a bathing-dress," said Dick, trying to wipe himself dry. "Really, I think somebody ought to stop Dame Washalot pouring her water away like that. How disgusting!"

"Oh, you'll soon get used to it, and dodge the water easily," said Jo. On they all went up the tree again, and at last came almost to the top. There they saw a door in the trunk of the tree, and from behind the door came the sound of voices.

"That's Moon-Face and the old Saucepan Man," said Jo, and he banged on the door. It flew open and Moon-Face looked out. His big round face beamed with smiles when he saw who his visitors were.

"Hallo, hallo, hallo," he said. "Come along in. The Saucepan Man is here."

Everyone went into Moon-Face's curious round room. There was a large hole in the middle of it, which was the beginning of the slippery-slip, the wonderful slide that went round and round down the inside of the tree, right to the bottom. Moon-Face's furniture was arranged round the inside of the tree trunk, and it was all curved to fit the curve of the tree. His bed was curved, the chairs were curved, the sofa and the stove. It was very queer.

Dick stared at it all in the greatest surprise. He really felt as if he must be in a dream. He saw somebody very queer sitting on the sofa.

It was the old Saucepan Man. He really was a very curious sight. He was hung all round with saucepans and kettles, and he wore a saucepan for a hat. You could hardly see anything of him except his face, hands and feet, because he was so hung about with saucepans and things. He made a tremendous clatter whenever he moved.

"Who's that?" he said, looking at Dick.

"This is Dick," said Jo, and Dick went forward to shake hands.

The Saucepan Man was very deaf, though he did sometimes hear quite well. But he nearly always heard everything wrong, and sometimes he was very funny.

"Chick?" he said. "Well, that's a funny name for a boy."

"Not Chick, but DICK!" shouted Moon-Face.

"Stick?" said the Saucepan Man, shaking hands. "Good morning, Stick. I hope you are well."

Dick giggled. Moon-Face got ready to shout again, but Silky quickly handed him her bag of Pop Biscuits. "Don't get cross with him," she said. "Look—let's all have some Pop Biscuits. They are fresh made to-day. And, oh, Moon-Face, do tell us—what land is at the top of the Faraway Tree to-day?"

"The Land of Topsy-Turvy," said Moon-Face. "But I don't advise you to go there. It's most uncomfortable."

"Oh, do let's," cried Dick. "Can't we just *peep* at it?"

"We'll see," said Jo, giving him a Pop Biscuit. "Eat this, Dick."

Pop Biscuits were lovely. Dick put one in his mouth and bit it. It went pop! at once—and he found his mouth full of sweet honey from the middle of the biscuit.

"Delicious!" he said. "I'll have another. I say, Jo—DO let's take our lunch up into the land of Topsy-Turvy. Oh, do, do!"

III

THE LAND OF TOPSY-TURVY

"What is Topsy-Turvy Land like?" asked Jo, taking another Pop Biscuit.

"Never been there," said Moon-Face. "But I should think it's quite safe, really. It's only just come there, so it should stay for a while. We could go up and see what it's like and come down again if we don't like it. Silky and I and Saucepan will come with you, if you like."

Moon-Face turned to the Saucepan Man, who was enjoying his fifth Pop Biscuit.

"Saucepan, we're going up the ladder," he said. "Are you coming?"

"Humming?" said Saucepan, looking all round as if he thought there might be bees about. "No, I didn't hear any humming."

"I said, are you COMING?" said Moon-Face.

"Oh, *coming*!" said Saucepan. "Of course I'm coming. Are we going to take our lunch?"

"Yes," said Moon-Face, going to a curved door that opened on to a tiny larder. "I'll see what I've got. Tomatoes. Plums. Ginger snaps. Ginger beer. I'll bring them all."

He put them into a basket. Then they all went out of the funny, curved room on to the big branch outside. Moon-Face shut his door.

Jo led the way up to the very top of the Faraway Tree. Then suddenly Dick gave a shout of astonishment.

"Look!" he cried. "There's an enormous white cloud above and around us. Isn't it queer!"

Sure enough, a vast white cloud swam above them—but just near by was a hole right through the cloud!

"That's where we go, up that hole," said Jo. "See that branch that goes up the hole? Come on!"

They all went up the last and topmost branch of the Faraway Tree. It went up and up through the purple hole in the cloud. At the very end of the branch was a little ladder.

Jo climbed the ladder—and suddenly his head poked out into the Land of Topsy-Turvy!

Then one by one all the others followed—and soon all seven of them stood in the curious land.

Dick was not as used to strange lands as were

the others. He stood and stared, with his eyes so wide open that it really seemed as if they were going to drop out of his head!

And, indeed, it was a strange sight he saw. Every house was upside down, and stood on its chimneys. The trees were upside down, their heads buried in the ground and their roots in the air. And, dear me, the people walked upside-down, too!

"They are walking on their hands, with their legs in the air!" said Jo. "Goodness, what a queer thing to do!"

Everyone stared at the folk of Topsy-Turvy Land. They got along very quickly on their hands, and often stopped to talk to one another, chattering busily. Some of them had been shopping, and carried their baskets on one foot.

"Let's go and peep inside a house and see what it's like, all topsy-turvy," said Jo. So they set off to the nearest house. It looked most peculiar standing on its chimneys. No smoke came out of them—but smoke came out of a window near the top.

"How do we get in?" said Bessie. They watched a Topsy-Turvy man walk on his hands to another house. He jumped in at the nearest window, going up a ladder first.

The children looked for the ladder that entered the house they were near. They soon found it. They went up it to a window and peeped inside.

"Gracious!" said Jo. "Everything really *is* upside down in it—the chairs and tables, and everything. How uncomfortable it must be!"

An old lady was inside the house. She was sitting upside down in an upside-down chair and looked very peculiar. She was angry when she saw the children peeping in.

She clapped her hands, and a tall man, walking on his hands, came running in from the next room.

"Send those rude children away," shouted the old woman. The tall man hurried to the window on his hands, and the children quickly slid down the ladder, for the man looked rather fierce.

"It's a silly land, I think," said Jo. "I vote we just have our lunch and then leave this place. I wonder why everything is topsy-turvy."

"Oh, a spell was put on everything and everybody," said Moon-Face, "and in a trice everything was topsy-turvy. Look—wouldn't that be a good place to sit and eat our lunch in?"

It was under a big oak tree whose roots stood high in the air. Jo and Moon-Face set out the lunch. It looked very good.

"There's plenty for everybody," said Jo. "Have a sandwich, Silky?"

"Saucepan, have a plum?"

"Crumb?" said Saucepan, in surprise. "Is that all you can spare for me—a crumb?"

"PLUM, PLUM, PLUM!" said Moon-Face, pushing a ripe one into the Saucepan Man's hands.

"Oh, *plum*," said Saucepan. "Well, why didn't you say so?"

Everybody giggled. They all set to work to eat a good lunch.

In the middle of it, Jo happened to look round, and he saw something surprising.

It was a policeman coming along, walking on his hands, of course.

"Look what's coming," said Jo with a laugh. Everyone looked. Moon-Face went pale.

"I don't like the look of him," he said. "Suppose he's come to lock us up for something? We couldn't get away down the Faraway Tree before this land swung away from the top!"

The policeman came right up to the little crowd under the tree.

"Why aren't you Topsy-Turvy?" he asked in a stern voice. "Don't you know that the rule in this land is that everything and everyone has to be upside-down?"

"Yes, but we don't belong to this silly land," said Jo. "And if you were sensible, you'd make another rule, saying that everybody must be the right way up. You've just no idea how silly you look, policeman, walking on your hands!"

The policeman went red with anger. He took a sort of stick from his belt and tapped Jo on the head with it.

"Topsy-Turvy!" he said. "Topsy-Turvy!"

And to Jo's horror he had to turn himself upside-down at once! The others stared at poor Jo, standing on his hands, his legs in the air.

"Oh, golly!" cried Jo. "I can't eat anything properly now because I need my hands to walk with. Policeman, put me right again."

"You *are* right now," said the policeman, and walked solemnly away on his hands.

"Put Jo the right way up," said Dick. So everyone tried to get him over so that he was the right way up again. But as soon as they got his legs down and his head up, he turned topsy-turvy again. He just couldn't help it, for he was under a spell.

A group of Topsy-Turvy people came to watch. They laughed loudly. "Now he belongs to Topsy-Turvy Land!" they cried. "He'll have to stay here with us. Never mind, boy—you'll soon get used to it!"

"Take me back to the Faraway Tree," begged Jo, afraid that he really and truly *might* be made to stay in this queer land. "Hurry!"

Everyone jumped to their feet. They helped Jo along to where the hole ran down through the cloud. He wasn't used to walking on his hands and he kept falling over. They tried their best to make him stand upright, but he couldn't. The spell wouldn't let him.

"It will be difficult to get him down through the hole," said Dick. "Look—there it is. I'd better go down first and see if I can help him. You others push him through as carefully as you can. He'll have to go upside down, I'm afraid."

It was very difficult to get Jo through the hole, because his hands and head had to go first. Moon-Face held his legs to guide him. Dick held his shoulders as he came down the ladder, so that he wouldn't fall.

At last they were all seven through the hole in the clouds, and were on the broad branch outside Moon-Face's house. Jo held on to the branch with his hands, his legs were in the air.

"Moon-Face! Silky! Can't you possibly take this spell away?" groaned he. "It's dreadful."

"Silky, what land is coming to the top of the Faraway Tree next?" asked Moon-Face. "Have you heard?"

"I think it's the Land of Spells," said Silky. "It should come to-morrow. But I'm not really sure."

"Oh, well, if it's the Land of Spells, we could easily get a spell from there to put Jo right," said Moon-Face, beaming. "Jo, you must stay the night with me and wait for the Land of Spells tomorrow. The others can go home and tell what has happened."

"All right," said Jo. "I can't possibly climb up the tree again if I'm upside down—so I'll just have to wait here. Mother will never believe it, though, when the others tell her why I don't go home. Still, it can't be helped."

They all went into Moon-Face's house. Jo stood on a chair, upside down. The others sat about and talked. Dick was sorry for Jo, but he couldn't help feeling a bit excited. Goodness—if this was the sort of adventure that Jo, Bessie and Fanny had, what fun things were going to be!

The others began telling him all the adventures they had had. Silky made some tea, and went down the tree to fetch some more Pop Biscuits. When it was half-past five Bessie said they must go.

"Good-bye, Jo," she said. "Don't be too unhappy. Pretend you are a bat—they always sleep upside down, you know, and don't mind a bit! Come on, Dick—we're going down the slippery-slip!"

Dick *was* excited. He took the red cushion that Moon-Face gave him and sat himself at the top of the slide. Bessie gave him a push.

And off he went, round and round the inside of the enormous Faraway Tree, sitting safely on his cushion. *What* a way to get down a tree!

IV

THE LAND OF SPELLS

Dick shot round down the inside of the Faraway Tree on his cushion. He came to the bottom. He shot out of the trap-door there, and landed on the soft green moss. He sat there for a moment, out of breath.

"That's the loveliest slide I've ever had!" he thought to himself. "O-o-oh – wouldn't I like to do that again!"

He had just got up from the moss when the trap-door at the bottom of the tree opened once again, and Fanny shot out on a yellow cushion. Then came Bessie, giggling, for she always thought it was a huge joke to slide down inside the tree like that.

"What do we do with the cushions?" asked Dick. "Does Moon-Face want them back?"

"Yes, he does," said Fanny, picking them up. "The red squirrel always collects them and sends them back to him."

As she spoke, a red squirrel, dressed in a jersey, popped out of a hole in the trunk.

"Here are the cushions," said Fanny, and the squirrel took them. He looked up into the tree, and a rope came swinging down.

"Moon-Face always lets it down for his cushions," said Bessie. Dick watched the squirrel tie the three cushions to the rope end. Then he gave three gentle tugs at the rope, and at once the rope was pulled up, and the cushions went swinging up the tree to Moon-Face.

"I wish Jo was with us," said Dick, as they all went home. "Do you suppose Aunt Polly will be worried about him?"

"Well, we'll have to tell Mother," said Fanny. "She is sure to ask where he is."

Mother did ask, of course, and the girls told her what had happened.

"I find all this very difficult to believe," said Mother, astonished. "I think Jo is just spending the night with Moon-Face for a treat. Well, he certainly must come back to-morrow, for there is work for him to do."

Nobody said any more. The girls and Dick felt very tired, and after some hot cocoa and potatoes cooked in their jackets for supper, they all went to bed. Bessie wondered how Jo was getting on at Moon-Face's.

He was getting on all right, though he was very tired of being upside down. It didn't matter how hard he tried to get the right way up, he always swung back topsy-turvy again. The policeman had put a very strong spell on him!

"You had better try to sleep in my bed," said Moon-Face. "I'll sleep on my sofa."

"I suppose I'll have to stand on my head all night," said poor Jo. And that's just what he did have to do. It was most uncomfortable.

Once he lost his balance when he was asleep, and tipped off the bed. He almost fell down the slippery-slip, but Moon-Face, who was awake, reached out a hand and caught his leg just in time.

"Gracious!" said Moon-Face. "Don't go doing things like this in the middle of the night, Jo. It's most upsetting."

"Well, how can I help it?" said Jo.

"I'll tie your feet to a nail on my wall," said Moon-Face. "Then you can't topple over when you are asleep."

So he did that, and Jo didn't fall down any more. When morning came he was most astonished to find himself upside-down, for at first he didn't remember what had happened.

"I'll just peep up through the hole in the cloud and see if by any chance the Land of Spells is there yet," said Moon-Face. "If it is, we'll go up and see what we can do for you."

So off he went up the little ladder and popped his head out of the hole in the cloud to see if the Land of Topsy-Turvy was still there, or if it had gone.

There was nothing there at all—only just the big white cloud, moving about like a thick mist. Moon-Face slipped down the ladder again.

"Topsy-Turvy has gone, but the next land hasn't come yet," he said. "We'll have breakfast and then I'll look again. Hallo—here's Silky. Stay and have breakfast, Silky darling."

"I came up to see how Jo was," said Silky. "Yes, I'd love to have breakfast. It's funny to watch Jo eating upside down. Hasn't the Land of Spells come yet?"

"Not yet," said Moon-Face, putting a kettle on

his stove to boil. "There's nothing there at all. But Topsy-Turvy is gone, thank goodness!"

They all had breakfast. Moon-Face cooked some porridge. "What do you want on your porridge?" he asked Jo. "Treacle – sugar – cream?"

Jo couldn't see any treacle, sugar or cream on the table. "Treacle," he said, "please, Moon-Face." Moon-Face handed him a small jug that seemed to be quite empty.

"Treacle!" he said to the jug in a firm voice. And treacle came pouring out as soon as Jo tipped up the jug. Silky wanted cream – and cream came out when Moon-Face said "Cream!" to the jug. It was great fun.

Moon-Face went again to see if the Land of Spells had come. This time he came back excited.

"It's there!" he said. "Come on! I'd better take some money with me, I think, in case we have to buy the spell we want."

He took a big purse down from a shelf, and then he and Silky helped Jo to walk upside down up the branch that led through the hole in the cloud to the little ladder. Up he went with great difficulty, holding on tightly to the rungs of the ladder with his hands. At last he was up in the Land of Spells.

This land was like a big market-place. In it were all kinds of curious little shops and stalls. All kinds of people sold spells. In some of the shops sat tall wizards, famous for magic. In some of them were green-eyed witches, making spells as fast as they could. Outside, in the market-place, sat all kinds of fairy folk at their stalls –

pixies, gnomes, goblins, elves—all crying their wares at the tops of their high voices.

"Spell to make a crooked nose straight!" cried one pixie, rattling a yellow box in which were magic pills.

"Spell to grow blue daffodils!" cried a gnome, showing a bottle of blue juice.

"Spell to make cats sing!" cried another gnome. Jo could hardly believe his ears. How queer! Who would want to make cats sing?

"Now, we must just see if we can possibly find a spell to make you stand up straight again," said Moon-Face, and he went into a little low shop in which sat a strange goblin.

The goblin had blue, pointed cars, and his eyes sparkled as if they had fireworks in them.

"I want a spell," said Moon-Face.

"What for?" asked the goblin. "I've a spell for everything under the sun in my shop! Very powerful spells too, some of them. Would you like a spell to send you travelling straight off to the moon?"

"Oh, no, thank you," said Moon-Face at once. "I know I look like the man in the moon, with my big round face—but I'm nothing at all to do with the moon really."

"Well, would you like a spell to make you as tall as a giant?" said the goblin, picking up a box and opening it. He showed Moon-Face a large blue pill inside. "Now, take that pill, and you'll shoot up as high as a house! You'll feel fine. It only costs one piece of gold."

"No, thank you," said Moon-Face. "If I grew as big as that I'd never get down the hole in the cloud back to the Faraway Tree. And if I did, I'd never be able to get in at the door of my tree-house. I don't want silly spells like that."

"Silly!" cried the goblin, in a rage. "You call my marvellous spells silly! Another word from you, stupid old Round-Face, and I'll use a spell that will turn you into a big bouncing ball!"

Silky pulled Moon-Face out of the shop quickly. She was quite white. "Moon-Face, you know you shouldn't make these people cross," she whispered. "Why, you may find yourself nothing but a bouncing ball, or a black beetle, or something, if you are rude to them. For goodness' sake, let *me* ask for the spell we want. Look—here's a bigger shop—with a nice-looking witch inside."

They all went in. The witch was knitting stockings from the green smoke that came from her fire. It was marvellous to watch her. Jo wished he wasn't upside-down so that he might see her properly.

"Good morning," said the witch. "Do you want a spell?"

"Yes, please," said Silky in her most polite voice. "We want to make our friend Jo come the right way up again."

"That's easy," said the witch, her green eyes looking in a kindly way at poor Jo. "I've only got to rub a Walking-Spell on to the soles of his feet—and he will be all right. The Walking-Spell will make his feet want to walk—and he will have to stand up the right way to walk on them—so he will be cured. Come here, boy!"

Jo walked over to the witch on his hands. She took down a jar from a shelf and opened it. It was full of purple ointment. The witch rubbed some on to the soles of Jo's shoes.

"Rimminy-Romminy-Reet,
Stand on your own two feet!
Rimminy-Romminy-Ro,
The right way up you must go!"

And, of course, you can guess what happened! Jo swung right over, stood on his two feet again, and there he was, as upright as Moon-Face and Silky. Wasn't he glad!

V

SAUCEPAN MAKES A MUDDLE

Jo, Silky and Moon-Face were so very pleased that Jo was the right way up again.

"It feels funny," said Jo. "I feel quite giddy the right way up after standing upside-down for so long. Thank you, witch. How much is the spell?"

"One piece of gold," said the witch. Moon-Face put his hand into his large purse. He brought out a piece of gold. The witch threw it into the fire, and at once bright golden smoke came out. She took up her knitting-needles and began to knit the yellow smoke into the stockings she was making.

"I wanted a yellow pattern," she said, pleased. "Your piece of gold came just at the right moment."

"Golly, this is a very magic land, isn't it?" said Jo, as the three of them walked out of the queer shop. "Fancy knitting stockings out of smoke! Don't let's go home yet, Moon-Face. I want to see a few more things."

"All right," said Moon-Face, who wanted to explore a bit, too. "Come on. I say, look at the gnome who is selling a spell to make cats sing! Somebody has brought his cat to him – I wonder if the spell will really work!"

The servant of a witch had brought along a big black cat. He handed the gnome two silver pieces of money. The gnome took the cat on his knee. He opened its mouth and looked down it. Then he took a silver whistle and blew a tune softly down the cat's pink throat. The cat swallowed once or twice and then jumped off the gnome's knee.

"Will it sing now?" asked the witch's servant. "I daren't go back to my mistress unless it does."

"It will sing whenever you pull its tail," said the gnome, turning to another customer.

The witch's servant went off with the cat following behind. Jo took hold of Moon-Face's arm and whispered to him:

"I'm going to pull the cat's tail. I do SO want to hear if it really will sing!"

Moon-Face and Silky wanted to as well. They giggled to see Jo running softly after the big black cat. He took hold of its tail. He gave it a gentle pull.

And then, oh, what a peculiar thing! The cat stopped, lifted up its head, and sang in a very deep man's voice:

"Oh, once my whiskers grew so long
I had to have a shave!
The barber said: 'It's not the way
For whiskers to behave,
If you're not careful, my dear cat,
They'll grow into a beard,
And then a billy-goat you'll be,
Or something very weird!'

"Oh, once my tail became so short
It hadn't got a wag,
The grocer said . . ."

But what the grocer said about the cat's short tail nobody ever knew. The servant of the witch turned round in surprise when he heard the cat singing, for he knew that he hadn't pulled the cat's tail. He saw Jo and the others grinning away near by, and he was very angry.

"How dare you use up the cat's singing!" he cried. "You wait till I tell the witch. She'll be after you. And *you* won't sing if she catches you!"

"Quick! Run!" said Moon-Face. "If he does fetch the witch we'll get into trouble."

So they ran away fast, and were soon out of

sight of the cat and the servant. They sank down under a tree, laughing.

"Oh, dear! That cat did sing a funny song!" said Jo, wiping his eyes. "And what a lovely deep voice it had. Do you suppose its whiskers really did grow very long?"

Just then the three heard a loud noise coming along: "Clankily-clank, rattle, bang, crash!"

"The Saucepan Man!" they all cried. "He's come up here, too!"

And sure enough, it *was* old Saucepan, grinning all over his funny face. He had so many kettles and saucepans on that day that nothing could be seen of him except his face and his feet.

"Hallo, hallo!" he said. "I guessed you were up here. Been having fun?"

"Yes," said Jo. "I'm all right again—look! It's so nice to walk the proper way up again. And oh, Saucepan, we've just heard a cat sing!"

Saucepan actually heard what Joe said—but he couldn't believe that he had heard right, so he put his hand behind his ear and said, "What did you say? I thought you said you'd heard a cat sing—but I heard wrong, I know."

"No, you heard right," said Moon-Face. "We *did* hear a cat sing!"

"Let's go and explore a bit more," said Jo. So up they got and off they went.

A witch was selling a spell to make ordinary broomsticks fly through the air. The four watched in amazement as they saw her rubbing a pink ointment on to a broomhandle belonging to an elf.

"Now get on it, say 'Whizz away!' and you can fly home," said the witch. The elf got astride the broomstick, a smile on her pretty face.

"Whizz away!" she said. And off whizzed the broomstick up into the air, with the elf clinging tightly to it!

"I'd like to buy that spell," said Jo. "I wonder how much it is."

The witch heard him. "Three silver pieces," she said. Jo hadn't even got one. But Moon-Face had. He took them out of his large purse and gave them to the witch.

"Where's your broomstick?" she said.

"We haven't got one with us," said Jo. "But can't you give us the ointment instead, please?"

"Well, I'll give you just a little," said the witch. She took a tiny pink jar and put a dab of the pink ointment into it. Jo took it and put it into his pocket. Now maybe his mother's broomstick would learn to fly!

At the next stall a goblin was selling a spell to make things big. The spell was in big tins, and looked like paint.

"Just think what a useful spell this is!" yelled the goblin to the passers-by. "Have you visitors coming to tea and only a small cake to offer them? A dab of this spell and the cake swells to twice its size! Have you a suit you have grown out of? A dab of this spell and it will grow to the right size! Marvellous, wonderful, amazing and astonishing! Buy, buy, buy, whilst you've got the chance!"

Saucepan heard all that the goblin said, for he was shouting at the top of his voice. He began to look in all his kettles and saucepans.

"What do you want?" asked Jo.

"My money," said the Saucepan Man. "I always keep it in one of my kettles or saucepans—but I never remember which. I simply *must* buy that spell. Think how useful it would be to me. Sometimes when I go round selling my goods a customer will say to me, 'Oh, you haven't a big enough kettle!' But now I shall be able to make my kettles just as big as I like! And we can dab the Pop Biscuits with the spell, too, and make them twice as big."

He found his money at last and paid it to the

goblin, who handed him a tin of the spell. Saucepan was very pleased. He longed to try it on something. He took the brush and dabbed a daisy nearby with the spell. The daisy at once grew to twice its size. Then Saucepan dabbed a bumblebee and that grew enormous. It buzzed around Moon-Face and he waved it away.

"Saucepan, don't do any more bees," he begged. "I expect their stings are twice as big, too. Look—let's go to that sweet-shop over there and buy some sweets. It would be fun to make them twice as big!"

They hurried to the shop—but on the way a dreadful thing happened! Saucepan fell over one of his kettles and upset the tin in which he carried the spell. It splashed up—and drops of it fell on to Moon-Face, Silky, Jo—and the old Saucepan Man, too! And in a trice they all shot up to twice their size! Silky grew to three times her size because more drops fell on her.

They stared at one another. How small the Land of Spells suddenly seemed! How little the witches and goblins looked, how tiny the shops were!

"Saucepan! You really *are* careless!" cried Moon-Face, vexed. "Look what you've done to us. *Now* what are we to do?"

Silky clutched hold of Moon-Face's arm. "Moon-Face!" she said. "Oh, Moon-Face—do you suppose we are too big to go down the hole through the cloud?"

Moon-Face turned pale. "We'd better go and

see," he said. "Comc on, everybody."

Frightened and silent, all four of them hurried to where the hole led down to the Faraway Tree. How little it seemed to the four big people now! Moon-Face tried to get down. He stuck. He couldn't slip down at all.

"It's no use," he said. "We're too big to go down. Whatever in the world shall we do?"

VI

WHAT CAN THEY DO NOW?

Jo, Moon-Face, Silky and Saucepan sat down by the hole and thought hard. Silky began to cry.

The Saucepan Man looked most uncomfortable. He was very fond of Silky. "Silky, please do forgive me for being so careless," he said in a small voice. "I didn't mean to do this. Don't cry. You make me feel dreadful."

"It's all right," sobbed Silky, borrowing Moon-Face's hanky. "I know you didn't mean to. But I can't help feeling dreadfully sad when I think I won't ever be able to see my dear little room in the Faraway Tree any more."

The Saucepan Man began to cry, too. Tears dripped with a splash into his saucepans and kettles. He put his arm round Silky, and two or three kettle-spouts stuck into her.

"Don't!" she said. "You're sticking into me. Moon-Face – Jo – can't you think of something to do? Can we possibly squeeze down if we hold our breaths and make ourselves as small as we can?"

"Quite impossible," said Moon-Face gloomily. "Listen – there's somebody coming up the ladder."

They heard voices – and soon a head popped up out of the hole in the cloud. It was Dick's! He stared in the very greatest surprise at the four enormous people sitting by the hole.

He climbed up and stood beside them, looking very, very small. Then up came Bessie and Fanny. Their eyes nearly fell out of their heads when they saw how big Jo and his friends were.

"What's happened?" cried Dick. "We began to be worried because you didn't come home, Jo – so we climbed up to see where you were. But why are you so ENORMOUS?"

Jo told them. Silky sobbed into Moon-Face's hanky. Bessie put her arm round her. It was funny to feel Silky so very big. Bessie's arm only went half round Silky's waist!

"And now, you see, we can't get back down the hole," said Jo.

"*I* know what you can do!" said Dick suddenly.

"What?" cried everyone hopefully.

"Why, rub the hole with the spell, and it will get bigger, of course!" said Dick. "Then you'll be able to get down it."

"Why ever didn't we think of that before!" cried Jo, jumping up. "Saucepan, where's that tin with the spell in?"

He picked up the tin—but, alas! it was quite, quite empty. Every single drop had been spilt when Saucepan had fallen over.

"Well, never mind!" said Moon-Face, cheering up. "We can go and buy some more from that goblin. Come on!"

They all set off, Dick, Bessie and Fanny looking very small indeed by the others. They went up to the goblin who had sold them the spell.

"May we have another tin of that spell you sold us just now?" asked Moon-Face, holding out the empty tin.

"I've not the tiniest drop left," said the goblin. "And I can't make any more till the full moon comes. It can only be made in the moonlight."

Everyone looked so miserable that the goblin felt sorry for them. "Why do you look so unhappy?" he said. "What has happened?"

Jo told him everything. The goblin listened with great interest. Then he smiled. "Well, my dear boy," he said, "if you can't get a spell to make the hole big, why don't you buy a spell to make yourselves small? My brother, the green goblin over there, sells that kind of spell. Only be careful not to put too much on yourselves, or you may go smaller than you mean to!"

They went over to the green goblin. He was yelling at the top of his voice.

"Buy my wonderful and most amazing spell! It will make anything as small as you like! Have you an enemy? Dab him with this and see him shrink to the size of a mouse! Have you too big a nose? Dab it with this and make it the right size! Oh, wonderful, astonishing, amazing. . . ."

Everyone hurried up. Moon-Face took some money out of his purse. "I'll have the spell, please," he said. The green goblin gave him a tin. The spell in it looked rather like paint, just as the other had done.

"Now go slow," said the goblin. "You don't want to get too small. Try a little at a time."

Moon-Face dabbed a little on Silky. She went a bit smaller at once. He dabbed again. She went smaller still.

"Is she the right size yet?" asked Moon-Face. Everyone stared at Silky.

"Not *quite,*" said Bessie. "But she is almost, Moon-Face. So be careful with your next dab."

Moon-Face was very careful. At the next dab of the spell Silky went to exactly her right size. She was so pleased.

"Now you, Jo," said Moon-Face. So he dabbed Jo and got Jo back to his right size again, too. Then he tried dabbing the Saucepan Man, and soon got him right. His kettles and saucepans went right, too. It was funny to watch them.

"Now I'll do you, Moon-Face," said Jo.

"No, thanks, I'll do myself," said Moon-Face. He dabbed the spell on to himself and shrank smaller. He dabbed again and went smaller still. Then he stopped dabbing and put the brush down.

"You're not quite your ordinary size yet," said Jo.

"I know," said Moon-Face. "But I always thought I was a bit on the short side. Now I'm just about right. I always wanted to be a bit taller. I shan't dab myself any more."

Everyone laughed. It was funny to see Moon-Face a bit taller than usual. As they stood there and laughed, a curious cold wind began to blow. Moon-Face looked all round and then began to shout.

"Quick, quick! The Land of Spells is on the move! Hurry before we get left behind!"

Everyone got a shock. Good gracious! It would never do to be left behind, just as everyone had got small enough to go down the hole in the clouds.

They set off to the hole. The wind blew more and more strongly, and suddenly the sun went out. It was almost as if somebody had blown it out, Jo thought. At once darkness fell on the Land of Spells.

"Take hold of hands, take hold of hands!" cried Jo. "We shall lose one another if we don't!"

They all took hold of one another's hands and called out their names to make sure everyone was there. They stumbled on through the darkness.

"Here's the hole!" cried Jo, at last, and down he went. He felt the ladder and climbed down that, too. The others followed one by one, pushing close behind in the dark, longing to get down to the Faraway Tree they knew so well. How lovely it would be to sit in Moon-Face's room and feel safe!

But down at the bottom of the ladder there was no Faraway Tree. Instead, to Jo's astonishment, there was a narrow passage, lit by a swinging green lantern.

"I say," he said to the others, "What's this? Where's the Faraway Tree?"

"We've come down the wrong hole," groaned Moon-Face. "Oh, goodness, what bad luck!"

"Well, where are we?" asked Dick in wonder.

"I don't know," said Moon-Face. "We'd better follow this passage and see where it leads to. It's no use climbing back and trying to find the right hole. We'd never find it in the dark—and anyway, I'm pretty sure the Land of Spells has moved on by now."

Everyone felt very gloomy. Jo led the way down the passage. It twisted and turned, went up and down steps, and was lighted here and there by the green lanterns swinging from the roof.

At last they came to a big yellow door. On it was a blue knocker, a blue bell, a blue letter-box and a blue notice that said:

"Mister Change-About. Knock once, ring twice, and rattle the letter-box."

Jo knocked once, very loudly. Then he rang twice, and everyone heard the bell going "R-r-r-r-r-ring! R-r-r-r-r-ring!" Then he rattled the letter-box.

The door didn't open. It completely disappeared. It was most peculiar. One minute it was there—and the next it had gone, and there was nothing in front of them. They could see right into a big underground room.

At the end of it, by a roaring fire, a round fat person was sitting. "That must be Mister Change-About!" whispered Dick. "Dare we go in?"

VII

MR. CHANGE-ABOUT AND THE ENCHANTER

Everyone stared at Mr. Change-About. At least, as he was the only person in the room, they thought that was who it must be. He got up and came towards them.

He was a fat, comfortable-looking person with a broad smile on his face. "Dear me, what a lot of visitors!" he said. "Do sit down."

There was nowhere to sit except the floor. This was made of stone and looked rather cold. So nobody sat down.

Something happened to Mr. Change-About when nobody obeyed him. He grew tall and thin. His broad smile disappeared and a frown came all over his face. He looked a most unpleasant person.

"SIT DOWN!" he roared. And everybody sat down in a hurry!

Mr. Change-About looked at the Saucepan Man, who had sat down with a tremendous clatter.

"Have you a nice little kettle that would boil enough water for two cups of tea?" he asked.

The Saucepan Man didn't hear. So Jo shouted

in his ear, and he beamed, got up, and undid a little kettle from the many that hung about him.

"Just the thing!" he said, handing it to Mr. Change-About. "Try it and see!"

Mr. Change-About changed again, and became a happy-looking little creature with dancing eyes and a sweet smile. He took the kettle.

"Thank you," he said. "So kind of you. Just what I wanted. How much is it?"

"Nothing at all," said the Saucepan Man. "Just a present to you!"

"Well, allow me to hand round some chocolate to you all in return for such a nice present," said Mr. Change-About, and fetched an enormous box of chocolates from a cupboard. Everybody was pleased.

Dick looked carefully into the box when his turn came. His hand stretched out for the very biggest chocolate of all. Mr. Change-About at once changed again and flew into a rage.

He became thin and mean-looking, his nose shot out long, and his eyes grew small.

"Bad boy, greedy boy!" he shouted. "You shan't any of you have my chocolates now! Horrid, greedy children!"

And at once all the chocolates changed to little hard stones. Bessie had hers in her mouth, and she spat it out at once. The others looked most disgusted. The old Saucepan Man gave a yell of dismay.

"I've swallowed mine—and now I suppose I've got a stone inside me. Oh, you nasty Mr. Change-About! I'll show you what I think of your chocolates!"

And to everyone's surprise Saucepan rushed at Mr. Change-About, knocked his box of chocolates all over the room, and began to pummel him hard.

Biff, smack, biff, smack! Goodness, how the old Saucepan Man fought Mr. Change-About. And Mr. Change-About fought back—but what was the good of that? Saucepan was so hung about with pans of all kinds that nobody could possibly hit him anywhere without grazing their knuckles and hurting themselves very much indeed!

Clang, clatter, clang, clatter, clash! The kettles and saucepans made an enormous noise, and everyone began to laugh, for really Saucepan looked too funny for words, dancing about on the floor, hitting and slapping at Mr. Change-About.

Mr. Change-About suddenly got very big and fierce-looking, but old Saucepan didn't seem to mind at all. He just went on hitting out at him, and shouted: "The bigger you are, the more there is to hit!"

So then Mr. Change-About got very small indeed, as small as a mouse, and ran squealing across the floor in fright. Quick as lightning, Saucepan picked him up, popped him into a kettle, and put the lid on him!

"Oh, Saucepan! Whatever will you do next?" said Jo, wiping tears of laughter from his eyes. "I've never seen such a funny fight in my life. Be careful Mr. Change-About doesn't squeeze out of the spout."

"I'll stuff it with paper," said Saucepan, tearing some from the box of chocolates. "Now he's safe. Well – what do we do next?"

"We'd better get out of here," said Jo, standing up. He turned towards the doorway – but what was this! There was no doorway – and no door! Only a wall of rock that ran all round the underground room now.

"Goodness! How *do* we get out?" said Jo, puzzled. "This is a very magic kind of place."

"There's no window, of course, because we are underground," said Dick. "What in the wide world are we going to do?"

"What about the chimney?" asked Fanny, running to the fire. "It looks pretty big. We could put the fire out and climb up, perhaps."

"Well, that looks about our only chance of getting out of here," said Jo. He looked round for some water to put out the fire. He saw a tap jutting out from the wall and went to it. He put a pail underneath and turned on the tap. The water was bright green, and soon filled the pail. Jo threw it on the fire. It made a terrific sizzling noise and went out at once, puffing clouds of green smoke into the room.

Jo stepped on to the dead fire and looked up the chimney. "There's an iron ladder going right up!" he called in excitement. "Come on! We shall get dirty, but we can't help that. Hurry, before anything else queer happens!"

Up the ladder he went. It was hot from the heat of the fire, but grew colder the higher he went.

"What an enormously long chimney!" called back Jo. "Is everyone coming?"

"Yes! Yes!" called six voices below him. Jo climbed steadily upwards. At last the ladder came to an end. Joe clambered over the top of it and found himself in a most peculiar place.

"This looks like some kind of cellar," he said to the others, as they scrambled up beside him. "Look at all those sacks piled up! What do you suppose is in them?"

"Let's look," said Dick, who was always curious about everything. He undid a sack—and, goodness gracious me!—out poured a great stream of bright golden pieces of money! Everyone looked at it in astonishment.

"Somebody VERY rich must live here," said

Jo at last. "I never in my life saw so much gold. I can't believe that *all* the sacks are full of it!"

He undid another sack—and out poured gold again. Just as everyone was running their fingers through it, marvelling at the gleam and shine of so much gold, there came the sound of quick footsteps overhead.

A door above them opened, and a gleam of sunlight shone on to a flight of stone steps leading up from the cellar to the door. A tall man in a pointed hat looked down.

"Golly! It's an enchanter!" whispered Moon-Face in a fright. "We must still be in the Land of Spells. Oh, dear!"

"Robbers! Thieves! Burglars!" shouted the enchanter in a loud voice. "Servants, come here! Capture these robbers! They are after my gold! See—they have undone two sacks already!"

"We don't want your gold!" cried Dick. "We only just wanted to know what was in all these sacks!"

"I don't believe you!" cried the enchanter, as about a dozen small imps came running past him down the steps into the cellar. "Capture them, servants, and tie them up!"

The little imps pulled everyone up the cellar steps into a big, sunlit room. Its ceiling was so high that nobody could see it. "Now tie them up," commanded the enchanter.

Moon-Face suddenly snatched a kettle from Saucepan and snapped the string that tied it to him. He went towards the enchanter fearlessly.

"Wait!" he cried, much to the astonishment of all the others. "Wait before you do this foolish thing! *I* am an enchanter, too – and in this kettle I have Mr. Change-About! Yes – he is a prisoner there! And let me tell you this, that if you dare to tie me up, I'll put *you* into the kettle, too, with Mr. Change-About!"

From the kettle came a small, squealing voice: "Set me free, Enchanter, set me free! Oh, do set me free!"

The enchanter turned quite pale. He knew it was Mr. Change-About's voice.

"Er – er – this is most peculiar," he said. "How did you capture Mr. Change-About? He is a very powerful person, and a great friend of mine."

"Oh, I'm not going to tell you what magic I used," said Moon-Face boldly. "Now – are you going to let us go – or shall I put you into this kettle, too?"

"I'll let you go," said the enchanter, and he waved them all towards a door at the end of the room. "You may leave at once."

Everyone rushed to the door gladly. They all ran through it, expecting to come out into the sunshine.

But, alas for them! The enchanter had played them a trick! They found themselves going up many hundreds of stairs, up and up and up – and when they came to the top there was nothing but a round room with one small window! A bench stood at one end and a table at the other.

The enchanter's voice floated up to them.

"Ho! ho! I've got you nicely! Now I'm going to get my friend, Wizard Wily, and he'll soon tell me how to deal with robbers like you!"

"We *are* in a trap!" groaned Jo. "Moon-Face, you were very clever and very brave. But honestly, we are worse off than ever. I simply don't see any way out of this at all!"

VIII

HOW CAN THEY ESCAPE?

Moon-Face looked all round the room at the top of the tower. "Well, we're in a nice fix now," he said gloomily. "It's no use going down the stairs again—we shall find the door at the bottom locked. And what's the good of a window that is half a mile from the ground!"

Jo looked out of the window. "Gracious!" he said, "the tower is awfully tall! I can hardly see the bottom of it. Hallo—there's the enchanter going off in his carriage. I suppose he is going to fetch his friend, dear Wizard Wily."

"I don't like the sound of Wizard Wily," said Silky. "Jo—Dick—Moon-Face—please, please think of some way to escape!"

But there just simply WASN'T any way. No one wanted to jump out of the window.

They all sat down. "I'm dreadfully hungry," said Bessie. "Has anyone got anything to eat?"

"I may have got some Pop Biscuits," said

Moon-Face, feeling in his pockets. But he hadn't. "Feel in *your* pockets, Jo and Dick."

Both boys felt, hoping to find a bit of toffee or half a biscuit. Dick brought out a collection of string, bits of paper, a pencil and a few marbles. Jo took out much the same kind of things—but with his rubbish came a pink jar, very small and heavy.

"What's in that jar?" asked Bessie, who hadn't seen it before. "Isn't it pretty?"

"Let me see—what can it be?" wondered Jo, as he unscrewed the lid. "Oh—I know. We saw a witch selling whizz-away ointment for broomsticks in the Land of Spells—and I thought it *would* be such fun to rub some on mother's broomstick and see it fly through the air. So we bought some. Smell it—it's delicious."

Everyone smelt it. Moon-Face suddenly got tremendously excited. "I say——" he began. "I say—oh, I say!"

"Well, say then!" said Jo. "What's the matter?"

"Oh, I SAY!" said Moon-Face, stammering all the more. "Listen! If only we could get a broomstick—we could rub this pink ointment on it—and fly away on it!"

"Moon-Face, that's a very good idea—if only we had a broomstick—but we haven't!" said Jo. "Look at this room—a table and a bench—no sign of a broomstick at all!"

"Well, I'll run down the stairs and see if I can possibly get a broomstick," said Moon-Face, getting all excited. "I saw some standing in a corner of that room we were in. I'll do my best, anyway!"

"Good old Moon-Face!" said everyone, as they watched the round-faced little fellow scurry down the hundreds of steps. "If only he gets a broomstick!"

Moon-Face hurried down and down. It did seem such a very long way. At last he came to the bottom of the stairs. An enormous wooden door was at the bottom, fast shut. Moon-Face tried to open it, but he couldn't. So he banged on the door loudly.

A surprised voice called out: "Hie, there! What are you banging on the door for? What do you want?"

"A broomstick!" said Moon-Face loudly.

"A *broom*stick!" said the voice, more astonished than ever. "Whatever for?"

"To sweep up some crumbs!" said Moon-Face, quite untruthfully.

"A dust-pan and brush will do for that!" cried the voice, and the door opened a crack. A dust-pan and brush shot in with a clatter and came to rest by Moon-Face's feet. Then the door shut with a bang and was bolted at the other side.

"A dust-pan and brush!" said Moon-Face in disgust. "Now, who can ride away on those?" He banged on the door again.

"*Now* what's the matter?" yelled the voice angrily.

"These won't do," said Moon-Face. "I want a BROOMSTICK!"

"Well, go on wanting," said the voice. "You won't get one. I suppose you think you'll fly away on one if I give it to you. I'm not quite so silly as that. What do you suppose my master would say to me when he came back if I'd given you one of his broomsticks to escape on?"

Moon-Face groaned. He knew it was no good asking again. He picked up the dust-pan and brush and climbed the stairs slowly, suddenly feeling very tired.

Everyone was waiting for him. "Did you get it, Moon-Face?" they cried. But when they saw Moon-Face's gloomy face and the dust-pan and brush in his hand, they were very sad.

They all sat down to think. Jo looked up. "I suppose it wouldn't be any good rubbing the whizz-away ointment on to anything else?" he asked. "Would it make anything but broomsticks fly away?"

"I shouldn't think so," said Moon-Face. "But we could try. What is there to try on, though? We haven't a stick of any sort."

"No—but there's a table over there, and this bench," said Jo, getting excited. "Couldn't we try on those? We could easily sit on them and fly off, if only the magic would work."

"But it won't," said Silky. "I'm sure of that. It's only for broomsticks. But try it, Jo."

Jo took off the lid of the jar again. He dabbed a finger into the pink ointment and rubbed some all over the top of the wooden bench, which was very like a form at school. "Now for the table," said

Jo. He turned it upside down, thinking that it would be more comfortable to sit on that way. They could hold the legs as they went!

He rubbed the ointment all over the underside of the table. As he was doing this everyone heard the sound of horses' hoofs clip-clopping outside. Silky ran to the window.

"It's the enchanter come back again—and he's got the Wizard Wily with him!" she cried. "Oh, do be quick, Jo! They will be up here in a minute."

"Moon-Face, Silky and Saucepan, you sit on the bench," said Jo. "You girls and Dick and I will sit on the table. Hurry now!"

Everyone scrambled to take their seats. Silky was trembling with excitement. She could hear the footsteps of the enchanter and the wizard coming up the steps.

"Now, hold tight, in case we really do go off!" said Joe. "Ready, everyone? Then WHIZZ-AWAY HOME!"

And, goodness gracious, the bench and the table began to move! Yes, they really did! They moved slowly at first, for they were not used to whizzing away—but as the children squealed and squeaked in surprise and delight, the table rose up suddenly to the window and tried to get out!

It stuck. It couldn't get through. "Oh, table, do your best!" cried Jo. "The enchanter is nearly here!"

The table tipped itself up a little—and then it could just manage to squeeze through the opening. The children each clung tightly to a leg, afraid of being tipped off. Then at last the table was through the window, and, sailing away upside down, its four legs in the air, carrying the excited children safely, it whizzed off over the Land of Spells!

Jo looked back to see if the wooden bench was coming, too. It had had to wait until the table was through the window. Just as it was about to jerk upwards to the window, the enchanter and the Wizard Wily had come rushing into the room. What would have happened if the old Saucepan Man hadn't suddenly thrown a kettle at them, goodness knows!

It was the kettle with Mr. Change-About in! The lid came off. Mr. Change-About jumped out and turned himself almost into a giant! The enchanter fell over him, and Mr. Change-About, not seeing who it was at all, began to pummel him hard with his big fists, crying: "I'll teach you to put me into a kettle!"

Wily hit out at Mr. Change-About, not knowing in the least who he was, or where he had suddenly sprung from. And there was a perfectly marvellous fight going on, just as the wooden bench flew out of the window. The enchanter saw it going and tried to get hold of it—but just at that moment Mr. Change-About gave him such a hard punch on the nose that he fell over, smack, again!

"Go it, Change-About!" yelled Moon-Face. "Hit him hard!"

And out of the window sailed the bench, with

Moon-Face, Silky and Saucepan clinging tightly to it. Far away in the distance was the upside-down table.

The table whizzed steadily onwards, over hills and woods, and once over the sea. "We've come a very long way from home since we've been in the Land of Spells," said Jo. "I hope the table knows its way to our home. I don't want to land in any more strange lands just at present!"

The table knew its way all right. Jo gave a shout as it flew over a big dark wood. "The Enchanted Wood!" he cried. "We're nearly home!"

The table flew down to the garden of the children's cottage. Their mother was there, hanging out some clothes. She looked round in the greatest astonishment when she saw them arrive in such a peculiar way.

"Well, really!" she said. "Whatever next! Do you usually fly around the country in an upside-down table?"

"Oh, mother! We've had such an adventure!" said Jo, scrambling off. He looked up in the air to see if the bench was following—but there was no sign of it.

"Where's the bench?" said Dick. "Oh—I suppose it will go to the Faraway, as that is where the others live. Gracious—I feel all trembly. Jo—I am NOT going into any more lands at the top of the Faraway Tree again. It's just a bit too exciting!"

"Right," said Jo. "I feel the same. No more adventures for *me*!"

IX

THE LAND OF DREAMS

The children had had enough of adventures for some time. Their mother set them to work in the garden, and they did their best for her. Nobody suggested going to the Enchanted Wood at all.

"I hope old Moon-Face, Silky and the Saucepan Man got back to the tree safely," said Jo one day.

Moon-Face was wondering the same thing about the children. He and Silky talked about it.

"We haven't seen the children for ages," he said. "Let's slip down the tree, Silky, and make sure they got back all right, shall we? After all, it would be dreadful if they hadn't got back, and their mother was worrying about them."

So one afternoon, just after lunch, Silky and Moon-Face walked up to the door of the cottage. Bessie opened it and squealed with delight.

"Moon-Face! So you got back safely after all! Come in! Come in, Silky darling. Saucepan, you'll have to take off a kettle or two if you want to get in at the door."

The children's parents were out. The children and their friends sat and talked about their last adventure.

"What land is at the top of the tree now?" asked Dick curiously.

"Don't know," said Moon-Face. "Like to come and see?"

"No, thanks," said Jo at once. "We're not going up there any more."

"Well, come back and have tea with us," said Moon-Face. "Silky's got some Pop Biscuits—and I've made some Google Buns. I don't often make them—and I tell you they're a treat!"

"Google Buns!" said Bessie in astonishment. "Whatever are they?"

"You come and see," said Moon-Face, grinning. "They're better than Pop Biscuits—aren't they, Silky?"

"Much," said Silky.

"Well—Fanny and I have finished our work," said Bessie. "What about you boys?"

"We've got about half an hour's more work to do, that's all," said Jo. "If everyone helps, it will only take about ten minutes. We could leave a note for Mother. I would rather like to try those Google Buns!"

Well, everyone went into the garden to dig up the carrots and put them into piles. It didn't take more than ten minutes because they all worked so hard. They put away their tools, washed their hands, left a note for Mother—and then set off for the Enchanted Wood.

The Saucepan Man sang one of his ridiculous songs on the way:

"Two tails for a kitten,
Two clouds for the sky,
Two pigeons for Christmas
To make a plum pie!"

Everyone laughed. Jo, Bessie and Fanny had heard the Saucepan Man's silly songs before, but Dick hadn't.

"Go on," said Dick. "This is the silliest song I've ever heard."

The Saucepan Man clashed two kettles together as he sang:

"Two roses for Bessie,
Two spankings for Jo,
Two ribbons for Fanny,
With a ho-derry-ho!"

"It's an easy song to make up as you go along," said Bessie, giggling. "Every line but the last has to begin with the word 'Two'. Just think of any nonsense you like, and the song simply makes itself."

Singing silly songs, they all reached the Faraway Tree. Saucepan yelled up it: "Hie, Watzisname! Let down a rope, there's a good fellow! It's too hot to walk up to-day."

The rope came down. They all went up one by one, pulled high by the strong arms of Mister Watzisname.

Fanny was unlucky. She got splashed by Dame Washalot's water on the way up. "Next time I go up on the rope I shall take an umbrella with me," she said crossly.

"Come on," said Moon-Face. "Come and eat a Google Bun and see what you think of it."

Soon they were all sitting on the broad branches

outside Moon-Face's house, eating Pop Biscuits and Google Buns. The buns were most peculiar. They each had a very large currant in the middle, and this was filled with sherbet. So when you got to the currant and bit it the sherbet frothed out and filled your mouth with fine bubbles that tasted delicious. The children got a real surprise when they bit their currants, and Moon-Face almost fell off the branch with laughing.

"Come and see some new cushions I've got," he said to the children when they had eaten as many biscuits and buns as they could manage. Jo, Bessie and Fanny went into Moon-Face's funny round house.

Moon-Face looked round for Dick. But he wasn't there. "Where's Dick?" he said.

"He's gone up the ladder to peep and see what land is at the top," said Silky. "I told him not to. But he's rather a naughty boy, I think."

"Gracious!" said Jo, running out of the house. "Dick! Come back, you silly!"

Everyone began to shout, "Dick! DICK!"

But no answer came down the ladder. The big white cloud swirled above silently, and nobody could imagine why Dick didn't come back.

"I'll go and see what he's doing," said Moon-Face. So up he went. And he didn't come back either! Then the old Saucepan Man went cautiously up, step by step. He disappeared through the hole—and *he* didn't come back!

"Whatever has happened to them?" said Jo in the gravest astonishment. "Look here, girls—get a rope out of Moon-Face's house and tie yourselves and Silky to me. Then I'll go up the ladder —and if anyone tries to pull me into the land above, they won't be able to, because you three can pull me back. See?"

"Right," said Bessie, and she knotted the rope round her waist and Fanny's, and then round Silky's, too. Jo tied the other end to himself. Then up the ladder he went.

And before the girls quite knew what had happened, Jo was lifted into the land above—and they were all dragged up, too, their feet scrambling somehow up the ladder and through the hole in the cloud!

There they all stood in a field of red poppies, with a tall man nearby, holding a sack over his shoulder!

"Is that the lot?" he asked. "Good! Well, here's something to make you sleep!"

He put his hand in his sack and scattered a handful of the finest sand over the surprised group. In a trice they were rubbing their eyes and yawning.

"This is the Land of Dreams," said Moon-Face sleepily. "And that's the Sandman. Goodness, how sleepy I am!"

"Don't go to sleep! Don't go to sleep!" cried Silky, taking Moon-Face's arm and shaking him. "If we do, we'll wake up and find that this land has moved away from the Faraway Tree. Come back down the hole, Moon-Face, and don't be silly."

"I'm so—sleepy," said Moon-Face, and lay down among the red poppies. In a trice he was snoring loudly, fast asleep.

"Get him to the hole!" cried Silky. But Jo, Dick and the Saucepan Man were all yawning and rubbing their eyes, too sleepy to do a thing. Then Bessie and Fanny slid down quietly into the poppies and fell asleep, too. At last only Silky was left. Not much of the sleepy sand had gone into her eyes, so she was wider awake than the rest.

She stared at everyone in dismay. "Oh dear," she said, "I'll never get you down the hole by myself. I'll have to get help. I must go and fetch Watzisname and the Angry Pixie and Dame Washalot, too!"

She ran off to the hole, slipped down the ladder through the cloud and slid on to the broad branch below. "Watzisname!" she called. "Dame Washalot! Angry Pixie!"

After a minute or two Jo woke up. He rubbed his eyes and sat up. Not far off he saw something that pleased him very much indeed. It was an ice-cream man with his cart. The man was ringing his bell loudly.

"Hie, Moon-Face! Wake up!" cried Jo. "There's an ice-cream man. Have you any money?"

Everyone woke up. Moon-Face felt in his purse and then stared in the greatest surprise. It was full of marbles!

"Now who put marbles there?" he wondered.

The ice-cream man rode up. "Marbles will do

to pay for my ice-cream," he said. So Moon-Face paid him six marbles.

The man gave them each a packet and rode off, ringing his bell. Moon-Face undid his packet, expecting to find a delicious ice-cream there—but inside there was a big whistle! It was most astonishing.

Everyone else had a whistle, too. "How extra-ordinary!" said Dick. "This is the kind of thing that happens in dreams!"

"Well—after all—this *is* Dreamland!" said Bessie. "I wonder if these whistles blow!"

She blew hers. It was very loud indeed. The others blew theirs, too. And at once six policemen appeared near by, running for all they were worth. They rushed up to the children.

"What's the matter?" they cried. "You are blowing police whistles! What has happened? Do you want help?"

"No," said Dick with a giggle.

"Then you must come to the swimming-bath," said the policeman, and to everyone's enormous astonishment they were all led off.

"Why the *swimming* bath?" said Fanny. "Listen, policeman—we haven't got bathing costumes."

"Oh, you naughty story-teller!" said the policeman nearest to her.

And to Bessie's tremendous surprise she found that she had on a blue and white bathing costume—and all the others had bathing suits, too. It was most extraordinary.

They came to the swimming bath—but there

was no water in it at all. "Get in and swim," said the policeman.

"There's no water," said Dick. "Don't be silly." And then, very suddenly, all the policemen began to cry – and in a trice the swimming bath was full of their tears!

"This sort of thing makes me feel funny," said Jo. "I don't want to swim in tears. Quick, everyone – push the policemen into the bath!"

And in half a second all the policemen were kicking feebly in the bath of tears. As the children watched they changed into blue fishes and swam away, flicking their tails.

"I feel as if I'm in a dream," said Dick.

"So do I," said Jo. "I wish I could get out of it. Oh, look – there's an aeroplane coming down. Perhaps we could get into it and fly away!"

The aeroplane, which was small and green, landed near by. There was nobody in it at all. The children ran to it and got in. Jo pushed down the handle marked UP.

"Off we go!" he said. And off they went!

X

A FEW MORE ADVENTURES

Everyone was very pleased to be in the aeroplane, because they thought they could fly away from the Land of Dreams. After a second or two Bessie leaned over the side of the aeroplane to see how high they were from the ground. She gave a loud cry.

"What's the matter?" asked Jo.

"Jo! This isn't an aeroplane after all!" said Bessie in astonishment. "It's a bus. It hasn't got wings any more. Only wheels. And we're sitting on seats at the top of the bus. Well! I *did* think it was an aeroplane!"

"Gracious! Aren't we flying, then?" said Jo.

"No – just running down a road," said Fanny.

Everyone was silent. They were so disappointed. Then a curious noise was heard. Splishy-splash! Splash! Splash!

The children looked over the side of the bus – and they all gave a shout of amazement.

"Jo! Look! The bus is running on water! But it isn't a bus any more. Oh, look – it's got a sail!"

In the greatest astonishment everyone looked upwards – and there, billowing in the wind, was a great white sail. And Jo was now steering with a tiller instead of with a handle or a wheel. It was all most muddling.

"This is certainly the Land of Dreams, no doubt about that," groaned Jo, wondering whatever the ship would turn into. "The awful part is—we're awake—and yet we have to have these dream-like things happening!"

An enormous wave splashed over everyone. Fanny gave a scream. The ship rocked to and fro, to and fro, and everyone clung tightly to one another.

"Let's land somewhere, for goodness' sake!" cried Dick. "Goodness knows what this ship will turn into next—a rocking-horse, I should think, by the way it's rocking itself to and fro."

And do you know, no sooner had Dick said that than it did turn into a rocking-horse. Jo found himself holding on to its mane, and all the others clung together behind him. The water disappeared.

The rocking-horse seemed to be rocking down a long road.

"Let's get off," shouted Jo. "I don't like the way this thing keeps changing. Slip off, Moon-Face, and help the others down."

It wasn't long before they were all standing in the road, feeling rather queer. The rocking-horse went on rocking by itself down the road. As the children watched it, it changed into a large brown bear that scampered on its big paws.

"Ha!" said Jo. "We got off just in time! Well – what are we going to do now?"

A man came down the road carrying a green-covered tray on his head. He rang a bell. "Muffins! Fine muffins!" he shouted. "Muffins for sale!"

"Oooh! I feel exactly as if I could eat a muffin," said Bessie. "Hie, muffin-man! We'll have six muffins."

The muffin-man stopped. He took down his tray from his head and uncovered it. Underneath were not muffins, but small kittens!

The muffin-man seemed to think they were muffins. He handed one to each of the surprised children, and one to Moon-Face and Saucepan. Then he covered up his tray again and went down the road ringing his bell.

"Well, does he suppose we can eat kittens?" said Bessie. "I say – aren't they darlings? What are we going to do with them?"

"They seem to be growing," said Jo in surprise. And so they were. In a minute or two the kittens were too heavy to carry – they were big cats!

They still went on growing, and soon they were as big as tigers. They gambolled playfully round the children, who were really rather afraid of them.

"Now listen," said Jo to the enormous kittens. "You belong to the muffin-man. You go after him and get on to his tray where you belong. Listen – you can still hear his bell! Go along now!"

To everyone's surprise and delight the great animals gambolled down the road after the muffin-man.

"He *will* get a surprise," said Dick with a giggle. "I say – don't let's buy anything from anyone else. It's a bit too surprising."

"What we really ought to do is to try and find the hole that leads from this land to the Faraway Tree," said Jo seriously. "Surely you don't want to stay in this peculiar land for ever! Gracious, we never know what is happening from one minute to another!"

"I feel terribly sleepy again," said Moon-Face, yawning. "I do wish I could go to bed."

Now, as he said that, there came a clippitty-cloppitty noise behind them. They all turned – and to their great amazement saw a big white bed following them, tippitting along on four fat legs.

"Golly!" said Dick, stopping in surprise. "Look at that bed! Where did it come from?"

The bed stopped just by them. Moon-Face yawned.

"I'd like to cuddle down in you and go to sleep," he said to the bed. The bed creaked as if it was pleased.

Moon-Face climbed on to it. It was soft and cosy. Moon-Face put his head on the pillow and shut his eyes. He began to snore very gently.

This made everyone else feel dreadfully tired and sleepy, too. One by one they climbed into the big bed and lay down, snuggled together. The bed creaked in a very pleased way. Then it went on its way again, clippitty-clopping on its four fat legs, taking the six sleepers with it.

Now what had happened to Silky? Well, she had found Dame Washalot, Mister Watzisname and the Angry Pixie, and had told them how the others had fallen asleep in the Land of Dreams.

"Gracious! They'll never get away from there!" said Watzisname anxiously. "We must rescue them. Come along."

Dame Washalot put a wash-tub of water on her head. The Angry Pixie picked up a kettle of water. Watzisname didn't take anything. They all went up to the ladder at the top of the tree.

"The Land of Dreams is still here," said Silky when her head peeped over the top. "I can't see that horrid Sandman anywhere. It's a good chance to slip up and rescue the others now. Come on!"

Up they all went. They stared round the field of poppies, but they could see none of the others at all.

"We must hunt for them," said Silky. "Oh, my goodness, look at that great brown bear rushing along! I wonder if he knows anything about the others." She called out to him, but he didn't stop. He made a noise like a hen and rushed on.

The four of them wandered on and on—and suddenly they saw something most peculiar coming towards them—something wide and white.

"What in the world can it be?" said Silky in wonder. "Goodness me—it's a BED!"

And so it was—the very bed in which the four children and Moon-Face and Saucepan were asleep!

"Oh, look, look, look!" squealed Silky. "They're all here! Wake up, sillies! Wake up!"

But they wouldn't wake. They just sighed a little and turned over. Nothing that Silky and the others could do would wake them. And, in the middle of all this, there came footsteps behind them.

Silky turned and gave a squeal. "Oh, it's the Sandman! Don't let him throw his sand into your eyes or you will go to sleep, too! Quick, quick, do something!"

The Sandman was already dipping his hand into his big sack to throw sand into their eyes. But, quick as lightning, Dame Washalot picked up her wash-tub and threw the whole of the water over the sack! It wetted the sand so that the Sandman couldn't throw it properly. Then the Angry Pixie emptied his kettle over the Sandman himself, and he began to choke and splutter.

Watzisname stared. He suddenly took out his pocket-knife and slit a hole at the very bottom of the sack. The sand was dry there. Watzisname took a handful of it and threw it straight into the choking Sandman's eyes.

"Now *you* go to sleep for a bit!" shouted Watzisname. And, of course, that's just what the big Sandman did! He sank down under a bush and shut his eyes. His sleepy sand acted on him as much as on anyone else!

"Now we've got a chance!" said Silky, pleased. "Help me to wake everyone!"

But, you know, they just would *not* wake! It was dreadful.

"Well, we can't possibly get the bed down the hole," said Silky in despair. Then a bright idea came to her. She felt in Jo's pockets. She turned out the little pink jar of Whizz-Away ointment. "There may be *just* a little left!" she said.

And so there was—the very tiniest dab! "I hope it's enough!" said Silky. "Get on the bed, Dame Washalot and you others. I'm going to try a little magic. Ready?"

She rubbed the dab of ointment on to the head of the bed. "Whizz-Away Home, bed!" she said.

And, good gracious me, that big white bed whizzed away! It whizzed away so fast that Silky nearly fell off. It rushed through the air, giving all the birds a most terrible scare.

After a long time it came to the end of the Land of Dreams. A big white cloud stretched out at the edge. The bed flew through it, down and down. Then it flew in another direction.

"It's going back to the Faraway Tree, I'm sure," said Silky. And so it was! It arrived there and tried to get through the branches. It stuck on one and slid sideways. Everyone began to slide off.

"Wake up, wake up!" squealed Silky, banging the children and Moon-Face and Saucepan. They woke up in a hurry, for they were no longer in Dreamland. They felt themselves falling and and caught hold of branches and twigs.

"Where are we?" cried Dick. "What has happened?"

"Oh, goodness, too many things to tell you all at once," said Silky. "Is everyone safe? Then for goodness' sake come into my house and sit down for a bit. I really feel quite out of breath!"

XI

UP THE TREE AGAIN

Everyone crowded into Silky's room inside the tree. "How did we get back to the tree?" asked Dick in amazement.

Silky told him. "We found you all asleep on that big bed, and we rubbed on it some of the Whizz-Away ointment, the very last bit left. And it whizzed away here. Oh, and we wetted the Sandman's sand so that he couldn't throw sand into our eyes and make us go to sleep."

"Watzisname was clever, too. He slit the bottom of the sack with his knife, found a handful of dry sand there and threw it at the Sandman himself!" said the Angry Pixie. "And he went right off to sleep and couldn't interfere with us any more!"

"It was all Dick's fault," said Jo. "We said we wouldn't go to any more lands—and he went up there and got caught by the Sandman. So of course we had to go after him."

"Sorry," said Dick. "Anyway, everything's all right now. I won't do it again."

"We'd better go home," said Bessie. "It must be getting late. Goodness knows when we'll come again, Silky. Good-bye, everyone. Come and see us if we don't come to see you."

They all slid down the slippery-slip at top speed. Then they walked home, talking about their latest adventure.

"It was so queer being awake and having dreams," said Fanny. "Do you remember the muffins that turned into kittens?"

"I wish a really *nice* land would come to the top of the tree," said Jo. "Like the Land of Take-What-You-Want. That was fun. I wonder if it will ever come again."

For about a week the children did not even go into the Enchanted Wood. For one thing they were very busy helping their parents, and for another thing they felt that they didn't want any more adventures for a little while.

And then a note came from Silky and Moon-Face. This is what it said:

"DEAR BESSIE, FANNY, JO AND DICK,

"We know that you don't want any more adventures just yet, but you might like to know that there is a most exciting land at the top of the Faraway Tree just now. It is the Land of Do-As-You-Please, even nicer than the Land of Take-What-You-Want. We are going there tonight. If you want to come, come just before midnight and you can go with us. We will wait for you till then.

"Love from
"SILKY AND MOON-FACE."

The children read the note one after another. Their eyes began to shine.

"Shall we go?" said Fanny.

"Better not," said Jo. "Something silly is sure

to happen to us. It always does."

"Oh, Jo! Do let's go!" said Bessie. "You know how exciting the Enchanted Wood is at night, too, with all the fairy folk about—and the Far-away Tree lit with lanterns and things. Come on, Jo—say we'll go."

"I really think we'd better not," said Jo. "Dick might do something silly again."

"I would *not*!" said Dick in a temper. "It's not fair of you to say that."

"Don't quarrel," said Bessie. "Well, listen—if you don't want to go, Jo, Fanny and I will go with Dick. He can look after us."

"Pooh! Dick wants looking after himself," said Jo.

Dick gave Jo a punch on the shoulder and Jo slapped back.

"Oh, don't!" said Bessie. "You're not in the Land of Do-As-You-Please now!"

That made everyone laugh. "Sorry, Jo," said Dick. "Be a sport. Let's all go to-night. Or at any rate, let's go up the tree and hear what Silky and Moon-Face can tell us about this new land. If it sounds at all dangerous we won't go. See?"

"All right," said Jo, who really did want to go just as badly as the others, but felt that he ought not to keep leading the girls into danger. "All right. We'll go up and talk to Silky and Moon-Face. But mind—if I decide not to go with them, there's to be no grumbling."

"We promise, Jo," said Bessie. And so it was settled. They would go to the Enchanted Wood that night and climb the Faraway Tree to see their friends.

It was exciting to slip out of bed at half-past eleven and dress. It was very dark because there was no moon.

"We shall have to take a torch," said Jo. "Are you girls ready? Now don't make a noise, or you'll wake Mother."

They all crept down stairs and out into the dark, silent garden. An owl hooted nearby, and something ran down the garden path. Bessie nearly squealed.

"Sh! It's only a mouse or something," said Jo. "I'll switch on my torch now. Keep close together and we shall all see where we're going."

In a bunch they went down the back garden and out into the little lane there. The Enchanted Wood loomed up big and dark. The trees spoke to one another softly. "Wisha, wisha, wisha," they said. "Wisha, wisha, wisha!"

The children jumped over the ditch and walked through the wood, down the paths they knew so well. The wood was full of fairy folk going about their business. They took no notice of the children. Jo soon switched off his torch. Lanterns shone everywhere and gave enough light to see by.

They soon came to the great dark trunk of the Faraway Tree. A rope swung down through the branches.

"Oh, good!" said Dick. "Is Moon-Face going to pull us up?"

"No," said Jo. "We'll have to climb up—but

we can use the rope to help us. It's always in the tree at night to help the many folk going up and down."

And indeed there were a great many people using the Faraway Tree that night. Strange pixies, goblins and gnomes swarmed up and down it, and brownies climbed up, chattering hard.

"Where are they going?" asked Dick in surprise.

"Oh, up to the Land of Do-As-You-Please, I expect," said Jo. "And some of them are visiting their friends in the tree. Look—there's the Angry Pixie! He's got a party on to-night!"

The Angry Pixie had about eight little friends squashed into his tree-room, and looked as pleased as could be. "Come and join us!" he called to Jo.

"We can't," said Jo. "Thanks all the same. We're going up to Moon-Face's."

Everyone dodged Dame Washalot's washing water, laughed at old Watzisname sitting snoring as usual in his chair, and at last came to Moon-Face's house.

And there was nobody there! There was a note stuck on the door.

"We waited till midnight and you didn't come. If you do come and we're not here, you'll find us in the Land of Do-As-You-Please.

"Love from

"SILKY AND MOON-FACE."

"*P.S.*—DO come. Just *think* of the things you want to do—you can do them all in the Land of Do-As-You-Please!"

"Golly!" said Dick, longingly, "what I'd like to do better than anything else is to ride six times on a roundabout without stopping!"

"And *I'd* like to eat six ice-creams without stopping!" said Bessie.

"And *I'd* like to ride an elephant," said Fanny.

"And *I* should like to drive a motor-car all by myself," said Jo.

"Jo! *Let's* go up the ladder!" begged Fanny. "Oh, do, do let's! Why can't we go and visit a really nice land when one comes? It's just too mean of you to say we can't."

"Well," said Jo. "Well—I suppose we'd better! Come on!"

With shrieks and squeals of delight the girls and Dick pressed up the little ladder, through the cloud. A lantern hung at the top of the hole to give them light—but, lo and behold! as soon as they had got into the land above the cloud it was daytime! How extraordinary!

The children stood and gazed round it. It seemed a very exciting land, rather like a huge amusement park. There were roundabouts going round and round in time to music. There were swings and see-saws. There was a railway train puffing along busily, and there were small aeroplanes flying everywhere, with brownies, pixies and goblins having a fine time in them.

"Goodness! Doesn't it look exciting?" said Bessie. "I wonder where Moon-Face and Silky are."

"There they are—over there—on that roundabout!" cried Jo. "Look – Silky is riding a tiger that is going up and down all the time – and Moon-Face is on a giraffe! Let's get on, too!"

Off they all ran. As soon as Moon-Face and Silky saw the children, they screamed with joy and waved their hands. The roundabout stopped and the children got on. Bessie chose a white rabbit. Fanny rode on a lion and felt very grand. Jo went on a bear and Dick chose a horse.

"So glad you came!" cried Silky. "We waited and waited for you. Oh – we're off! Hold tight!"

The roundabout went round and round and round. The children shouted for joy, because it went so fast. "Let's have six rides without getting off!" cried Jo. So they did – and dear me, weren't they giddy when they did at last get off. They rolled about like sailors!

"I feel like sitting down with six ice-creams," said Bessie. At once an ice-cream man rode up and handed them out thirty-six ice-creams. It did look a lot. When Jo had divided them all out equally there were six each. And how delicious they were! Everybody managed six quite easily.

"And now, what about me driving that railway engine!" cried Jo, jumping up. "I've always wanted to do that. Would you all like to be my passengers? Well, come on, then!"

And off they all raced to where the railway train was stopping at a little station. "Hi! hie!" yelled Jo to the driver. "I want to drive your train!"

"Come along up, then," said the driver, jumping down. "The engine is just ready to go!"

XII

THE LAND OF DO-AS-YOU-PLEASE

Jo jumped up into the cab of the engine. A bright fire was burning there. He looked at all the shining handles and wheels.

"Shall I know which is which?" he asked the driver.

"Oh, yes," said the driver. "That's the starting wheel – and that's to make the whistle go – and that's to go slow – and that's to go fast. You can't make a mistake. Don't forget to stop at the stations, will you? And oh – look out for the level-crossing gates, in case they are shut. It would be a pity to bump into them and break them."

Jo felt tremendously excited. Dick looked up longingly. "Jo! Could I come too?" he begged. "Do let me. Just to watch you."

"All right," said Jo. So Dick hopped up on to the engine. The girls, Moon-Face and Silky got into a carriage just behind. The guard ran up the platform waving a green flag and blowing his whistle.

"The signal's down!" yelled Dick. "Go on, Jo! Start her up!"

Jo twisted the starting wheel. The engine began to chuff-chuff-chuff and moved out of the station. The girls gave a squeal of delight.

"Jo's really driving the train!" cried Bessie. "Oh isn't he clever! He's wanted to drive an engine all his life!"

The engine began to go very fast—too fast. Jo pulled the "Go Slow" handle, and it went more slowly. He was so interested in what he was doing that he didn't notice he was coming to a station. He shot right through it!

"Jo!" cried Dick, "you've gone by a station. Gracious, the passengers waiting there did look cross—and oh, look, a lot of them in our train wanted to get out there!"

Sure enough quite a number of angry people were looking out of the carriage windows, yelling to Jo to stop.

Jo went red. He pulled the "Stop" handle. The engine stopped. Then Jo pulled the "Go Backwards" handle and the train moved slowly backwards to the station. It stopped there and Jo and Dick had the pleasure of seeing the passengers get out and in. The guard came rushing up.

"You passed the station, you passed the station!" he cried. "Don't you dare to pass my station again without stopping!"

"All right, all right," said Jo. "Now then—off we go again!" And off they went.

"Keep a look-out for stations, signals, tunnels and level crossings, Dick," said Jo. So Dick stuck his head out and watched.

"Level crossing!" he cried. "The gates are shut! Slow down, Jo, slow down!"

But unluckily Jo pulled the "Go Fast" handle instead of the "Go-Slow" and the train shot quickly to the closed gates of the level-crossing. Just as the engine had nearly reached them a

little man rushed out of the cabin near by and flung the gates open just in time!

"You bad driver!" he shouted as the train roared past. "You might have broken my gates!"

"That was a narrow squeak," said Jo. "What's this coming now, Dick?"

"A tunnel," said Dick. "Whistle as you go through in case anyone is walking in it."

So Jo made the engine whistle loudly. It really was fun. It raced through the dark tunnel and came out near a station.

"Stop! Station, Jo!" cried Dick. And Jo stopped. Then on went the train again, whistling loudly, rushing past signals that were down.

Then something happened. The "Go Slow" and the "Stop" handles wouldn't work! The train raced on and on past stations, big and small, through tunnels, past signals that were up, and behaved just as if it had gone mad.

"I say!" said Dick in alarm, "what's gone wrong, Jo?"

Jo didn't know. For miles and miles the train tore on, and all the passengers became alarmed. And then, as the train drew near a station, it gave a loud sigh, ran slowly and then stopped all by itself.

And it was the very same station it had started from! The driver of the train was there, waiting.

"So you're back again," he said. "My, you've been quick."

"Well, the engine didn't behave itself very well," said Jo, stepping down thankfully. "It just ran away the last part of the journey. It wouldn't stop anywhere!"

"Oh, I dare say it wanted to get back to me," said the driver, climbing into the engine-cab. "It's a monkey sometimes. Come along and drive it again with me."

"No, thank you," said Jo. "I think I've had enough. It was fun, though."

The girls, Moon-Face and Silky, got out of their carriages. They had been rather frightened the last part of the journey, but they thought Jo was very clever to drive the train by himself.

They all left the station. "Now what shall we do?" said Moon-Face.

"I want to ride on an elephant," said Fanny at once.

"There aren't any," said Bessie. But no sooner had she spoken than the children saw six big grey elephants walking solemnly up to them, swaying a little from side to side.

"Oh, look, look!" yelled Fanny, nearly mad with excitement. "There are my elephants. Six of them! We can all have a ride!"

Each elephant had a rope ladder up its left side. The children, Moon-Face and Silky climbed up and sat on a comfortable seat on the elephant's backs. Then the big creatures set off, swaying through the crowds.

It was simply lovely. Fanny did enjoy herself. She called to the others. "Wasn't this a good idea of mine, everybody? Aren't we high up? And isn't it fun?"

"It *is* fun," said Moon-Face, who had never even seen an elephant before, and would certainly never have thought of riding on one if he had. "Oh, goodness—my rope ladder has slipped off my elephant! Now I shall never be able to get down! I'll have to ride on this elephant all my life long!"

Everybody laughed—but Moon-Face was really alarmed. When the children had had enough of riding they all climbed down their rope ladders—but poor Moon-Face sat up high, tears pouring down his fat cheeks.

"I tell you I can't get down," he kept saying. "I'm up here for good!"

The elephant stood patiently for a little while. Then it got tired of hearing Moon-Face cry. It swung its enormous trunk round, wound it gently round Moon-Face's waist, and lifted him down to the ground. Moon-Face was so surprised that he couldn't speak a word.

At last he found his tongue. "What did the elephant lift me down with?" he asked. "His nose!"

"No, his trunk," said Jo, laughing. "Didn't you know that elephants had trunks, Moon-Face?"

"No," said Moon-Face, puzzled. "I'm glad he didn't pack me in his trunk and take me away for luggage!"

The children roared with laughter. They watched the big elephants walking off.

"What shall we do now?" said Jo. "Dick, what do you want to do?"

"Well, I know I can't do it—but wouldn't I just love to have a paddle in the sea!" said Dick.

"Oooh—that *would* be nice!" said Fanny, who loved paddling too. "But there isn't any sea here."

Just as she said that she noticed a sign-post near by. It pointed away from them and said, in big letters, "TO THE SEA."

"Goodness!" said Fanny. "Look at that! Come on, everyone!"

Off they all went, running the way that the sign-post pointed. And, after going round two corners, there, sure enough, was the blue, blue sea, lying bright and calm in the warm sunshine! Shining golden sands stretched to the little waves.

"Oh, goody, goody!" cried Dick, taking off his

shoes and socks at once. "Come on, quickly!"

Soon everyone was paddling in the warm sea. Moon-Face and Silky had never paddled before, but they loved it just as much as the children did. Dick paddled out so far that he got his shorts soaking wet.

"Oh, Dick! You *are* wet!" cried Bessie. "Come back!"

"This is the Land of Do-As-You-Please, isn't it?" shouted Dick, dancing about in the water and getting wetter than ever. "Well, I shall get as wet as I like, then!"

"Let's dig an ENORMOUS castle!" cried Moon-Face. "Then we can all sit on the top of it when the sea comes up."

"We can't," said Silky, suddenly looking sad.

"Why not? Why not?" cried Jo in surprise. "Isn't this the Land of Do-As-You-Please?"

"Yes," said Silky. "But it's time we went back to the Faraway Tree. This land will soon be on the move—and nice as it is, we don't want to live here for ever."

"Gracious, no," said Jo. "Our mother and father couldn't possibly do without us! Dick! Dick! Come in to shore! We're going home!"

Dick didn't want to be left behind. He waded back at once, his shorts dripping wet, and his jersey splashed, too. They all made their way to the hole that led down through the cloud to the Faraway Tree.

"We did have a lovely time," sighed Jo, looking back longingly at the gay land he was leaving behind. "It's one of the nicest lands that has ever been at the top of the Tree."

They all felt tired as they crowded into Moon-Face's room. "Don't fall asleep before you get home," said Moon-Face. "Take cushions, all of you."

They went down the slippery-slip, yawning. They made their way home and fell into bed, tired out but happy. And in the morning their mother spoke in surprise to Dick.

"Dick, how is it that your shorts and jersey are so wet this morning?"

"I paddled too deep in the sea," said Dick—and he couldn't *think* why his Aunt Polly said he was a naughty little story-teller!

XIII

THE LAND OF TOYS

One afternoon Silky came to see the children as they were all working hard in the garden. She leaned over the gate and called to them.

"Hallo! I've come to tell you something!"

"Oh, hallo, Silky dear!" cried everyone. "Come along in. We can't stop work because we've got to finish clearing this patch before tea."

Silky came in. She sat down on the barrow. "The old Saucepan Man wants to give a party," she said. "And he says, will you come?"

"Is it his birthday?" asked Jo.

"Oh, no. He doesn't know when his birthday is," said Silky. "He says he hasn't got one. This is just a party. You see, the Land of Goodies is coming soon, and Saucepan thought it would be a fine idea to go there with a large basket and collect as many good things to eat as he can find, and then give a party in Moon-Face's room, so that we can eat all the things."

"That sounds fine!" said Dick, who loved eating good things. "When shall we come?"

"To-morrow," said Silky. "About three o'clock. Will you be all right?"

"Oh, yes," said Bessie. "Mother says we've been very good this week, so she is sure to let us come to the Saucepan Man's party to-morrow. We'll be there! When is Saucepan going to get the goodies to eat?"

"To-morrow morning," said Silky. "He says that the Land of Goodies will be there then. Well, good-bye. I won't stay and talk to-day, as I said I'd make some Pop Biscuits and Google Buns for the tea to-morrow as well. I might make some Toffee Shocks, too."

Silky went. The children talked joyfully of the party next day.

"Hope there will be treacle pudding," said Dick.

"Treacle pudding! At a tea-party!" said Bessie.

"Well, why not?" said Dick. "It's most delicious. I hope there will be pink and yellow jelly, too."

Everyone felt excited when the next afternoon came. Mother said they might go, but she wouldn't let them put on their best clothes.

"Not if you are going to climb trees," she said. "And Dick, please don't get your clothes wet this time. If you do, you'll have to stay in bed all day whilst I dry them."

The children ran to the Enchanted Wood. They had to climb up the tree in the ordinary way, for there was no rope that day. Up they went, shouting a greeting to the owl in his room, to the Angry Pixie, and to Dame Washalot.

They reached Moon-Face's house. He and Silky were setting out cups and saucers and plates ready for all the goodies that Saucepan was going to bring back. Silky handed a bag round. "Have a Toffee Shock?" she said.

Now, all the children except Dick had had Toffee Shocks before, and, providing you knew, what the toffee did it was all right. But if you didn't, it was rather alarming.

A Toffee Shock gets bigger and bigger and bigger as you suck it, instead of smaller and smaller – and when it is so big that there is hardly room for it in your mouth it suddenly explodes – and goes to nothing. Jo, Bessie and Fanny watched Dick as he sucked his Toffee Shock, nudging one another and giggling.

Dick took a big Toffee Shock, for he was rather a greedy boy. He popped it into his mouth and sucked hard. It tasted most delicious. But it seemed to get bigger and bigger.

Dick tried to tell the others this, for it surprised him very much. But the Toffee Shock was now so big that he could hardly talk.

"Ooble, ooble, ooble!" he said.

"What language are you talking, Dick?" asked Moon-Face, with a giggle.

Dick looked really alarmed. His toffee was now so enormous that he could hardly find room in his mouth for it. And then suddenly it exploded—and his mouth was quite empty.

"Ooooh!" said Dick, opening and shutting his mouth like a goldfish. "Oooh!"

"Don't you like your sweet?" said Silky, trying not to giggle. "Well, spit it out if you like, and have another."

"It's gone!" said Dick. Then he saw the others laughing, and he guessed that Toffee Shocks were not quite the usual kind of sweets. He began to laugh, too. "Goodness, that did frighten me!" he said. "I say, wouldn't I like to give the master at my old school a Toffee Shock!"

Moon-Face looked at his clock. "Old Saucepan is a long time," he said. "It's half-past three now, and he promised to be really quick."

"Hallo—here's somebody coming now," said Moon-Face, hearing footsteps on the ladder that led up through the cloud. "Perhaps it's old Saucepan. But I can't hear his kettles clanking!"

Down the ladder came a wooden soldier. He saluted as he went past.

"Hie, hie!" shouted Moon-Face suddenly. "Wait a minute! How is it that you live in the Land of Goodies?"

"I don't," said the wooden soldier, in surprise. "I live in the Land of Toys."

"What! Is the Land of Toys up there now?" cried Moon-Face, standing up in astonishment.

"Of course!" said the soldier. "The Land of Goodies doesn't arrive till next week."

"Goodness!" groaned Moon-Face, as the soldier disappeared down the tree. "Old Saucepan has made a mistake. He's gone to the Land of Toys instead of to the Land of Goodies. I expect he is hunting everywhere for nice things to bring down to us – he's such a dear old stupid that he wouldn't know it wasn't the right land."

"We'd better go and tell him," said Silky. "You children can stay here till we come back, and then we'll have a nice tea of Pop Biscuits and Google Buns. Help yourself to Toffee Shocks whilst we are gone."

"We'll come too," said Bessie, jumping up. "The Land of Toys sounds exciting. I wish we'd brought Peronel, our doll. She would have loved to visit the Land of Toys."

"I suppose it isn't at all a dangerous land!" said Jo. "Just toys come alive?"

"Of course it's not dangerous," said Silky.

They all went up the ladder. They were very anxious to see what the Land of Toys was like. It was exactly as they imagined it!

Dolls' houses, toy sweet shops, toy forts, toy railway stations stood about everywhere, but much bigger than proper toys. Golliwogs, teddy bears, dolls of all kinds, stuffed animals and clockwork toys ran or walked about, talking and laughing.

"I say! This is fun!" said Bessie. "Oh, look at

those wooden soldiers all walking in a row!"

The children stared round, but Moon-Face pulled their arms.

"Come on," he said. "We've got to find out where the old Saucepan Man has got to! I can't see him anywhere."

The six of them wandered about the Land of Toys. Clockwork animals ran everywhere. A big Noah's Ark suddenly opened its lid and let out scores of wooden animals walking in twos. Noah came behind, humming.

The Saucepan Man was simply nowhere to be seen. "I'd better ask someone if they've seen him," said Moon-Face at last. So he stopped a big golliwog and spoke to him.

"Have you seen a little man hung about with kettles and saucepans?" he asked.

"Yes," said the golliwog at once. "He's bad. He tried to steal some sweets out of the sweet shop over there."

"I'm sure Saucepan wouldn't steal a thing!" said Jo angrily.

"Well, he did," said the golliwog. "I saw him."

"I know what happened," said Moon-Face, suddenly. "Old Saucepan thought this was the Land of Goodies. He didn't know it was the Land of Toys. So when he saw the sweet shop he thought he could take as many as he liked. You can in the Land of Goodies, you know. And people must have thought he was stealing."

"Oh, dear," said Silky, in dismay. "Golliwog, what happened to the Saucepan Man?"

"The policeman came up and took him off to prison," said the golliwog. "There's the policeman over there. You can ask him all about it."

The golliwog went off. The children, Moon-Face and Silky went over to the policeman. He told them it was quite true what the golliwog had said – Saucepan had tried to take sweets out of the sweet shop, and he had been locked up.

"Oh, we must rescue him!" cried Jo at once. "Where is he?"

"You must certainly not rescue him," said the policeman crossly. "I shan't tell you where he is!"

And no matter how much the children begged him, he would NOT tell them where he had put poor Saucepan.

"Well, we must just go and look for him ourselves, that's all," said Jo. And the six of them wandered off through the Land of Toys, shouting loudly as they went.

"Saucepan! Dear old Saucepan! Where are you?"

XIV

AN EXCITING RESCUE

The children, Moon-Face and Silky went down the crooked streets of the Land of Toys, calling the old Saucepan Man.

"Of course, Saucepan is very deaf," said Jo.

"He might not hear us calling him, even if he were locked up somewhere quite near."

They went on again, shouting and calling. The toys hurrying by stared at them in astonishment.

"Why do you keep calling 'Saucepan, Saucepan'?" asked a beautifully dressed doll. "Are you selling saucepans, or something?"

"No," said Jo. "We're looking for a friend."

Just then Silky heard something. She clutched Jo's arm. "Sh!" she said. "Listen! Do listen!"

Everyone stood still and listened. Then, floating on the air came a well-known voice, singing a silly song:

"Two trees in a teapot,
Two spoons in a pie,
Two clocks up the chimney.
Hi-tiddly-hie!"

"It's Saucepan!" cried Jo. "Nobody but Saucepan sings those silly songs. Where is he?"

They looked all round. There was a toy fort not far off, but, of course, much bigger than a proper toy fort. The song seemed to come from there.

"Two mice on a lamp-post,
Two hums in a bee,
Two shoes on a rabbit.
Hi-tiddly-hee!"

Jo laughed loudly. "I never knew such a stupid song in my life," he said. "I can't think how old Saucepan can make it up. It's coming from that fort. That's where he is locked up."

Everyone looked at the red-painted fort. Soldiers walked up and down on it. A drawbridge was pulled up so that no one could go in or out. When a soldier wanted to go out the drawbridge was let down and the soldier stepped over it. Then it was pulled up again.

"Well, Saucepan is certainly in there," said Moon-Face. "And, by the way, don't call to him, any of you. We don't want the guards to know that there are any friends of his here – else they may guess we'll try and rescue him."

"Oh, do let's try and let him know we're here," said Bessie. "He would be so very, very glad. He must feel so worried and unhappy."

"I know a way of telling him we are here, without anyone guessing we are friends of his," said Jo suddenly. "Listen."

He stood and thought for a moment. Then he raised his voice and sang a little song:

"Two boys in the high-road,
Two girls in the street,
Two friends feeling sorry.
Tweet-tweet-tweet-tweet-tweet!"

Everyone roared with laughter. "It's very clever, Jo," said Dick. "Two boys – Saucepan will know that's you and me – two girls – that's Bessie and Fanny – two friends, Silky and Moon-Face! Saucepan will know we're all here!"

A frightful noise came from the fort—a clanging and a banging, a clanking and crashing. Everyone listened.

"That's old Saucepan dancing round madly to let us know he heard and understood," said Jo. "Now the thing is—how are we going to rescue him?"

They walked down the street, talking, trying to think of some good way to save poor Saucepan. They came to a clothes shop. In it were dolls' clothes of all sorts. In the window was a set of sailor's clothes, too. Jo stared at them.

"Now, I wonder," he said. "I just wonder if they've got any soldier's clothes. Moon-Face, lend me your big purse if it's got any money in."

Moon-Face put his large purse into Jo's hand. Jo disappeared into the shop. He came out with three sets of bright red soldier's uniforms, with big, black, furry bearskins for hats.

"Come on," he said in excitement. "Come somewhere that we shan't be seen."

They all hurried down the street and came to a field where some toy cows stood grazing.

They climbed over the gate and went behind the hedge. "Dick, see if this uniform will fit you," said Jo. "I'll put this one on."

"But Jo–Jo–what are you going to do?" asked Bessie in surprise.

"I should have thought you could have guessed," said Jo, putting on the uniform quickly. "We're going to see if we can march into the fort and get old Saucepan out! I should think they will let down the drawbridge for us if we are dressed like soldiers."

"Is this third suit for me?" asked Moon-Face, excitedly.

"No, Moon-Face," said Jo. "I didn't think you'd look a bit like a soldier, even if you were dressed like one. You must stay outside and look after the girls. This third suit is for old Saucepan. The soldiers wouldn't let us take him out of the fort all hung round with kettles and saucepans! They would know it was the prisoner and would stop him. He'll have to take off his kettles and things and dress in this. Then, maybe we can rescue him quite easily."

"Jo, you are really very, very clever," said Silky.

Jo felt very pleased. He buckled his belt, and put on his black bearskin. My word, he did look grand! So did Dick.

"Now we're ready," said Jo. "Moon-Face, if by any chance Dick and I are caught, you must take the girls safely back to the Tree. See?"

"I see," said Moon-Face. "Good luck, boys!"

Everyone went out of the field and walked back to the fort. When they got near it, Dick and Jo began to march very well, indeed. Left, right, left, right, left, right!

They came to the fort. "Soldier, let down the drawbridge!" yelled Jo, in his loudest and most commanding voice. The sentinel peered over the wall of the fort. When he saw two such smart soldiers, he saluted at once, and set to work to let down the drawbridge. Crash! It fell flat to the ground, and Dick and Jo walked over it into the fort.

Creak, creeeee-eak! The drawbridge was drawn up again. Jo and Dick marched right into the fort. Soldiers saluted at once.

"I wish to talk to the prisoner here," said Jo.

"Yes, captain," said a wooden soldier, saluting. He took a key from his belt and gave it to Jo. "First door on the right, sir," he said. "Be careful. He may be fierce."

"Thanks, my man," said Jo, and marched to the first door on the right. He unlocked it and he and Dick went in and shut the door. Saucepan was there! When he saw the two soldiers, he fell on his knees.

"Set me free, set me free!" he begged. "I did not mean to steal the sweets. I thought this was the Land of Goodies."

"Saucepan! It's us!" whispered Jo, taking off his helmet so that Saucepan could see him plainly. "We've come to save you. Put on this uniform, quick!"

"But what about my kettles and saucepans?" said Saucepan. "I can't leave them behind."

"Don't be silly. You'll have to," said Jo. "Quick, Dick, help him off with them."

The two boys stripped off every pan and made Saucepan dress up in the red uniform. He trembled so much with excitement that they had to do up every button for him.

"Now march close to us and don't say a word," said Jo, when Saucepan was ready. His kettles and saucepans lay in a heap on the floor. He fell over them as he scrambled across to Jo and Dick. Jo opened the door. All three marched out, keeping in step. Left, right, left, right, left, right!

The other soldiers in the fort looked up but saw nothing but three of their comrades—or so they thought. Jo shouted to the sentinel:

"Let down the drawbridge!"

"Very good, captain!" cried the sentinel, and let it down with a crash. Jo, Dick and Saucepan marched out at once. Left, right, left, right, left, right.

Moon-Face and the girls could hardly believe that the third soldier was old Saucepan. He did look so different in uniform, without his pans hung all round him. Silky flew to hug him.

And then the sentinel of the fort yelled out in a loud voice: "I believe that's the prisoner! I believe he's escaped! Hie, hie, after them!"

"Goodness! Run! run!" cried Jo, at once. And they all ran. How they ran! Soldiers poured out of the fort after them, golliwogs and teddy bears joined in the chase, and dolls of all kinds pattered behind on their small feet.

"To the hole in the cloud!" shouted Jo. "Run, Bessie; run, Fanny! Oh, I do hope we get there in time!"

XV

A SHOCK FOR THE TOYS

How the children and the others ran! They knew quite well that if they were caught they would be put into the toy fort—and then the Land of Toys would move away from the Faraway Tree, and goodness knew how long they might have to stay there!

So they ran at top speed. Fanny fell behind a little, and Jo caught her hand to help her. Panting and puffing, they raced down the streets of the Land of Toys, trying to remember where the hole led down through the cloud to the Faraway Tree.

Jo remembered the way. He led them all to the hole—and there was the ladder, thank goodness! "Down you go!" cried the boy to Silky, Bessie and Fanny. "Hurry! Get into Moon-Face's room quickly."

Down the girls went, and then Dick, Moon-Face, Saucepan and Jo. Jo only just got down in time, for a large golliwog, with very long legs, had almost caught them up – and as Jo went down he reached out and tried to catch Jo's collar.

Jo jerked himself away. His collar tore – and the boy half slid, half climbed down the ladder to safety. Soon he was in Moon-Face's house with the others – but what was this? The toys did not stay up in their land – they poured down the ladder after the children and their friends!

"They're coming in here!" yelled Moon-Face. "Oh, why didn't we shut the door?"

But it was too late then to shut the door. Soldiers, golliwogs, bears and dolls poured into Moon-Face's funny round room – and Moon-Face, quick as lightning, gave them each a push towards the middle of his room.

The opening of his slippery-slip was there – and one by one all the astonished toys fell into the hole and found themselves sliding wildly down the inside of the tree!

As soon as Jo and the others saw what Moon-Face was doing, they did the same.

"Down you go!" said Jo to a fat golliwog, giving him a hard push – and down he went.

"A push for you!" yelled Dick to a big blue teddy bear – and down the slide went the bear.

Soon the children could do no more pushing, for they began to giggle. It really was too funny to see the toys rushing in, being pushed, and going down the slide, squealing and kicking for all they were worth. But after a while no more toys came, and Moon-Face shut his door. He flung himself on his curved bed, and laughed till the tears ran down his cheeks and wetted his pillow.

"What will the toys do?" asked Jo at last.

"Climb back up the tree to the Land of Toys," said Moon-Face, drying his eyes. "We'll see them out of my window. They won't interfere with us again!"

After about an hour the toys began to come past Moon-Face's window, slowly, as if they were tired. Not one of them tried to open the door and get into Moon-Face's house.

"They're afraid that if they don't get back into their land at once it will move away!" said Silky. "Let's sit here and watch them all – and have a few Google Buns and Pop Biscuits."

"I'm so very sorry to have caused all this trouble," said the Saucepan Man in a humble voice. "And I didn't bring anything back for tea either. You see, I really thought, when I got into the Land of Toys, that it was the Land of Goodies, because one of the first things I saw was that toy sweet shop. And in the Land of Goodies you can just take anything you like without paying – so of course I went right into the shop and began to empty some chocolates out of a box. That's why they put me into prison. It was dreadful. Oh, I *was* glad to hear Jo singing. I knew at once that you would try to rescue me."

This was a very long speech for Saucepan to make. He looked so unhappy and sorry that everyone forgave him at once for making such a silly mistake.

"Cheer up, Saucepan," said Moon-Face. "The Land of Goodies will soon come along – and we'll ALL go and visit it, not just you – and we'll have the grandest feast we have ever had in our lives."

"Oh, but do you think we ought to?" began Jo. "Honestly, we seem to get into a fix every single time we go up the ladder."

"I'll make quite sure that the Land of Goodies is there," said Moon-Face. "Nothing whatever can go wrong if we visit it. Don't be afraid. I say, Jo, you and Dick and Saucepan do look awfully grand in your soldier's uniforms. Are you always going to wear them?"

"Oh, gracious – I forgot we haven't got our proper clothes," said Jo. "Mother will be cross if we leave them in the Land of Toys. We left them under a hedge near the fort."

"And I left my lovely kettles and saucepans in the fort," said Saucepan in a mournful voice. "I feel funny without them. I don't like being a soldier. I want to be a Saucepan Man."

"I'd like you to be our dear old Saucepan Man, too," said Silky. "It doesn't seem you, somehow, dressed up like that. But I don't see how we are to get anything back. Certainly none of us is going back into the Land of Toys again!"

Just then three sailor dolls, last of all the toys, came climbing slowly up the tree. They were crying. Their sailor clothes were torn and soaking wet.

Moon-Face opened his door. "What's the matter?" he asked. "What's happened to you?"

"Awful things," said the first sailor. "We were climbing up this tree when we came to a window, and we all peeped in. And a very angry pixie flew out at us and pushed us off the branch. The Faraway Tree was growing thorns just there and they tore our clothes to bits. And then a whole lot of washing water came pouring down the tree on top of us and soaked us. So we feel dreadful. If only we could get some new clothes!"

"Listen!" cried Jo suddenly. "How would you like to have our soldier uniforms? They are quite new and very smart."

"Oooh!" said all the sailor dolls together. "We'd love that. Would you really give us those? We shall get into such trouble if we go back to the Land of Toys like this."

"We'll give you them on one condition, sailor dolls," said Jo. "You must find our own things in the Land of Toys and throw them down the ladder to us. We'll tell you where they are."

"We can easily do that," promised the sailors. So Jo, Dick and the Saucepan stripped off their smart uniforms and gave them to the sailor dolls who took off their torn blue clothes and dressed themselves in the red trousers, tunics and bearskin helmets. They looked as smart as could be.

"Now you *will* find our clothes for us, won't you?" said Jo. "We are trusting you, you see."

"We are very trustable," said the dolls, and ran up the ladder after Jo had told them exactly where to find everything.

Jo, Dick and Saucepan sat in their vests and pants and shivered a little, for the uniforms had been warm. "We shall look funny going home like this if those sailors don't keep their word!" said Dick. "As a matter of fact, I'd have liked to keep that uniform. I like it much better than my clothes."

"Look–something's coming down the ladder!" cried Moon-Face, and they all ran out to see. "How quick the sailor dolls have been–or soldier dolls, I suppose, we ought to call them now."

Two sets of clothes tumbled down the ladder and the children caught them. Then came a clatter and a clanging as kettles and saucepans came down too. Saucepan was delighted. He put on a pair of ragged trousers and a funny old coat that came down with the pans–and then Silky helped him to string his kettles and saucepans round him as usual.

"Now you look our dear old Saucepan again," said Silky. The boys dressed, too. Then Jo looked at Moon-Face's clock.

"We must go," he said. "Thanks for the Pop Biscuits and everything. Now, Saucepan, don't get into any more trouble for a little while!"

"Smile?" said Saucepan, going suddenly deaf again. "I *am* smiling. Look!"

"That's a grin, not a smile!" said Jo, as he saw

Saucepan smiling from ear to ear. "Now don't get into any more TROUBLE!"

"Bubble? Where's a bubble?" said Saucepan, looking all round. "I didn't see anyone blowing bubbles."

The children grinned. Saucepan was always very funny when he heard things wrong.

"Come on," said Bessie. "Mother will be cross if we're home too late. Good-bye, Moon-Face. Good-bye, Silky. We'll see you again soon."

"Well, don't forget to come to the Land of Goodies with us," said Silky. "That really will be fun. Nearly as much fun as the Land of Do-As-You-Please."

"We'll come," promised Bessie. "Don't go without us. Can I have a red cushion, Moon-Face? Thank you!"

One by one the four children slid swiftly down the slippery-slip to the bottom of the tree. They shot out of the trap-door, gave the red squirrel the cushions and set off home.

"I'm looking forward to our next adventure," said Dick. "It makes my mouth water when I think of the Land of Goodies! Hurrah!"

XVI

THE LAND OF GOODIES

The four children were rather naughty the next few days. Dick and Jo quarrelled, and they fell over when they began to wrestle with one another, and broke a little table.

Then Bessie scorched a table-cloth when she was ironing it—and Fanny tore an enormous hole in her blue frock when she went blackberrying.

"Really, you are all very naughty and careless lately," said their mother. "Jo, you will mend that table as best you can. Dick, you must help him—and if I see you quarrelling like that again I shall send you both to bed at once. Fanny, why didn't you put on your old overall when you went blackberrying, as I told you to? You are a naughty little girl. Sit down and mend that tear properly."

Bessie had to wash the table-cloth carefully to try and get the scorch marks out of it.

"I say, it's a pity all these things have happened just this week," groaned Jo to Dick, as the two boys did their best to mend the table. "I'm afraid the Land of Goodies will come and go before we get there! I daren't ask Mother or Father if we can go off to the Faraway Tree. We've been so naughty that they are sure to say no."

"Moon-Face and the others will be wondering why we don't go," said Bessie, almost in tears.

They were. The Land of Goodies had come, and a most delicious smell kept coming down the ladder. Moon-Face waited and waited for the children to come, and they didn't.

Then he heard that the Land of Goodies was going to move away the next afternoon, and he wondered what to do.

"We said we'd wait for the children – but we don't want to miss going ourselves," he said to Silky. "We had better send a note to them. Perhaps something has happened to stop them coming."

So they wrote a note, and went down to ask the owl to take it. But he was asleep. So they went to the woodpecker, who had a hole in the tree for himself, and he said he would take it.

He flew off with it in his beak. He soon found the cottage and rapped at the window with his beak.

"A lovely woodpecker!" cried Jo, looking up. "See the red on his head? He's got a note for us!"

He opened the window. Mother was there, ironing in the same room as the children, and she looked most astonished to see such an unexpected visitor.

Jo took the note. The bird stayed on the window-sill, waiting for an answer. Jo read it and then showed it to the others. They all looked rather sad. It was dreadful to know that the lovely Land of Goodies had come and was so soon going – and they couldn't visit it.

"Tell Moon-Face we've been naughty and can't come," said Jo.

The bird spread its wings, but Mother looked up

and spoke. "Wait a minute!" she said to the bird. Then she turned to Jo. "Read me the note," she said.

Jo read it out loud:

"DEAR JO, BESSIE, FANNY AND DICK,

"The Land of Goodies is here and goes to-morrow. We have waited and waited for you to come. If you don't come to-morrow we shall have to go by ourselves. Can't you come?

"Love from

"SILKY, SAUCEPAN AND MOON-FACE."

"The Land of Goodies!" said Mother in amazement. "Well, I never did hear of such funny happenings! I suppose there are lots of nice things to eat there, and that's why you all want to go. Well—you certainly have been bad children—but you've done your best to put things right. You may go to-morrow morning!"

"Mother! Oh, Mother, thank you!" cried the children. "Thank you, Aunt Polly!" said Dick, hugging her. "Oh, how lovely!"

"Tell Moon-Face we'll come as soon as we can to-morrow morning," said Jo to the listening woodpecker. He nodded his red-splashed head and flew off. The children talked together, excited.

"I shan't have any breakfast," said Bessie. "It's not much good going to the Land of Goodies unless we're hungry!"

"That's a good idea," said Dick. "I think I won't have any supper to-night either!"

So when the time came for the four children to

set off to the Enchanted Wood, they were all terribly hungry! They ran to the Faraway Tree and climbed up it in excitement.

"I hope there are treacle tarts," said Jo.

"I want chocolate blancmange," said Bessie.

"I simply can't begin to say the things I'd like," said greedy Dick.

"Well, don't," said Jo. "Save your breath and hurry. You're being left behind!"

They got to Moon-Face's, and shouted loudly to him. He came running out of his tree-house in delight.

"Oh, good, good, good!" he cried. "You *are* nice and early. Silky, they're here! Go down and call old Saucepan. He's with Mister Watzisname.

I'm sure Saucepan would like to come too."

It wasn't long before seven excited people were climbing up the ladder to the Land of Goodies. How they longed to see what it was like!

Well, it was much better than anyone imagined! It was a small place, set with little crooked houses and shops—and every single house and shop was made of things to eat! The first house that the children saw was really most extraordinary.

"Look at that house!" cried Jo. "Its walls are made of sugar—and the chimneys are chocolate—and the window-sills are peppermint cream!"

"And look at that shop!" cried Dick. "It's got walls made of brown chocolate, and the door is made of marzipan. And I'm sure the window-sills are gingerbread!"

The Land of Goodies was really a very extraordinary place. Everything in it seemed to be eatable. And then the children caught sight of the trees and bushes and called out in the greatest astonishment:

"Look! That tree is growing currant buns!"

"And that one has got buds that are opening out into biscuits! It's a Biscuit Tree!"

"And look at this little tree here—it's growing big, flat, white flowers like plates—and the middle of the flowers is full of jelly. Let's taste it."

They tasted it—and it *was* jelly! It was really most peculiar. There was another small bush that grew clusters of a curious-looking fruit, like flat berries of all colours—and, will you believe it, when the children picked the fruit it was boiled sweets, all neatly growing together like a bunch of grapes.

"Oooh, lovely!" said Jo, who liked boiled sweets very much. "I say, look at that yellow fence over there – surely it isn't made of barley-sugar!"

It was. The children broke off big sticks from the fence, and sucked the barley-sugar. It was the nicest they had ever tasted.

The shops were full of things to eat. You should just have seen them! Jo felt as if he would like a sausage roll and he went into a sausage-roll shop. The rolls were tumbling one by one out of a machine. The handle was being turned by a most peculiar man. He was quite flat and brown, and had what looked like black currants for eyes.

"Do you know. I think he is a gingerbread man!" whispered Jo to the others. "He's just like the gingerbread people that Mother makes for us."

The children chose a sausage roll each and went out, munching. They wandered into the next shop. It had lovely big iced cakes, set out in rows. Some were yellow, some were pink, and some white.

"Your name, please?" asked the funny little woman there, looking at Bessie, who had asked for a cake.

"Bessie," said the little girl in surprise. And there in the middle of the cake her name appeared in pink sugar letters! Of course, all the others wanted cakes, too, then, just to see their names come!

"We shall never be able to eat all these," said Moon-Face, looking at the seven cakes that had suddenly appeared. But, you know, they tasted so delicious that it wasn't very long before they all went!

Into shop after shop went the children and the others, tasting everything they could see. They had tomato soup, poached eggs, ginger buns, chocolate fingers, ice-creams, and goodness knows what else.

"Well, I just simply CAN'T eat anything more," said Silky at last. "I've been really greedy. I am sure I shall be ill if I eat anything else."

"Oh, Silky!" said Dick. "Don't stop. I can go on for quite a long time yet."

"Dick, you're greedy, *really* greedy," said Jo. "You ought to stop."

"Well, I'm not going to," said Dick. The others looked at him.

"You're getting very fat," said Jo suddenly. "You won't be able to get down the hole! You be careful, Dick. You are not to go into any more shops."

"All right," said Dick, looking sulky. But although he did not go into the shops, do you know what he did? He broke off some of a gingerbread window-sill – and then he took a knocker from a door. It was made of barley-sugar, and Dick sucked it in delight. The others had not seen him do these things – but the man whose knocker Dick had pulled off did see him!

He opened his door and came running out. "Hie, hie!" he cried angrily. "Bring back my knocker at once! You bad, naughty boy!"

XVII

DICK GETS EVERYONE INTO TROUBLE

When Jo and the others heard the angry voice behind them, they turned in surprise. Nobody but Dick knew what the angry little man was talking about.

"Knocker?" said Jo, in astonishment. "What knocker? We haven't got your knocker."

"That bad boy is eating my knocker!" cried the man, and he pointed to Dick. "I had a beautiful one, made of golden barley-sugar – and now that boy has eaten it nearly all up!"

They all stared at Dick. He went very red. What was left of the knocker was in his mouth.

"Did you really take his barley-sugar knocker?" said Jo in amazement. "Whatever were you thinking of, Dick?"

"Well, I just never thought," said Dick, swallowing the rest of the knocker in a hurry. "I saw it there on the door – and it looked so nice. I'm very sorry."

"That's all very well," said the angry man. "But being sorry won't bring back my knocker. You're a bad boy. You come and sit in my house till the others are ready to go. I won't have you going about in our land eating knockers and chimneys and window-sills!"

"You'd better go, Dick," said Jo. "We'll call for you when we're ready to go home. We shan't be long now. Anyway, you've eaten quite enough."

So poor Dick had to go into the house with the cross little man, who made him sit on a stool and keep still. The others wandered off again.

"We mustn't be here much longer," said Moon-Face. "It's almost time for this land to move on. Look! Strawberries and cream."

The children stared at the strawberries and cream. They had never seen such a strange sight before. The strawberries grew by the hundred on strawberry plants–but each strawberry had its own big dob of cream growing on it, ready to be eaten.

"They are even sugared!" said Jo, picking one. "Look–my strawberry is powdered with white sugar–and, oh, the cream is delicious!"

They enjoyed the strawberries and cream, and then Jo had a good idea.

"I say! What about taking some of these lovely goodies back with us?" he said. "Watzisname would love a plum pie–and the Angry Pixie would like some of those jelly-flowers–and Dame Washalot would like a treacle pudding."

"And Mother would like lots of things, too," said Bessie joyfully.

So they all began collecting puddings and pies and cakes. It was fun. The treacle pudding had so much treacle that it dripped all down Moon-Face's leg.

"You'll have to have a bath, Moon-Face," said Silky. "You're terriby sticky."

They nearly forgot to call for poor Dick! As they passed the house whose knocker he had eaten, he banged loudly on the window, and they all stopped.

"Gracious! We nearly forgot about Dick!" said Bessie. "Dick, Dick, come on! We're going!"

Dick came running out of the house. The little man called after him: "Now, don't you eat anybody's knocker again!"

"Goodness! Why have you got all those things?" asked Dick in surprise, looking at the puddings and pies and cakes. "Are they for our supper?"

"Dick! How can you think of supper after eating such a lot!" cried Jo. "Why, I'm sure I couldn't eat even a chocolate before to-morrow morning. No—these things are for Watzisname and Dame Washalot and Mother. Come on. Moon-Face says this land will soon be on the move."

They all went to the hole that led down through the cloud. It didn't take long to climb down the ladder and on to the big branch outside Moon-Face's house.

Dick came last—and he suddenly missed his footing and fell right down the ladder on the top of the others below. And he knocked the puddings, pies and cakes right out of their hands! Down went all the goodies, bumping from branch to branch. The children and the others stared after them in dismay.

Then there came a very angry yell from below. "Who's thrown a treacle pudding at me? Wait till I get them. I've treacle all over me. It burst on my head. Oh, oh, OH!"

Then there came an angry squealing from lower

down still. "Plum pie! Plum pie in my washtub! Sausage rolls in my washtub! Peppermints down my neck! Oh, you rascals up there – I'm coming up after you, so I am!"

And from still lower down came the voice of the Angry Pixie – and truly a very angry pixie, indeed, he was! "Jelly on my nose! Jelly down my neck! Jelly in my pockets! What next? Who's doing all this? Wait till I come up and tell them what I think!"

The children listened, half frightened and very much amused. They began to giggle.

"Plum pie in Dame Washalot's tub!" giggled Jo.

"Jelly on the Angry Pixie's nose!" said Bessie.

"I say – I do believe they really are coming up!" said Jo, in alarm. "Look – isn't that Watzisname?"

They all peered down the tree. Yes – it was Watzisname climbing up, looking very angry. The Saucepan Man leaned over rather too far, and nearly fell. Dick just caught him in time – but one of his kettles came loose and fell down. It bounced from branch to branch and landed on poor old Watzisname's big head!

He gave a tremendous yell. "What! Is it you, Saucepan, throwing all these things down the tree. What you want is a spanking. And you'll get it? And anybody else up there playing tricks will get a fine fat spanking, too!"

"A spanking!" said Dame Washalot's voice.

"A SPANKING!" roared the Angry Pixie not far behind.

"Golly!" said Jo in alarm. "It looks as if the Land of Spankings is about to arrive up here. I vote we go. You'd better shut your door, Moon-Face, and you and Silky and Saucepan had better lie down on the sofa and the bed and pretend to be asleep. Then maybe those angry people will think it's somebody up in the Land of Goodies that has been throwing all those things down."

"Dick ought to stay up there and get the spankings," said Moon-Face gloomily. "First he goes and eats somebody's door-knocker and gets into trouble. Then he falls on top of us all and sends all the goodies down the tree."

"I'm going down the slippery-slip with the children," said Silky, who was very much afraid of Mister Watzisname when he was in a temper. "I can climb up to my house and lock myself in before all those angry people come down again. Saucepan, why don't you come, too?"

Saucepan thought he would. So the children and Silky and Saucepan all slid down the slippery-slip. Just in time, too—for Mister Watzisname came shouting up to Moon-Face's door as Jo, who was last, slid down.

Moon-Face had shut his door. He was lying on his bed, pretending to be asleep. Watzisname banged hard on the door. Moon-Face didn't answer. Watzisname peeped in at the window.

"Moon-Face! Wake up! Wake up, I say!"

"What's the matter?" said Moon-Face, in a sleepy voice, sitting up and rubbing his eyes.

Dame Washalot and the Angry Pixie came up,

too. The Pixie had jelly all over him, and Watzisname had treacle pudding down him. They were all very angry.

They opened Moon-Face's door and went in. "Who was it that threw all those things down on us?" asked Watzisname. "Where's Saucepan? Did he throw that kettle? I'm going to spank him."

"Whatever are you talking about?" said Moon-Face, pretending not to know. "How sticky you are, Watzisname!"

"And so are you!" yelled Watzisname, suddenly, seeing treacle shining all down Moon-Face's legs. "It was you who threw that pudding down on me! My word, I'll spank you hard!"

Then all three of them went for poor Moon-Face, who got about six hard slaps. He rolled over to the slippery-slip, and slid down it in a fright.

He shot out of the trap-door just in time to see Silky and Saucepan saying good-bye to the children. They were most amazed when Moon-Face shot out beside them.

"I've been spanked!" wept Moon-Face. "They all spanked me because I was sticky, so they thought I'd thrown all the goodies at them. And now I'm afraid to go back because they will be waiting for me."

"Poor Moon-Face," said Jo. "And it was all Dick's fault. Listen. Silky can climb back to her house; but you and Saucepan had better come back with us and stay the night. Dick and I will sleep downstairs on the sofa, and you can have our beds. Mother won't mind."

"All right," said Moon-Face, wiping his eyes. "That will be fun. Oh, what a pity we wasted all those lovely goodies! I really do think Dick is a clumsy boy!"

They all went home together, and poor Dick didn't say a word. But how he did wish he could make up for all he had done!

XVIII

A SURPRISING VISITOR

The children's mother was rather astonished to see Moon-Face and Saucepan arriving at the cottage with the children.

"Mother, may they stay the night?" asked Jo. "They've been so good to us in lots of ways–and they don't want to go back to the tree to-night because somebody is waiting there to spank them."

"Dear me!" said Mother, even more surprised. "Well, yes, they can stay. You and Dick must sleep downstairs on the sofa. If they like to help in the garden for a day or two, they can stay longer."

"Oooh!" said Moon-Face, pleased. "That would be fine! I'm sure Watzisname will have forgotten about spanking us if we can stay away a few days. Thank you very much. We will help all we can."

"Would you like one of my very special kettles?" asked Saucepan gratefully. "Or a fine big saucepan for cooking soup bones?"

"Thank you," said Mother, smiling, for the old Saucepan Man was really a funny sight, hung about as usual with all his pans. "I could do with a strong little kettle. But let me pay you."

"Certainly not, madam," said Saucepan, hearing quite well for a change. "I shall be only too pleased to present you with anything you like in the way of kettles or saucepans."

He gave Mother a fine little kettle and a good strong saucepan. She was very pleased. Moon-Face looked on, wondering what he could give her, too. He put his hand in his pocket and felt around a bit. Then he brought out a bag and offered it to the children's mother.

"Have a bit of toffee?" he asked. Mother took a piece. The children stared at her, knowing that it was a piece of Shock Toffee! Poor Mother!

The toffee grew bigger and bigger and bigger in her mouth as she sucked it, and she looked more and more surprised. At last, when she felt that it was just as big as her whole mouth, it exploded into nothing at all—and the children squealed with laughter.

"Mother, that was a Toffee Shock!" said Jo, giggling. "Would you like to try a Pop Biscuit—or a Google Bun?"

"No, thank you," said Mother at once. "The Toffee Shock tasted delicious—but it *did* give me a shock!"

It *was* fun having Moon-Face and Saucepan staying with them in their cottage for a few days. The children simply loved it. Moon-Face was very,

very good in the garden, for he dug and cleared away rubbish twice as fast as anyone else. The old Saucepan Man wasn't so good because he suddenly went deaf again and didn't understand what was said to him. So he did rather queer things.

When Mother said: "Saucepan, fetch me some carrots, will you?" he thought she had asked for sparrows, and he spent the whole morning trying to catch them by throwing salt on their tails.

Then he went into the kitchen looking very solemn. "I can't bring you any sparrows," he said.

Mother stared at him. "I don't want sparrows," she said.

"But you asked me for some," said Saucepan, in surprise.

"Indeed I didn't," said Mother. "What do you suppose I want sparrows for? To make porridge with?"

When Saucepan and Moon-Face had been at the children's cottage for two or three days, Silky came in a great state of excitement.

She knocked at the door and Jo opened it. "Oh, Jo! Have you still got Moon-Face and Saucepan here?" she asked. "Well, tell them they must come back to the tree at once."

"Gracious! What's happened?" said Jo. Everyone crowded to the door to hear what Silky had to say.

"Well, you know the Old Woman Who Lives in a Shoe, don't you?" said Silky. "*Her* land has just come to the top of the tree! and the Old Woman came down the ladder through the cloud to see Dame Washalot, who is an old friend of hers. And when she saw that Moon-Face's house was empty, she said she was going to live there! She said she was tired of looking after a pack of naughty children."

"Oh, my!" said Moon-Face, looking very blue. "I don't like that Old Woman. She gives her children broth without any bread, and she whips them and sends them to bed when they are just the very littlest bit bad. Couldn't you tell her that that house in the tree is *mine*, and I'm coming back to it?"

"I did tell her that, silly," said Silky. "But do you suppose she took any notice of me at all? Not a bit! She just said in a horrid kind of voice:

'Little girls should be seen and not heard.' And she went into your house, Moon-Face, and began to shake all the rugs."

"Well!" said Moon-Face, beginning to be in a temper. "Well! To think of somebody shaking *my* rugs! I hope she falls down the slippery-slip."

"She won't," said Silky. "She peered down it and said: 'Ho! A coal-hole, I suppose! How stupid! I shall have a board made and nail that up.'"

"Well, I never!" cried Moon-Face, his big round face getting redder and redder. "Nailing up my lovely slippery-slip! Just wait till I tell her a few things! I'm going this very minute!"

"I'll come with you," said Saucepan. "Are you coming, too, children?"

"Mother, Saucepan and Moon-Face have got to go back home," called Jo. "May we go with them for a little while? We shan't be long."

"Very well," said Mother. Moon-Face and Saucepan went to say good-bye to her and thank her for having them. Then they and the four children and Silky sped off to the Enchanted Wood.

"I'll tell that Old Woman a few things!" cried Moon-Face. "I'll teach her to shake my rugs! Does she suppose she is going to live in my dear little round house? Where does she think *I'm* going to live? In her Shoe, I suppose!"

The children couldn't help feeling rather excited as they ran to the Tree. They climbed up it quickly and at last came to Moon-Face's door. It was shut. Moon-Face banged on it so loudly that the door shook.

The door flew open and a cross-faced old woman glared out.

"Do you want to break my door down?" she cried.

"'Tisn't your door!" shouted Moon-Face. "It's mine."

"Well, I've taken this house now," said the Old Woman. "I'm tired of all those naughty children, and I don't want to live in a shoe any more. I'm going to live by myself and have a good time. Dame Washalot is an old friend of mine and she and I will have lots of chats about old times." She slammed the door in the faces of everyone.

Moon-Face peered in at the window. He groaned. "She's nailed up the Slippery-Slip," he said. "She's put my bed across the board she's nailed there. Whatever am I to do?"

"*I'll* see if I can do something," said the old Saucepan Man unexpectedly. "You're a good friend of mine, Moon-Face, and I'd like to do something for you."

Saucepan began to clash his pans together and make a fearful noise. He shouted at the top of his voice: "Come out, you naughty Old Woman! Come out and let Moon-Face have his house! Your children are hungry!"

Now he was making such a tremendous noise that he didn't notice old Dame Washalot coming up the tree looking as black as thunder. She glared at the little company outside Moon-Face's house. She was short-sighted and she didn't see who they were. She thought that they were seven of the Old Woman's children who had come down from the Land above and were making themselves a nuisance.

"I'll teach you to shout and scream like that!" said Dame Washalot in a fierce voice – and before anyone quite knew what was happening they were all taken up one by one in Dame Washalot's strong arms and flung right up through the hole in the cloud into the Land of the Old Woman Who Lived in a Shoe!

And there they were, in a new and strange land again, out of breath and most astonished. How they stared round in surprise!

XIX

THE LAND OF THE OLD WOMAN

The children and the others were most surprised at being thrown up the ladder, through the hole in the cloud and into such a funny land.

It was quite small, not much larger than a big garden. It had a high wall all round to prevent the children from falling off the edge of the Land. In the very middle was a most peculiar thing.

"It's the Shoe!" said Jo. "Golly! I never imagined such a big one, did you?"

Everyone stared at the Shoe. It was as big as an ordinary house, and had been made very cleverly indeed into a cottage. Windows were let into the side, and a door had been cut out. A roof had been put on, and chimneys smoked from it. A rose tree climbed about it, and honeysuckle covered one side.

"So that's the Shoe where those naughty children live?" said Bessie, quite excited. "I never thought it would be quite like that. However did the Old Woman get such a big one?"

"Well, it once belonged to a giant, you know," said Silky. "The Old Woman did him a good turn, and asked him for an old boot. She had so many children that she couldn't get an ordinary house. So the giant gave her one of his biggest boots, and she got her brother to make it into a house."

"Look at all those children!" said Moon-Face. "They're not very well behaved!"

About twenty boys and girls were playing round the house. They shouted and screamed, and they fought and punched one another.

"I don't wonder the Old Woman wouldn't allow them bread with their soup, and whipped them and sent them to bed," said Silky. "They deserved it!"

The children suddenly saw Jo and the others and ran up to them. They pulled Bessie's hair. They tugged at Saucepan's kettles. They made fun of Moon-Face's round face. They dug Jo in the middle and pulled Dick's ears. They were very naughty and unkind.

"Now just you stop all this," said Moon-Face, looking fierce. "If you don't, I'll fetch the Old Woman."

"She isn't here, she isn't here!" shouted the naughty children, dancing round in delight. "She says she's going to go right away and leave us, and we're glad, glad, GLAD! Now we shall have bread with our soup—and we'll go to the larder and open tins of pineapple and bottles of cherries! We'll sleep out of doors if we like, and we'll go to the wardrobe and take out the Old Woman's best clothes to dress up in!"

"Whatever would she say to that?" said Bessie in horror, thinking what her own mother would say if she went to her cupboard and dressed up in her Sunday frocks!

"Oh, she would be SIMPLY FURIOUS!" cried the children. "But she's gone, so she won't know. Oh, we'll have a grand time now!"

One of the children in the Shoe called to the others. "Hie! I've opened a tin of pineapple! Come and taste it! It's lovely!"

With screams of joy the children rushed to the Shoe. Jo looked at the others. "I've just got an idea," he said. "What about telling the Old Woman about the children dressing up in her best clothes? She might rush back here then to get her precious clothes, and we could slip down the ladder, go to Moon-Face's house and bolt the door on the inside."

"That's a really good idea," said Silky. "Jo, you go down and tell her."

Jo was rather nervous about it. Nobody really wanted to go and see the fierce old lady again. At last Dick said he would. He badly wanted to make up for all the silly things he had done a few days before.

"I'll go," he said. And down the ladder he went. He banged hard at Moon-Face's door. The Old Woman opened it.

"Old Woman, do you want your best clothes?" began Dick. "Because if . . ."

"My best clothes! I'd forgotten all about them!" cried the Old Woman. "Those children will be messing about with them. Boy, go to my wardrobe, get out all my clothes and bring them down here. You shall have a sweet if you do."

"Well, I think . . ." began Dick. But the Old Woman wouldn't listen to him. She pushed him away and cried, "Go now! Don't stop to argue with me. Go at once!"

Dick ran up the ladder. He waited there a minute or two, his head sticking out into the Land above. He saw the naughty children coming out of the Shoe dressed up in the Old Woman's clothes, squealing with laughter, and *how* funny they looked dressed up in long skirts and shawls and bonnets! Dick grinned to himself and slipped down the ladder again. He banged at the door.

"Well, have you brought my clothes?" asked the Old Woman, opening the door. "You naughty boy, you haven't."

"Please, Old Woman, I couldn't bring them," said Dick in his most polite voice. "You see, your children have got them all out of your wardrobe and they're dancing about, wearing them – and they've opened your tins of pineapple – and they're going to pull their beds out of doors and sleep there – and . . ."

"Oh! Oh! The bad, naughty creatures!" cried the Old Woman.

She gathered up her black skirts and climbed the ladder at top speed. She appeared in the Land above and saw at once her naughty children dancing about in her best Sunday clothes. She broke a stick from a nearby tree and ran after the surprised children.

"So you thought you could do what you liked, did you?" she cried. "You thought I would never come back? Well, here I am, and I'll soon show you how to be sorry!"

She was so angry that she rushed round like a whirlwind. The children dragged off the clothes in fright, and ran away like hares. The Old Woman ran after them, so angry that she didn't notice that Jo and the others were not her own children. They got whirled in to the Shoe with the others. There they all were, about twenty-five or six of them.

There was a big saucepan simmering on the kitchen fire. It smelt of broth. "Get the soup-plates," ordered the Old Woman. "No bread for any of you to-night! Mary! Joan! Bill! serve out the plates and then come to me one by one for your supper!"

Jo and the others had plates given to them too.

They didn't dare to say anything. They went up for broth in their turn. The Old Woman ladled it out of the big saucepan. She stared at the Old Saucepan Man when he came up.

"You bad boy!" she said. "You've played a

game with my kettles and saucepans, I see! Wait till you've finished your broth and I'll give you a good whipping."

Poor old Saucepan trembled so much that his pans clashed together as loudly as a thunder-storm! He rushed back to his place at once, spilling his soup as he went.

"I want some bread," wailed a little boy. But he didn't get any. Everyone ate their broth, which was really very good.

"And now you will all go to bed—but first you know what happens to naughty children," said the Old Woman, and she took up her stick. All the children began to howl and cry:

"We're sorry we were naughty, Old Woman! We didn't mean to dress up in your clothes!"

"Oh, yes, you did," said the Old Woman. She beckoned to Dick. "Come here, you bad boy!"

Dick got up. He whispered to the others. "Look, I'll let her spank me, and whilst she's doing it you creep out and run to the ladder. Hurry! I'll join you as soon as I can."

Dick went boldly up to the Old Woman.

"Hold out your hands!" she said.

Spank, spank! Poor Dick, he didn't like it at all. He began to howl as loudly as he could so that the others could creep away without being heard. One by one they slipped out of the door and rushed to the hole, looking for the ladder that led down to the Faraway Tree.

"I say! I believe this Land is just about to move!" said Moon-Face, looking round. A peculiar wind had just got up and was blowing round them. Very often when the strange Lands at the top of the tree began to move away, this queer wind blew.

"Well, quick, let's get down the ladder!" cried Silky. "We don't want to live in the Land of the Old Woman! I should just hate that!"

They all scrambled down the ladder, glad to be on the broad branch at the bottom. When they were safely there Bessie began to cry.

"Poor Dick will be left behind," she sobbed.

Everyone looked very sad. The Land above the cloud began to make a strange noise.

"It's moving on," said Moon-Face. "We'll never see Dick again."

But just at that moment someone came slipping and sliding down the ladder—bump! bump! BUMP! And, hey presto, there was good old Dick, in such a hurry to get down before the Land moved right away that he had missed his footing and slid down the ladder from top to bottom!

"Dick! Dick! We're so glad to see you!" cried everyone. "What happened?"

"Well, the Old Woman spanked me, as you saw," grinned Dick. "And then when I went to take my place she saw you were all gone and sent me after you. I tore out—and she came, too. But I got to the ladder first, and now the Land has moved on, so we're safe!"

Moon-Face went into his house, and they heard him banging about loudly. They went to see what he was doing.

"He's taking up the board that nailed up the slippery-slip," giggled Jo. "Good old Moon-Face! I'm glad he's got his house back again for himself. Come on – we'd better go home. We promised Mother we wouldn't be long. It's a good thing we can use the slippery-slip!"

And down it they went, their hair streaming out as they flew down on their cushions. What exciting times they do have, to be sure!

XX

THE LAND OF MAGIC MEDICINES

For a few days the children had no time even to think of going to their friends in the Faraway Tree. Their mother was in bed ill, and the doctor came each day.

"Just let her lie in bed and keep her warm,' he said to the two girls. "Give her what she likes to eat, and don't let her worry about anything."

The children were upset. They loved their mother, and it was strange to see her lying in bed.

"There's all that washing that I had to do for Mrs. Jones," she said. "No, you girls are not to try and do it. It's too much for you."

Moon-Face and Silky came to visit the children one morning, and were very sorry to hear that the children's mother was ill.

"She worries so about the washing," said Bessie.

"She won't let us two girls do it. I don't know what to do about it!"

"Oh, we can manage *that* for you," said Silky at once. "Old Dame Washalot will do it for nothing. It's the joy of her life to wash, wash, wash! I believe if she's got nothing dirty to wash, she washes clean things. She even washes the leaves on the Faraway Tree if she's got nothing else to wash. Is that the basket over there? Moon-Face and I will take it up the tree now, and bring it back when it's finished."

"Oh, thank you, Silky darling," said Bessie gratefully. "Mother will be so pleased when I tell her. She'll stop worrying about that."

Silky and Moon-Face went off with the basket. They took it to Dame Washalot, and how her face shone with joy when she saw such a lot of washing to be done!

"My, this is good of you!" she said, taking out the dirty things and throwing them into her enormous wash-tub of soapy water. "Now this is what I really enjoy! I'll have them all washed and ironed by to-night."

Silky was pleased. She knew how beautifully Dame Washalot washed and ironed. She went up to Moon-Face's house to have dinner with him.

"I do so wish we could help make the children's mother better," she said. "She is such a darling, isn't she? And the children love her so much. Moon-Face, can't you possibly think of anything?"

"Well, I don't suppose Toffee Shocks would be

any good, do you?" said Moon-Face. "I've got some of those."

"Of course not, silly," said Silky. "It's medicine we want—pills or something—but as nobody is ill in the Faraway Tree there's no shop to buy them from."

That night they went to see if Dame Washalot had finished the washing. She had. It was washed and most beautifully ironed, done up in the basket, ready to be taken away.

"I've had a fine time," said the old dame, beaming at Silky. "My the water I've poured down the tree to-day."

"Yes, I've heard the Angry Pixie shouting like anything because he got soaked at least four times," said Moon-Face with a grin. "He's got plums growing on the tree just outside his house and he was picking them for jam—and each time he went out to pick them he got soaked with your water. You be careful he doesn't come up and shout at you."

"If he does I'll put him into my next wash-tub of dirty water and empty him down the tree with it," said Dame Washalot.

"Oooh, I wish I could see you do that," said Silky, tying a rope to the basket of washing, so that she might let it down the tree to the bottom. "Well, Dame Washalot, thank you very much. The person who usually does this washing is ill in bed and can't seem to get better. It's such a pity. I wish I could make her well."

"Why, Silky, the Land of Magic Medicines is

coming to-morrow," said the old dame. "You could get any medicine you liked there, and your friend would soon be better. Why don't you visit the Land and get some?"

"That's an awfully good idea!" said Silky joyfully, letting down the basket bit by bit. Moon-Face had gone to the bottom of the tree to catch it. "I'll tell Moon-Face, and maybe he and I could go and get some medicine.

She slipped down the tree and told Moon-Face what the old dame had said. Moon-Face put the basket of washing on his shoulder and beamed at Silky.

"That's good news for the children," he said. "Come on, we'll hurry and tell them."

The children were delighted to have the washing back so quickly, all washed and ironed. Dick set off with it to Mrs. Jones. Bessie ran to tell her mother that she needn't worry any more about it.

Silky told Jo and Fanny about the Land of Magic Medicines coming the next day to the top of the Faraway Tree. They listened in surprise.

"Well, I vote we go there," said Jo at once. "I'd made up my mind we'd none of us go whilst Mother was ill—but if there's a chance of getting something to make her better, we'll certainly go! One of the girls must stay behind with Mother and the rest of us will go."

So it was arranged that Jo, Dick and Bessie should meet at Moon-Face's house early the next morning. Then they would go up to the strange Land and see what they could find for their mother.

Fanny was quite willing to stay with her mother, though she felt a little bit left out. She said good-bye to Jo, Dick and Bessie soon after breakfast the next day, and promised to wash up the breakfast things carefully, and to sit with her mother until the rest of them came back.

They set off and arrived outside Moon-Face's house at the top of the tree very soon afterwards. Moon-Face and Silky were waiting for them. "Is old Saucepan coming?" asked Jo.

"Hie, Saucepan, do you want to come?" shouted Moon-Face, leaning down the tree.

Saucepan was with Watzisname. For a wonder he heard what Moon-Face said and shouted back:

"Yes, I'll come. But where to?"

"Up the ladder!" yelled Moon-Face. "Hurry!"

So Saucepan came with them and in a little while they all stood in the Land of Magic Medicines. It was just as peculiar as every land that came to the top of the Faraway Tree!

It didn't seem to be a land at all! When the children had climbed up the ladder to the top, they found themselves in what looked like a great big factory—a place where all kinds of pills, medicines, bandages and so on were made. Goblins and gnomes, pixies and fairies were as busy as could be, stirring great pots over curious green fires, pouring medicines into shining bottles, and counting out pills to put into coloured pill-boxes.

In one corner a goblin was stirring a purple mixture in a yellow basin. Bessie looked at it.

"It's a kind of ointment," she said to the others. "I wonder what it's for."

"It's to make crooked legs straight," said the goblin, stirring hard. "Do you want some?"

"Well, I don't know anyone with crooked legs," said Bessie. "Thank you all the same. If I did I'd love to have some, because it would be simply marvellous to make somebody's crooked legs better."

A pixie near by was pouring some sparkling green medicine into bottles shaped like bubbles. The children and the others watched. It made a funny singing noise as it went in.

"What's that for?" asked Jo.

"Whoever takes this will always have shining eyes," said the Pixie. "Shining, smiling eyes are the loveliest eyes in the world. Is it this medicine you have come for?"

"Well, no, not exactly," said Jo. "I'd like to have some, though."

"Oh, your eyes *are* smiley eyes," said the pixie, looking at him. "This is for sad people, whose eyes have become dull. Come to me when you are an old man and your eyes cannot see very well. I will give you plenty then."

"Oh," said Jo. "Well, I shan't be here then! I've only just come on a short visit!"

Dick called to the others. "I say, look!" he cried. "Here's some simply marvellous pills! Watch them being made!"

Everyone watched. It was most astonishing to see. First of all the pills were enormous – as large as footballs. A goblin blew on them with a pair of bellows out of which came green smoke, and they at once went down to the size of a cricket-ball. He then splashed them with what looked like moonlight from a watering-can. They went as small as marbles.

Then he blew on them gently – and they went as small as green peas, and each one jumped into a pill-box with a ping-ping-ping till the box was full.

"What are they for?" asked Dick.

"To make short people tall," said the goblin. "Some people hate being short. Well, these pills are made of big things – the shadow of a mountain – the height of a tree – the crash of a thunder-storm – things like that – and they have the power of making anything or anyone grow."

"Could I have some?" asked Dick eagerly.

"Take a boxful," said the goblin. Dick took it. He read what was written on the lid.

"GROWING PILLS. ONE TO BE TAKEN THREE TIMES A DAY."

Now Dick was not very tall for his age and he had always wanted to be big. He looked longingly at the pills. If he took three at once, maybe he would grow taller. That would be fine!

He popped three of the pills into his mouth. He sucked them. They tasted so horrid that he swallowed them all in a hurry!

And goodness, WHAT a surprise when the others turned to speak to Dick. He was taller than their father! He was as tall as the ceiling in their cottage! He towered above them, looking down on them in alarm, for he hadn't expected to grow quite so much, or quite so quickly!

"Dick! You've been taking those Growing Pills!" cried Jo. "Just the sort of stupid thing you *would* do! You're enormous! How in the world do you think you'll ever get down the hole in the cloud?"

"Oh, do something to help me!" begged Dick, who really was frightened to be so enormous. Everyone else looked so small. "Jo, Moon-Face – what can I do? I'm still growing! I'll burst out of the roof in a minute!"

The goblins and pixies around suddenly noticed how fast Dick was growing. They began to shout and squeal.

"He'll break through the roof! He'll bring it down on top of us! Quick, stop him growing!"

XXI

SOME PECULIAR ADVENTURES

Dick was enormously tall. He had to bend down so that his head wouldn't touch the roof. The little people in the medicine factory rushed about, yelling and shouting.

"Fetch a ladder! Climb up it and give him some Go-Away Pills! Quick, quick!"

Somebody got a ladder and leaned it up against poor Dick.

A pixie ran up it on light feet. He carried a box of pills. He shouted to Dick:

"Open your mouth!"

Dick opened his mouth. The pixie meant to throw one pill inside, but in his excitement he threw the whole box. Dick swallowed it!

And at once he began to grow small again! Down he went and down and down. He got to his own size and grinned with delight. But he didn't stop there. He went smaller and smaller and smaller—and at last he couldn't be seen! It was a terrible shock to everyone.

"He's gone!" said Bessie in horror. "He's so

small that he can't be seen! Dick! Dick! Where are you?"

A tiny squeak answered her from under a big chair. Bessie bent down and looked there. She couldn't see a thing.

"Listen, Dick," she said. "I've got a pill box here. Come running over to me and put yourself in it. Then we shall at least know where you are, even if we can't see you. And maybe we can get you right if only we've got you safely somewhere."

A tiny squeaking sound came from the pill box after a minute, so Bessie knew that Dick had done as he had been told and got into the box. But she couldn't see anyone there at all. She put on the lid, afraid that Dick might fall out.

She stood up and stared round at the wondering little folk there. "What can we do for someone gone too small?" she asked. "Haven't you any medicine for that?"

"It will have to be very specially made," said a Pixie. "We can't give him the Grow-Fast Mixture because he's really too small for that. We'll have to prepare a special little bath of powerful medicine, and get him to go into it. Then maybe he will grow back to his own size. But he shouldn't have meddled with our magic medicine. It's dangerous."

"Dick's so silly," said Jo. "He always seems to get himself and other people into trouble! I do hope you can make him right again. I wouldn't want him to live in a pill box all his life."

"We'll do our best to get him right," said the

little folk, and they began to shout here and there, calling for the most peculiar things to make the bath for Dick.

"The whisk of a mouse's tail!" cried one.

"The sneeze of a frog!" cried another.

"The breath of the summer wind!" cried a third. And as the children watched small goblins came running with little boxes and tins.

"What queer things their medicines are made of!" said Jo. "Well, let's leave them to it, shall we? I'd like to wander round this big factory a bit more. Come on, Saucepan."

Saucepan was very deaf because there was such a noise going on all the time. Fires were sizzling under big pots. Medicines were being poured into bottles with gurgles and splashes. Pans were being stirred with a clatter. Saucepan couldn't hear a word that was said—and it was because of that that he made his great mistake.

He stopped by a goblin who was pouring a beautiful blue liquid into a little jar. It shone so brightly that it caught Saucepan's eye at once.

"That's lovely," he said to the goblin. "What's it for?"

"To make a nose grow," said the goblin.

"To make a rose grow!" said Saucepan in delight. "Oh, I'd like some of that. If I had that I could make roses grow on the Faraway Tree all round Mister Watzisname's branch. He *would* like that!"

"I said to make a NOSE grow!" said the goblin.

"I heard you the first time," said Saucepan.

"It would be lovely to be able to grow roses. Do I have to drink it?"

"Yes – if you want your nose to grow," said the goblin, looking at Saucepan's nose.

Saucepan kept on hearing him wrong. He felt quite certain that the beautiful medicine was to make roses grow. He thought that if he drank it he would be able to make roses grow anywhere! That would be marvellous. So he took a jar of the medicine and drank it all up before the goblin could stop him.

"Now I'll make the roses grow out of my kettles and pans!" said Saucepan, pleased. "Grow, roses, grow!"

But they didn't grow, of course. It was his poor old nose that grew! It suddenly shot out, long and pink, and Saucepan stared at it in surprise.

The others looked at him in amazement.

"Saucepan! What has happened to your nose?" cried Jo. "It's as big as an elephant's trunk!"

"He *would* drink it!" said the goblin in dismay. showing the children the empty jar. "I told him it was to make a nose grow – but he kept on saying it was to grow roses, not noses. He's quite mad."

"No, he's just deaf," said Jo. "Oh, poor old Saucepan! He'll have to tie his nose round his waist soon. It's down to his feet already!"

"I can cure it," said the goblin with a grin. "I've got a disappearing medicine. I'll just rub his nose with it till it disappears back to the right size. I think you ought to watch him a bit, if he goes about hearing things all wrong goodness knows what may happen to him!"

Saucepan was crying tears that rolled down his funny long nose. The goblin took a box of blue ointment and began to rub the end of Saucepan's nose with it. It disappeared as soon as the ointment touched it. The goblin worked hard, rubbing gradually all up the long nose until there was nothing left but Saucepan's own pointed nose. Then he stopped rubbing.

"Cheer up!" he said. "It's gone, and only your own nose is left. My, you did look queer! I've never seen anyone drink a whole bottle of that nose medicine before!"

A shout came from behind the watching children. "Where's that tiny boy in the pill box? We've got the bath ready for him now."

Everyone rushed to where there was a tiny bath filled with steaming yellow water that smelt of cherries. Bessie took the pill box from her pocket and opened it.

A squeaking came from the box at once. Dick was still there, too small to be seen! But, thank goodness, his voice hadn't quite disappeared, or the others would never have known if he was there or not!

"Get into this bath, Dick," said Bessie. "You will soon be all right again then."

There came the tiniest splash in the yellow water. It changed at once to pink. A squeaking came from the bath and bubbles rose to the surface. Then suddenly the children could see Dick! At first it was a bit misty and cloudy—then gradually the mist thickened and took the shape of a very, very small boy.

"He's coming back, he's coming back!" cried Jo. "Look, he's getting bigger!"

As Dick grew bigger, the bath grew, too. It was most astonishing to watch. Soon the bath was as big as an ordinary bath, and there stood Dick in it, his own size again, his clothes soaked with the pink water. He grinned at them through the steam.

"Just the same old cheerful Dick!" said Bessie gladly. "Oh, Dick, you gave us such a fright!"

"Step out of the bath, quick!" cried the pixie nearby. "You're ready to be dried!"

Dick jumped out of the bath—just in time, too, for it suddenly folded itself up, grew a pair of wings, and disappeared out of a big window near by!

"Dry him!" cried the pixie, and threw some strange towels to the children and Moon-Face. They seemed to be alive and were very warm. They rubbed themselves all over Dick, squeezing his clothes as they rubbed, until in a few minutes he was perfectly dry. But his clothes were rather a curious pink colour.

"That can't be helped," said the pixie. "That always happens."

"Well, I suppose I look a bit funny, but I don't mind," said Dick. "Golly, that was a queer adventure."

"A bit too queer for me!" said Jo. "Now see you don't get into any more trouble, Dick, or

I'll never bring you into any strange land again. I never knew anyone like you for doing things you shouldn't. Now, look here everyone—I vote we try and get some medicine for Mother, and then we'll go. Fanny is waiting patiently for us to go back, and I really think we'd better go before Dick or Saucepan do anything funny again."

"What medicine do you want?" asked a goblin kindly. "What is wrong with your mother?"

"Well, we really don't know," said Dick. "She just lies in bed and looks white and weak, and she worries dreadfully about everything."

"Oh, well, I should just take a bottle of Get-Well Medicine," said the Goblin. "That will be just the thing."

"It sounds fine," said Jo. The goblin poured a bubbling yellow liquid into a big bottle and gave it to Jo. He put it carefully into his pocket.

"Thank you," he said. "Now, come along every-one. We're going."

"Oh, Jo—there's a medicine here for making teeth pearly," said Saucepan, pulling at Jo's arm. "Just let me take some."

"Saucepan, that's for making hair CURLY!" said Jo. "You've heard wrong again. Don't try it. Do you want curls growing down to your feet? Now take my arm and don't let go till we're safely back in the Tree. If I don't look after you, you'd have a nose like an elephant's, curly hair down to your toes, and goodness knows what else!"

They were not very far from the hole in the cloud, and they were soon climbing down the ladder, leaving behind them the Strange Land of Magic Medicines. Jo was very careful of the bottle in his pocket.

"Now we'll go straight home," he said. "I'm simply LONGING to give dear old Mother a dose of this magic medicine. It will be so lovely to see her looking well again and rushing round the house as she always did!"

XXII

WATZISNAME HAS SOME QUEER NEWS

Fanny was delighted to see Jo, Bessie and Dick back. "Mother doesn't seem quite so well," she said. "She says she has such a bad headache. Did you get some medicine for her, Jo?"

"Yes, I did," said Jo, showing Fanny the big bottle. "It's a Get-Well medicine. Let's give Mother some now. It smells of plums, so it should be rather nice."

They went into Mother's bedroom and Jo took a glass and poured out two teaspoonfuls of the strange medicine.

"Well, I hope it's all right, Jo dear," said Mother, holding out her hand for it. "I must say it smells most delicious—like plum tarts cooking in the oven!"

It tasted simply lovely, too, Mother said. She lay back on her pillows and smiled at the children. "Yes, I do believe I feel better already!" she said. "My head isn't aching so badly."

Well, that medicine was simply marvellous. By the time the evening came Mother was sitting up knitting. By the next morning she was eating a huge breakfast and laughing and joking with everyone. Father was very pleased.

"We'll soon have her up now!" he said. And he was right! By the time the bottle of Get-Well Medicine was only half-finished, Mother was up and about again, singing merrily as she washed and ironed. It was lovely to hear her.

"We'll put the rest of the bottle of magic medicine away," she said. "I don't need it any more – but it would be very useful if anyone else is ill."

A whole week went by and the children heard nothing of their friends in the Faraway Tree. They were very busy helping their parents, and they wondered sometimes what land was at the top of the Tree now.

"If it was a very nice Land Silky and Moon-Face would be sure to let us know," said Jo. "So I don't expect it's anything exciting."

One evening, when the children were in bed, they heard a little rattling sound against their windows. They sat up at once.

"It's Silky and Moon-Face!" whispered Jo.

"They've come to say there's a lovely Land at the top of the Tree," said Dick, excited. The boys went into the girls' room to see if they were awake. They were looking out of the window.

"It isn't Silky or Moon-Face," whispered Bessie. "I think it's old Watzisname!"

"Gracious! Whatever has *he* come for!" cried Jo.

"Sh!" said Fanny. "You'll wake Mother. Whoever it is doesn't seem to want to come any nearer. Let's creep down and see if it *is* Watzisname."

So they put on their dressing-gowns and crept downstairs. They went into the garden and whispered loudly: "Who's there? What is it?"

"It's me, Watzisname," said a voice, and Mister Watzisname came nearer to them. He looked terribly worried.

"What's the matter?" asked Jo.

"Have you seen Silky, Moon-Face or Saucepan lately?" asked Watzisname.

"Not since we all went to the Land of Magic Medicines," said Jo. "Why? Aren't they in the Faraway Tree?"

"They've *disappeared,*" said Watzisname. "I haven't seen them for days. They went—and never even said good-bye to me!"

"Oh, Watzisname! But what could have happened to them?" asked Bessie. "They must have gone up into some Land, that moved away from the top of the Tree—and that's why you haven't seen them."

"No, that's not it," said Watzisname. "The same Land has been there ever since the Land of Medicines moved away. It's the Land of Tempers. I'm quite sure that Moon-Face and the others wouldn't visit it, because it's well known that everyone there is always in a bad temper. No—they've gone—vanished—disappeared. And I DO so miss dear old Saucepan. It makes me very, very sad."

"Oh, Watzisname, this is very worrying," said Bessie, feeling upset. "Whatever can we do?"

"I suppose you wouldn't come back to the Far-away Tree with me, would you, and help me to look for them?" asked Watzisname. "I feel so lonely there. And, you know, somebody else has taken Moon-Face's house and Silky's house, too. They have come from the Land of Tempers, and I'm so frightened of them that I just simply don't dare to go near them."

"Good gracious! This is very bad news," said Jo. "Somebody else in Moon-Face's nice little house—and someone in Silky's house, too! Most extraordinary! I'm surprised you didn't hear anything, Watzisname. You know, I'm sure Moon-

Face would have made an awful fuss and bother if anyone had turned him out of his house. Are you sure you didn't hear anything?"

"Not a thing," said Watzisname, gloomily. "You know how I snore, don't you? I expect I was fast asleep as usual, and I shouldn't even have heard if they had called to me for help."

"Well, listen, Watzisname, we can't possibly come to-night," said Jo. "Mother likes us to get the breakfast, and since she has been ill we make her have her breakfast in bed. But we will come just as soon as ever we can after breakfast. Will that do?"

"Oh, yes," said Watzisname, gratefully. "That's marvellous. I shan't go back to the Tree to-night. It's too lonely without the others. May I sleep in that shed over there?"

"You can sleep on the sofa downstairs," said Jo. "Come in with us. I'll get you a rug. Then we can all start off together to-morrow morning."

So that night old Watzisname slept on the sofa. He snored rather, and Mother woke up once and wondered what in the wide world the noise was. But she thought it must be the cat, and soon went off to sleep again.

Next morning the children asked if they might go off with Watzisname. They explained what had happened.

"Well, I don't know that I like you going off if something horrid has happened," said Mother. "I don't want anything to happen to *you*."

"I'll look after everyone," said Jo. "You can

trust me, Mother; really you can. We'll be back soon."

So Mother said they might go. They set off to the Enchanted Wood with Watzisname, feeling rather excited. Whatever *could* have happened to Silky and the others?

They climbed up the Faraway Tree. It was growing peaches that day, and they were really most delicious. Dick ate far more than the others, of course, and nearly got left behind.

They came to Silky's house. It was shut. From inside came a stamping and a roaring.

"That's one of the people from the Land of Bad Tempers," said Watzisname in a whisper. "They're always losing their tempers, you know, whenever anything goes wrong. I just simply DAREN'T knock at the door and ask where Silky is."

"Well, let's go on up to Moon-Face's," said Jo, feeling that he didn't really want to go knocking at the door either.

So up they went, and at last came to Moon-Face's door. That was shut, too, and from inside came a banging and shouting.

"Golly, they have got bad tempers, haven't they!" said Jo. "I'm quite certain I shan't go visiting the Land of Tempers! Let's peep in at the window and see who's there."

So they peeped in, and saw a round, fat little man, with large ears, a shock of black hair, fierce eyes, and a very bad-tempered look on his face. He was looking for something on the floor.

"Where's it gone?" he shouted. "You bad, wicked button! Where did you roll to? Don't you know that I want to put you on my coat again? I'll stamp you into a hundred bits when I find you!"

Jo giggled. "If he does that it won't be much good trying to sew it on his coat!" he said.

Just then the black-haired man looked up and saw the four children peering in at him. He got up in a rage, flew to the door and flung it open.

"How dare you pry and peep!" he yelled, stamping first one foot at them and then the other. "How dare you look into my window!"

"It isn't your window," said Jo. "This house belongs to a friend of ours, called Moon-Face. You'd better get out of it before he comes back, or he will be very angry."

"Pooh! you don't know what you're talking about!" cried the bad-tempered man. "I'm Sir Stamp-a-Lot, and this is *my* house. My cousin, Lady Yell-Around, has taken the house a bit lower down. We've come to live in this tree."

"But don't you belong to the Land of Tempers?" asked Jo. "Are you allowed to leave your own land?"

"Mind your own business," said Sir Stamp-a-Lot. "MIND YOUR OWN BUSINESS!"

"Well, it *is* my business to find out what you are doing in my friend's house," said Jo firmly. "Now, you just tell me what has happened to Moon-Face—yes, and Silky and the old Saucepan Man, too."

"Moon-Face said I could have his house whilst he went to live for a while in the Land of Tempers," said Sir Stamp-a-Lot, doing a bit more stamping. "And Silky said the same. The old Saucepan Man went with them."

"Well, I just don't believe you," said Watzisname suddenly. "Moon-Face told me that the Land of Tempers had come, and he said nothing in the world would make him go there. So you are telling fibs."

That sent Sir Stamp-a-Lot into such a rage that he nearly stamped the bark off the tree branch he stood on! "How dare you talk to me like that?" he cried. "I'll pull your hairs out! I'll pinch your noses! I'll scratch your ears!"

"What a nice, kind, pleasant person you are," said Jo. "What a beautiful nature you have! What a sweet, charming friend you would make!"

This made Sir Stamp-a-Lot so angry that he kicked hard at Jo, who dodged. Stamp-a-Lot lost his balance and fell. He fell down through the tree, yelling loudly.

"Quick!" said Jo. "He'll be back in a minute; but we might just have time to pop into Moon-Face's house and see if there is any message from him!"

They all crowded into the little round house and hunted hard. Wherever could their three friends be? It was too puzzling for words!

XXIII

THE LAND OF TEMPERS

The four children and Mister Watzisname hunted in every corner of Moon-Face's house, but there was no message anywhere from their friends.

"I say—that's old Stamp-a-Lot coming back," said Fanny. "I can hear him shouting. Let's get out, quick!"

"We can go down the Slippery-slip," said Jo. But he was wrong! The Slippery-slip was stuffed up with all kinds of things—cushions, boughs, carpets, leaves—and nobody could possibly get down it. The children were all staring at it, puzzled, when Sir Stamp-a-Lot came back.

And, my goodness me, what a rage he was in! He had bumped his head and his back in falling down the tree, and he had a tremendous bruise on his left cheek. He came in bellowing like a bull!

"How dare you go into my house!" he stormed. "How dare you pry into my business! I'll throw you out! I'll throw you out!"

He tried to get hold of Fanny, but Joe and Dick stopped him. "We're five to one," said Jo. "You might as well keep your temper, or we may do a bit of throwing out, too. We're going because we can only get fibs out of you, and it's quite plain that our friends are not here. But you'll feel very sorry for yourself when we do find our friends and we all come back to tell you what we think!"

Stamp-a-Lot was furious. He began to throw

things after the children and Watzisname as soon as they had gone out of the house. Crash! That was the clock. Clatter! That was a picture. Bang! That was a chair!

"Oh, dear! Poor Moon-Face won't find a single thing in his house when he gets home," said Jo, dodging a soup plate that came flying past his head. "Now, what shall we do next? Perhaps we had better go down to Silky's house and see if we can find out anything from Lady Yell-Around or whatever her name is."

Nobody really wanted to see Lady Yell-Around – but they saw her before they expected to. As they climbed down to where Dame Washalot lived, they heard a fierce quarrel going on.

"You emptied your dirty water down on me just as I was going shopping!" yelled an angry voice. "You did, you did, you did!"

Then came Dame Washalot's voice. "I did, I did, I did, did I? Well, I'm glad! If people can't look out for my washing water, it's their own fault!"

"Look how wet I am; look at me!" came the other voice.

"I don't want to look at you, you're a most unpleasant person," said Dame Washalot. "Now, look out – here comes some more water!"

There was a sound of splashing – and then squeals and screams as Lady Yell-Around got the whole lot on top of her. The children began to giggle. They climbed down to where Dame Washalot was standing by her empty tub, grinning as she looked down the tree. Lady Yell-Around was hurriedly climbing down, dripping wet, her shopping basket still in her hand.

"Dame Washalot—have you heard anything about Silky and the others?" asked Bessie.

"Not a thing," said the old dame. "All I know is that that bad-tempered creature who calls herself Lady Yell-Around has taken Silky's house and says that Silky said she might have it, because she, Silky, wanted to go and live for a while in the Land of Tempers—a thing I don't believe at all, for a sweeter-tempered person than little Silky you could never find!"

"It's awfully funny," said Jo, frowning. "Silky, Moon-Face and Saucepan disappear—and these two awful people take their places. There's only one thing to do. We'd better just pop up into the Land of Tempers to see if by any chance they *have* gone there."

"Well, that's dangerous," said Dame Washalot. "Once you lose your temper up there you have to live there for always. And you might easily lose your temper with the cross lot of people who live there. I can't think how it is that these two have been able to leave."

"It does sound dangerous," said Jo. "But I think we could all keep our tempers, you know, if we knew we had to. Anyway, I simply don't know what else to do. Perhaps it would be best if I just went by myself—then the others wouldn't have to risk getting into danger."

But the others wouldn't hear of Jo going by

himself. "We share in this," said Dick. "If you can go to the Land of Tempers and keep your temper, we can, too. We need only go up and ask if Silky and the others are there. If they're not, we can at once come away."

"Well, then, we'd better go now," said Jo.

So up the Tree they went, and then up the ladder through the hole in the cloud – and into the Land of Tempers.

Well, it *was* a funny Land! There was such a lot of shouting and quarrelling going on – such a smashing of windows by people throwing stones in a rage – such a stamping and yelling!

"Goodness! I vote we don't stay here long!" said Jo, dodging to miss a stone that someone had thrown. "Look! Let's ask that man over there if he has seen Silky or the others."

So he asked him. But he glared at them and answered rudely.

"Don't come bothering me with your silly questions! Can't you see I'm in a hurry?"

He pushed Jo roughly, and the little boy at once felt angry. He was just about to push the man roughly too when Fanny whispered to him:

"Jo! Don't lose your temper! Smile, quickly, smile!"

So Jo made himself smile, for he knew that no one can really lose his temper when he is smiling. The man glared at him and went away.

"Well, I can see that it would be jolly difficult to live here without getting angry almost every minute of the day," said Jo. "Hie, there – do you know anything about our friends, Silky, Moon-Face and Saucepan?"

The boy he was calling to stopped and put out his tongue at Jo. "Yah!" he said. "Do you suppose I'm here to answer your questions, funny-face?"

"No, I don't," said Jo. "But I thought perhaps you might be polite enough to help me."

The boy made a lot of rude faces at all of them and then pulled Fanny's hair very sharply before he ran off.

Dick and Jo felt angry, because they saw the tears come into Fanny's eyes. They began to run after the boy, shouting.

"Dick! Jo! Come back!" cried Watzisname. "You are losing your tempers again."

"So we are," said the boys, and they stopped and made themselves look pleasant.

Watzisname went to meet them, and as he went two naughty little boys ran by. One put out his foot, and poor old Watzisname tripped over it, bang, on his nose. The boys stood and laughed till they cried.

Watzisname got up, his face one big frown. "I'll teach you to trip me up!" he cried. "I'll . . ."

"Smile, Watzisname, smile!" cried Bessie. "Don't look like that. You're losing your temper. Smile!"

And Watzisname had to smile, but it was very, very difficult. The two bad boys ran off. The children went walking on, telling themselves that they MUST remember, whatever happened, not to lose their tempers.

They met a very grand-looking fellow, wearing a gold chain about his shoulders. They thought he must be one of the head men of the Land of Tempers, and nobody liked to speak to him. But suddenly Fanny called to him.

"Do you know where Sir Stamp-a-Lot and Lady Yell-Around are?" she said. The haughty-looking man stopped in surprise.

"No, I don't," he said. "They have disappeared, and I am very angry about it. Do *you* know where they are?"

"Yes, I do," said Fanny boldly.

"Where are they, then?" asked the grand man.

"I'll tell you the answer to your question if you'll answer one of mine," said Fanny.

"Very well," said the man.

"Have our friends, Silky, Moon-Face and Saucepan come to live here for a while?" asked Fanny.

"Certainly not," said the man. "I've never heard of them. No one is allowed to live here unless they first lose their tempers and then get permission from me to take a house. And now—tell me where Stamp-a-Lot and Yell-Around are."

"They have escaped from your Land and are living in the Faraway Tree," said Fanny.

"But they are not allowed to do that!" cried the head man. "How dare they? I didn't even know we were near the Faraway Tree. Wait till I catch them! I'll shake them till their teeth rattle. I'll scold them till they shiver like jellies."

"Well, that would be very nice," said Fanny. "Good-bye. We're going."

The others joined her as she ran towards the hole in the cloud. "How brave and clever you are, Fanny!" said Jo. "I should never have thought of all that! I'm quite, quite sure that Silky and the others aren't up here."

"I was awfully afraid of that head man," said Fanny. "I just couldn't speak a word more to him. Hurry up—let's get back to the Tree. Silky isn't here. I can't imagine where they all are. There's something very, very mysterious about it."

They all climbed down the ladder to the Tree, thankful to leave behind the horrid Land of Tempers. They went down to Silky's house and peeped in at the window. Lady Yell-Around wasn't there.

"I vote we go in and have a look round," said Jo. But the door was locked and the key had been taken. Bother!

"Well, I'm sure I don't know WHAT to do," said Jo. "But we simply must do SOME-thing!"

XXIV

A MOST EXCITING TIME

As the children stood gloomily outside Silky's house, a voice called to them from farther down.

"Is that you, Watzisname? Any news of our missing friends?"

"That's the Angry Pixie," said Jo. "Let's go down and talk to him."

The Angry Pixie was looking very miserable.

"I can't understand all this mystery," he said. "I saw Silky and the others a few days ago—and then they suddenly disappear like smoke without a cry or a yell. It's funny."

"We've just been up in the Land of Tempers," said Fanny. "But they're not there."

"I thought of going up there to see," said the Angry Pixie, "but I was so afraid I'd lose my temper and have to stay there always. You know what a temper I've got."

"Yes," said Jo. "You certainly mustn't *dream* of going up there. You'd never come back."

They sat there, looking at one another—and then they all pricked up their ears. They could hear a very peculiar noise.

Boom, boom, boom! Knock, knock, knock! Boom, boom, boom!

"Whatever's that?" said Fanny, looking all round. "And where is it coming from?"

"I can't imagine," said the Angry Pixie. "I keep on hearing it. I heard it yesterday and last night and this morning. It just goes on and on."

Everyone listened. The noise stopped and then went on again. Boom, boom, boom! Knock, knock, knock!

"Where *does* it come from?" said Bessie.

"From the inside of the tree," said Watzisname, listening hard. "I'm sure of that!"

"Do you suppose – do you possibly suppose – that it might be Silky and the others – somewhere inside the tree?" said Fanny suddenly.

Boom, boom, boom! Knock, knock, knock! There it was again!

"I believe Fanny's right. I think Silky, Moon-Face and Saucepan are prisoners inside the slippery-slip. Stamp-a-Lot must have pushed them down there, and then stuffed up the hole with all those things," said Watzisname.

"But they would have shot out of the trap-door at the bottom," said Dick.

"We'll go down and open it and see if anything has been put there to stuff that up, too," said Jo. "Come on, everyone."

So they all went down to the tree to where the trap-door was at the bottom. Jo opened it. He looked inside and then gave a shout.

"This end is all stuffed up, too! These two horrid people from the Land of Tempers have got Silky and the others in there, I'm sure. Look – there's all kinds of things stuffed in here. The poor things can't get up or down. They're trapped!"

"Well, let's pull everything out and set them free!" said Dick, and he tugged at a great ball of moss. But it wouldn't move!

Everyone had a turn at tugging and pulling—but it was no use at all. Not a thing would move.

"They've stuffed everything in and then put a spell on it to make it stay where it is," said Watzisname at last. "It's no good. We'll never be able to move a thing. Look—there's Lady Yell-Around coming back from her shopping. We'll just see if we can't make her do something about this!"

But that wasn't any good either. Lady Yell-Around pretended that she didn't know anything about the stopped-up hole.

"What's the good of shouting at me and asking me something I don't know anything about?" she said. "You go and ask old Stamp-a-Lot. He'll tell you what you want to know."

"No, he won't," said Jo. "He's just as big a fibber as you are."

Anyway, no one wanted to see Stamp-a-Lot again. He was such a bad-tempered person. They all climbed back to the Angry Pixie's house, sat down, and looked gloomily at each other.

"*Can't* get in at the top of the Slippery-slip, and *can't* get in at the bottom," said Jo. "How in the world can we rescue poor Silky and the others? It's simply dreadful."

"They'll be starving!" said Fanny, beginning to cry. "Oh, Jo, do think of something!"

But nobody could think of anything at all. It was only when the woodpecker flew by to go to his hole in the tree that any idea came—and then Jo jumped up with his eyes shining.

"I know! I know!" he cried. "Let's ask the woodpecker to help us."

"But how could a bird help?" said Dick.

"Well, a woodpecker pecks holes in wood to make his nest," said Jo. "I've seen them pecking hard with their strong beaks. They make a kind of drumming noise, and can peck out quite a big hole in no time. If we asked him, I'm sure the woodpecker could peck a hole at the back of this room, right into the Slippery-slip—and then we could pull Silky, Moon-Face and Saucepan through the hole."

"Oh, that really does sound a marvellous idea!" said Fanny, beaming. "Let's call him now."

So they went outside on to a big branch of the Faraway Tree and called to the woodpecker.

"Woodpecker! Come here a minute!"

The woodpecker stared round in surprise. He was cleaning his wing feathers by running each one carefully through his beak. He was a lovely bird with his bright, red-splashed head. He spread his wings and flew down.

"What's the matter?" he asked.

Jo told him. The bird listened with his head on one side and his bright eyes shining.

"Do you think you could possibly help us to rescue Silky and the others by pecking a hole at the back of the Angry Pixie's house?" said Jo, when he came to the end of his story. "You have such a strong beak."

"Yes, I know I have," said the woodpecker. "The only thing is I generally only peck rotten wood – that's easy to peck away, you know. It just falls to pieces. But good, growing wood like the trunk of the Faraway Tree – well, that's different. That's very hard, indeed. It would take me ages to peck a large hole through that."

"Oh, dear!" sighed Jo. "I'm so disappointed. We daren't let Silky and the others stay in the Slippery-slip too long in case they starve. There's nothing to eat down there, you know. Whatever are we to do?"

Everybody thought hard. It was the woodpecker who had an idea first.

"I know!" he said. "I could fetch my cousins who live in the Enchanted Wood in another tree – and maybe if there were three or four of us all pecking hard together we could make a good hole quite quickly. I know I couldn't make one by myself without taking two or three days – but a lot of us working together might do it easily."

"Oh, good!" cried everyone. "Go and get your cousins, there's a dear. Hurry!"

The woodpecker flew off. Everyone waited impatiently. They heard the noise from the inside of the Tree again. Boom, boom, boom! Knock, knock, knock!

"Poor things!" said Bessie, tears in her eyes. "It must be so dreadful inside there in the dark, with nothing to eat or drink."

After about ten minutes the woodpecker came back, and with him he brought *five* others! They were all woodpeckers, with bright, red-splashed heads, strong-looking birds with powerful beaks.

"Oh, splendid!" cried Jo, and he took them all into the Angry Pixie's little house. "Peck away at the back, here."

The six birds stood in a row and began to peck as close to one another as they could. Peck, peck, peck! They pecked so hard and so very fast that they made a curious drumming noise that echoed through the little house. R-r-r-r-r-r-r-r! R-r-r-r-r-r! R-r-r-r-r-r-r!

They pecked hard for about an hour and then stopped for a rest. Jo pressed close to see how they were getting on. To his joy he saw that a small hole had been pecked right through into the Slippery-slip. He asked the Angry Pixie for a torch and shone it through the hole. Yes – there was no doubt about it, the woodpeckers had got right through the tree trunk just there.

"Now you've only got to make the hole bigger!" cried Jo joyfully. "Peck away, woodpeckers, peck away! You are doing marvellously!"

XXV

EVERYTHING COMES RIGHT

After a good rest the six woodpeckers set to work again at the hole they had made. R-r-r-r-r-r! went their strong beaks, drumming away at the wood. Everyone watched to see the hole getting bigger and bigger. Then a voice floated up, singing a mournful song:

"Two kettles for Silky,
Two saucepans for me,
Two dishes for Moon-Face,
We're sad as can be!"

"That's the old Saucepan Man!" said Jo in delight. "Did you hear his silly song? That's to tell us they are all there. Move aside a bit, woodpeckers, and let me call to them."

The woodpeckers made room for Jo by the hole. He stuck his head through it and yelled loudly: "Silky! Moon-Face! Saucepan! We're going to rescue you. We'll pull you through a hole we've made at the back of the Angry Pixie's room."

There was a squeal of delight from Silky, a

shout from Moon-Face, and a clatter of pans from Saucepan.

"We're coming, we're coming!" yelled Moon-Face. "We've got a rope to come up by. We shan't be long. Is the hole big enough to squeeze through?"

"Not yet," shouted back Jo. "But the woodpeckers are just going to set to work again, and they'll soon have made it bigger."

"R-r-r-r-r-r! R-r-r-r-r-r!" went the woodpeckers' strong beaks, and the hole grew larger and larger. At last it really was big enough for anyone to get through. Jo leaned through it, his torch shining into the Slippery-slip. He saw a light gleaming a little way down, and noticed a rope shaking near by, as if someone was holding on to it.

"They're coming up," he said to the others. "They've got a light of some sort, too. Oh!—it's a candle. I can see Moon-Face now. He's the first. And he's helping Silky up. The old Saucepan Man is behind. They'll soon be here! Angry Pixie, put on a kettle to boil some water. I expect they would like some hot cocoa or something. And have you got anything to eat?"

"I've got Pop Biscuits and Google Buns," said the Angry Pixie, looking into a tin. "They'll like those."

Moon-Face at last hauled himself right up to the hole. His round face looked white and rather worried—but he gave Joe a grin as usual. "Help Silky through first," he said.

Jo and Dick pulled Silky through the hole. She looked pale, too, but how glad she was to see all her friends! She flung her arms round Bessie and Fanny, and they all cried tears of joy down one another. Then Moon-Face squeezed through the hole, and last of all the old Saucepan Man, though he had to take off a few pans before he could get through!

"We never, never thought we'd be rescued!" said Moon-Face. "We'd quite given up hope. We kept knocking and banging, hoping someone would hear us."

"Yes, we did hear you," said Jo. "That's what made us think you might be trapped in the Slippery-slip. But Moon-Face, how did you get there? What happened?"

"Wait a minute – let them have something to eat and drink first," said Watzisname. "They must be terribly hungry, not having had anything to eat and drink for so long."

"Oh, we had plenty," said Moon-Face. "We didn't starve. But I'll tell you all about it."

Everyone settled down to hear his story.

"You see, one morning this week Silky, Saucepan and I were sitting up in my house talking," began Moon-Face, "and suddenly we saw two people from the Land of Tempers looking in at us."

"Yes – Sir Stamp-a-Lot and Lady Yell-Around!" said Jo. "*We* know them!"

"Well, they looked very fiercely at us," said Moon-Face, "and they told us that they wanted to leave the Land of Tempers because the head-man was very angry with them about something. I think they had broken his windows in a temper. Well, they had escaped, and they meant to live in the Faraway Tree. They had found out by accident that their Land was over it, you see."

"And they wanted your house!" cried Dick.

"Yes," said Moon-Face. "They had been down the tree and seen that Silky's house was empty, because Silky was up here with me, and had taken that for themselves. At least Yell-Around meant to have it for herself. And Stamp-a-Lot meant to have mine."

"And they said they had stopped up the trap-door at the bottom," said Silky, "and they meant to push us down the Slippery-slip, and then stop up the hole in Moon-Face's room, so that we would be prisoners in the slide!"

"Well, you can guess how frightened we were!" said Moon-Face. "Old Saucepan heard it all because Stamp-a-Lot shouted so loudly. And the clever old thing began to stuff his kettles and saucepans with food from my larder, and some candles, too, and matches—and a rope. I couldn't think what he was doing!"

"So, of course, when we were pushed into the Slippery-slip we had plenty of food!" said Silky, putting her arm round Saucepan and hugging him. "All because Saucepan was so clever."

"He managed to tie the rope on to something so that we had that to climb up and down on if we wanted to," said Moon-Face, "and we found a little sort of cubby-hole half-way down where we could sit and eat and drink. We lighted a candle, and then Silky thought of knocking and banging somewhere near to the Angry Pixie's house just in *case* you might be there and heard it."

"Oh, we were so worried about you," said Jo. "We just simply didn't know WHAT to do! I'm so glad we thought of the woodpeckers. So you're really not very hungry or thirsty after all?"

"No, not very," said Moon-Face. "But some of the cake we brought got rather stale. Woodpeckers, would you like it?"

It was a treat for the woodpeckers and they pecked up the stale cake eagerly before they flew off. They had been very pleased to help.

"And now what are we going to do about turning Stamp-a-Lot and Yell-Around out of our houses?" said Silky. "We can't all live with the Angry Pixie. His house is too small."

Just as she said that there came the sound of shouting and yelling some way up the tree. Everyone listened.

"That's Yell-Around, I'm sure," said Silky. "Let's go and see what's happening."

Well, quite a lot was happening! About eight people from the Land of Tempers, with the head-man leading them, had come down the tree to capture Stamp-a-Lot and Yell-Around! The head-man had remembered what Fanny had said, and had come to find the two escaped people. They had easily found Stamp-a-Lot, for he was asleep in Moon-Face's house, which was not far below the ladder leading up to the Land of Tempers.

But Yell-Around had not been so easily captured. She had seen the head-man climbing down the tree and had tried to escape. She had fallen, and had hung by one foot from a branch, yelling and squealing, because she was so afraid of falling. And the head-man picked her up by her foot and dragged her up the Tree like that, bumping her as he went.

Everyone watched in silence. Yell-Around was squealing loudly in a terrible rage, but nobody took any notice.

"I won't go back to the Land of Tempers!" she yelled. "I won't, I won't!"

But she had to! Up the ladder she was carried, upside down, and Stamp-a-Lot was pushed up, too.

"Serves them right," said Moon-Face. "Taking our houses from us and trapping us in the Slippery-slip like that. Let's go up to my house."

They all went up. Moon-Face was sad to see his house so untidy and so many of his things broken. Everyone helped him to put it right. Then they all looked at the stuffed-up Slippery-slip.

"The spell put on it will be gone now that those two horrid people have gone," said Moon-Face. "We can pull everything out."

So it wasn't long before the hole was free of all the things that stuffed it up. Moon-Face shook out his cushions and grinned at the children.

"Well, everything's all right again," he said.

"I'm so happy. It's lovely to have good friends like you."

"We'd better get home now," said Jo. "We've been away a long time."

"We can't slide down the Slippery-slip because it's all stuffed up at the bottom," said Fanny.

"Well, I'll send a message down to the red squirrel to clear it," said Moon-Face. He whistled to a sparrow sitting on a nearby branch.

"Hey, little brown bird! Fly down to the red squirrel and tell him to open the trap-door at the bottom of the tree, and clear the slide there, will you?" he asked. "Tell him to do it at once."

The sparrow flew off. Moon-Face handed round a tin of Toffee-Shocks, and everyone took one. "Just time to have one whilst the squirrel is clearing out the mess," he said. "Hark! I can hear the Land of Tempers moving off."

Sure enough there came the noise of the Land moving away – the curious creaking, groaning noise that the strange lands always made when they went.

"What Land will come next, I wonder?" said Jo.

"I know what it will be," said Watzisname. "I heard the head-man of the Land of Tempers say that the Land of Presents was due to-morrow."

"Oooooh!" said Moon-Face, his eyes shining. "We must all go to THAT! The Land of Presents! That's a marvellous land! We can all go and get as many presents as we like – just as if it was our birthday! Come to-morrow, will you? We'll all go! I can get some new carpets and things. Stamp-a-Lot spoilt so many of my belongings."

"We'll come!" said Jo as he slid down the Slippery-slip on a yellow cushion. "We'll all come! RATHER!"

XXVI

THE LAND OF PRESENTS

Next day all the four children woke up feeling excited. It was so lovely when a really nice Land was at the top of the Faraway Tree. They had been to the Land of Birthdays before, and the Land of Take-What-You-Want. The Land of Goodies had been nice, and the Land of Do-As-You-Please. The Land of Presents sounded just as exciting!

"I wonder who gives the presents—and if you can choose them," said Fanny. "I'd like a necklace of blue beads."

"And I'd like an enormous box of chocolates," said Dick.

"You would!" said Jo. "Anything to eat, and you're happy! I'd like a toy aeroplane that would fly from my hands and come back to them."

"I shall bring something home for Mother," said Bessie. "She wants a new purse. When can we start, Jo? I'm all ready."

They set off about eleven o'clock, when they had done all their work. They were very excited.

It was so lovely to think that Silky, Moon-Face and Saucepan were safe again and coming to enjoy the Land of Presents with them. Perhaps Watzisname, Saucepan and the Angry Pixie would come, too.

Well, everyone in the Faraway Tree had heard that the Land of Presents was at the top of the Tree that day; and, dear me, what a lot of people were steadily climbing up that morning! Brownies from the wood below, pixies and elves, even rabbits from their holes. The Angry Pixie's house was empty. He had gone already. The owl had gone, too, for he was not asleep in his little house as usual. Dame Washalot was gone, and no water came pouring down the Tree as the children climbed up.

"What a crowd there'll be!" said Jo happily. "I hope we aren't too late. I hope there will be some presents left for us!"

"Oh, goodness! Let's hurry!" said Dick in alarm. He didn't want to lose the big box of chocolates he wanted!

Moon-Face, Silky and Saucepan were waiting most impatiently for them. "Hurry, hurry!" cried Silky. "The Land of Presents goes in an hour! It never stays long! Quick! Quick!"

Up the ladder they all went, talking and laughing in excitement. And, my goodness me, what a wonderful Land it was!

There were Christmas trees hung with presents of all kinds! There were bran-tubs full of exciting parcels. You had to dip in your hand for those.

There were tables spread with the loveliest things. And, oh, the chattering and giggling that went on as people chose their presents and went off with them!

Dick marched up to a Christmas Tree because he saw hanging on it a most wonderful box of chocolates. A goblin was in charge of the Tree, and he smiled at Dick.

"I want that box of chocolates," said Dick.

"Who is it for?" asked the goblin, getting out some scissors to cut down the box.

"For myself," said Dick.

The goblin put away his scissors and shook his head gravely. "This is the Land of Presents," he said, "Not the Land of Take-What-You-Want. You can only get things here to give to other people. I'm sorry. This isn't a selfish land at all."

Dick looked very gloomy. He moved away. How stupid! He couldn't get anything for himself, then—and he had so much wanted the chocolates!

He saw a lovely blue necklace hanging on another tree, and he thought of Fanny. She had badly wanted a necklace of blue beads to go with her best blue frock. He went up to the goblin in charge of the tree.

"May I have that blue necklace to give to Fanny?" he asked.

"Where is she?" said the goblin, getting out his scissors. "Call her."

"Fanny, Fanny, come here!" cried Dick. "I've got something for you!"

Fanny came running up. The goblin handed

Dick the blue necklace and he gave it to Fanny.

"Put it round my neck for me and do up the clasp," she said. "Oh, Dick, thank you! It's lovely! Now – what present would you like me to get for *you*?"

"Oh, Fanny – I'd like that big box of chocolates," said Dick, beaming all over his face. "Would you like to get it for me?"

Fanny at once asked the goblin there for it and gave it to Dick. He undid the box and offered it to Fanny. "Have a chocolate?" he said.

Well, as soon as the children knew how to set about getting the presents, they had a most wonderful time. All except dear old Saucepan, who would keep on getting the wrong presents for everyone, because he kept hearing things all wrong.

"What would you like for a present?" he asked Bessie.

"Oh, Saucepan, I'd so like a frock!" said Bessie.

Well, Saucepan thought she said "clock", and off he went to find the biggest one in the Land. He managed to get one at last and put it on his back. It was a grandfather clock and so large that it quite bent him in two with its weight. Everyone stared in surprise as old Saucepan came up with it.

"Here you are, Bessie dear – here's your clock," said Saucepan, beaming at her.

"Saucepan, I said FROCK, not a *clock*," said Bessie, trying not to laugh. "A FROCK!"

Poor Saucepan. He simply didn't know what

to do with the clock after that, and in the end he left it in a field, striking all by itself very solemnly.

Then he asked Dame Washalot what *she* would like for a present.

"Well, I need a new iron," said the old dame.

"I'll get you one," said Saucepan. But, you know, he had heard quite wrong. He thought Dame Washalot said "*lion*", though if he had stopped to think one moment he would have known that she didn't want a lion—or a tiger or an elephant, either!

It was difficult to find a lion in the Land of Presents. But as the rule there was that whatever anyone wanted they must have, the goblins managed to produce one somehow.

He got a collar and a lead for it and took it back to Dame Washalot and the others. They all stared at him in amazement.

"What has Saucepan got a lion for?" said Jo.

"Dame Washalot, here is the lion you wanted," said Saucepan, beaming; and he put the lead in Dame Washalot's hand. She dropped it at once and backed away.

"Saucepan! Don't play this kind of joke on me. You know I'm scared of lions."

"Then why did you ask me to get you a lion?" asked Saucepan, astonished.

"I said an IRON, not a LION," said Dame Washalot quite snappily.

"Well, then, wouldn't you like to put it into your wash-tub and wash it clean?" said Saucepan.

But nothing would make Dame Washalot take

the lion, so in the end Saucepan had to take it into the field where the clock was, and let it loose.

"Perhaps it will eat the grass and be happy," said Saucepan.

"Oh, Saucepan—lions don't eat grass," said Jo with a laugh. "Now tell me—what do *you* want for a present?"

"Some more kettles and saucepans," said the old Saucepan Man at once.

So Jo went to a bran-tub and said what he wanted. He put in his hand and drew out four large, knobbly parcels—two shining kettles and two fine saucepans. The Saucepan Man was very pleased indeed. He put one of the new saucepans on for a hat.

Well, it *was* fun in the Land of Presents. Everyone went round getting something for the others. Dick got a toy sweet shop for Bessie. She was delighted. She got a fine aeroplane for Jo that flew from his hand and cleverly came back to it each time it flew. Jo got a new hat for Watzisname with a yellow feather in it. Watzisname got a pair of silver shoes for Silky, and she put them on at once.

"Are we allowed to take anything home for our mother and father?" Jo asked Moon-Face.

"Of course, so long as you say it is for them and no one else," said Moon-Face. So Jo went to where a Christmas Tree was hung with pipes and tobacco and got a grand new pipe and a tin of tobacco for his father. And Bessie got a large new purse for her mother.

Suddenly Jo looked at his watch. "It's almost twelve o'clock," he said. "The Land of Presents will be moving off in a minute. We'd better go. Anyway, we really can't carry anything more! Golly, what a lovely lot of things we've all got!"

So they left the lovely Land of Presents and went down the ladder to the Faraway Tree. They said good-bye to Moon-Face and the others, and sat carefully down on cushions, their presents on their knees so that they wouldn't break. And one by one they shot off down the Slippery-slip and out of the front door.

They heard a curious roar as they landed on the moss outside the tree. Jo looked up into the branches.

"Do you know, I believe that funny old lion followed us down the ladder!" he said. "Whatever will Dame Washalot do with him if he won't leave her! I guess she *will* wash him every day in her wash-tub!"

"Well, he'll wish he hadn't left the Land of Presents then!" said Bessie with a giggle. "Come on—let's go home to Mother. What a lovely adventure! I hope it won't be the last."

It won't, because the Faraway Tree is still there. But we must leave them now to have their adventures by themselves, for there is no time to tell you any more. There they all go through the Enchanted Wood, carrying their lovely presents—what a lucky lot of children they are, to be sure!

THE END

Enid Blyton

THE FOLK OF THE FARAWAY TREE

Jo, Bessie and Fanny are fed up when they hear that Connie is coming to stay – she's so stuck-up and bossy. But they don't let her stop them having exciting adventures with their friends Silky, the elf; Moon-Face and the Saucepan Man.

Together they climb through the cloud at the top of the tree and visit all sorts of strange places, like the Land of Secrets and the Land of Treats – and Connie learns to behave herself!

You can share more adventures of the Faraway Tree in

The Enchanted Wood

Enid Blyton

THE ENCHANTED WOOD

"Up the Faraway Tree,
Jo, Bessie and me!"

Jo, Bessie and Fanny move to the country and find an Enchanted Wood right on their doorstep! And in the wood stands the magic Faraway Tree where the Saucepan Man, Moon-Face and Silky the elf live. Together they visit the strange lands which lie at the top of the tree, and have the most exciting adventures – and narrow escapes.

More magical stories can be found in

The Folk of the Faraway Tree

Enid Blyton

MR MEDDLE'S MISCHIEF

"You're a tiresome, meddlesome creature, Mister Meddle!"

Mr Meddle is a very silly pixie. He's always getting in a muddle. He washes his hair with sherbet and cleans his teeth with glue; he feeds cake mixture to the pigs and worms to the budgies; he meddles with a conjuror's magic and drives an engine into the river. He just can't keep out of trouble!

You can have more fun with Mr Meddle in

Mr Meddle's Muddles

Enid Blyton

MR MEDDLE'S MUDDLES

"Will you keep away from me?" roared Meddle, getting angry. "You're a most annoying dream."

Mr Meddle can't do anything right. He's always getting into trouble, especially when he tries his best to be helpful. In these muddlesome stories, he throws away Aunt Jemima's luggage, has a fight with a kangaroo and is chased by an angry bull!

You can have more fun with Mr Meddle in

Mr Meddle's Mischief

A Distant Shore

Caryl Phillips was born in St Kitts and now lives in London and New York. He has written for television, radio, theatre and cinema and is the author of three works of non-fiction and six novels. *Crossing the River* was shortlisted for the 1993 Booker Prize. In addition to this he has won the Martin Luther King Memorial Prize, a Guggenheim Fellowship and the James Tait Black Memorial Prize, as well as being named the *Sunday Times* Writer of the Year 1992 and one of the Best of Young British Writers 1993.

ALSO BY CARYL PHILLIPS

Fiction

The Final Passage
A State of Independence
Higher Ground
Cambridge
Crossing the River
The Nature of Blood

Non-Fiction

The European Tribe
The Atlantic Sound
A New World Order

Caryl Phillips

A DISTANT SHORE

VINTAGE BOOKS
London

Published by Vintage 2004

8 10 9

First published in Great Britain in 2003 by Secker & Warburg

Vintage
Random House, 20 Vauxhall Bridge Road,
London SW1V 2SA

www.vintage-books.co.uk

Addresses for companies within The Random House Group Limited can be found at: www.randomhouse.co.uk/offices.htm

The Random House Group Limited Reg. No. 954009

A CIP catalogue record for this book is available from the British Library

ISBN 9780099428886

Printed and bound in Great Britain by Clays Ltd, St Ives PLC

I

England has changed. These days it's difficult to tell who's from around here and who's not. Who belongs and who's a stranger. It's disturbing. It doesn't feel right. Three months ago, in early June, I moved out here to this new development of Stoneleigh. None of the old villagers seem comfortable with the term 'new development'. They simply call Stoneleigh the 'new houses on the hill'. After all, our houses are set on the edge of Weston, a village that is hardly going to give up its name and identity because some developer has seen a way to make a quick buck by throwing up some semi-detached bungalows, slapping a carriage lamp on the front of them and calling them 'Stoneleigh'. If anybody asks me I just say I live in Weston. Everybody does, except one or two who insist on writing their addresses as 'Stoneleigh'. The postman told me that they add 'Weston' as an afterthought, as though the former civilises the latter. He was annoyed, and he wanted me to know that once upon a time there had been a move to change the name of Weston to Market Weston, but it never caught on. He was keen that I should understand that there was nothing wrong with Weston, and once he started I could hardly get him to stop. That was last week when he had to knock on the door for he had a package that wouldn't fit through the letterbox, and he said that he didn't want to squash it up ('You never know what's in it, do you, love?'). He told me that he had been instructed by head office to scratch out the name 'Stoneleigh' if it appeared on any envelopes. Should the residents turn out to be persistent offenders, then he was to politely remind them that they lived in Weston. But he told me that he didn't think that he would be able to do this. That actually if they wanted to live in cloud-cuckoo land, then who was he to stop them? He didn't tell this to his boss, of course, because that would have been his job. There and then, on the spot.

So our village is divided into two. At the bottom of the hill there is a road that runs west to the main town which is five miles away, and east towards the coast which is about fifty miles away. Everybody knows this because just before you enter Weston from the town side there's a sign that says it's fifty miles to the coast. Then after that there's the big sign that reads 'Weston' and announces the fact that we are twinned with some town in Germany and a village in the south of France. In the estate agent's bumf about 'Stoneleigh' it says that during the Second World War the German town was bombed flat by the RAF, and the French village used to be full of Jews who were all rounded up and sent to the camps. I can't help feeling that it makes Weston seem a bit tame by comparison. Apparently, the biggest thing that had ever happened in Weston was Mrs Thatcher closing the pits, and that was over twenty years ago.

The only history around these parts is probably in the architecture. The terraces on both sides of the main road are typical miners' houses, built of dull red brick; the original inhabitants would have had to bathe in the kitchen, and their toilets would have been at the end of the street. However, these houses have all long since been replumbed, and the muck has been blasted off the faces of most of them so that they now look almost quaint. Mind you, the people who live down there still have to deal with the noise of the traffic at all times of day and night, and I imagine it's murder to keep the windows clean. Besides the terraced houses there's a petrol station, a fish-and-chip shop, a newsagent-cum-grocery store, a sub-post office that opens three mornings a week, and behind the far row of houses a pub that sits smack on the canal, which runs parallel to the main road. There's also a small stone church, with nicely tended grounds, but I won't be needing to go in there. Stoneleigh is up a short steep hill and it overlooks the main road. We're the newcomers, or posh so-and-sos, as I heard a vulgar woman in the post office call us. There are not that many of us, just two dozen bungalows arranged in two culs-de-sac, but there are plenty of satellite dishes, and outside some of the houses there are two cars. Me, I don't drive. We don't have any shops up here, so if I do want anything I have to trek down the hill to the newsagent-cum-grocery store. Either that or catch the bus the five miles into town.

In May, I retired as a schoolteacher. Four years ago the school went comprehensive and since then standards have plummeted. It left me in a bit of a spot as I've spent most of my life banging on about how it would be better if kids of all levels and backgrounds could be educated together and learn from each other. It's what Dad believed. He hated seeing the grammar-school boys in their white shirts and ties, and their flash blazers, while the kids from the secondary modern could barely find a pair of socks that matched. I can still see him shaking his head and pointing. 'Class war, love,' he'd say. 'Class war before they're even out of short pants.' And then four years ago, the education authority scrapped grammar schools, turned us comprehensive, and they put me to the test. I was suddenly asked to teach whoever came into the school – we all were. Difficult kids I don't mind, but I draw the line at yobs. But then early retirement came along to save me, and when I saw the Stoneleigh advert in the paper I thought, why not, a change is as good as a rest. Four weeks later, I found myself standing at the door to this place and handing the removal men a twenty-pound tip. I watched the dust rise and then slowly cloud as their big van pulled away. It was only six o'clock and so I thought that rather than sort through my belongings and arrange everything, I'd wander down the hill and take a good look around.

I was surprised by how busy the main road was, with big lorries thundering by in both directions. It took a good while before there was a break in the traffic and I was able to dash across. As it turned out there was not much to see, except housewives sitting on their front steps sunning themselves, or young kids running around. Doors were propped wide open, presumably because of the heat, but I didn't get the impression that the open doors were indicative of friendliness. People stared at me like I had the mark of Cain on my forehead, so I pressed on and discovered the canal. It's a murky strip of stagnant water, but because I was away from the noise of traffic, and the blank gawping stares of the villagers, it looked almost tolerable. The skeletal remains of a few barges were tied up by the shoreline, and it soon became clear that the main activity in these parts appeared to be walking the dog. In the fields, the cows and sheep moved with an ease which left me in no doubt that, despite the public footpath that snaked across the farmer's land, this was their territory. I sat on a low wall underneath some drooping willow branches and looked around. The soft back-lap of the canal was soothing, although the jerky flight of a dragonfly buzzing about my head seemed out of place. This wall belonged to the village pub, The Waterman's Arms, whose garden gave out onto the canal. In the garden some young louts and their girlfriends were braying and chasing about the place. I watched them as they began to toss beer at each other, and then shriek with the phlegmy laughter of hardened smokers. I didn't want them to think that I was staring at them, so I turned my attention back to the relative tranquillity of the dank canal, and so time passed.

As the sun began to set, and the second dead fish floated by, the silver crescent of its bloated stomach gracelessly breaching the surface, I decided that I would quite like a drink. My throat was parched, and so I stood up and walked towards the pub. I could now feel eyes upon me, and for a few moments I wondered if some of these slovenly youngsters, with their barrack-room language, weren't pupils that I'd recently had the rare pleasure of teaching. However, I thought it best not to turn and look them full in the face, and I therefore made my way, without an escort and with eyes lowered, across the garden and up the half-dozen stone steps and into the public bar. Once inside I discovered that the small room was deserted, save for a courting couple snug in the corner, whose feverishly interlaced fingers suggested what was to come.

'Can I help you, love?' Despite the heat, the landlord was wearing a white shirt and a tie that suggested membership of some kind of club. He kept the place neat and tidy, and he'd decorated the walls with what looked like family photos and mementoes of his holidays. This stout man's private life was on display, and I imagined that the young couple in the corner might well be holding back their enthusiasm out of respect for this fact.

'I'll have a half of Guinness, please.' As the landlord carefully pulled the beer, I heard a loud cry and yet more jackalling from outside. The landlord glared through the leaded windows.

'Bloody hooligans.' Without looking in my direction he set

the half-pint of Guinness before me. 'One pound forty.' He continued to stare through the window, but his open hand snaked across the bar. I put two one-pound coins into his palm and his hand first bounced, as if to weigh the coins, and then it closed around them. 'Thanks, love.'

An hour later I adjusted myself on the bar stool as he set a second half-pint before me. It was dark now, but the youngsters were still making their noise in the garden, and in the corner behind me the courting couple had set aside decorum and were now practically sitting one on top of the other. Having finished my first drink I had stood up from the stool, but the landlord would hear nothing of my leaving. 'No, love, have one on the house. Call it a welcome if you like.' I still had to unpack, and the removal men had left the place in a tip, but I thought it would be rude to turn down his kind offer. I climbed back onto the stool and watched as he pulled the second glass.

'We used to have a doctor here. A young woman, but she didn't last long. The women didn't like the men seeing her.'

'But she's a doctor,' I said, taking a careful sip of the new drink.

'Yes, but she's a woman doctor, and you know how people are.'

I couldn't be sure if he was agreeing with the attitude of the villagers, or being critical, but then our attention was seized by the sound of breaking glass. During the past hour the landlord had twice been outside to ask the youngsters to calm down, but things were clearly out of control. I understood his frustration. This was his clientele and to bar them would be to effectively lose his business. The landlord tried to ignore the breaking glass and turned back towards me.

'These days if you need to see a doctor for anything then you have to go into town. You've got a doctor there, right?'

I nodded. I looked at the landlord and wished that we had

happened upon another subject for casual conversation. But he was hooked now, and it was proving difficult to shake him free and on to a different topic.

'There's a young Irish nurse who comes around to the health centre four afternoons a week, but with her you're not talking about proper treatment. She can take your blood pressure and tell you what to eat and all that, but not much more.'

Again I nodded. He paused, then looked over my shoulder at the courting couple in the corner.

'Everything all right back there with you two love-birds?' I didn't turn around, but I heard the sound of their nervous laughter. The landlord smiled at them, and then he glanced outside where he could see the hooligans tearing around his garden. Almost imperceptibly he shook his head, and then he swivelled his attention back towards me.

'Don't get me wrong. I liked Dr Epstein. Nice woman.' The landlord fell silent, and his eyes glazed over as if his thoughts were drifting aimlessly. I looked through the window and could see that two of the louts were now playing on the children's swings. They were swinging high, but in opposite directions to each other, and when the swings crossed they were anointing each other with beer. Their girlfriends looked on and screeched with laughter.

'But like I said, folks didn't take to Dr Epstein, what with her being a woman. Made her life a misery, and that of her husband and kids. Young they were, maybe five or six, a boy and a girl. Rachel and Jacob. Funny thing is they might be happier if they came here today. You know, now that Stoneleigh or whatever you call it is finished. Up there they might have fit in better, but living down here with us, well, it was difficult for them to mix.' Again he paused. 'Nobody cares much in the town, but around here they don't blend in. I mean, Rachel and Jacob. They weren't even trying. You know what it's like, you've got to make an effort. You've lived around these parts all your life, haven't you?'

'Well, like I said, mainly in town, but never out here.'

'Well, welcome again to Weston.' He raised his glass. 'To a long and happy retirement in Weston.'

I picked up my glass and smiled. I thought to myself, I'm glad that I live in a cul-de-sac. There's something safe about a cul-de-sac. You can see everything when you live near the far end of a cul-de-sac.

That night I walked up the hill under the moonlight. I think Mum would have liked Stoneleigh, but Dad would have hated it. She would have liked the idea that by living up the hill you'd moved on with your life and left something behind. But Dad wasn't burdened by her ambitions, which is one of the reasons why they argued and why Mum ultimately fell silent. But Mum should have known better, for Dad wasn't the type to take kindly to disagreement. Almost to the end there was a fire within him which only needed a conversational push, or the prod of an ill-timed comment, for the flames to start roaring. Dad liked to talk, but even as a girl it was obvious to me that Mum had given up on his temper. Instead Dad talked to me, and he tried to treat me like the son he'd never had. He loved nothing more than to sit with his pipe and his tobacco pouch, pressing rubbed flake into the bowl, and tell me about how he'd lost his own dad in the war, and how his mum had struggled to make ends meet.

He was twenty when the war ended, but by that time he'd started as a draughtsman and he'd decided to marry Mum, whom he always described as 'the prettiest of all the local lasses'. Whenever he said this he would look at her as though asking himself what on earth had happened to his 'pretty lass', but Mum never looked back and she would just carry on with whatever she was doing. Dad's responsibilities, and the lack of money, meant that he never went to university, and although he claimed to be glad that he had been spared the upheaval of leaving his home town, I never really believed him. When I finally went off to university at eighteen, I could see how proud he was, but he never did say anything to me, nor did he ever travel, apart from the one disastrous trip that he and Mum made to Majorca. His dad fell in Belgium and this seemed to have soured his attitude to anything that lay outside the orbit of his home-town life. So much so that whenever he swore, which he seldom did, he was always quick to say 'pardon my French', which, of course, made no sense unless one viewed it through the prism of contempt.

Unfortunately, while I seemed to get on with Dad, Sheila barely spoke to him. To begin with they used to get on. I may have been the 'son', but she was definitely the much-loved daughter. I was actually jealous of her for he used to dote on her, and take her to the allotments, and buy her presents, so much so that I used to call her 'Daddy's little pet'. But as she got older, and grew to know her own mind, Dad seemed to change towards her. I could see what she meant when she said that he seemed to be going out of his way to pick on her, but she didn't help herself. Any chance to misbehave, she took it, and of course that only made things worse. Mum sided with Sheila, but her voice didn't count for much with Dad, and so Sheila began to resent Mum's impotence in the household. And where was I in all of this? Either doing my homework or playing the piano. I knew I wasn't much use to Sheila, but when my sister started to smoke, and then stay out late, even though Dad had told her that she had to be back by ten, then I began to see his point of view. She was acting up, there was no question about it, and then I went and made it all worse by going off to university and leaving her alone with the two of them. I often wonder if things would have worked out differently if I'd stayed at home, or gone to the local college, or just got a job. Maybe I could have been more help to them all.

At the top of the hill I stopped and looked back at Weston. I remember seeing it clearly, for the full moon hung heavily in the sky, as though supported by an invisible column. Bathed in the moon's bright glare, Weston looked serene and unencumbered by the problems that continued to plague the town. I'm almost embarrassed to admit it, but these days whenever I go into town it's the homeless people who annoy me the most, and the frightening thing is they seem to be everywhere. There are dozens of them living beneath the underpass in boxes that used to hold fridges or big colour television sets, with their matted hair and their bottles of meths. It looks to me like they'll always be around as long as the church is happy to give them plastic cups of sweet tea and change their ulcerated bandages, without holding them accountable for anything. During the day they sit around the precincts playing the guitar like it's some kind of summer camp that they're attending. Why didn't they pay any attention at school? It's not too late to get their lives back on track. They've got their health, and they're not retarded. Well, at least not the younger ones. And they've even got some kind of talent. It's just a wilful waste, that's all, and I believe most of them are doing it on purpose because they're lazy and they want sympathy, but they never get it from me. When I refuse to give them money they scream at me, and I often feel scorn when I walk past them. I didn't used to, but I do now that they've started in on me and other passers-by. A few days ago I was coming back from the hospital when I caught one of them, a filthy beast, eating out of a dustbin like a dog. I didn't say anything, but I did look at him and then he started to shout. 'You can't hurt me any more,' he said. 'You can't hurt me.' Who said that I wanted to hurt him? I'm glad that Dad isn't here to see what's become of his town. I suppose I'm also glad that he's not here to see that I'm living up in Stoneleigh. He'd never say anything to me about it, but he'd find a way to let me know that he didn't approve.

I put the key in the door, slipped off my shoes and slumped down in my favourite armchair, surrounded by the mess of boxes and packing cases. In fact, I didn't even take off my coat. The walk up the hill, plus the two halves of Guinness, had taken their toll. Through the uncurtained window I could still see the powerful light of the moon. Dad would have liked The Waterman's Arms, that much I was sure of, for he regarded pubs as a place of refuge. He always used to say that they should be a sanctuary where you can be yourself and not have to watch your p's and q's, but this being the case you had to find a pub that fitted you. He'd remind me that they're all different, like people, and while some bring out the good in you and open you up, others close you down and make you quiet so that you just want to sit in the corner and nurse a pint. 'They're not about drinking' was his big line, but Mum would just roll her eyes and get on with her ironing or whatever she was doing. I'd listen though. He'd insist that they're about being yourself, and he'd stress that you had to keep looking around until you found a pub that you felt comfortable in. However, he never told me what to do if I found myself living in a place that only had the one pub. I don't think either of us ever imagined that anything like this could ever happen.

I've not been in the local pub since that first night, and that was three months ago. But I see everybody all the time. The young courting couple, the yobs who were playing outside, the landlord. You can't help it. You go for a walk, or you go to get a paper, or you wait by the bus stop, and there they all are, the cast of the village acting out their assigned roles. Those of us from Stoneleigh, the small group of extras who live up the hill, have yet to be given our parts. We're still strangers to each other, let alone to the other villagers. The somewhat undernourished coloured man in the small bungalow next door is the only one I see regularly. He's the caretaker for all the houses; if anybody needs a lock fixing, or a door rehanging, or the plumbing seeing to, then he's the man to call. Apparently, there were so many complaints when the bungalows were finished that some owners in both culs-de-sac threatened to sue the developers unless they did something about it. I must have been lucky for everything's fine with my place, but it turns out that I'm the exception. So, in order to keep everybody happy, they built a small bungalow for a handyman-cum-night-watchman and Solomon moved in. I can see him now, behind his blinds. He never pulls them fully closed, as though he always needs to have a little light coming into his place. Either that, or he's not sure how to make them work.

His car is parked out front in its proper place. It's clearly second-hand, but it's always carefully washed and clean. The other day I saw him take a cloth to it and go at the bodywork as though he was buffing up a piece of brass. I've thought about asking him why he takes so much trouble over a car, but there's no point because it fits in with how he behaves about everything. The way he dresses, or cuts the lawn, or combs his hair with that sharp razor parting. Everything is done with such precision. Like most of the folks up here, he keeps himself to himself, but unlike most of the folks up here, he lives by himself. Like me, he's a lone bird. There's me, there's him, and there's a man in the other cul-de-sac who has let it be known that he used to be something in the London jazz scene. He claims to have known all sorts of famous people, and played all the clubs, but he talks too much which, of course, makes me think that he's making the whole thing up. But Solomon is different. He'll be over in ten minutes. I know his routine by now, and I'll have to be ready for him so that he can drive me into town to see Dr Williams. In fact, I'm nearly ready. All I have to do is find my referral card and pull on my coat and I'll be ready to go. Dr Williams is not a proper doctor, more of a specialist. In psychological pressures. My old GP recommended him to me a few months ago, just after Sheila died. He thought it would do me good to talk with somebody, but after all this time I've still not been getting any real sleep, and so I asked Dr Williams to give me some tests, which he did. Today I expect him to give me the results.

As I wait for Solomon I glance at the mantelpiece. I recognise my sister's handwriting on the envelope. The lines are weaker, the shapes less aggressive. Strange, really, for it never occurred to me that handwriting can age, but it does. When I first saw the letter on the doormat I looked at it and felt afraid to touch it. Finally, I picked it up and then propped it on the mantelpiece where I could see it, but I knew that I'd have to be stronger before I could tackle it. I remember laughing. It's not a rugby-playing bloke, I thought, it's a letter. I don't have to tackle it, and so I left it where it was, but every day I find myself glancing at the handwriting. Weak or otherwise, it's still her handwriting. After all these years of silence my sister can still do this to me. And then I hear Solomon knocking at the door.

I like the way he corners the car. He always holds the wheel in two hands and he pushes and pulls it gently, as though he's making something, rather than spinning it around as though he's gambling. He also wears driving gloves, which I like. Not the tacky type with the Velcro backing; his gloves have studs which you push to and they snap into place, all snug. I like this about his driving. It's neat and careful, and it makes me feel safe.

'Will the doctor be giving you the results today?'

He asks the question, but Solomon does so without taking his eyes from the road. When he first did this I thought it was rude, however I now realise that it's just his way of being careful. It's simply a matter of safety first, that's all. Because I have not replied to his question, he continues.

'I hope you do not mind my enquiry?'

This time he throws a quick glance in my direction. He's a handsome man, which makes me feel uncomfortable. I've never asked him, but I'd guess he's in his early thirties, although it's difficult for me to tell. He returns his attention to the road.

'Of course I don't mind your asking.' I pause. 'The doctor said that he'd tell me today.' Again I pause, unsure as to whether I should be volunteering any more information. But I trust this man. He doesn't expect me to be perfect.

Again he glances at me. It's a worried glance which says, 'Is there something that you are not telling me?' I say nothing as he slows down now, and then he turns into the hospital car park. There is, of course, one thing that I've been meaning to tell him, but I haven't found the right opportunity. It's about all this washing of his car. I want to tell him that in England you have to become a part of the neighbourhood. Say hello to people. Go to church. Introduce your kids to their new school. You can't just turn up and start washing your car. People will consider you to be ignorant and stand-offish. But I've yet to find the proper moment to talk to Solomon about the way he flaunts himself in his driveway with that bucket of soapy water and his shammy.

Dr Williams is a balding man of about forty. He's at that place where men either tumble rapidly down the slope towards irreversible middle-age spread, or they start to exercise and take care of themselves in an attempt to hold on to some of their youth. My guess is that Dr Williams isn't sure what to do with himself. He asks me to please take a seat, but he doesn't get up from behind his desk. I sit down and place my handbag in my lap, and then I realise that I probably look like a Sunday School teacher. Sadly, it's too late. I've got butterflies in my tummy, but any change of position will suggest to him that I'm nervous, and I don't want to give out this impression.

'I have your results, Miss Jones, and everything seems fine.' He looks me full in the face and he tries to put on that stupid little doctor smile that they all have. 'But my nurse has passed on your messages, and if you say that you're still having problems sleeping, then perhaps we should talk.' He gives me that half-sad, half-cheerful chin-up thing that they all do, and then he opens my file and takes his pen from the top pocket of his white overcoat. He clicks the knob of the pen with his thumb, then he uses the pen as some kind of a marker as he traces his way through the unbound pages.

'You've been through a lot recently, haven't you?'

I look at him and wonder if he's really asking me, or if he's just telling me.

'Early retirement can be a problem, but you're still teaching music, aren't you? The piano. I mean privately.'

Why is he asking me this? It was his idea that I advertise myself in that vulgar way. Desperate woman available for music lessons.

'I'm trying to talk to you, Miss Jones. Staring at the wall isn't going to help either of us, now is it?'

I look at his chubby face and decide that it's my turn to give him the stupid smile.

'The death of your parents, your divorce, the death of your sister, early retirement, and then moving home, that's a lot of pressure for anybody to have to deal with in a short space of time.' He pauses to give me an opportunity to comment, but I have nothing further to say to him. 'You have to start planning a new life, Dorothy. Your sister has gone, but you're still a relatively young woman, and there's nothing wrong with you physically. You've still got a significant expanse of life ahead of you, and you must start to plan and reach out and take it. Am I making myself clear?'

Solomon and I usually have lunch in town before going back to Stoneleigh. While I'm at the hospital he tends to do a bit of shopping, although he never tells me what he buys. Mind you, I never ask him either. He'll come back to the hospital with whatever he's bought safely stashed in the boot of his car. Sometimes I'm already out and waiting under the green Outpatients awning, while other times I know that I've kept him waiting, but he never complains. He's a volunteer driver, and the village nurse will probably have told him that he has to be tolerant if he's going to be driving folks who are ill. Because I used to live and teach in the town, it's usually up to me to choose the place for lunch. Once upon a time I chose the Somalian and Mediterranean Food Hall and it now seems to have become our regular, although they could keep the place a little cleaner. Still, he seems to like it.

He glances up from his lamb kebab and looks at me with his big eyes, as though I've somehow betrayed him.

'You have not told me about your results.'

'Inconclusive,' I say, but I continue to eat. I stuff some pitta bread into my mouth so that it is momentarily impossible for me to continue.

'I see.' He waits until I have finished chewing. 'Will there be more tests?'

'I don't think the doctor knows what he's doing.'

'He still cannot diagnose the problem?'

'So he says.'

'This is very troubling.' He pauses for a moment and continues to stare at me. 'And your sister. Did you reply to her letter?'

I put down my fork, but before the words come out of my mouth I realise that I'm about to say too much to this man. 'I haven't read the letter yet.'

'You have not read it?' He now puts down his own fork and he looks across the table at me. 'But she is all that you have now that your parents have passed on. And you say that she lives only one hour away on the coast. I have told you, I am prepared to drive you there.'

This strange man. The caretaker at Stoneleigh. The estate handyman in his free bungalow. Solomon and his second-hand car. Not even a dog. Just him alone, hiding behind those blinds, waiting for a piece of guttering that needs fixing or a door handle that has to be replaced. At nights I see him out on patrol with his torch. The Irish nurse told me that if I didn't want to take the bus into town there were two volunteer drivers. And then one afternoon, of all people, he came and knocked on my door. My knight in shining armour with his polished chariot. And now Solomon wants to drive me to the coast so that I can spend some time with Sheila, and all I'm thinking is why doesn't he finish his lamb kebab? There's people in the world who are starving to death and who would do anything for a bit of lamb kebab.

In the evening I stare again at the letter on the mantelpiece. Before I open it I feel as though I ought to go and visit my parents' grave and ask their permission. At my age I shouldn't feel compelled to ask for their approval, but Sheila didn't treat them well and I don't want them to think that by reading Sheila's letter I'm betraying them. I pour a glass of white wine and look out of the window. After a few minutes it occurs to me that it's not so much their permission that I'm seeking, it's more that I'm simply informing them of what's going on. I suppose that's it. I just want to let them know what's what and I hope that they'll understand. The light is beginning to fade from the sky. One of the things I like most about this house are the evenings, for you can see the sun setting on the horizon from up here. To the west there is a clear uninterrupted view straight out to where the old railway viaduct marches across the valley on its strong stone legs. A train hasn't passed across it for over fifty years or so, and it's some kind of a monument now. Every evening the sun sets behind this viaduct, which means that I can sit at this window with a glass of wine and watch the day come to a peaceful conclusion.

I've not been up long before I hear the banging on the door. It's all right because I'm already washed and presentable. I've even had time to brush out my hair, before tucking it back up into its familiar bun. I long ago forswore the vanity of trying to disguise the grey, and leaving it natural saves me stacks of time. Even though I no longer have to be at school at eight in the morning, I've kept the habit of being an early riser. I've generally had a bowl of cereal and some orange juice by the time the cars are pulling out of the driveways and the kids are running off to catch the school bus. Again I hear the intemperate banging on the door, as though whoever it is has decided that I'm asleep and is determined to wake me up. I'm not altogether happy about this, for it suggests bad manners. I go to the door and Mrs Lawson is there, but without Carla. The two-piece navy linen suit, and the matching pale-blue scarf around her neck, tells me that she is on her way to work.

'I'm sorry for coming by so early, but I wanted to catch you before I went off.'

Well, I'd guessed that much, and from the way she was standing it was clear that she'd not come over to borrow a cup of sugar. Two days earlier, at her last piano lesson, Carla had refused to do her final lot of scales. Again I reminded her that sitting at the piano without any sense of propriety, her feet dangling uselessly above the pedals, was an insult to both teacher and instrument. I gently covered her hands with mine and asked her to feel it in her chest. To let it rise up from her body and out through the top of her head. I squeezed her hands, telling her that she must forget them, for they should be like lettuce, limp and useless. Then again, I reminded her that it all begins in the chest and that her performance must always be strong and passionate, but the girl was clearly unimpressed. In the end I snapped at her, and asked her if she thought that her mother was paying all this money out so that she could sit and stare into mid-air and give cheek. But this only made things worse. Carla began to snipe back, and then she banged the lid of the piano down, pushed back her chair and stood up. As she snatched her bag, she shouted, 'I'm going to tell my mother about you', and then she bolted from the house without closing the door behind her. I looked at the book of exercises that stood discarded on the piano, the corners carefully upended to make it easier to turn the page, and decided that enough was enough with this girl. I had half-expected to see Carla's mother within the hour, but when she didn't appear I wasn't surprised. In fact, when the mother had first answered my handwritten advert in the newsagent's window, which somewhat immodestly advertised my skills as a 'first-class' piano teacher, I was sure that Mrs Lawson was simply looking for the most convenient way of keeping her daughter out of trouble. She told me that she was the clerical manager at the big supermarket in town and that she often worked late. Apparently, she and Carla's father were separated, so most of the time the poor girl was left to her own devices. However, predictably enough, Carla soon became bored by both me and the piano, and it was inevitable that in the long run she would become obstreperous. And now the mother has shown up. I look blankly at the woman.

'It's about Carla,' she says.

'I'm sorry.' I blink and try to refocus on the woman. 'Please come in. Would you like some tea?'

'I can't stay for very long. Only a minute or two.' The woman squeezes past me and makes her way towards the living room as though she is a regular visitor in my home.

'Would you prefer tea or coffee?' I ask.

'Either, thanks. Whatever is easiest. Honestly, I really can't stay long.'

I follow her into the living room, sit her down and then go into the kitchen to pour her a cup of tea. In my house it's easy to carry on a conversation with somebody from the kitchen. You don't have to do any shouting or anything, so I wait for her to say what's on her mind, but she doesn't say anything, so I pour the milk into the tea and then stir.

After she has gone I begin to clear away the tea, and then the plate with the biscuits that she refused to eat. I pick up the plate and look through the window as she clip-clops her way, in her stupid high heels, down towards the end of the cul-de-sac where her new red hatchback is waiting for her. She does not look back, but rather than envying her confidence, I find myself despising it. She has, after all, just come into my home and very quickly stepped beyond the boundaries of decorum. As I set down the tea and biscuits before her, I asked her if she would like sugar. She shook her head vigorously as though I had offered her rat poison.

'Well,' I began, 'I suppose you have to ask yourself, does Carla really want to learn the piano?'

'I thought she did,' said the mother, 'but now I'm not so sure. She's at a difficult age, and she has strong opinions about certain things.'

'I see.' I took a biscuit. 'Such as playing the piano?'

'Well, not just this. There's your own behaviour to consider.'

'My own behaviour?' I replaced the biscuit on the plate and looked at the woman.

'I think you need help, don't you? Carla likes you all right, but she says you shout, and then at other times you're nice, but most of the time you just stare out of the window and you don't hear anything that she's saying to you. Can I ask you frankly, Miss Jones, what's the matter?'

'You're taking your daughter's word for all of this?' The woman stared at me with a piteous look that would have tried the patience of a saint. 'I see, so I'm to understand that I'm the one with problems concentrating.'

'Carla's a good kid, and she wouldn't lie. In fact, she's quite upset about you. I mean, she likes you, but she thinks you should get some help as you're behaving strangely.'

For a few moments I stared at this woman, and then it dawned on me that she was serious.

'More tea?' I asked. The woman glanced at her watch and then reached for her bag.

'You know, at least I tried. I've really got to be going.'

'As you please.'

The woman leaned forward now and she tried to appear sympathetic.

'I think you should remember, it's a small village, and like you I've been used to the town. But these people, they talk, you know.'

'About who?'

'About you, Miss Jones. There *are* good people in the village that you can spend time with. You don't have to be by yourself.'

'Well, I can't stop them talking.' It was difficult to remove the anger from my voice, and Mrs Lawson seemed to accept the fact that there was little further to be said on this, or any other, subject.

'Well, I'm sorry, but I really just came to tell you that Carla won't be coming back for any more piano lessons.' With this said, she got to her feet and bade me good morning. I look at her now as she leans forward and unlocks her car door. She climbs in and starts the hatchback's engine, and soon she is indicating right and then turning into the traffic and making her way to work.

There is a young man weeding in the graveyard. He is there almost every time I visit. What makes his labour strange is the fact that he does this job by hand. Not with a scythe, a trowel, or even a pair of scissors; this young man pulls out the weeds by hand and stuffs them into a black plastic bag that is looped to his belt with a piece of frayed rope. As I walk up the short incline I can see that he has finished my parents' grave. They lie side by side, Mum having died first and then Dad a year later. They planned this final resting-place together, and they arrived in almost perfect harmony. One day, while Dad was down at his allotment, Mum's heart gave out. He said goodbye to her in the morning and left the house which they had shared for almost fifty years. When he arrived home at the end of the day she was gone. According to the neighbours, she collapsed in the back yard while taking out the rubbish, and one of them called the ambulance while the others tried to bring her round. There had been a few minor scares over the years, including a mild stroke when they went abroad, for the first and only time, to Majorca. She had to be flown back, on insurance, and she spent a fortnight in hospital. But this final blow was swift and sudden, like a hammer falling, and there was no time to do anything but react. Dad phoned me and I travelled up from Birmingham. I made him a cup of tea and we sat together in silence, a banked fire glowing red in the grate, until the weak sun came up the next morning. I knew that he'd not be able to last long without her.

In the morning he asked me to get hold of my sister, and so I said I would, although I had an address but no phone number. It turned out her number was unlisted, but it wasn't that difficult to find Sheila's number in London and so I called her and broke the news about Mum. She was silent, and then when I asked her if she was coming to the funeral she simply said 'yes'. When, two days later, she turned up with her friend, it took all my self-control to stop myself from saying something to my younger sister. Now was not the time to be introducing Dad to such lifestyle choices, for he was fragile enough as it was. In fact, I couldn't remember a time when I'd been more angry, but luckily Dad was too grief-stricken to notice what Sheila had done. My so-called husband Brian played the role of peacemaker, and somehow we all survived the funeral. And then Dad started to get worse. His ailments seemed to all flare up together. The chest from all the years on the pipe. Then his hips, which had long been riddled with arthritis, went from bad to worse, and then finally his eyes started to mist over with glaucoma. Six months after we buried Mum he had become so bad that he couldn't go to the toilet, or take a bath, or do much of anything by himself. To start with, I was travelling up from Birmingham and spending every weekend with him, but his doctor finally told me that unless we got a nurse he'd have to go into a home. So I asked the doctor to be honest with me and say how long he'd got left. He knotted his fingers together and said maybe a year, but probably less, and so we arranged for a retired midwife to live in the spare room. Soon Dad couldn't leave his bed, but he still made the poor woman's life miserable, even going so far as to tell her that he didn't believe in good women, only women who lived under the influence of good men.

Less than a year after Mum went, he passed away in his sleep, and the sour-faced midwife made a performance out of leaving the house before his body was even cold. Again, I telephoned my sister, and this time I got her answering machine and left a message, but I heard nothing. I wasn't surprised, and if truth be told I was somewhat relieved that I would be spared a rerun of Sheila's selfishness. It had been her own wilful decision to leave home at seventeen, and for nearly thirty years Mum and Dad had hardly had any contact with her. It was something they'd reluctantly learned how to deal with, and they'd become well schooled in the practice of deflecting questions, telling half-truths and hiding their grief. Mum, in particular, seemed to suffer. Sheila's rejection of them both, and her determination to live her own life in the south, caused Mum to retreat even further from people and conversation. Mum began to eat by herself, and there was something deeply painful about seeing her sitting alone with her Bible and her face furrowed in lonely concentration. Dad had argued any real faith out from under me, but Mum still believed, although she didn't bother with actually going to church. I used to wonder if things might have been better for her if I could have given her some little ones to be proud of, but I soon came to realise that nothing would help. Mum had lost her youngest daughter, and even the blessing of grandchildren wouldn't have begun to compensate for this loss. Dad, on the other hand, continued to rail about every subject under the sun, but the one subject he refused to take on was that of our Sheila.

Over the years, whenever I'd returned home I always knew that I could find him in his shed. I'd go down past the old cottages, then across the wasteland till I came to the patchwork quilt of allotments, with their turnips and runner beans laid out in obedient rows. He'd be there sucking on his pipe and bemoaning the fact that we were giving up our English birthright and getting lost in a United States of Europe, or the fact that one never sees men in collars and ties on Sundays, or expressing his continued astonishment that ordinary folk could have any respect for the memory of Churchill, a man who during the 1926 General Strike had, as Dad had been telling me since I was a small child, referred to the workers as 'the enemy'. I would listen, knowing that I would never hear a word from either him, or Mum, about Sheila, but everything about their behaviour suggested a profound pain at having failed to hold on to one of their two children. It was, of course, easier for me; she was my younger sister, and although I missed having her in my life, I didn't depend upon her in any way. I never had.

The young man who is weeding among the tombstones recognises me. We have one of those 'nod and a wave' relationships. He seems to enjoy his work, or at least he never complains about it, which surprises me. I'm so used to young people who either don't want to work, or who make it clear that although they are working they are doing so reluctantly. This young man's work ethic seems to have been born in an earlier generation. In fact, he dresses as though he were from an earlier generation, with his flat cap and big boots. I stand and look down at my parents, their names freshly picked out with a wet cloth. I can feel the young man's eyes upon me, and it suddenly occurs to me to ask him if he's ever seen anybody else standing here looking at Mum and Dad. Maybe Sheila has visited out of some vaguely remembered sense of duty, choosing her times to coincide with my absences. For a moment I toy with the idea, but the truth is Sheila would never bother to cultivate such cunning. Not my Sheila, the seventeen-year-old girl who ran away from home while I was at university, and who showed up penniless on my doorstep. Once I'd recovered from the shock of opening the door on Sheila and her lopsided grin, I asked her in. She left her rucksack by the door and sat down on the edge of my single bed.

'Where have you been, Sheila? You look like a cat dragged you backwards through a hedge.'

She stared at the Jean-Luc Godard poster on my wall and said nothing, so I made her a cup of tea and waited for her to speak. I had concert practice that evening, but I knew that I wasn't going to make it. While the tea was brewing I quickly excused myself and dashed down the dormitory corridor. I slipped a note under my friend Margaret's door. I didn't feel like explaining anything to anybody, so a note was easier. I told Margaret that something had come up, which it had, and that they would have to manage without me tonight. I hurried back to my room and closed the door behind me, then locked it. Sheila didn't look up. I felt guilty, but I couldn't help but notice how much bigger on her chest she'd become. I poured us both a cup of tea and then sat next to my sister, ready to talk. But she wasn't ready to talk, and her eyes began to fill with tears that eventually spilled out and ran down her gaunt cheeks.

I must have lingered too long at the graveside, for it appears that I've missed the four o'clock bus. A woman of my age finds it both difficult, and a little undignified, to run. I sit on the bench by the bus stop and stare at the hordes of badly dressed schoolchildren milling about and shouting. I recognise the green sweatshirts, and the ties that hang down like cords that you might yank to turn on a light switch. Then I realise that I know some of the kids, so I look away and try to make myself as inconspicuous as possible. A double-chinned man, burdened with shopping bags, sits next to me. He was on the bus that brought us out from the village a few hours earlier, and he attempts conversation. 'It's still warm out.' I can't help him, and so I smile and silently beg his forgiveness. He registers my reluctance and opens a copy of the evening newspaper. I look around and wonder how I ever managed to live in this noisy, filthy town. Mercifully, I now live in Weston, or in the 'new development', which the man next to me has no doubt already guessed. I'm sure that he sits at home at the bottom of the hill, probably by himself, judging by all the shopping bags, and considers me and everybody else in the new development to be interlopers. All of us, disturbing a pattern that has gone on for decade after decade until Stoneleigh came along to make them feel as though their shrinking lives, which were already blighted by closures and unemployment, were even less important than they had hitherto imagined.

It's a little after five-thirty when the bus rolls slowly into the village. There are those who don't stir, for they will be alighting at one of the small towns or lonely villages beyond Weston. However, I watch as my bench partner gets to his feet and struggles with his shopping bags, and then two younger women make their way from the back of the bus and join him at the door. I bring up the rear. The driver is a polite young kid who seems to specialise in this route, and he wishes us all, individually mind you, a good night. Strange, I think, as it's still bright out, but I appreciate the gesture. Usually I would turn to the left and begin the short walk up the hill, but having read some of the back of the man's evening newspaper it occurs to me that catching up on the news would be a nice way to spend the evening. I wait until the bus has moved off on its way, and then I cross the main road. Carla sees me coming towards her and, at least to start with, she's a little shocked, as though I were the last person she wanted to see. Then she catches herself and looks somewhat nervously at me.

'Hello, Miss.' She is dressed to go out, with her eyes overly made-up and her hair neatly combed so that it fans down over her shoulders. If I'm not mistaken there's even a dusting of glitter on her face. I look at her, budding all over, and done up like a promiscuous little so-and-so, but there is nothing that I can say to her by way of admonishment for she is no longer one of my pupils.

'Hello, Carla. I'm sorry I won't be seeing you again.'

Carla shrugs, not with insolence, but as though to imply there's nothing that she can do about the situation.

'I'm sorry too, Miss.' She pauses. 'Is it true you'll be going into a home?'

I say nothing, but I'm taken aback.

'It's just that people are saying you're ill.'

I stare at Carla who, despite her mother, is not a bad girl. Christ, I've taught far worse. In fact, as far as delinquency and bad behaviour go, this girl is practically an angel. I begin to think of what I'd do with her if she were my child. But she's not my child or, if truth be known, even my friend. She asks this intrusive question because, like all young people today, she feels entitled; entitled to dress, behave, speak, walk, do whatever they please.

'Yes, Carla, I am ill, and it's a bully of an illness.' The girl looks momentarily alarmed. 'But you're all right. It's not catching.' Carla smiles weakly.

'What is it, Miss?'

'What is it? What do you think it is?'

Carla shrugs her shoulders. 'I don't know, Miss. Your nerves?'

I can see that the blushing girl wishes that she'd never asked the question, so I rescue her.

'I don't think I'm quite yet ready for a home, Carla, do you?' I throw her a parting smile and move off into the newsagent's, leaving her to wait for the bus that will no doubt take her into town for her night of teenage antics with her friends.

It's a bit of a pull up the last stretch of the hill and I begin to tire. It has already been a long day and my hip has started to hurt. Too many years of sitting at the piano in the same position, said my old doctor when I first went in to complain about it. 'You need regular exercise' was his solution, but some chance, I thought, looking after Brian, trying to teach all day and taking on more pupils at night to make some extra money. And so the hip just got worse, until it reached the stage where it was difficult for me to walk any distance. That's when the old doctor gave me the steroid shots and, miraculously enough, they seemed to do the trick. Now that I'm retired I do, of course, have a lot more time to exercise. But what use is it now? Dr Williams told me not to think like this, but Dr Williams is a specialist, not a proper GP. I can feel the evening newspaper getting damp in my grip, so I tuck it into my bag. And then, as I enter the cul-de-sac, I see Solomon. As usual, by himself, washing his car, oblivious to everything around him. He has a habit of keeping the car radio on, and a window wound down just a little bit, so that he can listen to light music on Radio 2. I hate this kind of mindless commercial rubbish, but I've never told him this for fear of offending him. He puts it on when he drives me, although he makes a point of asking first. I'm always accommodating and I say 'fine', so it's obviously my own fault. I'm sure he isn't going to throw a fit or anything if I say, 'No, I don't like it', but generally I try to be pleasant. As I come up to him I realise that today there's no music. He's washing his car in silence.

'Is everything all right?' Solomon asks me this without looking up at me. For a second or so I'm taken aback, but I understand that it's probably his way of being discreet. He's allowing me my space. I stop and look at him waxing the bonnet of his car.

'I think everything's all right,' I say. 'I missed the bus coming back, but that's about the highlight of my day.'

Solomon stares at me.

'You missed the bus? How did that happen?' He seems genuinely concerned, so I try to set his mind at ease.

'No emergency or anything. I just spent too much time with my parents.' He continues to look puzzled. 'At the cemetery. Time just flew by.'

'Oh, I see.' He puts down his cloth now. 'Miss Jones, it is true that sometimes life can be difficult, yes?' He turns to face me. The dying sun forms a halo around his head and for a moment I find myself more caught up with this image than with his enquiry. Solomon notices that my attention has drifted off, but he simply waits until my mind returns.

'I'm sorry,' I say. 'I must be tired after the walk up the hill.' He seems confused now, but we both know that his question still hangs in the air between us. 'Yes, Solomon, sometimes life can be difficult.' I pause. 'And why on earth do you still insist upon calling me Miss Jones.' I laugh now. 'For heaven's sake, I keep telling you to call me Dorothy. I don't employ you, you know.'

'Yes, Dorothy. I know this. I am just trying to be polite.'

I feel bad now, because I can see that he doesn't know if I'm mocking him.

'Solomon, you couldn't be any more polite if you tried. In fact, I sometimes wonder if you shouldn't be less polite. People will take advantage, you know.'

Solomon says nothing, he just smiles that same enigmatic smile that always seems to be on his face.

'I am sure that your parents were wonderful people.' He

isn't giving up. I set down my bag now, but he continues. 'I would like to learn more about your family.'

'Well, talking about my parents and my sister, these are not easy topics, Solomon.'

'But it is not good to keep these things locked up inside.'

I look at him and understand that he is only speaking to me because he wishes to help. However, we shouldn't be standing in the cul-de-sac, in the full view of others, talking like this.

'You know, Solomon, why don't you come inside and I'll brew a nice pot of tea. When you've finished your car, that is.'

Solomon raises his eyebrows.

'You want me to come inside for tea?'

'Well,' I say, 'only if you want to. I might even give you a biscuit, if you're lucky.' Solomon smiles and he throws down his cloth.

'A biscuit? Now the temptation is too great.'

'No rush,' I say. 'I've got to put the kettle on. You might as well finish your car.' He wipes the excess water from his hands by rubbing them along his overalls. Then he bends down and tips the bucket of soapy water into the gutter.

'I will just finish the waxing.'

'I'll see you in a minute.' As I turn to walk towards my house, the full glare of the dying sun hits me in the face. Solomon has been blocking out much of its force, but I now squeeze my eyes closed against its powerful light.

Solomon waits until he has had a second cup of tea before he asks his question. I look at him as he prepares himself. He is a thin man and he seems dwarfed by the armchair. Not that he's sickly, but his legs and arms seem a bit too long for his body. I offer him the whole pack of biscuits in an attempt to stem his question, but it is too late.

'You have not really spoken of your illness. I am sorry if I seem to be prying.'

'You're not prying.' I make a bowl with my hands and cradle the cup.

'But will you be fine?'

'Dr Williams says things are all right for now, but I need more tests.'

'But he does not understand the problem?'

'So he says.'

'But I do not understand. You appear to me to be strong.'

'I have difficulty sleeping. And sometimes my mind wanders. You must have noticed this.'

I look at Solomon, who now seems somewhat embarrassed that he has raised the subject, and we fall into silence. He stares at me, and I wish that he would look away, but I can see that he has no intention of doing so.

'That's enough about me,' I say, trying to strike a lighter tone.

'If you say so.'

'I do, I do.' Here is the moment that I've been hoping for. An opening into which I can place my own question. 'But what about you, Solomon? I hardly know anything about you.'

I look across at him, and he suddenly seems very tired. He has not yet finished his new cup of tea, and the cup hangs at an angle in his hand. It is politely balanced over the saucer, which he supports in the broad palm of his other hand, as though he were holding a small coin. He washes his car, he drives me to the hospital, he stays at home behind his blinds. At night he patrols the culs-de-sac. He smiles nervously in my direction, as though apologising for his inability to answer my question. But it doesn't matter. I look at him and feel sure that at some point soon he will lever his thin frame out of the chair and pretend that he has something that he must attend to. Always polite. Until then I am happy to watch him as his mind drifts beyond my question, his idle thoughts turning over like leaves in the wind. I am simply happy to be in Solomon's company.

Solomon left an hour ago. He suddenly snapped to attention, looked around and understood where he was. He was embarrassed that he had allowed himself to fall asleep, but I chuckled reassuringly as he made his excuses and then hurried away. And now I am alone again. There doesn't seem to be any point to cooking a dinner for one, so I'll just have a few more biscuits and another cup of tea. I see Sheila's letter staring down at me, and again I'm reminded of the time she turned up at my room at university. I handed her a cup of tea and sat next to her on the edge of the bed. I watched as she wiped away her silent tears.

'I've run away,' she said.

I couldn't stop staring at her skinny, unwashed body. Her new chest aside, my poor sister looked like a stick insect, with her dirty clothes hanging off her.

'I need some money and a place to stay. Just for tonight.'

I remember laughing. Nobody could ever accuse Sheila of not getting straight to the point about things.

'So, you want *me* to give you some money?'

'I'll pay you back, if that's what you're worried about.'

'Sheila, I'm not worried about that. I just want to know how you got yourself into this state in the first place.'

'What do you mean by "this state"?'

I could see she was angry now. She always bit her lower lip when something or somebody annoyed her; in this case, me.

'There's no need to get your mad up, Sheila. I'm just saying, you turn up looking like a drowned rat and, I mean, what am I supposed to think?'

'I'm off to London, and I just need a bit of money. I've had it with up here.'

'You've had it with Mum and Dad, or you've had it with the North?'

'Both. You're such a creep going to university in Manchester so you're not far away.'

'I'm not a creep. It's the only place that took me.'

'Well, I'm getting out of here.'

'You're not off anywhere tonight, are you?'

'I told you I need a place to stay for the night.'

'Sheila, why are you carrying on like this?'

'They think they own me. And you too. But I suppose they do own you, don't they?'

I felt the sting in her words, but I could also see that she was still upset. I tried to change the tone in my voice.

'Sheila, they just don't understand. Why can't you ignore them instead of always having to battle it out? You can always get your own way, but you've just got to be clever about it.'

'I can't be bothered.' A door slammed with this statement. She waited for a moment, and then she looked up at me and spoke quietly. 'It's my life and I don't see why I should have to play games.'

She spent the night with me, but neither of us really slept. When we weren't arguing, one of us was reminiscing about something in the past that made us laugh. Like the time that Mum decided to join the local choral association, but wouldn't accept the fact that she had the worst voice in the world. Or the time I entered the school swimming races, but forgot to tell anybody that I couldn't swim. I agreed to give her the money to go to London, where she was sure she could get a job, and in the morning she gave me that grin of hers and I waved my sister goodbye and watched her walk out of our lives. Once Sheila reached London, silence reigned between her and 'home'. In the first few years after college, I found reasons to go to London occasionally, either by myself or with Brian, and in this way I kept in some kind of contact with Sheila. But I never told Mum or Dad, for fear of upsetting them, and then, without really understanding why, Sheila and I just drifted apart. And now a letter on my mantelpiece. A single letter asking for what?

I make myself a cup of tea, pick up the letter and then sit in the chair by the window that Solomon was sitting in. I look out into the cul-de-sac and can see that the moon is lighting up the street, so that tonight there's really no need for street lights. There's no movement behind Solomon's blinds and I imagine that he must be out on his patrol. I try to imagine the inside of his bungalow and assume that it's probably as impossibly neat and tidy as he is, but I've no way of knowing this. The letter lies ominously in my hands and I understand that at some point I'll have to open it. I feel myself falling asleep in the chair, caught between the need to get some rest and the desire to discover what has happened to my sister's life. However, even as my head grows heavy on my shoulders, I can already feel the responsibility of having Sheila back in my life.

In the morning I wake up in the same place with the pages of Sheila's letter scattered about me like confetti. My neck aches from the awkward way in which I've been resting it on the edge of the chair, and I immediately recognise that I'm in some pain. But there is also another feeling, although I've no words to describe it. I glance out of the window, half-hoping to find Solomon washing his car, but there is nobody in sight. Then I understand the strange feeling that has come over me. Loneliness. Carla won't be coming today. I stare at the piano and realise that music lessons won't help me today, but before I fall into any kind of depression I know what I've got to do. I've seen enough programmes on the television about this condition, and I've read enough articles. I know that I've got to go out, and so I decide to take a shower and dress quickly before my mind can absorb any more thoughts.

The woman in the newsagent's shop at the bottom of the

hill knows me. In fact, I get the impression that she knows everybody, and their business. She beams at me and I wonder if she reserves this particularly foolish expression for me, or if she uses it for all of us from up the hill. She always breaks off her conversation with whatever customer she's dealing with so that she can take care of me. Today I buy a newspaper and a few groceries, and this gives her the opportunity to say, 'So I take it you'll not be going into town today then?' I beam back in her direction.

'No, I won't.'

'Lessons?' she asks. 'Has the card in the window brought you any luck?'

I'm sure she knows that only Carla has materialised as a result of the card, and now there's nobody.

'I've had some promising phone calls.' I say this in a manner which lets her know that there's nothing further to be said on the matter. The other woman stands in the shop and looks at me with a kind of pity. There's something about her which makes me angry. She has no right to be staring at me in this way, let alone thinking whatever it is that she's thinking. I take my change and turn from the pair of them. I hear the door-bell tinkle as I walk out, but I also feel their eyes upon my back and I know that as soon as the door closes their conversation will resume. It will be a highly different conversation, one that will, of course, include me as subject matter. I'm pretty sure that I've become the sort of person that Weston people feel comfortable talking about.

Once I reach the top of the hill I don't have any doubt as to what I have to do. I go straight to his bungalow and knock loudly. A somewhat crumpled Solomon opens the door and looks me up and down. He rubs his eyes and blinks vigorously, and then he politely stifles a cough with the back of his hand. It must be strange for him seeing me in the morning, standing on his doorstep with my few bits of shopping. Neither of us says anything, and then he speaks.

'We are not supposed to be going into the town today, are we? I have not forgotten, have I?' He seems embarrassed, but I let out a short laugh to assure him that everything is fine, and there's no need to worry.

'You haven't forgotten anything. It's just that I thought I'd come by to see if you were all right.'

He seems puzzled now. Again he looks me up and down as though trying to work out what has changed about me. He's looking for evidence of some change, but he won't see anything. At least I don't think he will.

'Well,' he says, 'you must come in.' He steps to one side. 'Or have you already decided the answer to your question?'

'What question?' He catches me by surprise now.

'You can ask your question when you come in.'

I edge past Solomon and into the house, and he closes the door behind me. It's much darker than I'd expected, but when he switches on the lights I feel a little easier.

'Please put down your shopping and let me take your coat. Coffee? Or would you prefer tea?'

'Whatever's easiest for you.'

'Please take a seat,' he says, pointing to the living room. 'I will be fast.' With this said, he disappears into the kitchen and leaves me by myself. There's not much in the way of furniture or home comfort to the room. In fact, it's really quite bare, but I am most taken by the absence of any pictures of his family, although strangely enough there is a framed photograph of a middle-aged Englishman. I'm looking for clues as to who this man is, but there are none. He shouts out from the kitchen.

'Do you take sugar in your coffee?'

'Two, please.' I pause. 'I know it's a bad habit.' He doesn't reply, which makes me feel anxious. He is, of course, right. I do have a question. Does he realise that he is also one of those people who Weston folk feel comfortable talking about? Does he care? As I look up he comes through with two cups of coffee, both of which he places on a small table.

'Taking sugar is not sinful. You have only yourself to please, is that not so?'

'Well, yes,' I say. 'I suppose that's true.'

'Biscuits?' Clearly he's remembering yesterday.

'No, thanks. I'm fine. But thanks anyhow.'

He sits now and picks up his coffee and takes a loud sip. Then he puts it back down and turns to look in my direction.

'Perhaps people have been talking to you about me?' he asks.

'No, they haven't, but I don't care what people say.'

He smiles, then laughs out loud. Then he stands and walks the three or four paces to a tall wooden chest, pulls out a drawer and claims a sheaf of letters. He shuts the drawer and puts the letters on the coffee table.

'What are these?' I ask.

'Letters. Perhaps from the same people who have been talking.'

'What do you mean?' I put down my cup of coffee now. 'I'm not following you.'

'Some people like to write to me.' Solomon laughs. He picks up his coffee again, which I take as a cue to pick up my own. 'What do they write to you about?'

I feel embarrassed, as though I am somehow responsible for these people, whoever they are. Solomon can see the predicament I'm in, so again he stands up.

'I am going for more coffee. Would you like some?' I shake my head. Solomon points to the pile of letters. 'This is

England. What kind of a place did I come to? Can you tell me that?'

'I don't know what you mean.'

'Do you like it here?' asks Solomon, his voice suddenly impassioned.

I look at Solomon, but I really don't understand. I feel as though he's blaming me for something.

'I really don't know anything else, do I? I mean, this is where I'm from, and I've not got anything to compare it to. Except France. I once went there on a day trip. I suppose that seems a bit pathetic to you, doesn't it?' Solomon shakes his head.

'No, but I am asking you, what do you think of this place?'

'It's where I'm from.'

He points again to the pile of letters. 'Then maybe you should not read the letters.' Solomon disappears into the kitchen and I hear the clatter of dishes, and water being noisily poured into a kettle. Solomon sounds angry, but I don't know what to do, so I simply stare at the letters.

After a few moments the noises stop, and then Solomon comes out of the kitchen and he sits opposite me. He seems calmer, and his eyes are softer, but I notice that his hands are shaking slightly. He carefully moves the cup up to his lips and then he replaces it on the saucer. When he's driving he holds on tightly to the wheel. He's in control and I feel safe with him, but sitting in this house he seems curiously vulnerable. He glances at the letters and I feel as though I have to say something.

'Do you want me to read them, is that it?'

Solomon laughs now, but he doesn't say anything. I realise that he's been hurt, and I watch him for a while and then decide that I should leave. As I stand up he also gets to his feet. It's awkward for both of us, but I don't think the relationship is in any way broken. Solomon reaches down and picks up an envelope.

'How do you open your letters?' He doesn't hand me the envelope, he simply lets it dangle between his fingers. I look at him unsure of how I'm supposed to answer his question.

'Well,' I begin. 'I just tear open the envelope.'

'Ah,' he says. He smiles now. 'Just tear open the envelope. I usually do this too, but for some reason I decided not to with this one.'

I'm not sure what I'm supposed to take from all of this, but I continue to listen.

'For some reason I took a knife to it. This was a fine decision, for somebody had sewn razor blades into a sheet of paper and carefully turned the page over so that I would grab the so-called letter and have my fingers sliced off. This is not very kind.'

He laughs slightly and tosses the envelope down onto the pile with the other letters.

'Love letters,' he laughs. 'From people who do not want me in this place.' Again he laughs. 'I am beginning to take this personally.'

I sit back down and stare at the pile of letters. Solomon sits too, and he asks me if I would like more coffee. I look across at him and nod. 'Would you mind?' He takes my cup and saucer and disappears into the kitchen.

'I'm not naïve.' I say this to myself. I whisper it under my breath. I'm not naïve. I've got stuck into these arguments in the past. With Mum and Dad, for starters, both of whom disliked coloureds. Dad told me that he regarded coloureds as a challenge to our English identity. He believed that the Welsh were full of sentimental stupidity, that the Scots were helplessly mean and mopish and they should keep to their own side of Hadrian's Wall, and that the Irish were violent, Catholic drunks. For him, being English was more important than being British, and being English meant no coloureds. He would no more listen to me than would the teachers at school, who also hated coloureds. When people were around, they'd go on about them not really adapting well to our school system, but in private they were always 'cheeky little niggers'. I know this is what people think, I'm not naïve, but why the hatred towards Solomon, who doesn't talk to anybody? Who washes his car. Who hasn't done anything. What do these people hope to achieve? In fact, who are these people? Are they the same people who write letters to the paper complaining about the new coins being too bulky, and the fact that telephone kiosks are no longer red? Do I know these people? Do I sit on the bus with them? I look up and Solomon has returned from the kitchen. He's watching me looking at the pile of letters.

'I'm sorry,' I say, as he sets down my coffee and takes up the seat opposite me.

'You are sorry for what?' he asks. 'I do not understand. You did not write any of these letters, did you?' He flashes me a smile. I don't know if it's appropriate to laugh, or if my laughter will somehow be interpreted as being disrespectful. But Solomon saves me. 'Do not worry,' he says. 'I know you did not write any of these letters. I am only making a joke.'

'But I'm sorry and I'm ashamed.'

'Well,' says Solomon. 'I too am ashamed.'

'But what have you got to be ashamed about? You shouldn't be ashamed of anything.'

'Why not? Sometimes the behaviour of my fellow human beings makes me ashamed.' He pauses. 'And I too am not without guilt. Who among us is?'

I look at Solomon as he bites into a biscuit. He looks up and catches my eye.

'Please,' he says, 'you must not apologise for these people. Most of them sign their names. They want me to know who they are.'

'But what do they want?'

'They want me to go away.'

'But why?'

Solomon sits back in the chair now. He seems nervous, but behind his uncertainty there is hurt.

'I do not know. They just want me to go. That is all.'

'But go where? I don't understand.'

'Away.' Solomon looks tired. It's still early in the morning, but there's an aspect of defeat about his demeanour. 'Just away, that is all.' He pauses and then he slowly shakes his head.

In the evening I decide to go to the pub for a second time. The landlord is friendly and he remembers me. He doesn't, however, remember what I drink and so he asks me what I'd like. I tell him a half of Guinness, but I'm never sure if I really should be drinking and undergoing Dr Williams's tests at the same time. As he begins to pour, I make a promise that I'll limit myself to the one drink.

'We don't see many of you folk down here.'

I'm not sure if I'm being criticised, or if this is a situation with which the landlord is comfortable.

'A lot of people work long hours. Two jobs some of them, I think.'

'Yes,' he says as he takes a plastic knife and smooths off the top of the Guinness. 'I expect they need to make some brass to pay off their fancy mortgages.' He laughs to let me know that this is his idea of wit. I smile to let him know that I'm not offended.

I hand him the exact money, and then I sit in the corner of the pub so that I can look out over the canal. In the garden, and seated around the wooden picnic tables, are the young hooligans, all of whom are drinking beer and gazing lovingly at their cluster of motorbikes as though worried that people might not realise that they're the ones who own them. There's only myself and the landlord in the pub, and an elderly man who watches over a pint in the corner opposite me. When I sat he nodded in silent acknowledgement, and I gave him the briefest of nods in return. It was, however, already clear that this would be the full extent of our intercourse.

I stare out of the window at the dark leaves of an old oak tree. Through its branches I can see the enlarged sun finally sinking in the west. I haven't given it much thought, and perhaps this is my failing, but Solomon is the only coloured person in the village. In the town there are plenty of dark faces, but in this village he's alone. And maybe he feels alone. Perhaps I should have invited him to come to the pub? It would have been easy to have said, 'Can we get together this evening? Maybe go for a walk by the canal, and then pop into the pub for a drink. Would you like to do this, Solomon?' But I didn't make any effort. Even tonight, as I was leaving the house to come out, I could have stopped by and asked him if he'd like to join me for a drink, but I didn't. The landlord is washing glasses behind the bar. I have Solomon's number on a piece of paper in my bag. I could ask the landlord if he has a public phone, and then call Solomon and suggest that he comes down and joins me in the pub, except that it would look like an afterthought and he might be insulted. I don't want Solomon to become a problem in my life, but today I get the feeling that this is what he's becoming and it's making me feel awkward. I lift the glass to my mouth and take another sip. I decide that I'll mind this drink until I see the sun disappear beyond the canal, and then while there's still some light in the sky I'll walk back up the hill to Stoneleigh. By the time I get to the top of the hill it will be dusk and I should be able to walk home without being seen.

I wait by the bus stop and worry that I might have got the time wrong. After a long night without sleep, I have made my decision and this morning I will act upon it. But I'm the only person standing here. Across the main road there are those villagers who are going into town. They talk to each other with casual ease, picking up conversations as though they have simply been set on the back burner for a few minutes. I stand by myself, going in the wrong direction, with a small suitcase by my side. I feel like I'm running away. In fact, I'm temporarily avoiding a man I don't really know. I'm leaving my home for a few days. A day? I don't know. But I'm alone at a bus stop waiting for a bus to come into view, and for the life of me I can't work out if I'm doing the right thing. A girl is waving at me. It's Carla, who's seated in a white van that's sitting outside the newsagent's. A boy in a leather jacket, and with one of those army crew cuts, comes out of the shop and gets behind the wheel. Carla turns from me to the boy. They say something to each other, and then the boy leans past Carla, looks at me, and then the hairless boy starts the van's engine. They pull off in the direction of town, and as they do so Carla waves me a final greeting. No doubt somewhere, down beneath the boy's waistline, desire is already leaping like a trout, but who am I to warn Carla of the ways of men? Maybe I'm imagining it, but I think Carla feels sorry for me. However, she shouldn't, for I'm quite resilient. People, especially young people, are always picking things up and dropping them again. Especially feelings. But I imagine Carla will find this out for herself in the fullness of time.

As I walk by the canal I keep looking around and wondering where exactly they found him. I know it was beyond The Waterman's Arms, and out towards where the double locks are. It seems stupid that I should be so concerned with this, but I am. Where exactly? As far as I know, he didn't go for walks down by the canal. In fact, he hardly left his bungalow apart from taking me to the hospital and patrolling Stoneleigh with his torch. It's been raining heavily so the towpath has turned muddy, and the odd puddle has formed here and there. Somewhere, behind the hedges, I can hear the rush of a stream that has been swollen by the recent rain, and over the canal there hangs a thin ribbon of mist, which makes the water look like it's sweating. At the best of times the stiles are an obstacle, but today it's like climbing Ben Nevis. I don't like traipsing about when it's like this. You seem to spend as much time looking at your feet as you do trying to take in the scenery. The other thing about wandering up the canal path is that there are no benches, so this means that you have to keep going. And these towpaths always remind me of work. Straight lines, no messing, keep walking. Unlike rivers, canals are all business, which makes it hard for me to relax by one. It's late morning, which probably accounts for why there's nobody around. Early in the morning or late in the afternoon, before or after work, people walk the dog or take a stroll to work up an appetite; these are canal times. But even then, there's hardly ever anybody by this canal, which is why it doesn't make any sense that Solomon should be down here by himself.

The police haven't a clue. They told me that there isn't necessarily anything suspect, although they detected some evidence of bruising to the head. The truth is I'm not sure how hard they're trying. I mean, there's no yellow police tape, or signs asking for witnesses. It's only two days ago that a man was drowned in this village, but everything is just going on as normal. I stop and peer over a hedgerow where a white-ankled horse stares back at me with that vacant quizzical look that they sometimes have. And your problem is? My problem is that my friend was found face down in this canal and nobody seems to care. I turn from the hedgerow, and the field's curious occupant, and begin now to walk back in the direction of the village. Face down in a canal because he said something to somebody? I just don't know. When I reach The Waterman's Arms I turn from the towpath and cross the sodden garden, dodging the discarded children's toys, until I come to the six stone steps that lead up to the public bar.

Inside the pub it's quiet. A few people have already settled in for a lunchtime pint, and they barely look up as I enter. As I walk to the bar the landlord surprises me by reaching for a half-pint glass. 'Half of Guinness, isn't it?' I smile and ease myself up and onto a stool. The landlord focuses on the drink, as people tend to when they're pouring a Guinness, and then he looks up at me.

'Friend of yours, wasn't he?' The landlord hands me the Guinness and I remember to answer the question.

'Yes,' I say. 'He was a friend of mine.'

'It's a sad business, isn't it? I'm sorry for him and I'm sorry for what it's doing to our village.'

I take the Guinness and wonder if I should leave this stool and go to the other side of the pub, but it's too late. It would look as though I was running away from something, which would, of course, be the truth.

'What it's doing to the village?'

'Well, it makes us look bad, doesn't it?'

'I still don't understand,' I say. This time I take a drink and stare directly at him.

'Well, it must have been an accident because there's nobody in Weston who would do anything like that.'

'I see.'

He looks over my shoulder at the other men in the pub. Now I understand. This is not a private conversation.

'If you've lived here as long as I have, love, and you've grown up with folks like these, you'd understand that there's not one among them capable of harming anybody. That's just how they are. Decent folk committed to their families and their community. We don't have murderers here. A few villains, some with light fingers, and a few who are quick with their fists, but that's about it. Nothing more than this.'

I nod, for I have no desire to upset his sense of community. I'm not sure that I want the rest of the Guinness, but to leave at this point would be to admit defeat, and out of respect for my friend I won't be doing that. Not with these people. And then the landlord suddenly reaches beneath the bar as though remembering something. He rips open a packet of crisps and offers the bag to me, but I shake my head.

'No, thanks.'

He withdraws the bag, and then thrusts his hand in and pulls out a half-dozen crisps at once. 'I can't help it,' he says, 'I'm addicted to the beggars, but only Bovril and maybe prawn. The others I can let go, but I'm addicted to Bovril.'

I watch this unselfconscious man and understand that until the bag is empty our conversation will remain on hold, which suits me fine.

I lock, and then bolt, the door behind me. The clock reminds me that it is only one in the afternoon, and I look around and realise that I've simply replaced the gloom of the pub with the gloom of my own house. It's early autumn, but it looks and feels like winter. The Guinness seems to have gone straight to my head, and not even the walk up the hill in the fresh air has sorted me out. I slump down into the chair nearest the fireplace and close my eyes. It was only yesterday afternoon that I came back from the seaside and went directly to the hospital. When the bus passed through the village I stayed put. The doctor had previously told me that I must come in straight away if I ever didn't feel right, and so I did as I was told. I had spent just the one night away, but I was in some discomfort and I could barely think. However, when I got to the hospital Dr Williams took a quick look at me, and then he stared at my suitcase. He asked me to sit and then he began to quiz me about where I'd been, and so I told him that I'd just been to see my sister. I knew this would upset him, and I was right. 'Dorothy,' he said, 'your sister is dead. She died earlier this year in London. You know you haven't been to see your sister, so where have you been?' I said nothing, for we'd already been through this enough times. He put on that caring face of his. 'Dorothy, you're going to have to learn to live without Sheila. I know it's difficult for you, but if you can't let go then we'll have no choice but to get you some help.' Again I said nothing and I just waited until he'd run out of things to say. Eventually he got fed up of me, and then I dashed to the bus stop for it looked like it might start to rain. I was standing on the bus going home when I felt it in my blood that something was wrong. It wasn't just the sight of burly, unemployed men sitting in the seats reserved for the handicapped and the elderly that was disturbing me, there was something else. I stared out of the window at the town's terraced houses, great stripes of them arranged in narrow, ramrod-straight streets which, as we made our way into the countryside, finally gave way to a desolate landscape of empty fields over which the sun now hung ominously low.

I got home and had barely set down my suitcase before I heard the knock on the door. Standing there in the dark was a policeman and a policewoman, both in uniform, so there was no need for them to introduce themselves. I felt my stomach lurch. They asked me if I was Miss Dorothy Jones, and when I said 'yes', they asked me if they might come in for a minute. I stepped to one side and tried to work out just what they were doing round at my place. I mean, why would the police come banging on my door? They wiped their feet on the mat, took off their hats and I ushered them into the living room. However, even before they said anything it suddenly dawned on me who it was they had come to talk to me about. The woman spoke up.

'It's about Solomon Bartholomew.'

'Yes,' I said. 'Please take a seat.' They looked around and then, hats in hand, they backed gently into the sofa. I was going to offer them a cup of tea, but this seemed ridiculous. I wanted to hear what they had to say. The man spoke now.

'So you know Solomon Bartholomew?'

'Yes, he drives me to the hospital. He's a very nice chap, who lives just there.' I pointed. 'The green car is his.'

Now it was the turn of the policewoman.

'And when was the last time that you saw Mr Bartholomew?'

'Just before I went away. I've been at the coast for the past day. Well, one night and two days. In fact, I've only just come back. Is something the matter?'

Again the woman spoke. 'And you're returning directly from there, are you?'

'Well, no. I stopped in town at the hospital.'

'But what I mean is you've not been here, in the village, for the past two days?'

'I've just told you, I've only just got back.'

The policewoman looked at the man, as though giving him the cue to assume his seniority.

'I'm sorry to have to tell you, but Mr Bartholomew has been found dead. He was found drowned, face down in the canal.'

I don't know what expression crossed my face, but the look obviously registered something with him for he felt compelled to go on.

'You know the canal we're talking about?'

'What happened?' I knew that I was whispering, but I couldn't find my breath.

'Well, there was some bruising to the head so we can't rule out foul play. But as I'm sure you appreciate, we don't want to jump to any conclusions for there isn't necessarily anything suspect.'

The woman leaned forward and lowered her voice.

'I'm sorry. We thought it best to come and tell you ourselves as people said you knew him.'

It was after the police had gone that Carla came to see me. I hardly ever have anybody come to my door, so to have two visits in rapid succession was disturbing. I got out of the chair and imagined that it was somebody else wanting to tell me about Solomon. Young Carla stared up at me with sad eyes, and so I asked her in. She wiped her feet and then sat down somewhat heavily in the armchair that I had just vacated. She did so without taking her eyes from me the whole time, which made me feel nervous. I asked Carla if she'd like some tea or coffee, but she just shook her head and then, for the first time, she spoke.

'It's about your friend. The black guy.'

'Solomon.'

'Yeah, him.'

I looked at her and waited for her to go on, but she said nothing. She lowered her eyes and stared at the space between her trainer-clad feet. 'What's the matter, Carla?'

'I really shouldn't be here. Paul will kill me if he knows I'm here.'

I sat now, and it was my turn to watch her closely.

'I've no idea what you're talking about.'

Carla twisted herself around and reached into the back pocket of her jeans and pulled out a letter. As she handed it to me, she looked up.

'I found this and it's addressed to the black guy. They're out of order, Miss. I'm not stupid. I know what they're like.' Carla paused. 'I'm sorry, Miss.'

'You're sorry about what?'

I looked closely at Carla, who was now leaning forward so that she was sitting on the edge of the armchair.

'They'll kill me, Miss, if they find out I'm here.'

'Who's "they", Carla?'

'Paul and his mates. Paul's my boyfriend. They're just stupid bullies.'

'Does anyone know you're here?'

'No. Course not.'

'Have you put yourself in danger?'

'I don't think so.' Carla looked puzzled and then she sat back in the armchair. 'What do you mean?'

'Carla, where did you get this letter?'

'I nicked it out of Paul's pocket. I told you, they're bullies. They've been writing stuff like this for a while now. They think it's a laugh, but I've told them it's bang out of order.'

I looked at an agitated Carla, who was clearly ready to leave now.

'Did they harm Solomon, Carla?'

'I think they just wanted to frighten him. But I didn't want any part of any of it, Miss. None of it.'

'Any part of what?'

Carla stood up now. She began to fumble with the zip on her jacket.

'Miss, maybe you should go to the police, but you can't tell them anything about me.'

'Perhaps *you* should go to the police, Carla. Unless, of course, you're simply making the whole thing up?' Carla flashed me a look that was initially disbelief. Then I saw her face change as she became angry. 'Listen, Carla, if you've got something to say, then please say it. We shouldn't be falling out. Not over something as serious as this.'

'We've not fallen out, Miss.'

I looked at her as she finished zipping up her jacket.

'I mean, I brought you the letter. What else do you want me to do?'

'I want you to tell me the truth, Carla.' For a moment Carla looked at me as though she was going to storm out, and then she sighed and shook her head.

'I'm sorry, Miss, but they told me to fetch him, so I did.'

'They?'

'Paul and his mates, Dale and Gordon. I knocked on the black guy's door and asked him to give us a hand pushing Paul's van as it wouldn't start. He was okay about it, but when he came out they jumped him and tied him up. That's when I didn't want nothing to do with it any more.'

'But did you help Solomon?'

Carla lowers her eyes. 'No, Miss.' She pauses. 'They drove him down to the canal, then out towards the quarry. They just wanted to have some fun, but when they opened the back of the van to let him out, he went nuts, Miss. He'd undone the ropes and he started to attack them like a madman. It was scary, and he was shouting and carrying on, and then he had a go at Paul. The others grabbed him and then Paul bricked him.'

'He did what, Carla?'

'They were by the quarry, Miss. Paul picked up a stone and smacked him on the head and he went down. Then they all started to brick him, but it didn't take long before he wasn't moving no more. Miss, I was scared. I didn't know what to do, but Paul said it was self-defence and they'd be okay. But the others didn't want to know, so they decided to push him in to make it look like an accident.' Carla looked up at me. 'Miss, he was terrifying. I thought he was gonna kill them, honest. They'll never say anything, but I could see that they were scared stiff. He kind of went mad, Miss, talking about how he was a bird that could fly, and he kept mentioning you.'

'But Carla, they murdered him, and you helped.'

'I know, Miss.' Her voice broke and tears began to roll down her face. 'I'd best go now.'

'What'll you do, Carla?'

'I ain't got much choice now, have I, Miss?' She paused. 'Paul and his mates are off on holiday on Monday, so I'll have to tell the police before then.'

'And you will tell them? Everything you've told me?'

'I will, Miss. I told you, I promise.'

I watched as Carla left the room, and I decided to leave her alone. There was no need to see her out. I waited for the door to slam shut, and then I looked at the grubby envelope with Solomon's name and address painstakingly scrawled in capital letters.

When I wake up it's dusk. I've fallen asleep in the chair by the fireplace and slept the afternoon away. Obviously the half-pint of Guinness took hold of me. I look out of the window and see the green car standing alone. Without Solomon, Weston suddenly seems like a strange and empty village, and it feels as though a whole lifetime has passed since the day that Solomon came calling. I have a doorbell, so it was unusual to hear somebody knocking at the door. In fact, it seemed a bit rude, so I opened the door somewhat gruffly. I saw Solomon standing there in his Sunday best, his hands clasped in front of him as though he were about to pray. I'd seen him cleaning his car, of course, and I'd noticed him walking about, especially in the evenings, but I couldn't for the life of me work out what he thought he was playing at, knocking at my door like this.

'I saw you at the bus stop yesterday. And before this, in the rain.' I looked him up and down and waited for him to go on. However, I realised that he wasn't going to say anything further until I said something to him.

'Yes,' I said. 'I was going into town. I go once or twice a week.'

'Yes, I know. I have seen you as I have driven past. But I am not really sure if I should stop.'

'Stop where?' I wrinkled my forehead.

'Stop to ask you if you would like me to drive you into the town. After all, we are neighbours. I am the night-watchman for the Stoneleigh estate.' He gestured all around him. 'This is my job.'

I nodded. I knew who he was, but he was being a bit strange, so it seemed best to say nothing more. I thought about just closing the door, but then he spoke again.

'Please, when are you going to town again?' Suddenly I felt sorry for him, for I could see now that he was harmless. Obviously he didn't have any friends, and it seemed stupid to have him standing on the doorstep like he was some kind of Jehovah's Witness.

'Would you like to come in?' He stared at me, but he did not reply. Didn't he want to come in? I looked over his shoulder to see if there was anybody else in the cul-de-sac watching, but I couldn't see anybody.

'You have not answered my question,' he said. 'If you need some time to consider my offer, then I will understand.'

Very generous, I thought, but at least he seems more peculiar than he does dangerous.

'I'll be going in tomorrow. I've got to see the doctor regularly these days.'

'I am sorry. Is everything all right?'

'Well, hardly.' As soon as the words came out of my mouth I felt terrible. I knew there was no need to speak to him in this way. He was only trying to be helpful, and the truth was he had done nothing to deserve this kind of reply.

'I'm sorry,' I said. 'I think I've just had a bad few days.'

'Well, standing at the bus stop does not help one's spirit.'

'No, you're right,' I said. 'It doesn't help at all.' I paused for a moment, and then I realised that this was the first real conversation I'd had in weeks.

'What time is your appointment?'

'Noon. What I mean is I have to be there by noon.'

'Then I shall collect you at eleven-thirty precisely.'

'Eleven-thirty,' I said. I watched as he bowed slightly, and only then did he turn and move to go away. It seemed to me a strange way to leave somebody, and so I didn't shut the door. Instead, I watched as he practically marched the short distance back to his bungalow. As he put the key into his door he didn't turn around. Perhaps he could feel my eyes upon him? Perhaps he was already lost in some thoughts of his own? Whatever it was, I sensed that this man was lonely and in need of conversation.

The next morning, instead of walking over, and then the two of us walking back to where his car was, he drove the short distance, kept the engine running, and then came and knocked on my door. I wanted to laugh when I saw what he'd done, but I didn't know if this would cause offence. For the first few minutes he was silent, and then he began to talk. He wanted to know if it was serious, whatever it was that I was going to the hospital for, but I didn't answer him.

'I do not mean to pry. I just thought that it might please you to have somebody to talk with.'

I found the gloves the most unusual part of his costume. It was hot, yet he was wearing gloves and a collar and tie, but I appreciated the formality.

'The doctor says I'm suffering from stress, whatever that means.'

He didn't say anything, but he did give a slight nod as though to let me know that he had heard.

'But apparently it's difficult to get to the bottom of it. It's always difficult to know what to do.'

'I am sorry to hear this unfortunate news.' He looked across at me now. 'But you look well. You look very well.'

'Thank you.' I paused. 'I'm doing all right, I suppose.'

'Do you have anybody to help?'

'Help?' I asked. 'I'm not sure what you mean by help.'

We looked at each other now.

'I mean somebody to talk to. Somebody to assist you with this difficult situation.'

'Do I look like I need help?'

'No, that is not what I meant.'

I knew that he was trying to make me feel more comfortable. I appreciated this, but I didn't want him to do anything more than just drive me. In fact, I wasn't sure if I even wanted him to do this.

'I am sorry.' He had an apologetic tone to his voice, and the look on his face was pained. 'I did not mean to interfere.'

During the bus journey back from the seaside I had thought of poor Solomon sitting alone in his bungalow, with only his memories for company, wondering where I'd gone to. Wanting me. The journey itself was dull and uneventful. I sat near the front and looked over the driver's shoulder at the road ahead. I could see everything from his point of view, but there was nothing inviting about the coarse, bracken-strewn landscape that swam out flat to either side of the road and so I closed my eyes. When I opened them again the sky had already begun to turn dark, and I was being blinded by lights either flashing past us red, or barrelling towards us white. When the bus reached the town I stood up and remained hopeful that Dr Williams might still be seeing patients, for the splitting headache that had plagued me during the previous night had returned. 'Have a good evening, love,' said the driver, but I didn't reply. I was clutching my suitcase with one hand and gripping the hand rail with the other, and trying hard to concentrate so that I didn't fall down the three stairs.

The half of Guinness has really done for me. I'm still tired. Not surprising though, for I didn't sleep much last night. In fact, yesterday was difficult. First, I'd had to endure a day of sitting alone on a windswept promenade. Then the tedious bus journey, followed by yet another encounter with Dr Williams in which he didn't appear to want to take me seriously. Then the police. Then Carla and the stupid letter. After Carla left I maybe got a couple of hours at most before the sound of car doors slamming woke me up. And this morning I walked by the edge of the canal in the dreary autumn haze, and I thought of my friend lying face down in the water like a dead fish. It's hard to believe that there will be no more trips to the Somalian and Mediterranean Food Hall, or conversations with him in my house, or time spent with him in his house trying to work out who exactly the strange man is in the photograph on the mantelpiece. I worry over who will look after his car, or tell his family. I don't even know if he has any family. The poor man may as well have been living on the dark side of the moon. It was only after I'd been to the pub and had the half of Guinness, and then walked back up the hill, that it finally dawned on me. I slumped down in this chair and realised that there's no way that I can live among these people. I don't think they care about anybody apart from their stupid selves, and if this is true then I too may as well be living on the dark side of the moon.

Out beyond the viaduct, and through the evening gloom, I can see that night has paused on the horizon. In a minute I'll get up out of this chair and pull the curtains. Weston is simply not the place that I hoped I might be retiring to. I suppose I knew this yesterday when the policeman and policewoman came to tell me about Solomon as though they were enquiring about an unpaid parking ticket. And then there was poor confused Carla, who was obviously terrified of the boyfriend who'd been doing Lord only knows what with her for the past few months. I listen to the birds singing as the day finally begins to fade behind the viaduct. I turn Solomon lightly over in my mind. Maybe I should visit the small stone church and say some kind of a prayer for my friend? And then one final trip to town to put flowers on Mum and Dad's grave? And then what? Off to some tropical place to tell Solomon's family? And then? Back here and live with Sheila by the seaside? If I mention Sheila to Dr Williams he only gets annoyed, so it's perhaps best to say nothing further to him on this topic. Maybe Sheila and I can go abroad together. For the first time I want to leave England. To see Spain or Italy. England has changed.

I decide to take Carla's boyfriend's letter to the pub. I have to do something because I don't want it in the house with me for another night. After I've had breakfast, I put on my jacket, but then I realise that it's still too early. So I sit with my jacket all buttoned up, and with my handbag on my lap, and I wait until just before eleven. Then I get up and go out. It is a nice morning. I double-lock the door behind me. Strange really, because I only used to do that when I lived in town, and then only when I was going away for any length of time. Here, at Stoneleigh, there doesn't seem to be any reason to double-lock. This is a residential area, and I don't get the idea that we're in any danger of being broken into. There's also a night-watchman and so it has never occurred to me to double-lock. But maybe that's it. We don't have a night-watchman any more.

As I walk down the hill I realise that I've been foolish

because instead of just sitting in the house for three hours staring into mid-air, I could have gone for a walk. That would have been the sensible thing to do. Get some exercise, or do some shopping, but I've already failed to make proper use of this day. There is an early autumn chill in the air, and I can tell that winter is just around the corner waiting to pounce. There won't be many more days like this and so there's something sinful about having wasted the better part of the morning. At the bottom of the hill I see a few of the villagers, but I ignore them. Especially now, after what they've done. I stop at the main road and wait for the traffic to clear. It looks to me like it might take for ever as the cars and lorries are streaming by in both directions. I feel uncomfortable standing helplessly where everybody can see me, and I think about just dashing out into the road and making them stop for me. But I know that I'm just being silly. I'll have to wait like everybody else.

I am the first one into The Waterman's Arms. I knew I would be, for it is only a few minutes past eleven. I shut the door behind me and walk the few paces to the bar. There is no sign of the landlord, but I can hear voices. Somebody is around. In fact, somebody has to have drawn back the curtains and unbolted the door. My guess is that the landlord was simply not expecting anybody this early so he's gone round the back to finish off some chores. Fair enough, I think, I'll wait. There's a bell, but I don't want to sound it off like I'm in a hurry, or annoyed, so I sit on a stool and stare out of the window. I don't know how long I've been staring, but it seems like ages before I hear the landlord's voice. At first he frightens me, and then I turn and see him smiling at me from behind the bar. He's caught me by surprise, but I've also caught him by surprise for he's still doing up his tie.

'Well, you're keen, aren't you?'

'Good morning.' I hope this will put him in his place. After all, if he's going to wear a collar and tie, he can at least make the effort to conduct himself as though he's familiar with the type of behaviour that generally goes with civilised dress. He seems a bit taken aback that I've chastised him, but I can see that he's also keen to pretend that he hasn't been scolded. No doubt this better suits his ego.

'And it's a blooming nice morning at that. What'll you have? Your usual?'

'I'll have a half-pint of Guinness, please.'

He's already pulling the half-pint from the pump, but he stops for a moment and looks puzzled. Then he continues. However, it is his own fault for being too familiar. He ought to know his place. He hands me the small glass of Guinness, and I hand him a five-pound note and then smile sweetly when he produces my change.

'There you are, love.'

I'm sure he assumes that I'm going to sit with him at the bar, but I take the money and the drink and I walk to a small table by a window where I turn side-on to him so that when I look up there can be no accidental eye contact. For a few minutes I can hear him tidying up around the bar, but the truth is there isn't really any tidying up to be done. He's only just opened up and everything is in order. He's just embarrassed that I've walked away from him, but he can't pick a fight with a middle-aged lady. I let him stew for a while and then I hear his voice, which is somewhat less assertive than usual.

'I'll just be out back finishing off a few things.'

I turn and look at him, as though shocked to discover that he is still present. And then I smile, as I might smile at a pupil, just to let him know that he is dismissed now.

I don't really want the beer. As soon as he goes through to the back I push it away from me. I want to do what I have to do, and then go before anybody else comes in. I stand up and walk over to the small notice board. Aside from a small postcard-size piece of paper asking for volunteers for the village rugby team, there is nothing else pinned up. I take the envelope from my handbag, slip the letter out, open it up, and then I take a drawing pin from the bottom left-hand corner of the rugby notice and pin the abusive letter into place. I've 'mailed' it back to them. I don't need it in my house, for it doesn't belong there. They can have it back.

Once I reach the top of the hill I walk straight past my house and towards Solomon's bungalow. It is actually getting warm now and so I slip off my jacket. When I get to the bungalow I stop and stare at it. I think about what secrets I might find inside, were I to sneak in and rummage around. The one time that I visited Solomon, I saw nothing which gave me a clue about his past or his present. Besides, that is, the photograph of the Englishman on the mantelpiece. I don't even know what Solomon liked. Except, of course, his precious car, which still stands in the driveway. I put down my bag, then scrunch my jacket up into a ball. The least I can do for him is to polish it. It's getting dusty and Solomon would never have let it deteriorate into such a state. And so I start to polish his car, but I try to copy the way that he used to do it. All careful, with small circular movements like you're gently stirring a bowl of soup.

I suppose it's when I see them standing in the street and just staring at me that I know something is wrong. I have to ask myself, is it that fascinating watching me trying to keep Solomon's car clean? Don't they wash their own cars? Of course they do, and I don't come and stand and look at them, so I don't see the point of this communal gawping. Not everybody has come out, but there's enough of them to make me feel awkward and so I stop. The car is almost spotless anyhow, so it isn't like I haven't done a good job or anything. It's just that I don't want to be putting on a show, and that's how I feel. But I also don't want to stay in Stoneleigh with them any more. I resolve to use the day sensibly and go into town and talk with my parents. I uncrumple my jacket and fold it up and push it into my bag. It is far too dirty to wear, but I don't want to go back into my house and feel trapped there, so I secrete it in my bag where nobody can see it. I just have to hope that the weather doesn't change, otherwise I know I'll get cold.

When I get to the cemetery the boy is nowhere to be seen. I'm surprised because he always seems to be there with his seemingly unstoppable enthusiasm. But today of all days he isn't around. I spread the jacket out on the grass by Mum and Dad's grave and then I sit down and begin to talk to them. I tell them everything about Solomon that I can think of. I know Dad has some opinions about coloureds, and that he won't be totally sympathetic to a lot of what I'm saying about Solomon, but I still want to tell them. Dad doesn't say much. After a while Mum starts to cry and she asks me what it was about Solomon that made me want to be seen with him. I think for a while, and I then tell her that there was nothing in particular, it was just that Solomon was a proper gentleman. In fact, one of the first gentlemen that I'd ever met, with his smart driving gloves. He really showed Brian up for the slob that he is, but I don't have a chance to say anything for Mum hasn't finished. She goes on, but she's so upset that she can hardly get the words out. Didn't I understand what people would say about me if I were to be seen with a coloured, and particularly one as dark as this Solomon? She'd not brought me up to be that type of girl. Why, she wants to know, why would I want to do this to them both? There's no point in looking to Dad for any help, for I'm not going to get any from him. I try again and tell them that Solomon treated me with respect, but they don't want to hear this for their minds are already made up. Eventually neither of them will speak to me, and so I begin to plead. I just wanted to be happy, I say, and I could tell that Solomon was a man who could have made me happy. Mum continues to weep, but Dad has his one ugly word, and I could have predicted it before he even opened his mouth. Slag. He doesn't even want to look at me any more, that's how bad it is. As it starts to get dark, I reckon that I'd better leave them alone. This isn't going anywhere and I'm starting to get cold. I stand up, pull on my filthy jacket and look around one final time to see if I can spot the boy, but there's no sign of him.

On the way back to the bus station I see a few of them. They are staring as though there's something the matter with me, but I try to ignore them. Really, they should be ashamed of themselves with their hands out, begging for decent people's money when there's no reason at all why they shouldn't be working and earning their own. I'm retired and I don't have anything to give to them. And even if I did, why would I? They should go and get a job. I tell this to one of them and he just laughs and shows me his yellow teeth. Like an animal, he is crouched in a doorway. They're disgusting, dragging themselves and the country down like this. Just behind the bus station I see a large group of them gathered around an oil-drum which they've set alight. It has bits of wood sticking out of it, and they are huddled together and vigorously rubbing their hands and stamping their feet. It makes me feel angry just to look at them.

'What you looking at?' says one of them. It's a woman, which somehow makes it worse. She looks and sounds like a gypsy, with her black hair, and her black eyes, and her grimy black hands. Sheila and I have always been scared of gypsies and Mum had told us to run away if any of them ever spoke to us. They are nasty, and they like to take away people's children, everybody knows that much. So I don't say anything back to this woman, but when she spits in my direction I feel my blood beginning to boil. It's awkward, for I'm not dressed how I want to be dressed. There isn't much dignity to a crumpled jacket, but I'm not going to let this stop me from speaking my mind. But I don't know what to say.

The policewoman says that they found Dr Williams's phone number on the referral card in my bag. That's how come Dr Williams finds himself at the police station, sitting across a table from me, nervously kneading his hands together as though he's making bread. I still don't know what I'm doing here, but I suppose that something bad must have happened. I'm just waiting for either Dr Williams or the policewoman to speak, for I know that one of them will have to explain to me what the gypsy woman did. After all, I'm covered in bruises and I'm still bleeding.

'Are you all right, Dorothy?' Dr Williams is looking at me, but I can see that he is worried. I stare back at him, but what am I supposed to say? I don't know if I'm all right. I don't even know what happened.

'What time is it?'

The doctor looks at his watch and then he arches his eyebrows. 'It's getting late. Nearly eleven.'

'At night?'

Dr Williams nods and I stare first at him, then at the policewoman, then back at him.

'I don't think you're well, Dorothy. Shouting and brawling with homeless people, well, that's just not you.'

I remember something now. She spat and I spat back, and then the shouting started, and then I struck her, and the police arrived. Maybe this policewoman was one of them, but no matter how long I stare at her I can't remember if she was there or not. The policewoman looks at Dr Williams as though asking for his help, but why? I'm not doing anything wrong. I'm just looking at her and trying to work something out, but that's how it seems to go these days. I can't do anything right at all, can I?

I turn to Dr Williams. 'I don't want to be in this police station.'

He is smiling at me, but I need something more than this. I'm afraid smiling isn't good enough any more.

'I don't want to be in this place! Can't you hear me? I don't want to be in this place!'

'Dorothy, I think you need to spend some time convalescing in an environment where you can get better, don't you?'

'I don't understand what you're saying.'

I look closely at him, but his words make no sense. I know I'm sick. I still have problems sleeping, but unless there's been some serious change that he hasn't told me about, then I should be going home. That's where I belong. I shouldn't be at this police station talking about convalescing. Perhaps I've got Sheila's cancer, but I've been managing with it all right, haven't I? My jacket is a bit crumpled, I can see that. In fact, it's dirty, but it just needs a wash and then everything will be fine, won't it? It will be all right. I'm all right. It occurs to me that if I just stare at Dr Williams then I can make him believe me when I say that everything is all right, but he simply looks back at me and the longer I stare, the more I begin to feel like a fool.

Apparently I am convalescing. They always keep a light on somewhere. In the corridor, or on the other side of the room. I confess, I can't sleep properly. I've told them this, but they said that if the tablets and the hot milk don't help, then they can always give me the needle. But I'm not sure that they really listen to me. When I went to the seaside I didn't sleep. It took just over an hour to get there, and as we entered the town I saw a big field with maybe a hundred caravans set down on top of thick concrete slabs. In the corner of the field there stood a row of rusting tin sheds that I presumed to be the toilets and showers. Kids were drinking from standpipes, and recent rain had turned the whole place into a huge sea of mud. Once I got off the bus there was nowhere to go, so I lugged my suitcase into the bus-station café and found a seat in the far corner. I noticed a sticky mess of honey on the table where it had not been properly wiped off, so I was careful not to put my elbows up. A pregnant young girl came across and stood with pocketed hands. Before I could say anything she announced, 'We're all out of buns, but we've got cellophane-wrapped fruit cake and sandwiches.' I just wanted tea, and when it finally arrived it did so with a clatter. I sat in the bus station for a while and had one cup of tea after another and watched the pregnant girl, who was clearly stupid with confidence. She ashed her cigarette into a tea cup that was similar to the one that I was drinking out of, and then she started to gyrate to imaginary pop music as she stacked the saucers on top of the side plates. I felt my arms fold up across my chest, like the sleeves of a shirt after it's been ironed, and I stared at the creature.

Eventually it got dark, and little Miss Know-it-all made it clear that she needed to close up the café. She gave a deliberate yawn in response to my question, and then pointed me towards a small hotel that overlooked the promenade. It had one of those signs outside that advertised the name of the hotel, then beneath it there were two hooks where they could hang a sign that said 'vacancies' or one that said 'no vacancies'. I was lucky, for the sign said they had 'vacancies', but judging by the dismal state of the place, I imagined that on most days they would have vacancies. The woman asked me if I'd like dinner in my room or in the dining room with the other guests, but I saved her any bother by letting her know that I didn't want dinner, full stop. I wasn't nasty about it or anything, but I felt that I had to make myself clear so there would be no confusion on her part. She asked me if I wanted a hot water bottle, as mine was an attic room and it could get a bit nippy, but I let her know that there would be no need for a hot water bottle. Fatigue had begun to cloud my mind like a thick fog, and I didn't want to be disturbed.

The room smelled of mice and unwashed clothes. There was a single bed, a severe upright wardrobe, a pine dresser, and in the corner a metal chair over which a white towel was draped. There was also a paraffin heater, but it didn't look like anyone had used that in a while. The bed felt warm and clammy, as though somebody had recently crawled out of it, and so I reached for the towel, which was as rough as sandpaper. I spread it on top of the brown bedspread, and then listened. I heard feet pass my door and then fade away down the corridor. A door opened and then closed with a powerful echo, and I turned and glanced in the mirror on the dresser. I was tired, and I looked terrible, but I knew that I wouldn't be able to sleep in a single bed. For most of my adult life I'd associated them with not being grown-up, and they always made me feel like I'd stepped back into an era that I remember being anxious to leave behind. I kicked off my shoes, and then lay on the towel and looked up through the unadorned skylight. There was no bedside lamp or radio, and I now understood that I would have to survive till morning staring at the black night through this skylight window.

Dawn broke without emergency. I had been presented with the gift of the whole night to think everything through. I wanted Solomon to understand that he wasn't going to be able to just take me for granted. I wanted to be able to tell him about my adventures with my sister, and then I would wait a few weeks and disappear again. Lonely Solomon. I wanted to keep him on his toes until he realised for himself that he really didn't like it if I wasn't around all of the time. Then he would want me. I swung my legs down off the side of the single bed and felt the damp chill of the floor. I remembered something else about single beds that I didn't like. They reminded me of when Sheila turned up at university with her rucksack. After I'd cancelled my music practice for that evening, I sat back on the edge of my bed with her and we both cradled our cups of tea in our hands. And then she told me. I knew I should have made more effort to help her instead of just staring at her, but it wasn't easy to hear what she had to say. I kept trying to get the conversation back onto more pleasant things like Mum's embarrassing attempts at singing, but Sheila would have none of it. She kept asking me why I wouldn't believe her, and why did I think that she would lie about something like that? 'You *know* he used to take me to the allotments with him. I mean, what's the matter with you? Why can't you believe me?' The problem, of course, was that I did believe her. I knew she was right when she said that the fact that it had stopped now didn't make it any better, but underneath it all the real question that I wanted answered was how come I escaped his attention? Did he love her more than me? I knew that he loved me more than he loved Mum, but why take Sheila down to the allotments with him? Of all people, why our Sheila? I tried again to change the subject, but Sheila still wasn't having any of it. She wanted to make sure that I'd heard her, and I had. I eventually slipped my arm around my sister's shoulders, but her weeping had now given way to silence. Trying to change the subject was stupid, and I'd not said the right things. I'd failed her, and we both knew that something had changed between us. In those few moments, sitting on the edge of my single bed, a part of my sister simply disappeared from view. The rest of her life had not been very satisfactory. Including our brief time together in London. After nearly thirty years we tried once more to be together, but it was too late. Following that night in my dormitory room, Sheila couldn't talk to me again, and her grief was not something that I could simply penetrate by sympathy. We were civil with each other, but I'd lost her that night, with her rucksack standing by the door. After Sheila died I wrote to myself and pretended it was her doing the writing. It was all I had left of her. My imaginary Sheila who likes me and still needs my help. But my cowardice had lost me my real sister. My poor, grieving Sheila. Daddy's little pet.

My memory is getting stronger. I think that's a part of convalescing. If so, then it's a good part for I don't want to forget things. The people in this place give me tablets and hot milk, but although they don't help me to sleep, they help me to remember. I checked out of the depressing hotel and spent my second day by the sea sitting on a bench on the promenade. The water was being lashed and torn, and it leaped upwards in great buffalo-headed waves. What I really desired was a steady, comforting beat, with the surf printing its pattern like lace against the sand, but instead I had been presented with an angry summer sea. The wind was making a clown of my scarf, and it kept blowing strands of grey hair across my face. Regular as clockwork I had to take the loose hairs and pull them back from my eyes, but there was not much to see. A cargo ship far out on the horizon, and just beneath the promenade an energetic dog acrobatically fielding a Frisbee that its bored owner was dispatching with increasing impatience. I kept wondering what he'd be doing right now, whether he'd be knocking at the door to make sure that I was all right, or just peering from behind his blinds and wondering where I'd got to. By the time the afternoon came it was starting to get a little chilly, so I picked up my suitcase and began to make my way to the bus station. I thought about killing some more time by popping into a pub, but the only one that I saw had a garden out front whose grass was worn bald, no doubt by yobbo powwows, and wooden tables that were covered with empty pint glasses and overflowing ashtrays. I pressed on, and I waited in the station until a bus was leaving for Weston. Once on board I sat near the front so I could look over the driver's shoulder. Across the aisle a blowsy woman proceeded to annoy me, for she slapped sand from her unshod feet onto the floor of the bus, where she no doubt imagined that somebody less important than her would clean it up. I decided not to get off at Weston, and instead I went straight through to town and saw Dr Williams, which was a waste of time. But the truth was I just wanted to take up a bit more time so that Solomon would miss me even more. However, an hour or so later, when I finally got back to the village, I knew that something was wrong. When I saw the policeman and the policewoman standing at the door I felt my stomach lurch. I told them to come in, and they took off their hats as they did so. Then they told me.

II

Gabriel wipes the blood from his friend's eyes. An hour earlier Said had fallen from the bottom bunk and onto the hard concrete floor, and although Gabriel had immediately jumped down and made an effort to haul Said back into bed, he soon realised that his friend should not be moved. Said had hit his head as he fell, and Gabriel continues to mop the petals of blood from the floor with a paper tissue. Said does not seem to notice the blood, and he lacks the energy to wipe the vomit from his mouth. For much of the past hour Gabriel has been kneeling beside this man, and hoping that Said might talk to him. When not kneeling beside him, Gabriel has been holding on to the bars of the cell and begging the night warder to call for a doctor. But the night warder continues to watch television with his boots up on the desk, his legs crossed casually at his ankles and the flickering glow of the screen illuminating his face. Suddenly Gabriel looks up as the man in the next cell once more kicks the wall.

'Can't you lot just fucking shut it with your puking and carrying on?'

Gabriel climbs to his feet and crosses to the door of the cell. He prepares to launch yet another appeal for a doctor, but his neighbour's outburst has won the night warder's attention. The boots swing down off the desk and the man walks slowly towards Gabriel. The night warder is a tall stocky man, and his dark uniform, and the jangling keys that hang from his belt, suggests a severity that is betrayed only by his boyish face. He stops short of Gabriel, who watches as the man places both hands on the bars of the cell next door. For a moment the night warder simply stares. Gabriel imagines that, faced with this display of authority, his loud-mouthed neighbour will now be backing down, for he is sure that this man is a coward. The night warder continues to stare, and then the neighbour speaks, but this time in an almost helpless voice.

'What am I supposed to do? I can't get no fucking sleep with them going on like that.'

The night warder leans forward. 'I told you to be quiet, sunshine.' He pauses. 'I'm trying to watch the telly.'

'How can you watch the telly with all that fucking puking? It's disgusting.'

Gabriel watches as the night warder lifts one hand from the bars of the cell and points directly at its occupant.

'I don't want to hear another word, right?' The night warder does not blink. He repeats himself. 'Right?'

Gabriel hears a short grunt, and then the creak of a bed as his neighbour sits back down.

Now that he is satisfied, the man turns towards Gabriel. He speaks as he walks. 'He's not getting any better then?'

Gabriel steps to one side so that the night warder can look in and see for himself.

'What's the matter with him?'

'Please, I have seen this type of illness before. It is like malaria, but it is something more than this. I think Said is dying if we do not find a doctor.'

The night warder peers into the cell, but he seems reluctant to get too close. The pools of vomit are beginning to congeal, and the smell is ripe. The man pulls a crumpled handkerchief from his pocket, and clasps it to his face with one hand, and he points with the other.

'It would help if you cleaned up that shit.'

'Please, Mr Collins. Said needs help, that is what I am telling you.'

The night warder looks from Gabriel to Said, and then back to Gabriel. His brow furrows, and he understands that a decision is being forced upon him.

'I'll see what I can do.'

Gabriel is quick to react. 'Thank you, Mr Collins. And perhaps some water for Said while we wait for the doctor?'

The night warder says nothing. He turns on his heels and begins to amble his way back towards his desk, all the while keeping the handkerchief pressed closely to his face.

Gabriel is once again enveloped by a silence that is disturbed only by the night warder's television set. There are no windows to this cell, but Gabriel knows that it is night time. Beyond this prison there is England. Three days ago, when they first locked him in this cell with Said, Gabriel began to doubt that he would ever again see England. As his cellmate began to speak, Gabriel could see that the man was ailing, for his hands were shaking and his eyes were damp with fear.

'They say I robbed an Englishman and his wife on a train.'

Gabriel waited for Said to tell him what had actually occurred, but Said simply shrugged his shoulders.

'It is not exactly how it happened.' He thought for a few moments and then continued. 'Yes, I was on a train and I was talking to some English people. My English is good. In my country I am a teacher. I practise hard with my English. I was talking to some English people, for I am not afraid. I know that when the train gets to the town I will ask for asylum at the police station. That is the way. I am a human being who has paid over United States dollars three thousand, everything that I have, to come from my country in a small space under a truck. From Iraq I travel like this like an animal, but maybe worse than an animal, but I do not care for I know that in England they will give me money and some kind of voucher and let me work. Everybody wants to keep out the Muslim, but in England freedom is everything. They can change the law, but you cannot change the culture of the people and so I am not afraid. British people are good. I have friends who tell me the truth. I do not hate Americans, but they are not gentlemen. Why should I be afraid?'

He looked at Gabriel as though expecting an answer, but Gabriel said nothing.

'And then an Englishman and his wife they asked me if I would watch their bags while they go to the restaurant car, and I say yes, of course, yes. And then they come back and look at their bags, and the woman says that I have taken their money and she runs to get the man in the red jacket, the train manager. But why would I come all the way from my country to make a new life here and then take their money? I cannot go back. I sold my land and animals to pay for my journey. I have nothing to go back to. My wife and family are with my brother and waiting for me to send money so they can come to England. I have two hands, I can work. One day I can buy a television and a radio. A fridge. A carpet. Maybe, one day, a car. I have two hands.'

Said showed Gabriel his hands, but his hands continued to tremble and Gabriel noticed the beads of sweat on Said's brow.

'The police,' he said. 'When the train stopped, the police, they come for me. I told them, I have lost everything. My family, I have left my family behind. Despite my education I cannot feed my family. I am no longer a teacher. I am here to begin my life again and I have the appetite to do this so they must help me, yes? I told them I have a case to present, but they do not listen to me. I tell them, please do not send me back to my country. Not there. The policemen they ask me, what happened to you in your country? I told them that I cannot talk of this or I will lose what little appetite I have left. The policemen looked at me, so I ask them, is it true? Is it true that in England you can smell freedom in the air? That it is a different air? But they will not answer me. I say, I have smelled a little of the air and it is good, but why are you putting me in this prison? I do not want these filthy trousers, or this grey T-shirt that another man has worn. I will not wear your slippers. England is not my country. I have done nothing. I am not a criminal man. I have never been a criminal man. I have two hands, I can work.'

Gabriel asked his new cellmate if he was all right, but Said shrugged his shoulders.

'I am cold, but I have no money to see a doctor. And now maybe I will never see England again. But have you noticed? The light in England is very weak. It depresses me. They have taken the sun out of the sky.'

Said looked forlorn, and so Gabriel suggested that he try to sleep. Gabriel squeezed his friend's shoulder, and then he climbed onto the top bunk and stretched out. He listened as beneath him Said continued to cough and splutter. Sadly, for the past three days, his cellmate's condition has only deteriorated.

And now the night warder arrives back at the cell, and he javelins a wet mop and then tosses a roll of paper towel through the bars.

'Here, clean up this shit, Gabriel. It will make everybody feel happier.'

Gabriel looks down from his bunk, but the night warder is already walking back to his television set. Gabriel climbs from his perch, and he picks up the mop and the roll of paper towel and he begins to clean up the floor around Said's prostrate body. His friend continues to breathe in a rasping whisper, and although his eyes are still open he appears now to be incapable of focusing on anything. Gabriel bends down and he places the roll of paper towel underneath Said's head so that it becomes a squashed tubular pillow. During the past three days, the story of Said's life in Iraq has become increasingly improbable and riddled with contradictions, but Gabriel has been a patient audience. He re-adjusts the roll of paper towel under his friend's head, and listens once more as Said struggles to make himself heard.

'Please,' whispers Said. 'My brother and my children. You must tell them.'

Gabriel takes his friend's hand and squeezes hard.

'Said, you must continue to allow hope to grow.'

'Please, you must tell them.'

And then Said's eyes fall shut. Gabriel leaps to his feet, scattering the mop to the far side of the cell.

'Mr Collins, it is Said. Please, we need a doctor.'

The night warder abandons his precious television set, and he moves quickly to the cell. For the first time Gabriel can see concern on the face of the man. The night warder speaks to Gabriel, but without taking his eyes from Said.

'I'll call the doctor, but they do everything in their own sweet time.'

The night warder leaves Gabriel marooned with his friend. According to Said, his brother is still in Iraq, but at other times he is in America. And sometimes Said has a wife, and at other times he is a bachelor. But he always has children, a boy and a girl. Gabriel looks at Said until he cannot bear to look any more, and then he slumps down to the floor and rests his back against the bars of the cell.

It is the sound of keys in the cell door that alerts Gabriel to the fact that he has fallen asleep. A tall, thin man ignores Gabriel and steps quickly into the cell. The night warder follows him. The man puts down a brown leather bag, and he kneels beside Said. Gabriel stares at this reed of a man, who now stands and turns to face the warder.

'He's been gone for some time.' The night warder looks shocked, but the doctor is ready to leave. 'I suppose we've got some paperwork to sort out, right?'

The night warder waits for the doctor to stride from the cell, and then he locks back the door. Gabriel clambers to his feet.

'Please, Mr Collins, you cannot do this. You must take him away!'

The night warder does not trouble himself to look at Gabriel. He calmly escorts the doctor back in the direction of the television set, and Gabriel retreats to the furthest corner of the cell and huddles his body into a tight ball. He slides to the floor.

Eventually, the day warder arrives. He is a short, but powerfully built, man who looks as though at one time he might have enjoyed a career in professional sport. He stands by the door to the cell and looks contemptuously at Gabriel.

'So what's the problem then? What are you wailing about? He's dead. He ain't gonna bite.'

The man in the cell next door starts to laugh.

'You should make him eat him. Fucking noisy cannibal.'

The warder steps to his right and looks into the neighbour's cell.

'And you can shut it, you stupid little cretin.'

Obviously these few words are enough, for immediately there is silence. The warder steps back and looks at Gabriel, who now realises that the impossibly thin doctor is standing with this man.

The doctor peers into the cell, and then he simply instructs the warder to 'open up'. Gabriel climbs slowly to his feet. The doctor whispers something to the day warder, who begins to peel off his jacket.

'Well, sonny, what's with all the shouting? You losing it up here?' The day warder taps the side of his head.

Gabriel stares at the warder, and then slides back to the floor and curls himself into an even tighter ball. The warder shakes his head in disgust and turns to the doctor.

'You might have to help me get him up and onto the bunk.'

The doctor puts down his leather bag and he now slips out of his jacket. Unlike the warder, whose jacket lies in an untidy heap, the doctor folds his neatly and places it on top of his bag.

'What's he in here for?'

'You don't want to know.'

'He's not an illegal then?'

'Oh, he's that all right, but that's only half the problem.'

The warder takes Gabriel's legs while the doctor grabs his arms. Gabriel begins to kick out, but he is powerless in the grip of these two men.

'Which bunk?' asks the doctor, who is now struggling to keep control of Gabriel's flailing arms.

'It doesn't matter. Stick him on the bottom.'

Gabriel continues to kick and wrestle, but they easily lift their malnourished patient onto the bottom bunk and the warder reaches into his pocket and pulls out four strips of rubber. He passes two to the doctor, and they begin to strap Gabriel to the frame of the bed.

'This should hold the bugger in place,' says the warder. He gestures, with his head, towards Said. 'What about him?'

The doctor pulls his final knot tight and then takes a step back. He begins to slip his jacket back on.

'They should be here for the body before too long. But who knows.'

A terrified Gabriel watches as the doctor opens his bag and pulls out a syringe and long needle.

'Don't tell me,' says the warder. 'Cutbacks, right?'

'There's just not enough ambulances. In some boroughs they're using private cars.'

The doctor sits on the edge of the narrow bed and focuses on Gabriel.

'This won't hurt, but you'll feel a slight scratch.'

Gabriel squirms as the needle comes closer to his arm, and then he flinches as it breaks his skin. Finally the doctor pulls out the needle, places it in a plastic pouch, and then gets to his feet. Gabriel watches as the man picks up his bag, steps around Said, and then leaves the cell without saying another word. The warder seems somewhat surprised by the abruptness of the doctor's exit, and he hurries after him, first slamming and then locking the cell door.

Gabriel begins to feel warm. He wants to rub his nose, but his hands are tightly bound. He feels a low sigh leave his body, and then he cranes back his neck and looks at Said. Gabriel concentrates hard and stares at his friend, whose own eyes are firmly closed.

Gabriel watches from the cupboard and tries not to breathe. First they will shoot Gabriel's ageing father. He looks at his father's tired face, his confidence polluted by the ordeal of having to protect his family during the prolonged absence of his adult son. They laugh as they make the old man lie flat on the ground with his arms spread out to his sides as though they are wings. There are six soldiers dressed in khaki fatigues with red bandannas around their heads. Gabriel soon learns that they all have nicknames. 'Cassius.' 'Jacko.' 'O. J.' 'Brutus.' 'Big Dog.' 'Smokin'

Joe.' But, unlike Gabriel, they are young men. Boys. As the bullets hit Gabriel's father he jumps, but he does not fly.

Now they line up the rest of the family. 'Big Dog' kicks Gabriel's father until he cries out in pain. He is still alive. 'Big Dog' asks him if he will not beg for mercy, like a man? Does he not love his family enough to beg for their lives? Gabriel understands that this is sport. The boys are playing with his father, and then 'Smokin' Joe' puts his gun to the back of Gabriel's father's head. While the others continue to laugh and taunt his father, 'Smokin' Joe' casually pulls the trigger and the skull explodes. Small pieces of brain fly in all directions, and Gabriel's mother and two sisters begin to scream. 'Big Dog' shouts in a fake American accent, and admonishes 'Smokin' Joe' for spoiling the party.

'How can you do this, man? Nobody gave you the order to shoot.'

Gabriel's mother and sisters throw themselves across the body of the dead man. Gabriel is used to the sound of gunfire. The brutality is familiar to him. He looks on without emotion for he knows what is to come. 'Smokin' Joe' raises his voice, and as he does so he appears to grow in stature.

'Fuck you, man. This is business. I don't have time for no games.'

The shouting among the men becomes louder, and then 'Brutus' quietly steps forward and drags Gabriel's mother and two sisters from the father's body, and he forces them to lie face down on the floor. 'Brutus' unclips his pistol and pumps a single bullet into the back of both sisters. He turns to his colleagues, but nobody dares to offer a dissenting voice.

'Are you all happy now?' They look somewhat sheepishly at 'Brutus'. Authority has been restored. 'We are not here to argue.' 'Brutus' points with his pistol towards the two bleeding girls. 'You want your food, then turn them over and take it. But be quick.' 'Brutus' knows that the men are not interested in the mother.

'Jacko' is the last to mount the younger sister, but by now 'Brutus' is losing patience. He claps his hands. 'Enough.' 'Jacko' clambers to his feet, and rearranges himself. His colleagues look on and laugh as 'Jacko' struggles to make himself appear decent. Gabriel can see that his youngest sister has a thin ribbon of blood running down the inside of her leg, which pools near her ankle. She also appears to have lost consciousness.

'Finish them off,' says 'Brutus', pointing to the sisters, 'but you can leave the old woman. She is no use to anybody.'

Two bullets from 'O. J.', the smallest of the soldiers, drum into each girl's forehead. And then, as an afterthought, 'O. J.' shoots Gabriel's mother in the chest. An irritated 'Brutus' shakes his head. The boys laugh raucously, but 'Brutus' has seen enough.

'Come, let us go.'

As they leave, each man spits.

As darkness falls, Gabriel realises that he cannot stay hidden for much longer. He listens to the high-pitched chorus of insects, and in the distance he is able to discern the occasional human voice and the frequent staccato of gunfire. Gabriel knows that he will have to make the effort to leave this place, and so he opens the cupboard door and steps carefully into the darkness of the room. His legs and arms are stiff, and he walks with great difficulty. He stands over his mother, and although she is bleeding profusely he can see that she is still alive. She breathes loudly, as though her lungs are filled with sand, but Gabriel dare not remain with her for too long. He crosses to the door and slowly opens it, but there is no moon and the few stars in the sky give off little light. For a moment Gabriel hesitates, and then he begins to run. Out of the corners of his eyes he sees people huddled in doorways and lurking in shadow, but no voice is raised ordering him to stop, and no shot is fired.

Gabriel arrives at his uncle's house and discovers that everything is shrouded in darkness. He waits at the back door and tries to catch his breath, but his chest continues to heave. Gabriel imagines that his uncle is inside, but anything could have happened. As his breathing returns to normal, he places his head against the cold stone wall to calm himself down. The wall is pock-marked with bullet holes as though some giant bird has furiously pecked at the masonry in a desperate attempt to find a weak spot. Gabriel stands back upright and then he wraps his palm around the door handle and quietly turns it. He closes the door behind him and then, in the darkness, he reaches for the banister and edges forward until he can feel the first step of the wooden staircase. As he puts his full weight upon the stair, it fires off a volley of snapping sounds which causes his heart to leap. Gabriel hovers on this lowest stair and then decides to climb quickly, ignoring the sounds. He remains light on his feet, but he knows that people must be able to hear him. At the top of the stairs, he gropes his way towards the door in front of him, but he already understands that this door will be firmly barred.

'Joshua?' he whispers, but there is no answer. The cloying night heat is beginning to overpower Gabriel, and he can feel his head spinning. He calls again, 'Joshua?'

And then, from behind the door, he hears Joshua's whispered voice.

'Who is it?'

'Gabriel. I am here by myself.' There is a momentary pause, and then Joshua opens the door a few inches.

'Gabriel?' He opens the door a little more, and now Gabriel can clearly see his uncle's face. He is a dark-skinned man in his late fifties, with a short-cropped mesh of grey hair. His uncle's teeth are slightly too large for his mouth, and he has a tendency to lift a hand to his mouth before speaking. And, true to form, he lifts his hand. Joshua glances quickly all about himself and then whispers, 'Come in, come in.'

As Gabriel squeezes past Joshua he can see that this small storage room at the top of his uncle's warehouse has been transformed into an eerie chamber of light and shadow by small stubs of candle whose flames flicker in the fetid gloom. Scattered about the room are a dozen or so men who squat on the floor, some with their heads held in their hands, others with heads thrown back against the wall. In the corner there is a single bucket for bathing, and another, somewhat filthier, bucket for the men to relieve themselves in. Joshua closes the door behind his nephew and then turns to face him.

'Gabriel, why are you here?'

Gabriel looks at the older man, but the words will not come. He feels his lower lip begin to tremble, and then the pain of what he has just witnessed begins to rise through his body. Joshua places his hand on Gabriel's shoulder and encourages him to sit. They both squat beside the door, and Joshua decides to wait a few moments until his nephew has regained his composure. Gabriel stares intently at the space between his feet, and as the silence deepens, Joshua realises that the situation is his to repair.

'Did they find your family?'

Gabriel looks up at Joshua.

'They were not hiding.'

'Gabriel, did they kill everybody?' Gabriel ignores the question, but he knows that through the gloom Joshua will be able to see that tears are now streaming down his face. 'Gabriel, you must tell me. Did they kill everybody?' Gabriel shakes his head. 'Your mother?' Gabriel shakes his head. 'But everybody else, is that it?' Gabriel nods quickly. 'And your mother, where is she?'

'At the house.' Gabriel wipes his tears with the back of his hand.

'Gabriel, what will you do? They say you massacred innocent women and children, and then ran away. You know they will keep looking for you.'

'I did nothing wrong, but I know I have to leave this country. If I stay here they will kill me.'

Joshua nods, and under his breath he speaks to himself. 'You know, Gabriel, how can God ever forgive us for this shameful situation?' Gabriel looks at his uncle, who is temporarily lost in his own thoughts.

A few moments later Joshua climbs slowly to his feet. Gabriel watches him, and then he also stands. A weary Joshua takes his sister's man-child by the shoulder and he gestures to the other men in the room. He speaks in a whisper.

'Blood is blood, Gabriel. I want nothing more than to take you in as family, but these men have all paid two thousand dollars to leave. They have sold everything that they have.'

'But I must leave,' protests Gabriel. 'This is not my home any more.'

Joshua stares at his nephew, but he knows that words are all that Gabriel has to offer.

'Gabriel, if you can bring me two thousand dollars then you too will be leaving. But you have only a few hours. This is all that I can do for you.'

Gabriel looks at his uncle. He understands that Joshua is both accepting him and rejecting him at the same time. And then Gabriel glances at the other men in the room, all of whom are staring back at him. Gabriel averts his guilty eyes and concentrates on the dark water stains on the walls, where mould is growing and forming strange shapes and patterns. He knows that it will be impossible for him to travel with these men unless he does so on equal terms.

As Gabriel steps into the street he senses that dawn will soon break. The sky is still black, but buildings are beginning to recover an outline, and the noises of animals stirring and cocks crowing are a herald of what is to come. Gabriel walks quickly, but without fear, for he knows that the government soldiers prefer to operate under the cover of darkness. He passes a man who is wrapped in the national flag and pushing a wheelbarrow in which there is a computer. And then, in the distance, he sees a government soldier whose arm is held in a sling and whose legs are swaddled in blood-stained bandages, but he knows that this man will not trouble him. The lamps that line the street do not work, and until the city has regained electricity the street lamps will remain as mere ornaments. Gabriel passes by the city's one luxury hotel. Even at this distance he can smell the rotting carpets, and peering through the wire fence he can see beer bottles and furniture floating in the stagnant water that fills the swimming pool.

When Gabriel reaches the shop he sees that the shutters to the hardware store are already open and his friend is in the process of displaying, on a table outside the door, what little stock he has left. Ill-matching saucepans, metal pails, batteries, garish neon torches; once upon a time Felix's store was the place to come if you wanted any household or electrical item. If Felix did not have it, then it did not exist in the country, but Gabriel can see that since the onset of the war his former employer's stock has been severely depleted. Gabriel walks towards his elderly friend who, although a member of the ruling tribe, has never displayed any prejudice against those, like Gabriel, whose blood marks them off as the nominal enemy. As Gabriel moves closer, Felix looks up and then sets down the pile of white crockery that he is holding. He stares at Gabriel as though looking at a ghost, and then a small smile creeps across his weather-beaten face and he lets out a short laugh of astonishment.

'Gabriel? It's really you?' Felix holds his hands out in a gesture of disbelief. 'Gabriel?'

Gabriel smiles now and takes Felix's small hands in his own.

'But Gabriel, I heard they were looking for your family.' Then Felix remembers himself. 'Come inside, come inside. You really should not be out on the streets.'

Gabriel hesitates. 'Please, I do not wish to cause any trouble.'

Felix hooks his arm through Gabriel's and pulls the younger man through the door.

'First, we have to find a place to hide you.'

'But your wife and daughter, they still live upstairs?'

Felix looks puzzled. 'Of course.'

Gabriel is crestfallen. 'Felix, I must go. I cannot put your family in danger. It is only a matter of time before they come here and search your place.'

'Gabriel, they have already been.' Felix laughs and shows Gabriel the bruises on his arms and the scars on his legs.

'Felix?' Gabriel speaks slowly now, but the one word hangs foolishly in the air.

Felix raises both eyebrows, urging his young friend to continue.

'Felix, I need some money. I am sorry that I have to ask you.'

Felix says nothing, and so a nervous Gabriel continues.

'I must leave the country. If I pay him, my uncle will arrange it.'

Felix puts a finger to his lips and he glances upwards. Gabriel understands that he must lower his voice.

'I am sorry.'

They stare at each other, but neither man says a word. And then, after what seems to Gabriel an age, his former employer nods, having reached a conclusion to whatever private debate he was conducting.

'Please wait here.'

Gabriel feels Felix's hand on his shoulder, and then his friend disappears downstairs and into the basement. Gabriel knows that Felix keeps his money in a metal box that he hides beneath three loose floorboards, and he knows also that Felix scatters dirt on top of the boards to make it look as though the filthy basement contains nothing of any value. Moments later, Felix returns with his right fist tightly clenched. The nervous man slowly opens his heavily veined hand, and he reveals a small bundle of United States dollars.

'I am not a wealthy man, Gabriel. I have a wife and child, and I know that soon I will lose what is left of this shop, but please take this money.'

Gabriel takes the few notes from Felix's proffered hand, and he pushes them into his pocket.

'Perhaps your uncle will sympathise with your situation.'

Gabriel nods, and he watches as Felix turns and nervously scans the street. Gabriel knows that he will have to act quickly, and so in one swift movement he picks up the rusting metal clock that hangs behind the door and he brings down its full weight onto the head of Felix. His friend lets out a stunned cry, but it is the noise of Felix's body as it hits the wall and then buckles to the floor that alarms Gabriel. He tries not to look at his former employer as he quickly steps over him and then through the door which leads to the stairs.

Downstairs it is dark, but Gabriel knows exactly where to go and he rushes to the far corner of the empty basement. In the old days, when he worked for Felix, the place was crammed so full of supplies that it was often difficult to move down here. But now there is nothing at all. Gabriel kicks away the dirt with the outside of his foot and then he quickly pulls up the three boards so that the box is exposed. Gabriel grabs the box, but he sees that it is secured with a heavy padlock. It had not occurred to him that Felix would keep the box locked, but he has little time to ponder on this. He runs back upstairs and fishes in Felix's trouser pockets for his keys and then, having found them, he rushes back downstairs. When Gabriel opens the box he sees a thick pile of dollar bills and his hands begin to shake. He grabs the bills, and the two gold rings that are inside, and he pushes them into his pocket. Then Gabriel throws down the keys, and the box, and he leaves everything in disarray. There is no reason to cover his tracks. He runs to the stairs and then up and into the shop, where he notices that the pool of blood around Felix's head is blossoming.

Gabriel cracks the door open, but he waits for a moment before stepping out and into the street. There is a strange man on the corner who is looking in his direction, and he decides to wait until this man moves off. However, this man continues to stare at Gabriel and he shows no sign of moving on his way. In fact, the man begins now to walk towards the shop, and when he reaches Gabriel he pushes open the door and stares at the wounded figure of Felix.

'What has happened here?'

Gabriel looks at Felix as though this is the first time that he has noticed his bleeding friend, but the man is now angry.

'I know who you are. What have you done to him?'

Gabriel realises that there is little that he can say, so he steps into the street and begins to walk off, all the while looking over his shoulder. When the strange man begins to shout, Gabriel increases his pace and then he breaks into a panic-stricken run.

Eventually Gabriel turns into Joshua's street, where he once more slows to a walk, and he tries to compose himself. He climbs the stairs without any consideration of the noise that he is making, and when he reaches the storeroom he bangs quietly, but firmly, on the door and it opens before him. Joshua looks at Gabriel as though he is gazing upon a crazy man. Once they are safely inside the candlelit room, the older man turns to face his nephew.

'You are covered in sweat, and what is this? Blood?'

'I have your money.' Gabriel pushes his hand deep into his trouser pocket and he produces the crumpled notes. Joshua takes the money, but he neither counts it, nor does he take his eyes from his nephew's face.

'Gabriel, you must tell me what you have done.'

Gabriel can see that the eyes of the other men in the room are once again upon him.

'Please, Joshua. I have the money.'

Joshua looks to the money and begins to count the notes.

'Gabriel, this is not two thousand dollars.'

Gabriel puts his hand into his pocket and pulls out the two gold rings.

'I have nothing else.' Gabriel presses the rings upon Joshua and resigns himself to his fate, but his uncle simply points to a corner of the dark room.

'Try to get some sleep. We will leave tonight.'

Gabriel nods.

A hand pushes Gabriel's shoulder. He opens his eyes and sees Joshua bent over him. Beyond Joshua, Gabriel can see that the other men in the room are standing by the door clutching their bundles of belongings. The heat in the room suggests night. Gabriel rubs his eyes and climbs slowly to his feet.

'We have to go now. Are you all right?'

Gabriel shakes his head quickly as though trying to clear his mind. 'Yes,' he says. 'I am ready.'

Joshua turns from his nephew and addresses the group in a barely audible whisper. He instructs them to wait while he goes outside to check that everything is all right. He closes the door behind him and leaves the men alone in the candlelit room. The exhausted men look quizzically at each other, but nobody dares to speak. And then Joshua bursts back into the room and orders everybody to follow him. One after another the men tumble down the stairs, and as they run into the night they can hear the bursts of gunfire in the distance. Joshua points to a truck, and orders the men to quickly throw in their belongings and then climb up and into the vehicle.

'Lie down flat and be quiet.'

Gabriel is the last man to climb in, and no sooner has he found a small space in which to lie than he feels the oppressive weight of a heavy tarpaulin being tossed over him and tightly secured to the sides of the truck. As the engine roars to life, Gabriel realises that, trussed as they are like cargo, this first part of their journey is not going to be pleasant. He can feel the dampness of other men's perspiring bodies, and it is not possible to distinguish whose arm or leg is pressing up against him. As the truck sets off through the narrow streets of the town, it sways first one way and then the other before the engine strikes a regular tone, which informs Gabriel that they must now be on the highway. Tiredness begins to conquer his body, but his fatigued mind is suddenly shipwrecked against images of his mother and poor Felix. Gabriel knows that if he is going to live again then he will have to learn to banish all thoughts of his past existence. There can be no sentiment. Hurtling blindly down this highway, he knows that if he is lucky the past will soon be truly past, and that with every gasp of the acrid air beneath the heavy tarpaulin, life is taking him beyond this nightmare and to a new place and a new beginning.

Gabriel opens his eyes. There is a putrid smell in the air. He tries to move his hands, but both his hands and his feet are strapped down and he cannot move. Above him there is another bed that acts like an artificial ceiling. His head feels light on his shoulders and Gabriel wonders how long he has been asleep. And then he remembers the tall, thin doctor and the needle, and being lifted onto this bed, and Said lying on the floor and nobody coming to help him. Gabriel looks out of the corner of his eye and he can see that they have removed the body of his friend, but the smell remains. Gabriel coughs, but immediately he feels a rasping dryness in his throat and he calls out.

'Please, I need some water.' His voice is surprisingly weak. The man in the next cell shouts back at him.

'Shut your mouth, scum.'

Gabriel waits a while, but after a few moments his thirst gets the better of him.

'Please, I need water.'

Gabriel can hear the television set in the distance, and he knows that the night warder will have his feet up on the desk. He also knows that the difficult man will only stir himself when the noise of Gabriel's demands becomes too loud for him to concentrate properly. Gabriel closes his eyes and tries to ignore his thirst, but after a few minutes he hears the door to his cell being opened and he turns his head and sees the night warder holding a metal tray of food. The man puts the tray down, and as he does so he spills some of the weak tea out of the plastic cup. He leans over and begins to untie Gabriel.

'Bit bloody ripe in here, isn't it?' The night warder stands back and watches as Gabriel rubs his wrists and ankles to make sure that the blood is flowing properly through them.

'I'll come back for the tray when you're done with it.'

Gabriel sits on the edge of the bed, but he waits until the man has left the cell before leaning over and picking up the tray and placing it on his knees.

'You fucking animal. I don't know why they bother to feed you.'

Gabriel ignores the man and he begins to stuff the white bread and jam into his mouth as quickly as he can. Soon all of the food is gone and Gabriel is no longer hungry, but a raging thirst still causes his throat to burn. Gabriel finishes the tea and then slowly stands and crosses to the door of the cell. Once there, he looks down the corridor and sees the back of the television set and the man's feet up on the desk.

'Please, Mr Collins, some water.'

'Drink your own piss. Isn't that what you lot do in the jungle?' The man next door begins to laugh at his own humour.

Gabriel says nothing and he simply focuses on the night warder's feet, but they do not move. He watches the reflected light from the television set flickering against the wall, and then Gabriel turns from this strange cinema and climbs up onto the top bunk. He lies flat on his back, but then he realises that having been tied up like this he would prefer to adopt a different position. Gabriel rolls over onto his side, which somehow makes him feel less tense, and he faces the door to his cell so that if anybody tries to enter he will see them. However, having eaten, he once again feels tired, and so he closes his eyes, and soon his mind and body begin to feel heavy.

The heat of the day gives way to the noises of the night, but Gabriel is in pain, for his bladder is full and he is stiff with cold. When the truck finally stops, the dozen men are able to escape from beneath the tarpaulin. They climb to the ground, and as they relieve themselves they look around, but nobody seems to know exactly where they are. Once he has emptied himself, Gabriel sits with his uncle at the side of the dark road and stares at the star-speckled sky. Joshua asks his nephew if he has heard any voices of disquiet among the group, but Gabriel lets him know that despite the difficult conditions he has heard none of the men complain. The night-time stop lasts a little over an hour, and then as light begins to appear on the horizon, the men are once more shepherded onto the truck and the tarpaulin is pulled tightly into place. As the temperature begins to rise, and the blazing heat of the second day bears down upon them with full force, Gabriel cuts two holes in the tarpaulin so that air might pass through with greater ease. Having done so, he once more submits to the dull, uncomfortable rhythm of the journey.

Again day gives way to night, and just when Gabriel fears that the men will no longer be able to endure their confinement, the truck comes to an abrupt stop. Gabriel listens closely, and he can hear his uncle talking with men whose voices are charged with anger. After what seems an age, the tarpaulin is finally peeled back and the cargo is encouraged to step from the truck. Gabriel immediately realises that this stop marks the end of the first stage of their journey, for he can see that they are on the perimeter of an airfield. In the distance stands a large plane. Momentarily forgetting his hunger and his thirst, Gabriel stares blankly at the aircraft, for this is the first real evidence that he will be abandoning his country. He stretches his cramped limbs and looks across at his uncle, who is conversing with two men in military garb. Joshua says something to both men and then, as though late for an appointment, the men sprint to their jeep and begin to roar across the tarmac in the direction of the one-storey terminal building. Dust rises in their wake, and as they pass out of sight Joshua moves around to the back of the truck and prepares to address the men. Gabriel positions himself so that he is standing next to his uncle, and together with the rest of the men he waits to hear what their fate might be.

'The plane over there will take you to Europe.' Joshua lifts a weary arm and points. 'However, we have to hurry for the aircraft must leave within one hour.'

Gabriel is surprised to hear himself speaking up.

'And what will happen to us when we reach Europe?'

Joshua turns to Gabriel, aware that his nephew has asked the question that most of them wish to have answered.

'I will tell you in Europe, for I am coming with you.'

Gabriel is helpless to prevent his mouth from falling open in astonishment. However, before he can ask any further questions, his uncle continues.

'When we reach Europe I will tell you of the next stage, and if you wish to follow me, then you must do so. But if you choose to go on your own, then I will respect your decision.'

For some moments Gabriel stares at his grey-haired uncle, and then the older man breaks the silence. He turns to the driver of the truck.

'Do we have more water?' The man nods, and Joshua continues. 'Pass out the water, and after everybody has drunk their fill you must all return to the truck and we will leave.'

As the driver begins to pass round the gourd of water, Gabriel touches his uncle's arm.

'Is everything all right?'

Joshua looks all about himself before answering.

'Gabriel, there has been another massacre. I cannot go back.'

'And your family?' asks Gabriel.

Joshua shakes his head and the two men stare at each other.

When the truck reaches the shadow of the plane, the dozen men climb down and wait eagerly on the tarmac. They huddle together, while all around them men with powerful guns shout instructions to each other in a language that Gabriel cannot understand. Joshua raises his voice in order to be heard.

'This way. We must hurry now.'

A flight of steps has been pushed up against the plane, and Joshua leads the way. At the top of the steps, Gabriel turns and looks down at the one-storey terminal building, and the dimly lit runway, and the dark bush that spreads out flat in every direction as far as the eye can see. And then a man pushes past him, and then another, and Gabriel realises that he should not linger. Once he is inside, Gabriel is surprised to see that there are already perhaps one hundred men and women who are seated on the floor with their backs to the wall of the plane. There are no seats, and to Gabriel's eyes the interior looks like a large tubular warehouse. Those who have not been lucky enough to find wall space squat awkwardly.

From where he is sitting Gabriel is able to peer through one of the small round windows, but all he can see is blackness. The plane quickly levels out and the noise of the engines achieves a monotonous roar. Soon Gabriel begins to feel cold. He steals warmth from his uncle's body, and he tries desperately to fall asleep, but each time he closes his eyes he feels compelled to open them again, for he knows that in order to stay warm he must concentrate. He notices a man to the side of him with one leg and an unwashed blue rag covering his stump. The man looks in pain, and his eyes are brimming with tears, but Gabriel looks away and imagines this plane cutting neatly through the clouds with the bush carpet, and then the sand carpet, and then the water carpet way down beneath them.

The loud jolt of the plane hitting the tarmac wakes Gabriel up, and he tumbles into his uncle's lap. The runway lights race by, briefly illuminating the interior of the plane, and as Gabriel regains his balance it is clear to him that some of the women and men, including his uncle, appear to be sick. He gently pushes the older man, who speaks without opening his eyes.

'I'm fine, Gabriel. Everything is just fine.' But his uncle sounds weak.

Gabriel follows a frail Joshua down the steps and into the warm air. It is night time, and in the distance it is possible to see the bright lights of a great city. Once they reach the tarmac Gabriel is able to see that they are still some distance from the large terminal building, and should they be expected to walk, then he is sure that this task will prove too much for his uncle. An unshaven white man hands them a single paper cup of water, and the man is careful to make sure that they each receive only one cup. They gulp down their water and then hold their cups in their hands as though unsure of what to do next. Joshua's group of a dozen men, who two days earlier began their journey under a tarpaulin in the back of a truck, stand together. As though obeying some unheard order, the other voyagers have reclaimed their natural groups, and they all stand idly in the shadow of the huge plane that has carried them out of Africa. Dust begins to rise, and Gabriel watches anxiously as a fleet of buses races towards them, but he remains unsure whether the buses are hostile or friendly.

Once the buses reach the terminal building the new immigrants are all ushered through a narrow door, on the other side of which are stationed men with guns who look upon them without respect. The air inside this building is stifling. Joshua leaves his dozen men and approaches a uniformed white man who appears to be in charge of the whole operation. Gabriel eyes his uncle closely and tries to guess what is happening, but it is only when Joshua returns, and gathers his men around him, that it becomes clear what the next stage will entail. Joshua holds a hand up to his mouth, and tells them that they are to be transferred to a room where they will be able to wash themselves, and then the same buses will take them to a place where they will make a short journey across some water in a boat.

After this they will be in Europe proper, and then they will board a train to France and then on to England. Joshua reminds them that once they have crossed the water they are free to strike out on their own if they wish. Joshua pauses, but nobody speaks, and so he says that they must hurry because they must cross the water and board the train before the sun rises.

Gabriel barely has time to step out of his clothing and pile it onto a bench before a white man is shouting at him, and pushing and prodding his naked body into a powerful stream of icy water. Some men around Gabriel scream and rush to reclaim their clothes, while most seem grateful for the water and try to drink as much as possible. Gabriel runs quickly through the water and pulls on his clothes, despite the fact that his body is still dripping wet. As they pass through the city Gabriel looks out of the window and can see that the buildings are tall, but most of them are boarded up on the ground floor. On the higher floors, windows are open and curtains flutter in the breeze, but there is nobody to be seen. However, it is the neon glare from petrol stations, the signs in garish reds and greens, which catch Gabriel's attention. The men stare at the lights, which seem to suggest festivity, but one by one they all tire and adopt the fatigued position of lowering their heads onto the back of the seat in front of them or into their sweating, cupped palms.

Gabriel had imagined that the bus journey would be a short one, but they seem to have been trundling into the night for ever. Through the window he can see that they are now travelling along narrow country roads, with only the occasional house on either side. An exhausted Joshua leans against his nephew, and his head bobs first one way and then the next, causing him to roll from side to side like a puppet. Although it makes him feel guilty to notice, Gabriel can smell Joshua's unwashed body and he turns away from his poor uncle. As he does so the noise of the raucous engine begins to change, and the bus slows down and then pulls to a halt. Gabriel shakes Joshua, who wakes up with a start. He seems embarrassed that he has fallen asleep.

'Is this where we take the boat?'

His uncle rubs his eyes and stands up without answering Gabriel. He walks to the front of the bus to speak with the driver.

Gabriel continues to stare out of the window. He can see that there is a small pier and moored against the pier there is a boat. Far across the water he sees a low line of lights, which suggests that this is a very wide river. One by one his fellow travellers wake up, and then stretch, and then they too stare out of the window at the water, and at the land in the far distance. Gabriel turns his attention back to his uncle, who is still talking with the driver of the bus. The conversation is becoming increasingly loud, and then Joshua gesticulates angrily with both hands and walks back down the aisle. Once again he takes up his seat next to Gabriel, and then he turns to his nephew.

'We have to wait for other buses.'

Gabriel looks puzzled. 'How long do we wait?'

'This is the problem,' says Joshua. 'We do not know.'

'And what if the other buses do not arrive?'

Joshua ignores his nephew's question.

Gabriel huddles next to his uncle in the boat as the cold wind whips off the water and stings their faces. He can see that the boat's cumbersome engine is tracing a dull line in the moonlit water, a line that quickly disappears as the shallow swell erases all evidence of it. The heavily laden boat inches along with a laboured bearing, and Gabriel listens to the muted whisper of the water talking to itself. Out here on this night river that is full of the reflection of stars, the stiffening wind threatens to become spiteful and Gabriel feels a series of shivers course through his slender body. Above them the sky is beginning to relinquish its black pallor, but as yet there is no sign of dawn. Gabriel gazes ahead to the shoreline where the ribbon of lights moves ever closer, and then he hears the boat's engines being cut and he feels the vessel beginning to drift. A barefoot boy jumps up on the prow of the boat and tosses a rope to some scruffy-looking men on the quayside whose cigarettes glow especially bright in the twilight. And then the boy disembarks. Gabriel's eyes hurt, for his pupils feel as if they have shrunk so that they are now too small to hold the imminent daylight. However, as he looks around a sense of relief warms his empty stomach. This is Europe. Tired, hungry and disorientated, the weary migrants stumble ashore.

Joshua stands in the doorway to their cramped train compartment and explains to them all that under no circumstances are the plastic window screens to be raised. He then requests that Gabriel join him in the corridor. Gabriel is worried, for he is sure that he will now lose his coveted seat by the window, but Joshua waits patiently for his nephew to stand. Once they are in the corridor, Gabriel can see that stationed at either end of the carriage there is a uniformed man with a gun.

'Until we reach France, you will be in charge.' His uncle scratches furiously at his mesh of grey hair. 'Nobody must move in or out, unless it is to use the toilet. And then only with your permission. The customs police have been paid, but they do not wish to see us.'

Gabriel nods. His uncle knows that he was a major in the rebel army, and Gabriel imagines that Joshua assumes that his nephew is therefore familiar with issuing orders and having men obey him. But Gabriel knows that issuing orders is one thing; having men obey you is something entirely different.

When Gabriel returns to the compartment he has to force

himself down and into a new space for, as he suspected, his seat by the window has been taken and everybody has spread out and made themselves more comfortable. Gabriel explains that they will have to stay in this compartment for two, maybe three, days. Whenever the train stops they will not be allowed into the corridor, and under no circumstances are they to look out of the window. They listen to Gabriel, who tells them that they will be passing through Italy before they reach France, and that when they reach France it will be a relatively short journey to England. Everybody listens intently, but Gabriel feels somewhat awkward in this new role of leader and so, having finished what he is expected to say, he soon falls silent.

Gabriel looks over at the young woman in the corner. She had been in one of the other groups, but had apparently found it difficult to understand everything that they were saying because she did not share the same language. When she heard Joshua's group on the boat she realised that they might help her. Gabriel sneaks surreptitious glances at this quietly beautiful woman with large almond eyes, whose child is sleeping among the bundles of cloth that are swathed around her body. She looks up and catches Gabriel staring, and so he quickly lowers his eyes and listens intently to the sound of the train. Gabriel can feel his head beginning to roll about on his shoulders, but he continues to concentrate and think about what he will do once this journey is over and he has reached England. Some hours later Gabriel opens his eyes and he can see that his fellow passengers, with the exception of the woman, are now all asleep. She is breast-feeding her child, and when she feels Gabriel's eyes upon her she looks up. Gabriel is momentarily embarrassed, but although he knows that the decent thing would be to look away, this time he continues to stare at her. To his surprise the woman ignores him.

In the morning, Gabriel eases himself out of his seat

without waking the others, and he slides back the door and steps into the corridor. Through the partially shaded corridor windows he can see that the train is moving slowly through what appears to be pasture land. His uncle is seated on the floor with his back to the compartment, and, having cast a surreptitious glance at the uniformed men to his left and right, Gabriel takes a seat next to him.

'How much longer?'

'Suddenly you are impatient?' Gabriel says nothing, and so his uncle continues. 'Are the men becoming restless, is that it?'

Gabriel glances behind him and whispers.

'What is the woman doing among us?'

Joshua smiles. 'My nephew, everybody is leaving to go to a better place. Is she causing problems?'

'No, no.' Gabriel is quick to speak now. 'I do not know what to think about the child.'

'Well, is the child your problem?'

'Of course not.'

Joshua chuckles under his breath.

'Gabriel, the woman would not be here among us if she did not know how to take care of herself and her child. Do not worry about her. We have enough troubles of our own.'

Gabriel turns to face his uncle. 'What do you mean?'

'We are going only to Paris. These men say that if we wish to go to England, then we will have to do so by ourselves.'

'But we have paid our money for England. That is where they have to take us.'

Joshua shakes his head. 'They say they can take us to a place on the coast of France, and then we can try to pass through the tunnel to England. But it is heavily guarded.'

'But the French will not give us papers.' Again Gabriel glances at the guards at either end of the corridor, and then he looks again to his uncle. 'We cannot stay in France.'

'At least in France they will not kill us.'

Gabriel stares at his uncle and understands that their conversation is at an end. It is his responsibility to go back into the compartment and, when the time is right, tell the others. His uncle has closed his tired eyes, and his head is now beginning to fall towards his chest.

When Gabriel opens his eyes it is the afternoon and he realises that against his will he has slept. Everyone in the compartment is awake, although they are all clearly distressed with the heat. Gabriel looks at them and then decides that he should pass on to the group the news that his uncle entrusted to him. Having done so, some of the men begin to raise their voices, feeling understandably betrayed, but Gabriel encourages them to remain calm. He assures them that there are many Africans in Paris, and that they will find people who will help them. But Gabriel realises that most of them wish to go to England, and that nothing he says will assuage their sense of disappointment. The news that they are to be set down in France has triggered a volley of conversations, but the woman seems to have nothing to say. For the rest of the afternoon, as the train furrows its slow way across Europe, Gabriel steals glances at this beautiful woman and her child.

The man's screaming startles Gabriel and he sits bolt upright.

'Take your fucking hands off of me.'

Gabriel blinks vigorously and looks all about himself. The noise from the cell next door suggests that a fight of some kind is in progress. There is a loud thud, and then once again the man cries out, but this time in a half-muffled scream as though somebody is stuffing a piece of cloth into his mouth.

'Bastards.'

Gabriel climbs down from the top bunk and moves to the

bars of his cell. Two policemen are wrestling his neighbour down the corridor. Once the man has passed out of sight, Gabriel sits on the bottom bunk and hears his stomach begin to growl, so he gets up and goes again to the cell door and calls to the day warder.

'Please, I am hungry.' There is no answer, so he waits a few moments before calling again. 'Please, I am hungry and I need water.' Almost immediately he hears a reply from the irritated warder.

'All right. I'll sort you out in a minute, okay?'

Gabriel returns to his seat on the bottom bunk and contemplates the silence. He does not know this man as well as the night warder, but it worries Gabriel that this man harbours some silent resentment towards him. However, he understands that there is nothing that he can do about this, and so he continues to sit and he runs his tongue across his teeth. He craves a piece of chewing stick. Back home he liked to use his finger to pick out the bits of stick that got trapped in the gaps in his lower teeth, but it has been many days now since Gabriel has seen a piece of chewing stick. Gabriel looks up and sees the day warder holding a tray with one hand, and struggling to open the door with the other. He realises that even as he was shouting at the warder, the man must have had the tray ready to bring out to him. As the door opens, Gabriel levers himself to his feet, and he takes the tray and offers his thanks. The stocky warder nods slightly, as though to acknowledge that he has been shown some respect, and then he quickly retreats from view. Then, just when Gabriel has stuffed his mouth full of food, the warder reappears at the cell door. He looks at Gabriel as though studying an animal in a zoo, and then he finally speaks.

'You've got a visitor. You'd better come now.'

Gabriel puts the tray down on the bed and he hurriedly

swallows his food. The warder waits until Gabriel is at the cell door before pointing to the tray.

'You can't leave that there. You'll have to give it back to me.'

'But I have taken only half of the food, and I have not finished my drink.'

'Tough. Either you stay here and finish it or you see your visitor. You can't do both.'

Gabriel hovers uneasily.

'I don't have all day,' hisses the warder.

Gabriel has little choice but to pick up the tray and carry it through the open door and into the corridor. The man bangs shut the door to the cell and locks it. As they move off, Gabriel gazes at the empty cell next door. Only the bottom bunk has been slept in, and the top bunk supports an undressed mattress. The door has not been locked back and it sits open-mouthed on its hinges. The warder looks at Gabriel and laughs.

'Want him back, do you?' He amuses himself with his own wit. 'Bet you don't half-miss him, right?'

Gabriel says nothing, but the warder continues to laugh to himself as he leads Gabriel past the television set that is perched on the edge of the desk.

'Here,' says the warder, pointing to a space on his desk. 'Put it down there. You can grab the water if you like, but it's the last you'll see of that tray.'

Gabriel takes the plastic tumbler of water, swallows it in one and then wipes his mouth on the back of his sleeve.

'Please,' says Gabriel.

The warder stops and looks at him. 'Don't tell me,' he says, 'you've changed your mind. You don't want no visitors, is that it?'

'No, no.' Gabriel feels awkward. 'It is my friend, Said, the man who was in the cell with me.' The warder waits for him to go on. 'Perhaps I can contact his family? He asked me.'

The confused warder looks at Gabriel. 'He asked you what?'

'He asked me if I could be in contact with his family. He was worried about them.' The warder shakes his head, but he says nothing. He opens up the door and ushers Gabriel into an empty room. 'Please, what happened to Said?' The warder slams the door behind them.

'What happened to him?' the man laughs. 'What the hell do you think happened to him? He died and they'll soon be shoving him in the ground where he belongs.'

'But his family have to be told. That is what he wanted.'

The warder puts his palm on Gabriel's chest and pushes him back against the wall.

'You think you have any right to know anything after what you've done?'

Gabriel looks the man in the eyes, and he speaks calmly and clearly.

'I am only saying to you that I am worried, for his family do not know what has happened.'

The warder raps his knuckles against Gabriel's chest.

'You had better watch who you're getting lippy with.'

They stare at each other and Gabriel decides to say nothing further, but he is not afraid. Not of this man.

'Do you want to see your visitor or have you changed your mind?'

'Yes, please, I want to see my visitor.'

The, warder continues to stare at him.

'We've got a lot of things to work out, you and I, don't we?' Gabriel stares back at the warder, who begins now to laugh. 'You don't understand the trouble you're in, do you? Once they bang you up properly, your life will be hell, mate.'

The warder steps to one side and unlocks yet another door. As he pushes it open, Gabriel recognises the small woman who dresses in men's trousers. She is sitting at a table with a man, and on top of the table there is a pile of papers. The warder changes his tone now that others can see them.

'Well, come on then, these people have been waiting here to see you.'

Gabriel edges past the warder and into the room. Katherine stands up and extends her hand, and as she does so her face suddenly brightens.

'Gabriel, what took you so long?' She does not wait for an answer. 'This is Stuart Lewis, who will be your solicitor.'

The man stands and holds out his hand.

'Pleased to meet you, Gabriel. Stuart Lewis.'

The man is also short, and he wears a dark-blue suit and a bright-yellow tie. He looks like a schoolboy with his mousy hair and round spectacles, and Gabriel peers closely at him. He had been expecting an older, more intimidating man, and somehow this Stuart Lewis does not seem right. Gabriel shakes hands with the man and then he hears the door close behind him. He turns and sees the warder standing with his arms folded across his chest and staring into the middle distance. The woman notices that Gabriel seems perturbed by this and she places her hand on his shoulder.

'Gabriel, don't worry. You must talk freely, and you must speak honestly and from the heart. If you do, then Stuart can help you with the charges.'

Stuart Lewis nods in agreement and then he sits down. The woman removes her hand and points to the chair on the other side of the table, and then she also sits.

'Take a seat, Gabriel, and let's begin. I'm not sure how much time we have, but let's try and get through as much as possible.'

Gabriel sits down and then Stuart Lewis leans forward and begins to speak.

'Gabriel, may I call you Gabriel?' Gabriel nods, and the

lawyer smiles and then laughs. 'Well, thank you. It doesn't pay to assume too much unauthorised informality.'

Gabriel looks at the woman, who is also smiling, but her smile is etched somewhat less firmly to her face. He notices that today her short hair is pulled back and tied with a red band so that it doesn't fall into her eyes.

'You see,' continues the lawyer, 'I'm preparing the details of your case so that I can brief the barrister who will, in the fullness of time, represent you.'

Gabriel listens, but without really understanding a word of what is being said. He looks at the woman who continues to smile, as though reassuring Gabriel that he should not worry. Stuart Lewis hardly misses a beat.

'I have some questions to ask you, and you must answer as best you can. If you're not sure about the question, just let me know. There's no need to be frightened if you tell the truth.'

Gabriel nods, but he is suddenly aware that the eyes of the warder are on his back. The woman is quick to speak.

'Do you understand, Gabriel?'

Again Gabriel nods. Stuart Lewis glances at her, but she continues to address Gabriel.

'I'm just taking notes so that if everything goes well with this case, then I'll be able to present the relevant facts to the immigration authorities. You don't mind my taking notes, do you?'

Gabriel stares at the woman.

'You see, when they are making a judgement as to your suitability to remain in this country they'll want to know everything. And this is a very serious case, which is why you will have to have Mr Lewis plus another lawyer.'

Gabriel's mouth is dry, but there is no water to drink. He peels open his lips, which feel as though they have been glued together.

'I am ready to answer any questions. I have nothing to hide.'

The woman is happy, and she nods and then turns and looks at the lawyer. Stuart Lewis pushes his glasses further up the bridge of his nose and then he coughs.

'Well, shall we make a start?' Gabriel watches as the man looks at his watch and then carefully writes down the date and the time. He then turns to the woman. 'I'll also be keeping full notes, so we can always cross-refer.' He turns back to Gabriel. 'I'm afraid in situations like this it's impossible for us to have our secretaries in here. We could tape-record the proceedings, but it's never satisfactory. This being the case, it just means that it will take a while for us to go through everything and I may have to ask you to repeat some things, if you'll bear with me.' Gabriel looks blankly at the man. 'Right, then, let's make a start. Do you know on what day you arrived in France?'

'I do not know. I was travelling for a long time.'

'We can make a guess,' says the woman. 'I mean, by working backwards we can come up with a rough date.'

The man looks at the woman.

'I know, but I think we need to have the specifics for a criminal case.' He turns again to Gabriel. 'So you have no idea whatsoever, is that it?'

Gabriel shakes his head.

'And how long were you in France, do you have any idea?'

'A few days.'

'I see.'

The lawyer writes on the pad and then speaks without looking up at Gabriel.

'And you would have no idea whether a few was three or four, or seven or eight, am I right?' Gabriel thinks for a moment.

'I am sorry. It was not always possible to be sure if it was day or if it was night.'

The lawyer continues to write, and again he speaks without looking up.

'I understand, Gabriel, but tomorrow I am going to have to present the best possible case for you, and so we'll have to find some way of ascertaining these facts.'

The woman coughs as though eager to add something, and Stuart Lewis looks up at her. She speaks on cue.

'I've already been over some of this with Gabriel and it's very hard for him because of the personal trauma he suffered just before his having to flee for his life.' The lawyer looks quizzically at her, so she continues. 'You know, the massacre of Gabriel's family. This has had a profound impact on his memory and his ability to absorb anything, let alone details such as dates and times. It really is very difficult for him at the moment.'

The lawyer waits patiently until she has finished, and then he leans back in his chair.

'I understand what you're saying, Katherine, but I'm only trying to establish dates, not state of mind. I'll come to that later.'

The woman nods and Gabriel looks from one to the other and can now sense the frustration that is flowing between them. It is apparent to Gabriel that this is not the first time that the two of them have argued, and he is sure that he is the source of their disagreement. Stuart Lewis turns his attention back to Gabriel. He taps his pen against the pad in front of him, and he speaks slowly.

'Now then, Gabriel. You don't know what date you arrived in France? And you have no idea on what date you arrived here in Great Britain? Am I correct in my assumptions?'

Gabriel nods. Again, Katherine speaks up.

'As I keep telling you, Stuart, it's impossible for Gabriel to know all of these things, but we can make an educated guess at most of the dates and move on. Nobody's ever going to be able to verify them, are they? I mean, I'm not trying to tell you how to do your job, but shouldn't we focus more on the situation with the girl in the time that we have left?'

Stuart Lewis glances at his watch and then returns his attention to Katherine.

'You know, I appreciate that you're trying to help, but in criminal cases we need to do a lot more fact-checking than in civil litigation. So unless he can substantiate these dates for me, the case will, whether he likes it or not, be weaker.' Stuart Lewis ignores both Katherine and Gabriel and begins to write on his pad.

Gabriel watches the man making notes in his spidery hand, and then he looks across at the woman, who is also writing. As though wishing to draw attention to himself, Stuart Lewis flamboyantly underscores a passage from his own text with two heavy lines, and then puts down his pen and clasps his hands in front of him. The woman continues to write.

'Now then, Gabriel, I have to ask you some questions about the girl, do you understand?'

Gabriel nods, but he can feel thin streams of sweat beginning to trickle down the back of his neck.

'You do understand what I'm asking, don't you?'

Again Gabriel nods.

'All right then. When did you first meet the girl?'

Gabriel hears the question, but his mind blocks it, like a boxer might parry a blow. He stares blankly at the lawyer.

'Gabriel, when did you first meet the girl, that's all I need to know.'

Again Gabriel blocks the question. Katherine leans forward.

'Gabriel, you'll have to answer the question in court so you may as well tell us. After all, we're on your side.'

Gabriel looks at the woman and then lowers his eyes.

Stuart Lewis takes this as a good sign and he rephrases the question.

'Gabriel, tell me when you first met the girl and what made you talk to her. That's all I need to know at the moment. We can sort out the rest of it after I've got these details.' Gabriel looks up at the lawyer, but he says nothing. It is clear that this man is frustrated by Gabriel's silence, but Gabriel cannot remember any details that might help him. He is sorry. The short-haired woman smiles at Gabriel, and then leans over and looks directly into his eyes.

'You must remember when you first saw her, Gabriel? That much must be clear to you?'

Gabriel looks blankly at her. He feels betrayed. Why is she no longer defending him?

'This is no use at all.' Stuart Lewis pushes the pad in front of him to one side. He snaps the top of his pen back into place and picks up his briefcase from the floor.

'Stuart, wait.' Katherine seems alarmed by this man's willingness to abandon the interview so quickly. 'We must give Gabriel a chance.' She turns now to Gabriel. 'Gabriel, you remember her name at least. Surely you can remember that much?'

Gabriel looks at the woman, and slowly, as though suddenly realising that he can trust neither of them, he begins to shake his head. No, he cannot remember.

'You don't remember her name?' asks an incredulous Katherine.

Gabriel looks at the papers that lie on the table in front of him. He wonders about the contents of these papers, and if it is possible that they all refer to him, or perhaps some of them are about other people? The lawyer speaks to Katherine.

'Katherine, it's no good. If he wants to carry on in this manner, then he'll just have to take his chances in court. But there's not much that I'm going to be able to do to help him if he won't help himself.' The lawyer begins to stuff the papers into his briefcase. He leaves the notepad until the very end, and then he clicks his briefcase shut. Stuart Lewis tucks his pen into his inside jacket pocket and then he stands. He speaks to Katherine in a resigned, but irritated, manner. 'So, that's it then. We take our chances in the morning, right?'

Katherine looks from Stuart Lewis to Gabriel, and then back to Stuart Lewis.

'You know, Stuart, just give me a few minutes alone with Gabriel. I won't be long.'

The lawyer nods, and without saying anything further to Gabriel he walks towards the warder, who steps aside and unlocks the door. When Stuart Lewis has passed from view, the warder locks the door again and remains 'on guard'. Katherine waits for a few moments and then she begins to speak.

'Gabriel, I know it's difficult, but you've got to try, really you have.' Gabriel says nothing. The warder coughs.

'Five minutes, Miss. That's all you've got left, I'm afraid.'

Katherine ignores the man.

'We're talking about the girl, Gabriel. You do know who I'm talking about?'

Gabriel nods. He knows who she is talking about.

'But you don't remember when you first saw her? Is that it?'

Gabriel speaks quietly. 'It is difficult to remember everything. It all happened so quickly. I get confused.'

'Yes, of course you get confused. Who wouldn't? But tomorrow you will be in a very difficult position if you cannot remember these things. Remember, you have no rights in this country and they can just throw you out. If the worst comes to the worst, you might have to go to prison for a very long time on these charges relating to the girl. Either way it's not good for you. I'm sure that you can see this.'

'I understand.' Gabriel pauses, and then he continues. 'Can

you please send a letter to the family of the man who used to be with me in my cell. He asked me to help him before he left the earth and went to heaven.'

'He died? How did he die?'

'He died in the cell and they let him lie there on the floor like a dog.'

The woman looks up at the warder.

'Is this true? You left this man in a cell with a dead man?' Katherine glares at the warder. 'Well, is this true?'

'You'll have to speak to the boss. None of my business. Anyhow, your time's up, Miss. I'm afraid you'll have to go now.'

The woman turns back to Gabriel. As she stands up she straightens her trousers. 'I'll look into this, and if there's any way of contacting his family I'll let you know.'

Gabriel gets to his feet.

'He asked me to inform his brother. I promised Said that I would do this for him.'

The woman reaches up and places a hand on Gabriel's shoulder.

'Get a good night's rest and I'll see you in the morning. And try to remember anything that you can about the girl. The more you remember, the better it will be for you. Stuart may be a little blunt, but he's your best hope.' Gabriel nods. 'Think about it, Gabriel. You must remember something about the girl. Anything will help.'

The warder takes a step forward.

'I'm sorry, Miss, but you're already way beyond your time.'

Katherine picks up her bag and hooks it over her shoulder.

'Until tomorrow, Gabriel.'

The warder points to Gabriel.

'You can sit down there and wait. I'll be back in a moment.'

Gabriel listens as the door is unlocked and then locked back again. He sits alone in the room and looks at the empty table. He knows that at some point in the future he will probably have to start to remember about the girl, but he is not ready. Not yet.

During the day there is a thin strip of light at the edge of the plastic window screens, but at the moment everything is black. Everybody in the compartment is asleep apart from Amma, who takes this opportunity to feed her child without having to endure the heavy scrutiny of men's eyes. Gabriel speaks to her in a whisper, repeating the same plea that he has been making in a variety of ways for much of the past hour.

'But you must try and reach England. They are friendly and will give you food and shelter. We are not welcome in France. I will help you.'

Amma listens and then she looks at her child. She speaks without raising her eyes.

'I do not wish to be a burden to anybody. My husband told me that if they kill him, then I must learn to be by myself. I must trust nobody.'

Gabriel reaches into the pocket of his jacket and offers her a piece of bread that he has hidden there. Amma takes the bread and thanks him. Gabriel watches as she breaks off a small piece, then carefully breaks the small piece into even smaller pieces and feeds them to her child.

The door slides open and Joshua's exhausted face is suddenly staring at them. Gabriel understands and he climbs slowly to his feet. He tries not to disturb any of the other men as he slips out into the corridor, and he carefully closes the door behind him. The uniformed men still stand guard at either end of the carriage, but they ignore Gabriel and his uncle.

'Is everything all right?' asks Gabriel.

'We will be in Paris within an hour. The train will stop just outside of the station and everybody must get off. For those who want to go to England, there will be a bus that will take them as far as the tunnel.'

'And what happens then?'

'They keep telling me that it is possible to go to England. That is all that I know.' Joshua pauses, and then he lowers his eyes. 'I will not be coming with you. Another journey, and this time without these men.' Joshua glances down the corridor and then shakes his head. 'It is too much for me.'

Gabriel stares at the older man, but he knows that it would be disrespectful to argue with an elder.

'Do not say anything, my nephew. Go back inside and get ready. Everything will be fine.'

But Gabriel already knows that for many of them everything will not be fine. In the past few days his uncle has aged many years, and Gabriel feels as though he too has added considerably to his thirty years. Despite his uncle's assurances, Gabriel knows that in many ways their journey is only now beginning. And only the strongest among them will survive.

When the train stops, Gabriel opens his eyes. He listens to the thunder of footsteps as people rush by in the corridor, and then he hears a knock on the door and once again his uncle's tired face appears in the doorway. Gabriel jumps to his feet and then everybody stands and begins to gather their belongings about them. Gabriel positions himself closest to the door, but Joshua blocks their path into the corridor. A constant stream of men flows past them, and then one of the uniformed guards appears and bellows at Joshua.

'Now!'

Joshua steps to one side, and Gabriel follows the uniformed man the full length of the train corridor, through the open train door, down onto a metal step, and then he makes a short leap onto the dirt below. Gabriel dusts himself off and then stands to one side ready to catch those who will jump after him. One by one they jump, until Amma appears. Gabriel reaches up his hands for the child, whom she passes to him, and then she leaps and pitches forward, but two of the men catch her. After Amma there is only Joshua, who looks around before edging his way down onto the step, all the while clutching the hand rail. Joshua looks directly at his nephew and then jumps. Gabriel moves forward to pick him up, but Joshua is already climbing to his unsteady feet and dusting himself off. Joshua points towards a man with a rifle slung over one shoulder.

'If you wish to go to England, then you must go with that man.'

Without bidding farewell to his nephew, Joshua begins to half-limp, half-run towards an embankment, and then he slithers over the edge and disappears from view. In the distance Gabriel can see a wide ocean of lights, and he realises that this must be Paris. Amma waits patiently for Gabriel to either move towards the man with the rifle or say something, but Gabriel remains silent. Somewhere in the pit of his stomach Gabriel knows that should he fail in his efforts to reach England, then there might yet be an attempt to lose himself among these lights.

Three hours later the bus stops for the first time. Gabriel rubs his eyes, but having found it impossible to achieve any sleep he has been simply drifting in and out of consciousness. However, the others on the bus have not only been sleeping, but most of them remain asleep. Gabriel looks at Amma, who lies sprawled on the back seat of the bus, her child so tightly wrapped up in the folds of her dress that it is impossible to see him. He wishes that he had some water to offer to her, but his thoughts are interrupted by the driver, who stands and opens the door and then turns around and stares at his two dozen passengers. He claps his hands and begins to shout, achieving his desired effect of startling everybody. Then he claps his hands again and redoubles his shouting. This time he points into what Gabriel can now see is the twilight that precedes dawn. 'Go! Go!' Clearly this is his only word of English and he is using it with vigour. Those at the front of the bus begin to stand and leave. Gabriel makes sure that Amma is awake, and then he stumbles down the aisle. Once they have all alighted, the bus pulls quickly away and they now realise that they have been set adrift in the French countryside. Gabriel looks around and sees that to either side of them are wheat fields, and before them lies a narrow country road which quickly disappears into a tight bend. His fellow travellers look helplessly at each other, but as the sky brightens it is clear to Gabriel that in the field beyond the one to their left, there is a cluster of tents and he can also see plumes of smoke twisting into the air.

Gabriel scans the fatigued group, which contains many whose faces and languages are new to him, and he can see that these people appear to have adopted him as their leader. Despite his desire to protect Amma, he is reluctant to formalise this arrangement, and he therefore decides to move off in the direction of the tents without saying anything to any of them. He clambers through a gap in the hedge, holding back the branches between finger and thumb so that he will not be injured on the spikes, and then he steps into the first field. Now that it is brighter he can see that this brown field, and all the fields around him, are the colour of stale blood. The ground is damp underfoot, as though it has been recently raining, but it is only when Gabriel is halfway across the field that he decides to turn around and see if the people are following him. One by one they have made their way through the gap in the hedge and into the muddy field, and like a band of pilgrims they are strung out, one behind the other, with Gabriel at their head.

When Gabriel reaches the far side of the field he passes through another gap, one which he finds easier to squeeze through, for there are no thorns or brambles blocking its entrance. He sees a man in a white coat and black boots striding towards him across the muddy expanse. The man seems to be neither angry nor hostile, and Gabriel immediately senses that he is some kind of official. When he reaches Gabriel he speaks slowly, but Gabriel knows that this man's English is not the English of an Englishman.

'How many are you?'

Gabriel looks behind him. 'I am not sure.'

'And of course, the men who dropped you on the road, they are gone, yes?'

Gabriel nods.

'Are there more of you?'

Gabriel is not sure what the man means, and so he hesitates.

'Are there more of you in France?'

'Yes, in Paris.'

'Many? One hundred? Two hundred?'

'No, no.' Gabriel is adamant. 'Perhaps one hundred, but they are not coming here.'

The man sighs loudly. 'Well, I am happy. The truth is we can take no more. It will be difficult with this many of you.'

Gabriel says nothing, and together with the man he waits until the whole group gathers together. The man then leads them towards a large tent which seems to be unstable in the light breeze. The flaps at its entrance are blowing noisily, but the man takes little notice of this. He escorts them inside and points to the empty cots in the far corner.

'Some people left last night and I doubt if they will be coming back. Please rest, and later there will be food.'

Gabriel looks around at the scene of lethargic misery, and he can see others in the tent who either lie on the cots or sit cross-legged on the floor. These sullen people look up at the new migrants as though keen to understand the mystery of their origins. Gabriel turns his attention from their prying eyes to the recently vacated cots. These flimsy canvas beds, set atop thin metal frames, look hardly fit to bear the weight of a grown person. Gabriel walks over to Amma and leads her to the first cot, which he discovers to be surprisingly sturdy. Most of the others move slowly, but a few of the men appear to be squabbling and they make a desperate rush to secure a place for themselves. Gabriel says nothing, but he makes clear his displeasure by the manner in which he stares at these men. And then he looks again at Amma, and he sees that she has already discovered a coarse-looking blanket and is lying down curled around her child. Gabriel lies down on the cot next to her, but as he closes his eyes and prepares to sleep he hears a noise to the side of the cot. He opens his eyes quickly, and sees a man with thick glasses and bushy hair standing over him.

'Please, listen.' The man's eyes dart around in his head as he speaks. 'I take you to England, but you decide quickly. I can take only three.'

Gabriel sits up and looks at this man in disbelief. He assumes him to be French, for he speaks with the same accent as the man who led them into the camp, but there is a wild energy about this man's speech and his gestures.

'I come for you tonight after dark. In this place we live for the night.'

Gabriel continues to look at the man and he wonders why he has chosen him.

'Of course, I need money from you.'

'I have no money.'

'I have money.' Amma's voice is quiet but firm.

The man turns to look at her and he speaks quickly. 'I need two hundred United States dollars from each person.'

Gabriel looks at the child.

'But nothing for the child.'

'The two of you and the child, four hundred dollars.'

Gabriel looks at Amma, and then he turns back to the man.

'Please, allow us a few minutes to talk.'

'It is a good price,' says the man. 'You make a new life, new friends, and forget your stinking country. In England everything is given to you. Food, clothes, house. You live like a king.'

Gabriel repeats himself. 'Please, a few minutes.'

The man shrugs his shoulders, then turns and walks reluctantly to the entrance of the tent. Amma speaks first.

'You are angry with this man, is that it?'

Gabriel shakes his head. 'No, but I cannot accept any money from you. You must save it for yourself and your child. I will find my own way of getting to England and I will meet you there.'

'Are you sure?'

'I will come with you tonight and make sure that this man does not cheat you.'

The impatient man returns, as though on cue.

'Well?'

'Just the woman and the child.'

The man seems unconcerned, and he now squints at Amma as though he is having difficulty focusing his eyes.

'I come for you after dark. If you have identity papers, please lose them so they cannot send you back to where you are from. And wear many clothes, for sometimes it is cold.'

With this said the man turns and walks quickly out of the tent.

As the light begins to fade fast from the sky, Gabriel and Amma follow the guide towards the entrance to the camp. Gabriel notices two men with short, cropped hair and stubbled faces standing by the makeshift wooden gates, and as they reach the gates the guide stops. In the evening gloom he speaks a few hurried words with the men, and then he points at Amma, and Gabriel understands that these men are being told that Amma is to be their travelling companion. On receiving this news, the men begin to gesticulate and they eye Gabriel and Amma with barely disguised disgust. The guide returns to Gabriel and Amma.

'Filthy gypsies. Now we go to the train, but I must have money.'

Amma reaches into her clothes and hands the man some crumpled twenty-dollar bills, which he carefully counts and then tucks into his pocket. Gabriel looks angrily at the bushy-haired guide, for he neither seems grateful, nor does he appear to understand what it has probably cost a woman like Amma to acquire such a sum of money. Amma, sensing Gabriel's rising anger, simply puts her hand on Gabriel's arm.

Gabriel and Amma follow the three men out of the camp and down a deserted narrow lane where the hedgerows have cut off any possibility of a view, which makes Gabriel feel as though they are walking through a long tunnel without a roof. Night is beginning to fall and Gabriel tries to memorise the route, for he knows that later tonight he will have to return to the camp.

They walk on in silence for what seems an age, until the guide steps into a cornfield to relieve himself. Having finished, he then produces a cellular phone from his back pocket and conducts a short, whispered conversation before folding the phone in half and once more tucking it into his pocket. Gabriel watches him carefully, as do the two other men, fearful that he may try to bolt with their money. Having completed his phone call, the guide now returns to the narrow roadway. He cleans his thick glasses on the sleeve of his jacket, and then he replaces them. He points to a glow in the sky just a short way off.

'It is the place for the train.'

As they move in the direction of the light, Gabriel reaches over to take the boy from Amma, and for the first time since she jumped from the train she allows him to feel the weight of her child. She walks on, unburdened, and Gabriel feasts his eyes upon the graceful lines of her body.

A few hundred yards beyond where the guide relieved himself, he stops and gathers them around. Although there is no need to whisper, the man speaks quietly.

'We cannot go the whole distance by this road, for there are guards and police between here and the train. However, beyond this turning there is a bridge. The train passes below the bridge and you will drop down onto the top of the train.'

Gabriel can hardly believe what he is hearing.

'Onto the top of the train?'

The two other men are equally animated in their disbelief, but their guide is indignant. He raises his voice now and begins to gesticulate.

'What did you expect? Did you expect to travel in the train?'

Gabriel speaks up. 'Yes, in the train, please. In the train.'

The man simply laughs. 'You people are stupid.'

Gabriel turns to Amma, who seems unperturbed by this news.

'We must demand the return of your money. This seems too dangerous.'

Amma shrugs her shoulders. 'Let us wait and see the bridge. It may be possible.'

But Gabriel is adamant. 'You have your child. You cannot jump from a bridge with your child!'

'We have come this far. Let us at least take a look at the bridge.' Gabriel stares at her, but Amma will not back down. The guide turns and walks off in the direction of the glow in the sky, and his charges have little choice but to hasten after him. A few hundred yards down the road he stops abruptly and again he points.

'Now we cross this field to the bridge.'

The man leads them up off the road, and they begin to make their way across a deeply rutted field that is thickly overgrown with thistles and brambles. Amma reaches for her child to relieve Gabriel of the burden, but Gabriel makes it clear that he is comfortable with the boy's weight.

When they reach the far side of the field they see the bridge, which has a slight arch so that the middle part is higher than the rest. It is a narrow bridge, not broad enough for a car, but wide enough for two people to walk across, shoulder to shoulder. To reach the bridge the guide pulls back a piece of fencing that looks like it has already been cut. Lying discarded by this gap in the fence is an empty Coca-Cola can and a half-dozen chocolate wrappers. There are muddy footprints, which make the grass slick, but one after the other they all pass through the fence and then step onto the bridge. Gabriel looks over the edge to see how far the drop is, and he is relieved to discover that it is not nearly as far as he had feared. The two other men also look and then laugh, but theirs is a nervous laughter. The guide watches them, but he seems agitated, as though he is ready to leave. He looks first one way and then the other, but Gabriel is scrutinising this man who, for the first time, seems unsure of himself.

'The train will come from this direction.' The guide points towards the light. 'You will jump from here as it emerges on the other side.' He stands now in the middle of the small bridge and glances at his watch. 'The train will be here in one minute.'

Gabriel looks at Amma, but she seems calm. The guide continues.

'It is better to drop down onto the train. Better than to jump. And you must land on the wagons at the rear of the train, for these are for cargo. Nobody will hear you if you drop on top of these carriages. Now please, you must get ready.'

Amma busily ties her child securely into her bosom, wrapping yet another layer of cloth around him. The restless guide rubs the lenses of his thick glasses with his fingers.

'You must lie flat and still on top of the train. You will pass through a long tunnel, but do not be frightened. Then it will be England, but do not get up or show yourself until you reach London. You will know that it is London, for you will be in a big station with a roof. The train will stop and doors will open and you will hear people and announcements. If the train stops before this you must not get up, do you understand?'

The two men nod. Amma finishes binding her child to her bosom, and then they hear the noise of the train approaching. The guide jams his glasses back into place.

'Remember you must lie flat.'

Gabriel looks at the train as it comes into view, but he can immediately see that it is travelling too fast for Amma to jump. The two men are already hanging over the side of the bridge, and now the guide turns to Amma, but Gabriel moves to stand in front of her. The guide is flustered.

'Quick, you must hurry.'

Gabriel raises his voice over the noise of the approaching train. 'It is going too quickly. She cannot do this.' Gabriel can see that Amma wants to speak, but he is adamant. He takes a step towards the guide and holds out his hand. 'The money.'

The guide laughs and turns from Gabriel. The train is now passing underneath the bridge. Gabriel can feel Amma tugging at his sleeve, but without bothering to turn around he simply cries, 'No.' Gabriel watches as the two men let go of the bridge and fall on top of the train. They roll onto their sides and then one man reaches out and grabs the other in order to prevent him from falling. And then suddenly they are gone from sight as the train speeds into the distance. The guide turns from the train and looks at Gabriel.

'What is the matter with you?' He holds his hands out wide. 'The girl could have been on the train.'

'It was going too fast,' says Gabriel.

The guide laughs and begins to walk off, but Gabriel shouts.

'The money.'

The guide stops and turns around to face Gabriel.

'I have to pay the guards. If there are three people, then I pay for three. If only two jump, then it is not my problem.'

Amma takes Gabriel by the arm. 'Please, the money is not important.'

Gabriel, however, is determined. 'You have stolen our money.'

The guide walks back towards Gabriel. 'Please do not call me a thief.'

Gabriel is adamant. 'You have taken Amma's money.'

The man now points towards Amma. 'She decided not to jump. This is not my fault. If I am caught I will be imprisoned. But I take this risk.' He bangs his hand into his chest as he speaks. 'I take the risk. You understand?'

Amma turns and moves away from the bridge. She passes back through the gap in the fence and then she begins to walk across the field. Gabriel wants to say something more to this man, but he cannot take his eyes from Amma. He turns and runs after her, but when he reaches Amma she ignores him.

'Are you angry with me?'

Amma continues to walk.

'I am trying to help you, yet you treat me as though I have done something that has offended you.' Amma stops in the middle of the thorny field, and for the first time Gabriel can see the tears in her eyes.

'Why,' she asks, 'do you insist on arguing with this man? He is not going to give you the money and he may be dangerous. You put us in danger. You put my child in danger.'

Gabriel listens and he is shocked by how emotionally distraught Amma appears to be.

'I am sorry.' He speaks quietly, and as he does so he moves to hold her arm, but she pulls away. 'I did not know that you were frightened.'

Amma's eyes continue to blaze. 'Of course I am frightened. The man can keep the money, I have a child to protect.'

'I am sorry.'

'Why are you sorry?' She looks contemptuously at Gabriel. 'It is men like that man who raped me and made me sick.'

'Men like that?'

'Angry men. They killed my husband, and because of the rape his family did not want me any more. That is why I am here, just me and my child. We have nobody and we do not wish to make men angry.'

'But you have me, Amma.'

'I cannot have a man again, do you not understand? It is not possible. I am no use to you, no use at all.'

Gabriel stares at her, but Amma shakes her head and then she begins to walk back in the direction of the camp. Gabriel watches her for a few moments, and then he follows.

As they pass into the tent Gabriel notices that there are

new people who look closely at both of them. However, in the far corner of the tent, he sees familiar faces. He imagines that it must be clear to them that this is not the right time to begin questioning either of their distraught-looking fellow travellers. Amma sits down and begins to free the child from the cloths which bind him to her body. Gabriel sits heavily on the cot next to hers and he stares at her. And then he whispers.

'So what will happen with us?'

Amma says nothing, and she will not meet Gabriel's eyes. She lies on her side with her hands between her knees, as though she is praying, and she concentrates on her child. Knowing that he is effectively beaten, and that there is no way to make Amma talk against her will, Gabriel rolls over onto his cot and closes his eyes. He is tired, and he can feel sleep beginning to flood his body.

And then Gabriel sees his mother crawling on all fours like a dog. She is wailing, but without making any noise. Her head is craned back and she opens her mouth and reveals toothless gums. Her eyes bulge, but it is not immediately clear why she is in so much pain. And now she is surrounded by a group of men in khaki uniforms with red bandannas wrapped around their heads. They form a human circle inside of which Gabriel's mother crawls, and as she does so they kick her. Gabriel watches at some distance, and then one of the men turns around and sees Gabriel. The man has on dark glasses, and then all of the men turn and look at Gabriel so that he can now see that they are all wearing dark glasses. Gabriel's mother has collapsed into a heap and she is no longer able to crawl. But the men have finished with her and they stare now at Gabriel. And then Gabriel's two sisters walk into view. They are still in their blue and white school uniforms, and they carry their satchels over one shoulder. The men notice these two girls, and the older sister stops and holds the arm of the younger sister, who screams, and the two girls turn on their heels and begin to flee. A satchel drops from a shoulder, but it is impossible to tell who it belongs to. The men take off in pursuit of the girls and leave Gabriel standing alone with his mother. He waits for a few moments, but his mother does not pick herself up from the dirt. Gabriel is not sure if he should approach her, but in the end he decides to try and help. His mother is curled in a ball with her back to him.

'Mama?' Gabriel speaks quietly, as though not wishing to rouse her from an afternoon nap. 'Mama, are you all right?'

She says nothing in return, and so he bends down to touch her.

'Mama?'

'I have not had my blood in many months.'

He hears her voice, but she does not turn around to face him. He reaches down and pulls back her shoulder in order that he might look into her eyes, but there is no face. It is as if somebody has taken a piece of cloth and rubbed out her features. Gabriel jumps back in alarm, and then he opens his eyes and sees one of his travelling companions looking down at him.

'Gabriel, are you all right?'

Gabriel says nothing, and he simply stares at Bright.

'Gabriel, you were screaming. My brother, you are covered in sweat.'

Gabriel realises where he is. Beyond this man, and beyond the people who lie idly on their cots, he can see daylight through the open flaps of the tent. It is morning. Gabriel sits upright and wipes his damp brow with the sleeve of his jacket, and then he gestures to the empty cots.

'Where is everybody?'

'They have gone back to Paris to try to find Joshua.'

Gabriel looks to the cot where Amma used to lie. Bright reads his mind, and he speaks before Gabriel has time to frame the question.

'Yes, the woman too. She seemed sad to leave you. I think she wanted to wake you to say goodbye, but you were sleeping very heavily.'

Gabriel is disappointed with Amma, but there is little point in his letting Bright know this. Gabriel sits upright and looks around, and then Bright laughs, a loud, almost hysterical laugh, and he slaps Gabriel on the back.

'Come, let us get some food before these people eat it all.'

Gabriel follows Bright out of the tent. His friend is heavily built, but without being fat, and Gabriel guesses him to be in his mid-twenties. During the journey he has said very little to Gabriel, but even in the most difficult of times he has noticed a quiet determination about this man, Bright. They line up to collect their metal plate of rice and vegetables, and their hunk of bread, and then they both squat in the sunshine and eat. The ground is too muddy for them to sit, but it is too depressing to go back inside the tent. Bright eats quickly, as though unconcerned by what he is shovelling into his mouth, and when he finishes the food he tosses the plate to the ground and then turns to Gabriel.

'I think we should try to reach England tonight. I have been speaking to one of those men.' Bright gestures towards an unusually tall Chinese man in a red woollen hat who, judging by the manner in which he pulls his thin jacket around him, appears to be suffering badly with a cold. Suddenly this man bends almost double, and begins to cough loudly into his chapped hands.

'He told me that we can smuggle ourselves onto a boat. It is better than the trains, for everybody is trying the trains. The boats are unprotected most of the time.'

'Bright, you are sure about this?'

'The Chinese man told me that for those with no money, the only way into England is the boats. If we do not try, then we are defeated.' Bright pauses. 'This man says that he is coming with us.' Again Bright pauses and he looks directly at Gabriel. 'It is either this or Paris. But I am an Englishman. Only the white man respects us, for we do not respect ourselves. If you cut my heart open you will find it stamped with the word 'England'. I speak the language, therefore I am going to England to claim my house and my stipend.' For a moment Bright falls silent, and then again he begins to speak. 'My brother, this is difficult to talk about, so I will just say it once and then we can forget it. In our country they put me in prison and did terrible things to me to try to make me talk. If it was not for a cousin who brought me money so I could pay the guards and eat, I would not be here. I got dysentery from the one chamber pot that fifty of us were forced to share. I got lice from the damp mattress on the floor. The half-cooked rice in palm oil soothed my pain, but it made me very sick. I know we have all been afflicted, but I, this man, cannot go back ever. I hate it. I want to forget Africa and those people. I am an Englishman now. I am English and nobody will stop me from going home. Not you, not these people, nobody.'

Gabriel smells the sea, but he says nothing. The three of them continue to edge their way down the dark road, until they are greeted with a bank of floodlights which reveal a bustling scene of trucks and people, all of whom are bathed in the dazzling pool of bright fluorescent light. The Chinese man points to the bulk of a huge ship and then he speaks to Bright in a whisper, all the while glancing towards the vessel. Bright listens and then turns to Gabriel.

'He says that we are to move quickly through the trucks till we get close to the ship. Then we run to the ropes that secure the ship to the harbour, take them in our hands and drop over the side. There is a ledge on the side of the ship that we put our feet on, and we must hold on to the ship.'

Gabriel seems unconvinced.

'When do we do this?'

'Now.'

The Chinese man is not listening. He looks intently all about himself, and then suddenly his red hat is moving quickly through the trucks. Bright notices that they have been abandoned and he is quick to follow. Gabriel chases after his younger friend, and the two men scamper quickly in an effort not to lose sight of the Chinese man. They hide behind the truck that is closest to the ship, and all three of them wait until they have caught their breath. Then the Chinese man points first to himself, then to Bright, and then to Gabriel so that it is clear that they are to move off in this order. Without waiting to see if his instructions have registered, the man dashes to the side of the ship and swings himself off the quayside and down into the narrow gap between the sea wall and the vessel. Gabriel and Bright look at each other, but neither says anything. Bright glances all around and then scurries off. Gabriel watches as Bright grabs a rope and then disappears over the quayside. And now Gabriel runs out, his heart pounding, and he too grabs the rope and lowers himself until he can feel the ledge beneath his feet. He releases the rope and grabs holds of a metal chain, and he follows Bright and the Chinese man, who are edging their way towards the front of the ship. Once there they edge along the far side of the ship where nobody can see them. And then they stop and wait. Gabriel looks down and can see that there is nothing between this thin ledge and the sea below, and he clings tightly to the metal chain. Occasionally he glances at Bright, but Bright's eyes are tightly shut and he will not meet his friend's gaze.

Eventually, the hooter on the ship sounds a half-dozen shrill blasts and the ship begins, almost imperceptibly, to move off and into the open water. As she does so, Gabriel can feel the greasy swell lazily swinging the ship up, and then letting her down again as though having changed its mind. Gabriel notices that a terrified Bright has opened his eyes, but, as though sensing danger, he quickly shuts them again. As the ship moves out into the sea, and her movements become more energetic, water begins to spray up and over Gabriel so that he is instantly sodden, and it is now Gabriel's turn to close his eyes. As the ship moves forward, Gabriel can feel it hitting a tall ridge of water and then plunging down the far side of the ridge and into a trough, and for a moment he is totally submerged. Soon Gabriel can no longer feel his hands, but he fights with a soldier's concentration to keep his mind alert.

Gabriel hears the ship's engines falling quiet, and he notices that the lurching of the ship is becoming less violent. He hears people shouting to each other, and then the shouting becomes increasingly urgent. For a moment Gabriel wonders if this is the afterworld, and then he realises that it is his own name that is being shouted out. He opens his eyes. The ship is approaching a coastline that looks like a long, thin black shadow decorated with speckles of white light, and Gabriel blinks repeatedly, for the sea water is burning his eyes. He can see that Bright is gesturing wildly to him, but there is no sign of the other man. Bright now clings on to the metal chain with just one hand, and with the other hand he is pointing to the black water. 'Jump!' Before Gabriel has a chance to reply, Bright leaps down into the water and Gabriel jumps after him. As he hits the water Gabriel feels his leg snap back, as though it has struck something hard. The pain shoots through him like a bullet, and Gabriel opens his mouth to cry out in pain, but water rushes in. Bright is already swimming towards the shore, and Gabriel begins to flail after him although it causes him intense pain to do so. Gabriel decides to turn on his side, and he trails the leg behind him as though it were a semi-discarded article of clothing. As he thrashes his way towards the lights, the cinema of his mind fades to black and then it is suddenly flooded with disturbing, yet familiar, images.

We were the smaller tribe. We worked hard and we did not harm anybody. We tried to do what was best for ourselves, and what was good for our young country. We wanted only to live in peace with our brothers, but it became clear that this was not possible. My father told me they were jealous of us, for our people ran many businesses; not just in the capital city, but in our tribal land to the south. We formed the backbone of the economy, and therefore we had much influence. It was only after one of our people was elected to the presidency that the real trouble began; the killings. The army rebelled, and the government troops spilled out from their barracks and cruised the streets in vehicles with machine guns pointing out of the windows. They began to drink and kill, and kill and drink, and soon my terrified father had little choice but to take me to one side.

'You are my eldest child. My only son.' My father looked directly at me as he spoke, but on his breath I could smell wine. Father did not know how to cope with this new situation, and there were portions of his cheek that he had forgotten to shave. 'My son, these people are roaming the streets in aimless packs like disturbed hounds. This morning I saw with my own eyes as they took a woman, wrapped her in a blanket, poured kerosene on her and watched her burn alive. Out on the beach, beside the piles of rotting garbage, I saw this with my own eyes.'

I stared at my father who began now to shake his head.

'Power has not gone to the heads of these soldiers, it has gone to their bellies. They are fat and fleshy. They do not know how to fight, only how to kill. You must go to the south and join our people there. Soon they will kill our president and their army will take charge. I feel this in my blood. Our one hope will be you men in the south.' He paused. 'You must go now. You are my only son and it is my duty to send you to the liberation army. You will be trained to become a soldier, and the day will soon come when you will march triumphantly into the capital with your head held high. On this day I will throw petals at your feet, and strangers will rush to you and embrace you with tears of gratitude in their eyes. Your mother and your two sisters will weep with joy, for it is this day that we are all dreaming of. It is this day that we are waiting for.'

I was twenty-nine years old when my poor father said these words to me. The next morning, before dawn, I clambered up and onto the back of a truck with four other 'recruits'. My occupation was that of messenger clerk, and before this I had worked for many years at a hardware store. I was not prepared for the life of a soldier. My job as a messenger clerk was to run errands for civil servants and ministers in the government; I worked for the type of men who drove large foreign cars and who travelled freely to Europe and even to the United States. I would take them an envelope, or a pot of soup, or a new cell phone, or whatever it was that I was told to take to them, and I would wait in case they had something that they wished me to take away for them. In this way I hoped to gain influence and to one day secure for myself a position as a junior civil servant. This is how the system worked in my country. One had to be patient, but some days it was very difficult for I was no longer a young man.

Every day I would go into the ten-storey government

headquarters, and up the urine-stained steps, for we were not permitted to use the elevator. I would climb through the miasma of piss, and up the unfortunate stairwell where rats played in the corners, and then enter into the brightness of the neon-lit outer offices that were crammed with secretaries and typists, girls who spent their money on hot combs to make their stubborn hair smooth, and who wasted hours using skin-bleaching creams in the hope that they might render themselves more attractive to the men who promised these over-scented women a cosmetics shop of their own, or a half-dozen sewing machines, in exchange for their agreeing to lie back clumsily like upturned buses. I knew the names of some of these women, but such women would never be seen with me. They were goods in a shop, but I had no money. These fat men with greasy skin, who sweated underneath their tight western suits, they had already made a down payment on ruby-lipped Madonna, or fat Baby, or Pleasure with her blonde wig. These women did not consider me to be a man. A messenger clerk is not a man: I was a thing to be tolerated, a creature in a T-shirt and torn pants who was not much better than the cockroaches that skittered noisily across the floor. What did I know of Johnnie Walker Black Label? If the minister or civil servant had nothing for me to take back down the rotten stairwell, then one of these women would dismiss me with a flourish of her red nails and I would once more join the other clerks who squatted in the street rolling dice or playing cards, and I would sit and read until there was another message to be delivered. And then one night my father spoke to me, and in the morning he took me to a truck with no side mirrors, and with no indicators or windscreen wipers. Everything that could be peeled or ripped off from the truck had been taken, and he shook hands with me and reminded me that I was going south to become a soldier and wage war for my people.

He pushed a crumpled pack of cigarettes into my hand. He knew that I did not smoke, but he told me that I might be able to use the cigarettes as currency with which to bribe somebody and perhaps smooth my path for what lay ahead. There are, he reminded me, men who value tobacco more than bread.

Never before had I left the capital. As we passed through the shanty towns which clung to the edges of our main city, I stared in disbelief at the corrugated tin shelters which sprouted out of what looked like foul rubbish dumps. Although I had not seen these places with my own eyes, such tin-roofed slums, where beggars patrolled the streets, were widely known to be home for the disabled and maimed, places where huge rats bred freely and roamed by day and by night. I continued to stare in disbelief. This was our city? We soon passed into the countryside and sped south along the narrow strip of asphalt that had been laid clumsily over loose earth. The frayed edges of the asphalt had already been chewed by the red soil, and it was clear that at some point in the near future this 'road' would disappear. I looked to either side, but there was nothing except a dark curtain of bush.

The truck rolled and swayed like a drunk, and as we pressed further south we began to pass hundreds of displaced persons walking towards us with mattresses, cooking pots, and bundles of possessions on their heads. We soon grew accustomed to the barricades of burning tyres that occasionally blocked the road, and finally one of our escorts climbed wearily to his feet. He steadied himself by holding on to the side of the truck, and we stared at him as he stood before us resplendent in his grimy New York Jets T-shirt with his belt of neat bullets, like long chocolate fingers, that was wrapped around his waist and across his chest. He was chewing some kind of nut and the juice was dribbling down his chin, but either he did not care or he did not notice, for he made no attempt to dam the black rivulet at the corner of his mouth. He looked through his gold-rimmed glasses at all five of us in turn, and then he began to speak without enthusiasm, as though his words carried no weight.

'We are fighting for a purpose. Our aim is to liberate our land from these unscrupulous men who hate us. They outnumber us two or three to one, but they are mosquitoes. They suck our blood, but you will be trained so that you can squash them, do you understand?'

We looked at this man and nodded, and he stared at each one of us in turn and then, as though suddenly overcome with fatigue, he carefully lowered himself to the floor of the truck and once again rolled over and onto his side and closed his eyes. I watched him, for I was sure that this was some trick of his to test us, but soon I was convinced that the man had truly fallen asleep and the rest of our journey passed in silence.

In the south we were held in the bush far away from the nearest village. Those who trained us were boys, but they walked with the authority of old men in their plastic flip-flops. Their painted nails, and the teddy bears that many clung to, initially caused me to be confused. I soon learned that the currency of the camp was weed that you smoked, and this gave these soldiers a feeling of invincibility so that holding a stuffed toy, or wearing a Donald Duck mask, or daubing oneself with bright-pink lipstick, could never undermine their manhood. For my own part, beyond the dark sunglasses which we all craved and needed, I decided not to decorate myself, and perhaps because of my conservative bearing, and the fact that I was some ten years older than most of the men, I was chosen to be the leader of a brigade. I was different, for I had more education than the others, and more ambition to make something of myself in the world, and for these reasons they listened to me whenever I chose to speak. However, I was not a man to waste words, and most of the time I remained silent, which is why they took it upon themselves to christen me 'Hawk'.

Our first raids were a great success. I would lead the men into a village and we would drive out the government troops. We discovered many villagers with swollen stumps where their arms and legs used to be, the skin stretched and sewn together with makeshift stitching. These men had been tortured by the government troops, and many of our own people had now begun to resort to the same tactics in order to extract information, but I refused to allow my men to hack off limbs. When we had either killed or captured our enemy, the grateful villagers would re-emerge and shout and cheer for Hawk and his men. We showed restraint and, rather than just taking, we always waited for the liberated villagers to reward us. Sometimes they would cook food for us, rice with spicy sauce, cassava-bread pancakes, fresh roasted yam or soup; what little they had they would share with us, and even those who were not of our tribe knew that we would treat them better than the government soldiers. They knew that we were fair men, and when we left, my men always carried new gifts: a shower cap, a wedding headdress or a pair of women's shoes. Patrick, my second-in-command, enjoyed smearing his face in mud and he took to wearing a wig with one long braided pigtail. Never without the weed, Patrick soon appropriated the name 'Captain JuJu' and shortly after his rebirth he would not answer to any other title.

'Patrick,' I would ask him, 'what juju are you using?' and he would laugh as though my question was the opening gambit in a game. Patrick would cackle and pass me the joint.

'Hawk, you are a funny man.' And then Captain JuJu, who had long forgotten that my name was Gabriel, would flap his arms and begin to run around and screech, 'Only Hawk can fly' while the rest of the men clutched their sides with laughter. 'Only Hawk can fly.' And I would take the weed and watch crazy Patrick with a quiet smile on my face. 'Only Hawk can fly.'

For over a year this was our life, moving stealthily from one village to the next, driving back the government troops and waiting for news from the rest of the country, or a message from our leader back at the training camp. His headquarters was a small tin-roofed hut that was circled by bodyguards, and there he would sit with only his satellite telephone for company and plan the liberation campaign. Approximately once every month, our leader would call his commanders to him, and at such times a jeep would arrive and I would travel back south, leaving the troops in Patrick's charge.

Colonel Bloodshed never removed his Ray-Ban glasses or his Nike training shoes. Inside his hut he had glossy photographs of American film actresses stuck to the wall, and while I waited for him to look up at me, or finish a telephone call, I would stare at the fading pictures and wonder why *these* girls in particular? The miracle of electric light was produced by the roar of the leader's private generator, but above the noise of the engine I could still sometimes hear the sound of screaming as sand was being pushed into the ears of government soldiers, or I would hear cries for mercy as fresh captives were being hung upside down over the septic tank. Colonel Bloodshed seldom killed prisoners, this much I knew. Fear was enough to make the enemy talk, but I disliked hearing the noise. When the leader spoke to me from behind his glasses he enjoyed calling me Hawk, and he loved speaking in riddles and telling me that there were no more devils downstairs in hell, for they were all up here on earth visiting our country. He loved reminding me that guns must liberate, but they must never rule.

'Major Hawk,' he would say, 'you are one of my ten chiefs. Remember, in war there are casualties, and we all do things that we wish we had not done.' Our leader would pause. 'But remember. Guns must never rule, and I say this as a soldier.' Again he would pause, and then he would lift up his eyes as though trying to peer at me over the top of his Ray-Bans. 'Hawk,' he would whisper. 'To *not* be buried in one's own land. Now *that* is the ultimate insult. You understand, don't you?'

I would nod, but Colonel Bloodshed never listened to me, and I assumed he never listened to any of his 'chiefs'.

'Hawk, I am a good-looking man, do you not think so? A showman, yes?' Our leader stood and began to pace the floor with rhythmic deliberation. 'You can see how I dress, can't you? In the latest fashions, and always the best. Once upon a time I was a professional dancer in a night club, did you know that? Look, admire me, there is nothing to be ashamed of.' Our leader threw his hands into the air and spun on his axis, and then when he was once more facing me he began to laugh out loud. 'I used to dream of going to Europe. Of becoming a "been-to". But I knew that such a journey would cost me five years of savings and cause me five years of debt. So instead, in the capital, I used to service the wives of the diplomats and the tourists in the hope that one of them would take me to Europe. There I would be the toast of the town. The brown toast. I would never be one of the "been-tos" who come back as a ghost of the man they once were, their African souls crushed by these people. My body and my soul would return to Africa in triumph. Brown toast. Look at these feet.' He pointed to his Nike training shoes. 'These feet were not made to suffer dirt. When I go to Europe I will walk everywhere on soft material and they will worship my black beauty. They will fall at my feet and proclaim my power and how handsome I am. I will stamp on their violins and piss on their classical music CDs. I will bring them black Africa.'

At such moments I had learned that it was best to say nothing and simply listen.

'How are the dogs?' By this I knew Colonel Bloodshed meant my troops.

'Sir, they are well.'

'It is hard for the dogs. If they are afraid, you must let them smoke the cannabis and mix it with gunpowder. Then they will have no fear of spilled blood coming back to haunt them. They will no longer see people, only chickens that have to be slaughtered. You must encourage them to harvest the chickens. It is time for the men of our country to reap the harvest and eat chicken.'

At some point, having provided him with a patient and obedient audience, Colonel Bloodshed would tire of my presence and unceremoniously fall asleep, and I would find a jeep or a truck that was available and begin the long journey back north to my men.

Sometimes I would take out my book with its curled cover and mottled pages, and I would try to reread some of the notes that I had made, for I was in the habit of copying out passages from books that appeared to me to be memorable. However, on this particular night, as the light faded, I simply stared into the dark undergrowth. As I passed through a village that we had liberated only a few weeks earlier, I looked at the long line of women waiting at the solitary well for water, and the naked children running around in circles and playing the game of hitting each other with switches pulled from trees, and I wanted to weep for both tribes of my country. My own father had sent me to be a part of this slaughter and for the life of me I could not understand what he hoped to achieve. He meant well, that much I understood, but what did my father know of war?

When I arrived back at our camp I discovered that in my absence Patrick had led a group of men back to the village that we had most recently captured. Apparently the men had heard that the local prostitutes were prepared to go 'live' with a man who did not wear a condom. These women liked dry sex, rough, quick and without lubrication, and Patrick and the men were eager to offer up trinkets in exchange for these women's bodies. I sat by the campfire with the handful of men who remained behind, and I encouraged them to clean their weapons, for too many of them were rusting up in the humidity. I reminded the men that a weapon that jammed might well cost them their lives. They looked at me in silence. I cleaned my own rifle, but said nothing further.

In the morning Patrick and his men had still not returned and so I sent two men to search them out. When they finally appeared, Patrick was dressed in black pantyhose and he was still drunk. The others were high on pills and they continued to smoke weed. The men staggered towards me as streaks of light began to colour the tops of the trees. Patrick smiled his gap-toothed smile and placed a welcoming hand on my shoulder.

'Hawk,' he whispered. 'Hawk, you have never tasted women like these. I am sorry, my brother, but nothing like these women. Never. Nothing like these.'

I looked at Patrick and then turned away, for these men were suffering enough in this hellish war without enduring the lash of my tongue. In fact, I had no words on my tongue with which to lash them. These were young men who were fighting because somebody had given their family a bag of rice or promised them a car. For over a year they had simply eaten what they were given, and they had all lost friends. I walked to the shade of a tree and sat and closed my eyes. When I opened them it was evening.

The following morning we moved north and began our assault on the next village, but the mood had changed. As we cut through the bush, Patrick would not meet my eyes, and the other men avoided me. I felt as though I was marching alone, but I said nothing. When we reached the village we stopped and took up our crouching positions. We waited for signs of government troops, but we saw nobody. I stared at Patrick, who was wearing a new shower cap on top of his wig, but he simply looked at Major 'Hawk' and laughed, and I could see it in his eyes that he had already taken something.

'Hawk. We are ready. Are you ready? Hawk, we are ready to fly.'

I zipped my forefinger across my lips to encourage him to be quiet, but he simply giggled. And then others among the men began to laugh. I continued to look straight ahead at the village, but I could see no movement at all.

After a few moments, I stood up and beckoned everybody to gather around. I told them that the village was clear and that the government troops must have retreated. I suggested that we pass through, and accept food if the villagers wished to give some to us, but we would just move on. Patrick stepped out in front of me and held up his hand.

'No. The women last night told us that this village is friendly towards the government troops. These villagers are traitors.' I had heard this and I knew that there was a possibility that it was true, but before I could say anything Patrick continued. 'Captain JuJu says we take control of this village.'

The men began to nod and to move from one bare foot to another. They were already tired under the weight of shells and the heavy pieces of equipment that were strapped to their narrow backs, but their hearts were strong with amphetamines and dope. I spoke quietly.

'We will leave this village alone.'

Patrick stepped closer so that I could now smell the weed. 'I am Captain JuJu. They will follow me. To stop them you must kill me.' Patrick's eyes were stained red with blood, and he was laughing at me. 'You are a coward, Hawk. Somebody has clipped your wings and you cannot fly. This is war and in war you must kill. You must kill and then eat the hearts of your victims to make yourself more powerful. Come!' Patrick cocked his gun and signalled to the men to follow him into the village. The men removed their guns from their shoulders and made ready for war. Patrick pointed his weapon at me. 'If we find you, Hawk, we will kill you, for you are not a man, you are a woman, and you have no place among dogs.' He laughed and then suddenly choked back his amusement and spat. 'We mistake your silence for strength.' He then stepped forward and kissed me on the forehead, leaving behind a smear of lipstick. 'There.' He pointed for all to see. 'You have the mark of a woman upon you.' And then he cackled at his own humour.

I remained rooted to the spot and watched as Patrick led the men towards the village. Some time later, I listened to the rapid firing of their weapons and the chorus of screaming from the villagers. Captain JuJu was right. I did not have the heart for this savagery. My father had sent me to fight, and I could fight and kill if necessary. But only if necessary. Now I had little choice but to make my way back to the capital and warn my family. Everybody knew that these were my men, and it was clear that the government troops would blame me for this massacre and take bloody revenge on my mother and father and two sisters. This was the shameful manner in which we conducted our war. I stood for a few moments in the bush, my weapon by my side, and I listened to Patrick and his men mowing down innocent women and children. I remembered our leader's words. In war there are casualties and we all do things that we wish we had not done. Long before the last bullets ceased flying, I had begun the long walk north towards the capital. To reach my mother and father and two sisters, this was now the full extent of my ambition.

When Gabriel opens his eyes he can feel Bright pushing into his chest.

'Gabriel, breathe out. Breathe out!'

Gabriel can feel the water dribbling helplessly around his mouth, and he realises that there is no dignity to his present predicament.

'Gabriel, can you hear me?'

Gabriel tries to nod, but his head will not respond. He keeps his eyes firmly fixed on Bright, who again pushes on Gabriel's chest. This time Gabriel coughs loudly, but no water comes up. Then Bright feels Gabriel's leg, but the pain causes Gabriel to grimace. He looks down and sees that his right trouser leg is ripped so that the skin is exposed, but there is neither blood nor bruising.

With Bright's help, Gabriel sits upright and he can now see that he is on a stony beach. Only a few yards to his left the deafening sea is pounding into the shore. Gabriel looks around himself and then fixes his gaze upon Bright.

'England?'

Bright laughs out loud. 'If this is not England, then wherever it is, I am staying.' Bright reaches down a hand and pulls his friend to his feet.

Gabriel winces in pain, and is immediately aware that he cannot put much pressure on his right leg. He holds on to Bright's arm, but the slippery stones beneath his feet make his movement painfully slow.

Together they walk up the short incline, with Gabriel leaning heavily against his friend's portly body, and when they reach the deserted road they stop and stare at the lights of a distant harbour town. There, in the docks, Gabriel can see the ship that has brought them on this final leg of this journey, for its illuminated bulk dwarfs everything else. Bright points.

'We should walk towards the town.'

Gabriel says nothing, and he decides to conserve his energy. This first English night is causing him much pain, and he knows that to try to speak will prove too much for him, but he feels sure that Bright understands. And then suddenly, as they continue along the empty road, the thought strikes a guilty Gabriel.

'Bright, where is the other man?'

Bright continues to walk, assisting his friend as he does so. 'He fell into the sea a long time before we reached England. The water swallowed him.' Gabriel tries not to appear shocked, but Bright has not finished. 'What could I do? Follow him into the mouth of the sea? The man has passed over and now he is at peace.' Suddenly Gabriel's heart feels heavy, but he knows that it would be foolish for him to think any further on this subject, and so he resolves to forget the tall Chinese man with the red hat.

The two men continue to walk slowly, one supporting the other, both silently fearful of discovery, but it soon becomes clear to Gabriel that he cannot walk much longer. Gabriel feels guilty that he is holding back his friend, but just when he realises that he may have to insist that Bright leave him behind, they both see a small house to the side of the lonely road. Bright speaks first.

'Perhaps we should ask these people for help.'

Gabriel looks at the house, and notices that one of the upstairs windows is broken, and that the garden is badly overgrown with weeds. It occurs to him that this house is possibly abandoned.

Bright knocks at the door and waits, and then he turns the door handle, but the door is locked and it will not give way. Gabriel leans against the gatepost, and he can see Bright visibly gain some confidence now that he realises that nobody is in the house. His friend walks to the edge of the building and peers around the corner.

'You must wait here while I look.'

Bright disappears from view, and Gabriel looks back down the road in the direction that they have just travelled. Out at sea a ship that is decorated like a wedding cake slides slowly by, but this is all that Gabriel can see. And then the door in front of him begins to open slowly. As it does so the hinges make a loud, grating sound, as though they have been rusted shut for some time. Gabriel navigates the short path by himself, and an excited Bright reaches out a hand to help him over the threshold.

'Nobody lives here. There's some old furniture and a bed, but nothing else.' Bright closes the door behind them and Gabriel's eyes begin to adjust to the darkness. 'I climbed in through a window, but it's filthy back there.'

Gabriel topples into a seat. As he sits, a cloud of dust rises around him. He watches Bright, who stands by the window and peers outside and into the darkness. His friend's mind appears to be racing, but Gabriel decides not to ask any questions for he imagines that when he is ready, Bright will choose to share his thoughts. And then, without saying a word, his friend turns and crosses the room and slumps into a chair that Gabriel can see is leaking stuffing from old wounds.

When Gabriel wakes up the sun is shining directly into his eyes and Bright is no longer in the chair. He tries to stand, but the pain shoots through his right leg and he falls back down. He looks around the room and can see now that the house looks as though nobody has lived in it for quite some time. Every object is coated in a thin layer of dust, and the air feels heavy and stale. Gabriel tries again to get to his feet, and this time he manages to do so. As he moves to the window, he is careful to put as little pressure as possible on his injured leg. He lifts his hands to shield his eyes from the sun, and then he sees Bright walking up the path towards him with a small bag in his hand. Bright is grinning all over his face and he waves to Gabriel and then opens the door with a flourish.

'How is your leg?'

Gabriel hobbles to meet his younger friend, who hands him a plastic bottle with water in it. Bright continues, leaving Gabriel little time to answer his question.

'The town is small but it seems friendly, and at the train station the trains go directly to London. I think it will be easy to get on board and ride for nothing.'

Gabriel takes a drink from the bottle and then holds it out, but Bright sits down and refuses to accept the bottle.

'Please, you must finish it yourself. I have already had my fill in the town.'

Gabriel immediately tips the bottle up to his mouth and drains it. He puts down the bottle and stares at Bright, who suddenly seems tired. Although Gabriel is extremely hungry, he does not want to mention this fact for fear that Bright might think him ungrateful. As though sensing Gabriel's unease, Bright gets to his feet and moves to the window where he positions himself in such a manner that the afternoon light catches him full in the face.

'My God, I see somebody.' An alarmed Bright speaks without turning towards Gabriel. 'She is coming in this direction.'

Gabriel stands, and suddenly the pain in his leg is no longer a problem as he crosses to the window and joins Bright. Gabriel can see that the girl is young, and that she is walking right up to the house. She pushes at the door, and as she walks in she stops and lets out a small scream.

'My friend has hurt his leg,' says Bright. 'If this is your house, we are sorry, but we needed to stay somewhere for the night.'

The girl is small in height, but her body is large. She is dressed in a red jacket and she wears a matching skirt and black tights. Gabriel assumes this to be her school uniform, but beyond her initial shock the girl does not panic.

'Who are you?' she asks. Bright gestures nervously.

'This is Gabriel, who has hurt his leg, and I am Bright. But please, we are leaving now.' The girl comes into the house, but she does not close the door behind her.

'You don't have to go anywhere. This isn't my place. Nobody lives here any more. Well, at least not since the accident.' Bright seems puzzled now.

'The accident?'

'It happened a few years ago, I think. Somebody died here, but it wasn't like a murder or anything. Probably fell off the roof.'

Gabriel looks closely at the girl, who speaks quickly and with confidence.

'I'm serious, you don't have to go nowhere.' She speaks directly to Bright, who gestures to the seat opposite Gabriel.

'Please, you must take a seat. There is no reason for you to remain standing.'

The girl sits and looks suspiciously at Gabriel, and then she turns back to Bright.

'What's your names again? I've forgotten.' The girl runs a hand back and through her short blonde hair. 'I'm Denise.'

'Denise, I am Bright, and this is Gabriel.'

'I like your names. They're kind of simple. Does everybody in your country have simple names?'

Bright laughs. 'People have all kinds of names.'

They fall silent for a moment, and suddenly Denise seems nervous.

'Are you from Africa?'

Bright nods.

'You're illegals, aren't you?'

Bright looks at Gabriel, who says nothing. Denise notes the glance and is quick to speak.

'I'm not going to tell nobody, I promise. It's just that I've seen you people in town. Not Africans so much, but people from other places. Indians. Chinese. That lot. You want to go to London, don't you? Is that where you're heading?'

Bright nods.

'On the train?'

Again Bright nods, and then he speaks.

'We only arrived yesterday so we don't really know what to do.'

'Are you hungry?' Denise stands now.

Gabriel looks at the young girl, trying to decide whether they should trust her, but Bright appears to have already made this decision. The girl hooks her bag over her shoulder.

'I can get you some food, but not tonight. I have to be back home or my dad will wonder what's going on with me. But tomorrow I'll come back with some food.'

Bright stands and faces the girl.

'Is it possible you could bring something for my friend's leg? A bandage, perhaps?'

'Is a bandage all you need?'

Bright nods, and then he speaks.

'Are you sure that you will not be tempted to tell somebody about us?'

Denise laughs now. 'I thought you lot turned yourself in to the police. Isn't that what you do to get your asylum?'

'Yes. But we wish to go to London first.' Bright shrugs his shoulders. 'If we do it here, they may put us straight back on the boat.'

'So you came on the ferry?'

'We came on a boat, but it was not easy.' Denise stares at Bright, and then suddenly she seems nervous.

'I have to go now, but I promise I'll come back tomorrow with food. And I'll try to bring something for his leg.'

Denise moves towards the door and Bright follows her. Gabriel watches them both, and then he stands up and limps across to the window, where he sees that the sun has now hidden itself behind a cloud. He looks at Denise as she makes her way down the path, her bag swinging casually on her shoulder. As she disappears out of sight it worries him that she does not even bother to turn around. Bright playfully slaps his friend on the arm.

'I can see that you do not trust this girl.'

Gabriel continues to stare at the path.

'Bright, the girl will tell her people. Perhaps we should leave now and try to reach London before she returns.'

Bright seems taken aback by Gabriel's certainty. 'Are you able to leave now?'

'I do not know, but I can try.'

Gabriel leaves Bright by the window and sits down. He thinks for a few moments and then he glances up at his younger friend.

'We should leave together, but in the morning. I do not think that she will say anything tonight, do you?'

Bright shrugs his shoulders. 'I do not know. I cannot read the stupid girl's mind.'

Gabriel looks at Bright in surprise.

Gabriel dreams of his mother. He gazes at her, but she will not speak to him. He brushes her face with the back of his hand. It feels hot, flushed with anger. His mother is not only physically hurt and bruised, she is also mentally damaged. He can see it in her eyes. Sadly, the muscles in her face are no longer strong enough to bear the weight of a smile. He implores her to flee with him, to let him rescue her, but she looks at him with scorn. She will not run away. Gabriel tries again.

'You must come with me. I can take you to a place where you will be safe. I am a major.'

His mother looks him up and down with a barely perceptible movement of her eyes, and then she laughs.

'Major? Major son.'

Gabriel is angry now. He is a major in command of many men. They are fighting a war for their country and her son is a leader of men. She has no right to laugh at him. Again, he tries to reason with his mother.

'I can save you, but you must come with me now.' Gabriel can hear his men outside. They are becoming restless. Most of them have already lost their families in this war, and they are jealous of the fact that Gabriel still has a mother. Gabriel can see the lighted butts of their cigarettes burning brightly. He looks again at his mother and tries once more to persuade her that she should abandon her house and the material possessions that she appears keen to cling to.

'These things mean nothing. I am talking about your life, that is what is important. You have to protect your life. You know I am telling you the truth, my mother, so why will you not listen? Why are you behaving in this stubborn manner?'

Gabriel continues to dream of his mother. He listens to the increasingly impatient sounds of his men outside. He knows that unless he is able to persuade her to leave with him, then he might never again see her. But what can he do? Carry her out with him? If she does not wish to come with him, then he has no choice but to accept her decision. He continues to look at his mother, who is staring back at her 'Major son' with contempt that she seems incapable of disguising.

And then, some time later in the day, Gabriel imagines that he sees Amma and Joshua walking together along the banks of a broad river. Amma's child is now a small boy, and he dances in between the legs of the adults. Gabriel watches them, but they can not see him, and he realises that he has been betrayed. He understands now why Amma has chosen Paris over their future together. He understands now why Joshua refused to come to England. These two people have cast him aside and it hurts. He watches them closely, hoping that in their very movements he might pick up some clue as to what is passing through their minds. However, it is clear that Amma is giving to Joshua the love and attention that Gabriel sought from her.

Gabriel watches the child skipping happily, but it is only when the child turns around and looks in Gabriel's direction that he recognises just what it is about this free-spirited child that disturbs him. The child has Felix's face. Not just a resemblance, or a similarity, the child is Felix, and now the child points at Gabriel and begins to laugh. Joshua and Amma turn around, but they can see nothing and they wonder why the child is laughing. The boy begins to laugh even louder, and now Gabriel begins to panic. He turns and flees, but the boy chases after him, and no matter how quickly Gabriel runs, the boy runs faster until Gabriel realises that he has no choice but to stop and confront this young Felix. How can he apologise to this young boy for what he has done to him? He hurt him, and then left him to die, and Gabriel knows that he is guilty. Gabriel turns to face the boy, who immediately stops. The two of them stand alone, and then the young Felix begins to cry, and Gabriel realises the degree of hurt that is buried in the boy's soul. He takes a step towards the young Felix, but the boy backs away.

'Are you all right?' Gabriel speaks softly, but the boy is frightened. Gabriel takes another step towards young Felix, but the sobbing boy turns on his heels and runs for his life. He moves quickly, and soon he is out of sight and Gabriel knows that it will be futile to chase after him, for the boy will soon be safe in the arms of Amma. No doubt Joshua will also comfort the boy, and together they will resume their walk by the side of the great river so that to all who look on they might appear to be the perfect family.

Gabriel looks around himself and he now realises that he has no idea of where he is. His dream is becoming a nightmare. He hears a voice shout to him, 'Gabriel!', but he does not know how to find this person. Suddenly the street is in total darkness and he can see nothing. Then again the voice cries out, 'Gabriel!', and he realises that he is being lured by this man. The light begins to improve, and as Gabriel follows the voice, people begin to mill about. French people. He is still in Paris. Shops and cars appear, and Gabriel feels as though he has walked from death into life. He begins to relax now and walk freely. Gabriel no longer hears the voice calling to him, but he seems to know exactly where he is walking. He crosses a busy highway and turns into a side street, where he stops by a pavement café and looks at the man who is the centre of attention. The man is surrounded by a group of fellow Africans, and they hang on his every word as he tells his tales and orchestrates their communal laughter. Then Gabriel recognises the voice that has led him out of darkness and to this present place. It is the voice of Bright. His young friend does not look across at Gabriel, he simply continues to talk, and Gabriel listens, and then Gabriel realises that none of the men can actually see him. Should he go and sit down among them, they still would not be able to see him. Bright has clearly made something of his life, but Gabriel is surprised to see him in Paris. He had imagined that Bright would, after all the effort that he had made to get to England, at least have tried to reach London. 'Bright,' he says. He waits for Bright to respond, but Bright continues to ignore him. Gabriel tries again, but then Gabriel realises that, like the other men, Bright cannot hear him. He shouts one final time, 'Bright!'

When Gabriel opens his eyes he can tell that it is dawn. The birds outside are singing, and the light is weak. He feels rested now, not only from the terror of the ride on the side of the ship, but from the whole journey. He moves his leg slightly, and although it still hurts, the pain does not shoot through it in the same manner. It is only now, however, as he moves to stand, that he notices that Bright is not in the room. Gabriel walks to the door, and although it still troubles him to place his full weight on the leg, he can at least move with some freedom. He opens the door and steps outside, and then he looks up at the house. In the morning light, the true extent of its abandonment is now clear. At first he had noticed that only one window was broken, but he can now see that most of the windows are either cracked or have small holes in the panes of glass as though stones have been pelted through them. The woodwork on the house lacks paint and is peeling, and the guttering is falling from the structure. In between the bricks spout tufts of grass, and in places some bricks are either dislodged or missing altogether. Gabriel walks around the house and discovers that the dereliction is the same on all sides. However, at the back of the house the state of disrepair seems to be greater still, for not a single pane of glass is intact, and birds appear to have taken to nesting in what used to be the kitchen. To the side of the kitchen wall he notices roses climbing wildly on some rickety trelliswork, but their red splendour serves only to reinforce the misery of the place.

Gabriel wanders round to the front of the house, and as he does so he wonders what might have happened here. England was not enduring a period of war, so why would somebody flee from a grand house like this? He walks down the short path to the road and looks first to the left and then to the right, but he can see nobody. As he turns to go back inside the house, Gabriel hears a noise behind him. For a moment he stands still, not daring to turn around.

'It's only me.'

He hears Denise's voice, and then her laughter, and then he turns to face her. He sees that she is wearing the same red uniform with black tights that she wore the previous day and she is holding a plastic bag, which Gabriel hopes contains food. She pushes past him with her tank-like body, and then she dashes up the path and into the house, and Gabriel follows her.

'Scared you, did I?' She doesn't wait for Gabriel to answer. 'I brought you some food and some drinks. Where's your friend?'

'Bright?'

'Yes, Bright. I thought he was going to be here.' Gabriel can barely take his eyes from the bag of food, which the girl now passes to him. 'Take what you want, it's for you.'

Gabriel takes out a loaf of bread and tears off a large piece. As much as he wishes to eat slowly and with some dignity, he cannot restrain himself from cramming the bread into his mouth, for his stomach burns with hunger. Denise sits down now and stares at him.

'Hungry, are you?' She starts to laugh, and Gabriel realises that she is laughing at him. He glares at her, but an unperturbed

Denise continues to laugh. As he chews his food, Gabriel studies this girl, who appears to be younger than his own sisters, and who wears her school uniform with neither pride nor dignity. The skirt is too short and it rides up one leg so that half of the girl's thigh is exposed. Gabriel looks at her, and her exposed thigh, and then he attempts to open the bottle of water, which starts to bubble when he finally unscrews the metal cap.

'I don't think Bright's coming back, do you?' Gabriel begins to drink, but he does not answer. He decides instead to wait for her to continue. 'I saw him this morning by the train station.' Gabriel stops drinking. 'He didn't tell you anything, did he?' Gabriel says nothing. 'Well, don't worry, I'll look after you till you're ready to go. I couldn't find any bandages, but I haven't told anybody that you're here, honest.'

Gabriel looks away from this girl. He needs time to think, but he can feel the girl's eyes upon him. She is staring at him and waiting for him to say something, but Gabriel has nothing to say to this disrespectful girl. He does not even wish to look upon her. Gabriel can sense that she is about to ask another question and so he closes his eyes against the girl, and the bright sunlight, in an attempt to control his anger.

The day warder unlocks the final door and moves to one side so that Gabriel can pass into the room where the woman and the man are already sitting at the table waiting for him. As he walks in, Katherine stands up and smiles. Today she is dressed formally in black, but he can see that she has not surrendered her love for men's trousers. Stuart Lewis remains seated, his face a mask of concentration, and he studies the papers that are spread out before him. Gabriel hears the door bang shut behind him and he knows that the warder is standing guard behind his back.

'Sit down, Gabriel,' says Katherine, gesturing to the chair on the other side of the table.

Gabriel sits, but Stuart Lewis does not look up at him. The man continues to shuffle through the pile of papers in front of him.

'Gabriel, we just want to know if there's anything that you'd like to tell us before we go to court this morning.' Katherine pauses, and the man finally looks up. He adjusts his glasses.

'Gabriel, since we last met I've spent some time looking through the files. Given the circumstances, there's little point in having a barrister present.' Katherine sighs, but she remains silent. 'I think that only by saying something along the lines that you "think" this thing never happened will you really have a proper opportunity to help yourself. Do you understand?'

Gabriel says nothing. The man begins now to tap his pen and then he quickly shakes his head and pushes back his chair. Katherine leans across the table.

'Are you sure, Gabriel? I mean are you really sure that you remember nothing?'

Gabriel lowers his eyes. Stuart Lewis stands and begins to push the papers into his briefcase. Now it is Katherine's turn to get to her feet.

'We'll see you in court, Gabriel. And don't worry, we're on your side.' Katherine makes an attempt to look cheerful, but a disappointed Stuart Lewis does not look again in Gabriel's direction.

As the police van twists and turns its way through the narrow streets, Gabriel peers through the blackened windows at the English people going about their daily business. The driver and the policeman next to him talk and occasionally they throw a comment back in the direction of Gabriel, who sits behind the metal grille.

'I hear they're gonna put you in with some nice football boys.'

Gabriel does not understand everything they say.

'Chelsea fans, you prefer them, do you?' The men laugh out loud, but Gabriel ignores them and continues to stare out of the window. To Gabriel's eyes, English people look unhappy, and he notices that they walk with their heads down as though determined to avoid one another. It is strange, but nobody is looking at anybody else, and it would appear that not only are these people all strangers to one another, but they seem determined to make sure that this situation will remain unchanged.

And then suddenly there is no longer a view. They are in a dark underground car park, and both men are now serious. They leave the van together, doors slamming on either side like noisy metal wings. Gabriel hears them unlocking the back door, and then the driver grabs Gabriel by the collar of his shirt. 'Come on, sunshine, get up.' Gabriel finds it difficult to maintain his balance with his hands handcuffed together, and as they drag him out he bangs his head on the roof of the van. He notices others now, including a half-dozen police officers, and some men with cameras who begin to take pictures, their shutters firing like gunshots and their bright lights flashing in his face. He feels a policeman push down his head so that he is now looking at his shoes, and he is quickly pulled in the direction of an open door. Inside the building there seems to be less commotion. The policeman takes his hand from the back of Gabriel's head, and Gabriel looks up. They are in a brightly lit corridor. At the end of the corridor, Katherine and Stuart Lewis are waiting for him. As he reaches them, Katherine pats Gabriel on the back, and he notices that since he last saw her she has unfastened her hair so that it is now drifting into her eyes.

'We've got a few minutes before the hearing. Are you all right?'

Gabriel nods and looks all about himself. The corridor is filled with policemen who are staring at him, but at least nobody is taking any pictures. Katherine points.

'Come on, we can go in here.'

Stuart Lewis remains in the corridor while Katherine leads the way into a small room, where Gabriel immediately notices that the fluorescent light is blinking on and off. There are a table and four chairs, but on the walls there are neither pictures nor posters, and there are no windows. Gabriel sits across the table from Katherine, and then Stuart Lewis and a policeman come in and the lawyer sits next to Gabriel. Suddenly Stuart Lewis seems relaxed, and he even smiles at Gabriel, who can now see that today the man has what looks like a slight coffee stain on his yellow tie.

'How are we this morning?'

Gabriel is confused by this sudden change of tone. He glances at Katherine, who also seems somewhat puzzled.

'Everything all right, Stuart?'

'Oh yes, everything's all right.' The lawyer looks at his watch, and then he begins to drum his fingers against the table top.

Katherine waits for a few moments and then she speaks again.

'Stuart, what's going on?'

The policeman looks at them all in turn, and then he suddenly gets up. He opens the door and steps out into the corridor. Stuart Lewis looks at his watch and then he too stands.

'Stuart, what on earth is going on? I think Gabriel has some right to know, don't you?'

The lawyer glances again at his watch, and then he looks smugly at Katherine.

'Well, that's it. The Crown's lawyer has failed to turn up, and the girl is refusing to testify, so it's over. I've informed the police that you're taking care of his application for asylum, and so as long as you've filed his papers, he's all yours.'

'So all criminal charges are dropped?'

'The chief witness for the prosecution won't co-operate, so that's pretty much it. The case is over, but Mr Gabriel is not a popular man in these parts. You *have* filed his papers for asylum?' Katherine nods. 'Well, while things are being processed, I would suggest that Mr Gabriel get as far away from here as possible.'

Katherine stares at Stuart Lewis, who straightens his tie and then pushes his glasses up the bridge of his nose.

'Are you going?'

Stuart Lewis seems surprised by the question.

'Of course I'm going. Without the girl there's no case, and I've got other things to attend to. Is there anything else?'

Gabriel looks now at Katherine, who seems confused. She holds her arms out in a gesture of helplessness.

'Well, I suppose not. It's just that it's all a bit sudden.' The lawyer moves towards the door.

'Good luck.' He pauses and then looks at Gabriel. 'To you both, I mean.' He closes the door after he leaves, and Gabriel and Katherine are left alone.

'Did you understand all of that?' Gabriel does not answer, so Katherine edges her way around the table and sits next to him. 'Gabriel, it's over. The girl has refused to co-operate, so the Crown has had to drop the case. You're free to go, but Stuart is suggesting that you go far away. I think he's right. It's not going to be easy if you stay around here, but that's not what you want, is it?' Gabriel shakes his head. 'Look, I'll be honest with you, love. Your application's in and you're supposed to stick around here, where they'll house you and feed you as a refugee till they decide if they'll accept you. My colleagues in the local office here will take care of you.' Katherine pauses. 'But the truth is, love, with this hanging over your head, people around here are not going to forget you. You'll not get a fair hearing.'

Gabriel does not know what to say, and so he waits for Katherine to say something further that will break the silence. Then Katherine takes out a small notepad from her handbag and she begins to write in it.

'Gabriel, I'm going to give you my address in London.' Katherine tears a piece of paper out of her pad and hands it to Gabriel. 'Drop me a line if you need anything, but between you and me, your best bet is to do a runner. I shouldn't be telling you this, but it's true. Stuart's right, the press have been all over this case. In fact, even London will be a bit dodgy, given the publicity that you've had. Go north. You've not really got any papers, so call yourself something else. Take a chance up there as they won't know who you are.'

'But I did nothing wrong.'

Katherine touches his arm.

'I'm not disputing this, Gabriel. It's just that people always assume that there's no smoke without fire. I know it's unfair, but that's how it is.'

Gabriel looks closely at the piece of paper that Katherine has given him.

'Can you read it?'

Gabriel nods and Katherine smiles.

'Well, that's it then.'

'Will I be going back to the prison?'

'I shouldn't think so. You don't really have anything, do you?' Gabriel produces his crumpled book from his pocket. 'Well, if that's it, then you're all set. I'd give you a lift as far as London, but I've got to go across to Dover for another case.' Katherine pauses. 'You haven't any money, have you?'

He watches as Katherine reaches into her purse and takes out some notes. First the woman is sharing her private address with him, and now she is offering him money, but Gabriel will not take the money, for this is too much. He looks away, but Katherine is insistent.

'Gabriel, I am going to leave it right here on the table and I want you to take it. You never know.'

'I do not need your money.'

'I beg your pardon?' Katherine's voice is suddenly filled with indignation.

Gabriel is shocked by his words and he speaks again. 'I am sorry. Thank you.'

'Good.' Katherine stands. 'I know one of the policemen pretty well. I'll ask him to give you a lift to the train station in the next town so you can get away from the journalists. I'll tell him I'm meeting you there later or something. Wait until he goes, and then you're on your own.' She momentarily stares at him. 'But I expect you're used to that, aren't you?'

Gabriel stares back at her.

'Good luck, Gabriel.' Katherine closes the door behind her.

Gabriel sits and stares at the money. Then he reaches over and picks up the two notes and pushes them into his trouser pocket.

Gabriel feels the weight of a hand upon his shoulder and the sour smell of a man's breath on his face.

'Keep it down, mate. You'll have the whole of Scotland Yard down on our heads if you're not careful.'

Gabriel looks at the scruffy, unkempt man, whose straggly beard momentarily frightens him. The man's skin is pale, almost waxen, and now that the man is sure he has Gabriel's attention, he takes a step back. Gabriel looks around himself and he begins to remember. The policeman bundled him into the back of a car, but this policeman did not handcuff him, nor did he wait for a driver. He pulled his door closed, and then he began to drive out into the countryside. As he did so he tormented Gabriel, asking him about the girl, and what it was like, and how Gabriel would feel if he were to do the same thing to Gabriel's sister or to his mother. Gabriel had no choice but to listen, but the longer this man talked, the more convinced Gabriel became that the man intended to beat him, or take him to a place where a group of his friends would be waiting to kill him.

Just as Gabriel was beginning to think that in order to save his life he should open the door and jump out and run into a field, they began to approach another town. The policeman did not drive as quickly, and he stopped talking. Eventually the man turned off the engine and sauntered around to the back of the car, where he held open the door and simply said, 'Get out.' Gabriel quickly stepped out and onto the pavement, and the man slammed shut the door and said nothing further. Gabriel watched as the car raced off. He felt in his pocket to make sure that he still had the money that the woman had given to him, and then he turned and walked into the train station and towards the place where people were buying tickets.

Some hours later a cold and hungry Gabriel found himself wandering the overcast streets of London, a city bathed in the weak yellow glare of afternoon street lights. The sky was a grey blanket that hung limply over Gabriel's head, while all around him traffic roared so that no matter which direction he walked in, it was impossible to escape the terrible noise. He discovered the broad majesty of the river, where the crowds were less dense, and he stared in wonder at the great buildings that lined each bank. However, Gabriel could take no pleasure in these incredible sights for there was, as yet, no order to his life. He was lost. He wandered to the centre of one of the many bridges, and he stared down into the blackness and, for a moment, Gabriel wondered what it would be like to drop down into the cool water, having first spiralled through his own reflection. Perhaps he might find peace in the silence and stillness that lay beneath London's silvery vein. As a sudden washing of traffic across the bridge shook him to his senses, Gabriel decided to leave this river and once more give himself purpose by searching for Bright among the endless streets of the city. However, as a troubled day gave way to the consternation of the night, this task began to overwhelm Gabriel and he was soon eager to abandon his quest.

Night fell quickly, and Gabriel was concerned that a policeman might apprehend him and start to ask difficult questions. He had walked for many miles and his right leg had now begun to distract him, and Gabriel not only wished to feel safe, but was also in desperate need of a place where he might rest. At the point when Gabriel thought that he could probably walk no further, he stumbled upon an unlit park where, through the gloom, he noticed that many men appeared to have settled down to sleep on the benches. The first bench that he sat on disgusted him, for it was only after he leaned back and stretched out that he realised he was sitting next to a used condom that looked as though it had been filleted and opened like a cleaned fish. Gabriel found a different bench and as he lay down he kept his eyes open. Although he was tired he did not feel safe, so he stared at the tree above his head, the large branches hanging over him like a big black canopy. And then he noticed more of them, hanging in the branches like discarded rubber fruit, but he was too tired to move. He rehearsed the events of the day in his mind, a day which had begun in an English prison and was now ending with him lying on a park bench in the capital city of London. And then suddenly the man with the waxen face was upon him, and the sky was bright and clear, and Gabriel realised that he must have fallen asleep.

'You've got to keep it down round here.' The man steps back towards Gabriel and sits down on the edge of the bench. 'You're new, aren't you? I can always tell a new one. You're disturbed.' The man taps the side of his head with his finger. 'Up here. That's where you're disturbed. I'm right, aren't I?' He does not wait for a reply. 'You're worried about your family. You can't figure out how you got yourself into this situation, that's it, isn't it? I know I'm right, aren't I?' The man laughs quickly and slaps Gabriel's thigh. 'Well, go on, admit it.' The man continues to chuckle to himself.

'For me this is not a good situation.'

The man seems somewhat mystified by Gabriel's response, so he waits, but Gabriel says nothing further.

'What do you mean, it's not a good situation?' Gabriel knows that it is foolish to trust the first stranger that he meets, so he decides that he will not tell this man any more. 'You're one of those refugee blokes, aren't you?' The man seems to visibly relax now that he imagines that he has solved the mystery of Gabriel's identity. 'You're one of those blokes, aren't you? Coming into this country to sponge off the welfare state. That's what they say about you lot.' Gabriel looks at this man, and then he speaks slowly.

'I have not come to this country to take from anybody.'

His new friend seems immediately cheered by this news.

'Well, that's good then. Here, my name's Jimmy.' He sticks out a grubby hand, which Gabriel shakes cautiously. 'Well, come on then, cat got your tongue? What's your name?'

'Gabriel.' He utters his one word and then waits for the man to speak again.

'Nice name, Gabriel.' The man pauses and he points to Gabriel's book, which is falling out of his pocket. 'So what you got in there?'

'My book.' Gabriel pushes the book back into place.

'Oh, you're a big reader then, are you?'

'Sometimes I write things down.'

'Well, that's handy. Helps you to remember, right?' Gabriel looks at the man, but he says nothing. The man continues. 'You know, if you're so much of a reader, we can go and get some mags and get busy.' Gabriel looks puzzled, but the man continues. 'You know, the guide mags. Buy 'em for half the price that we sell 'em for. Keep the rest.' Gabriel has no idea what this filthy man is talking about, but he does not want to give him the wrong impression.

'I am poor. I do not have any money.'

'None at all?' Gabriel shakes his head. 'Well, sometimes they might trust you if you've got a friendly face.' The man looks closely at Gabriel. 'You know, you've got a lucky face. Anybody ever tell you that?' Gabriel shakes his head. 'I used to think I was lucky till I was had up for drunken driving twice in one week. That's when my luck ran out.' He laughs now. 'It ran out all right, and the bugger's never come back to me.'

Gabriel follows this man out of the park, across a wide road that takes them an age to negotiate, and then through a succession of streets that seem to dead-end into each other, until they come to a tall office block, which is clearly their destination. There are other 'Jimmys' both going into and coming out of the building, and Gabriel begins to panic, fearing that this man might be about to trick him out of his money. He pushes his hands deep into his trouser pockets and clutches the single note and loose coins, and then he reminds himself that, if necessary, he will fight this man, and any others, who attempt to treat him ill. Once they pass inside the building, Gabriel relaxes, for the man appears to know exactly what to do and there are many others present. His new friend approaches a woman who sits behind a desk and he hands her a fist full of coins. The woman counts the money, and then she begins to count ten copies from a bank of magazines that are piled up in front of her.

'How are you today, my love?'

Jimmy grins. She looks at Gabriel and then she looks back to Jimmy. She gestures with her head.

'Friend of yours, is he?'

The man says nothing as he tucks his magazines under his arm. Gabriel, however, notices scorn in the pout of the woman's lips.

Once they return to the street, Jimmy's eyes blaze. 'Fucking bitch.'

Gabriel is taken aback by this outburst, but he says nothing to the man, who now hands him half the magazines.

'It's best if we find two different places. We can meet up this evening and you can give me half the money and you keep the rest for yourself.' The man points across the street to an empty doorway. 'You take that spot. Hold the magazine up and just say, "Only a quid" or something like that. You understand the money, don't you?'

Gabriel does not understand the money, but he thinks it best not to trouble his friend any further so he nods and says, 'Yes.' Jimmy points towards the other end of the street.

'I'll be somewhere down there if you need me. I might be around the corner, but I'm around.'

With this said, the man walks off, and Gabriel watches him until he is swallowed up by the pedestrians and disappears from view.

Left by himself, Gabriel crosses the street and stands in the doorway as instructed. He holds the magazines aloft, but none of the passers-by seem in the slightest bit curious and none of them will meet his eyes. And then, after nearly one whole hour of enduring people looking through him as though he did not exist, Gabriel decides that he will find his new friend and regretfully return the magazines. He will thank him for his kind offer of help, but explain that he is in search of a friend, Bright, and he must focus on this one task. Gabriel rolls up the magazines and carefully places them in his jacket, but as he prepares to move off he notices that a man has stopped in front of him, and the man is looking at Gabriel as though he has suddenly recognised a long-lost relative. The man seems to be incapable of speech, and so Gabriel speaks first.

'Do I know you?'

The man now points his arm at Gabriel, like a gun. 'I am not sure. Perhaps. I think you are from my country.'

Gabriel waits for the man to say more, but the man seems incapable of further speech. Gabriel says the name of his country, and suddenly the man is overcome with emotion and he looks as though he is going to cry. He opens both arms wide.

'My brother, I cannot believe this. I have been here in England for so long and now I am finally with a countryman.' He laughs and offers his hand to Gabriel. 'Emmanuel. They call me Emmanuel.'

Gabriel shakes the man's hand, but an excited Emmanuel seems reluctant to let go.

'Come, let us go for a drink and talk about what is happening.'

'Right now?'

'Do you have anything else to do? Please, you will come with me. There is plenty of time for selling of papers. And besides, now is not the best time while everyone is at work. Come, please. This is just unbelievable.'

Emmanuel leads the way, taking left turns and right turns in quick succession, and Gabriel hurries after him, too embarrassed to explain to this excitable man that his injury prevents him from rushing like this.

At this time of the morning the pub is half-empty, but Gabriel is fascinated by the velvet-clad wooden chairs and the dimly lit chandeliers, and the torn curtains. In the dark, smoky atmosphere a few people are reading the newspaper, but most are simply alternating between drinking and staring into mid-air. Emmanuel suddenly looks embarrassed.

'Have you any money, my brother?'

Gabriel reaches into his pocket and takes out what is left of the money that Katherine gave to him. Emmanuel takes the single note and the few coins and he points to a seat.

'You wait there. I will bring the beer.'

Gabriel does as he is told, but he keeps a wary eye on Emmanuel, who goes to the bar and says something to the barman. The barman pours the beer into glasses and hands them to Emmanuel, who offers him some money and then waits for the change. Gabriel notices that Emmanuel pockets the money before bringing the two large glasses of beer over to where Gabriel is seated awkwardly with his knees steepled in the narrow gap between the chair and the edge of the low table.

'The nectar of life,' says Emmanuel, as he sits. He raises his glass. 'Cheers.'

Gabriel holds out his hand.

'You have money for me?'

Emmanuel laughs. 'Of course, but we are having more drinks. Do you not trust me?'

Gabriel tries not to sound too threatening, but his tone is clear.

'I prefer to have my money in my own pocket.'

Emmanuel laughs and puts his hand into his pocket and pulls out a handful of coins.

'You can count it, it is all there.' Gabriel cannot tell if it is all there, but he immediately pushes the coins into his pocket. Emmanuel takes another deep drink of his beer, and then he takes out a crumpled cigarette packet and raps it on the table top as though an actor in a movie. He offers the packet to Gabriel, who politely holds up his hand, but Gabriel is unable to stem the volley of questions. He watches the blue spurt of an ignited match as Emmanuel lights a cigarette and then blows out a huge circle of smoke. And then Emmanuel continues to fire off questions, and he asks his new friend how long he has been in England, and why he came, and how he arrived, and if he came alone, and Gabriel carefully answers all of Emmanuel's questions, but the more this man asks, the clearer it becomes to Gabriel that he is not going to reveal anything of himself to Emmanuel. His countryman drains his glass of beer and bangs it back down upon the table.

'Another, my brother?'

Gabriel pushes his hand into his pocket and hands some coins to Emmanuel.

'I am just going to the toilet and then I will be back.'

Gabriel narrows his eyebrows, and Emmanuel registers the look of suspicion.

'Or maybe you would like to go to the bar for the drinks?' He holds out the money for Gabriel to take, but Gabriel shakes his head. Emmanuel laughs and gets to his feet. 'Finally, you are learning to relax, man. You are in England now. If we do not trust each other, then how are we going to get along? The English think they are superior so they do not care about us. We have only each other. Every day people come up to me and abuse me, but there is nothing that I can do. I have no choice but to be here. And in order to survive among these people, I have to be private and quiet. But when I meet somebody from back home I want to be myself, I want to open up.'

Gabriel watches as Emmanuel pads his way across the dirty

carpet towards a door marked 'Gentlemen'. Gabriel still has some of his beer to drink, and as he lifts the glass to his mouth he looks around at these people. This is not the England that he thought he was travelling to, and these shipwrecked people are not the people that he imagined he would discover. Under this sad roof, life is stripped of ambition and it is broken. Gabriel takes another sip of the warm beer, but this beer is not to his taste. He decides to ask Emmanuel to order a different type of beer, but there is no sign of Emmanuel. Gabriel continues to wait, until the thought finally crosses his mind that he might be alone. Abandoning his beer, he slowly stands up and crosses the room until he reaches the door marked 'Gentlemen'. Once inside he can see that Emmanuel has climbed out of the open window. It is so simple. Gabriel leaves the filthy toilet and walks back into the pub and then out onto the street. He looks first left, then right, but Gabriel is unsure of which direction he should turn in order that he might find Jimmy. He imagines that Jimmy will be thinking that he has sold the magazines and made off with the money. Gabriel puts his hand into his pocket and pulls out the few coins that he has left. He also pulls out a piece of paper and notices Katherine's address.

The London sky has darkened like a bruise, and Gabriel still does not recognise a single building that he walks past, or a junction that he crosses, or a street that he turns into. For hours he has searched for first Jimmy, then Emmanuel, and finally Bright, but he now understands that these directionless streets were not laid out to welcome the feet of newcomers. And then it begins to rain, and umbrellas open up all around him like impatient flowers, and those without umbrellas move hastily as though they are trying to step between the drops of rain, and a sodden Gabriel simply holds the piece of paper before him as though it were a passport of some kind. He asks an

Englishman in a suit and tie if he knows the way to Katherine's address, but the man stares at Gabriel as though he is in the presence of a madman and he barely looks at the damp piece of paper. Gabriel asks another man, who waves him away, and then another man who studies the paper for a while. He is a younger man and he dresses casually, as though he is on his way out for the night as opposed to going home from work. Finally the man gives the paper back to Gabriel, and then he points.

'Get a bus down there. Number thirty-eight. Ask the conductor to put you out on Upper Street, and then just ask anybody.'

'Thank you. I am very grateful.' Gabriel smiles at the man.

'Got any money?'

Gabriel nods. 'I have a little.'

'Well, if you smartened yourself up a bit, I could show you how to make some easy money.'

Gabriel looks at the man, who points to the copies of the magazines that are sticking out of his pocket.

'There are easier ways of making money than that, or has nobody told you the facts of life?'

Gabriel remains baffled.

'You don't get it, do you?'

Gabriel begins to walk away from this man, who now laughs and shouts after him.

'Let me know if you need somebody to be your daddy.'

Gabriel does not turn around. In his own country he would have killed this man and nobody would have held him responsible for his actions. A disgusted Gabriel can barely contain his anger as he walks, and then he discovers the bus stop and he joins a short line. He stands behind a poverty-stricken woman who carries her small child in her arms. Gabriel looks closely and is surprised to see that the child has two earrings in each ear, but it is the small nose, which looks as though it has been finger-moulded out of damp clay, that shocks him, for it contains a large gold stud.

When the bus comes he follows the woman onto it, but he sits downstairs in a seat by himself. Gabriel is relieved that the bus conductor is a West Indian man, and he holds out his coins.

'I wish to go to Upper Street, please.'

The man takes a single coin. 'I'll let you know, mate.' He winks at Gabriel as he says this.

Gabriel is too frightened to respond, so instead he looks out of the window. His mind drifts and it occurs to Gabriel that he might arrive at Katherine's house and then discover that she is not there. She may still be working, or she may have gone out for the evening, but as he continues to think about these possibilities his eyes begin to close.

'Upper Street, mate.'

Gabriel stands up and the conductor points to his rolled-up magazines.

'You selling them or wearing them?' The man laughs.

'Would you like one?' Gabriel peels a single copy out of his pocket, and the man laughs and gives Gabriel a coin in exchange for the magazine.

'You'll have to be a bit more in-your-face if you want to get rid of them.'

Gabriel steps from the bus and looks around as it pulls away. He takes out the piece of paper with Katherine's address on it, and he approaches a man who, even at this late hour, is still selling newspapers. Gabriel simply says, 'Please', and shows the man the piece of paper. The man pushes his glasses up and onto the top of his head so that they are nesting in his hair, and then he squints at the writing in the gloom.

'Over there, mate.' He points across the road. 'Just go down the street over there. It's on the left.'

Gabriel thanks the man, and as he crosses the road, the London sky once again begins to weep gentle rain. He holds his gaping jacket together, and he walks cautiously down the side street until he comes to number twenty-seven. He can see that this is an affluent neighbourhood, for the houses have gardens at the front that are neat and well maintained. Also, the cars that are parked on this street are all expensive models that Gabriel recognises as the type that ministers or businessmen in his country liked to drive. However, there is one car that disturbs Gabriel, for a metal coat hanger has been twisted into the shape of a crushed diamond, then hopelessly inserted into a hole in the bonnet to serve as a radio aerial. This car suddenly reminds Gabriel of home, and of his own dreams of one day owning a vehicle, but he turns from the car and its makeshift aerial and realises that he has finally discovered the house.

The lights are on, so Gabriel knows that Katherine is at home, but he is now unsure of what he might say to her. He unfastens the gate and walks gingerly up the path. Once he reaches the door, Gabriel presses the bell, but nothing happens, so he knocks at the door, and as he waits he hears, somewhere in the distance, the thin, high-pitched whistle of what he imagines to be a passing train. After a few moments, Katherine appears before him with a book in one hand. She is wearing dark-rimmed glasses, which make her appear older.

'Gabriel? What are you doing here?'

Gabriel does not know what to say. Katherine is not being particularly friendly, which only deepens his embarrassment.

'I'm sorry,' he stammers. 'I should not be disturbing you like this, but I have no money. I have been robbed.'

Katherine looks alarmed, and then the door opens wider and a much older man with grey hair appears at Katherine's shoulder. Katherine turns to him.

'Leonard, this is Gabriel. The man I was telling you about from the coast. The one whose case was dismissed.'

Leonard speaks to Katherine without taking his eyes from Gabriel. 'Yes, of course I remember him. What's he doing here?'

Katherine is now visibly angry. 'Leonard!' she snaps, but the man just turns from Gabriel and disappears inside. Katherine sighs deeply, and then she looks again at the stranger on her doorstep.

'Just give me a minute, Gabriel.' Katherine pushes the door closed, and she leaves Gabriel by himself.

Gabriel hears raised voices and it is clear that both people are angry, but the louder the man shouts, the more Katherine seems to be able to match him in volume and intensity. As Gabriel listens he wonders if he should just leave now, for clearly he is the cause of this conflict. As he thinks about whether to turn and walk away, Katherine reappears at the door with her coat on.

'Come on, Gabriel.' Katherine slams the door behind her and marches down the garden path, leaving Gabriel in her wake. 'Trust me, Gabriel, you don't want to stay here.' Katherine opens the door to a small blue car and then climbs in. She leans over and pushes open the passenger door for Gabriel. 'Get in, get in.'

Gabriel folds himself into the small car and he sits next to Katherine.

'Seat belt.' Gabriel looks blankly at her. 'Put on your seat belt.' Katherine leans over and somewhat impatiently straps him into place. Gabriel feels embarrassed, for although he knows what seat belts are, he is not used to seeing people use them. Katherine lights a cigarette, and then she starts the engine. She holds the packet of cigarettes out to Gabriel, but he shakes his head. Katherine pushes them back into her bag, and then she engages the gear and swings the car out into the street and screeches away. Katherine drives for some minutes before she speaks.

'Gabriel, I'm sorry about that. Leonard knows about the case and, like everybody else, he thinks that there's probably something to it.'

Gabriel says nothing and Katherine shoots him a quick glance.

'I'm talking about the girl, Gabriel. I told him, and he also read about it in the papers.'

Gabriel nods so that Katherine will know that he understands what she is talking about. Katherine continues to drive, and Gabriel stares out of the window, where the rain seems to be getting heavier.

'Gabriel, I'm taking you to the motorway so that you can hitch a ride. Just ask to be put out somewhere in the North. Lorry drivers love having people to talk to, especially at night.' They stop now at a traffic light, and Katherine reaches into her bag and pulls out a single note. 'You weren't hurt when you were robbed, were you?'

Gabriel shakes his head.

'No, it was one of my own people. He tricked me.'

Katherine laughs. 'Welcome to England. Look, tuck this away for emergencies.' She pushes the note into Gabriel's hand, then changes gear and pulls away from the traffic light. 'It might help with food or something. I'm sure you'll find some kind of work in the North, and you really should become somebody else, Gabriel. I know you don't want to do this, but it will really help.' She pauses. 'Unfortunately, there's plenty of Leonards in the world.'

Gabriel does not know what to say in reply to this, so he simply looks out of the window as they drive on in silence through the seemingly endless streets of London. Katherine turns on the radio, but the pop music only seems to deepen the sense of embarrassment that Gabriel feels. It is shameful to have placed himself at the mercy of this woman, and to have troubled her life in this manner. However, as hard as he tries, he can think of nothing he might say that would repair the damage between them. As he once more turns to look out of the window, he feels Katherine beginning to slow the car down, and then she pulls over to the left-hand side of the road.

'I'm going to let you out here, Gabriel.' She pauses. 'Not much I can do about the rain, I'm afraid.' She points now to where the road divides. 'I'm going to the right, but you should just walk around the corner to the left and you'll soon get a lift, if you start to hitch. You know, put out your thumb, like this.' Katherine demonstrates. 'Just remember you want to go north.' Gabriel nods. 'Gabriel, I'm sorry I can't do more for you than this, but as you can see I've got things to sort out at home.'

Gabriel prepares to open the door to the car. Although he knows that Katherine is dismissing him, he is not angry.

'Thank you, Katherine.'

She smiles at Gabriel. 'I'm sorry, love.' Katherine points to the copies of Jimmy's magazine. 'You can leave them. You won't be needing them where you're going.'

Gabriel takes them from his pocket, hands them to Katherine, and then he climbs out of the car and into the rain.

'Good luck.' Katherine tosses the magazines onto the now empty passenger seat, then she leans over and blows Gabriel a kiss. 'I feel bad putting you out in this weather, but don't you worry, somebody will soon take pity.' Katherine pulls in the car door. Gabriel stands and watches as Katherine indicates, then moves out and into the traffic. He stares at her small blue car until it disappears around the corner and out of sight.

Gabriel walks towards the point where the road divides. There are no other people in sight, only cars and lorries that roar past him at high speed. Gabriel sees a figure in the windswept, sodden gloom with a thumb turned up in the manner that Katherine demonstrated. This makes Gabriel feel somewhat better as he has no desire to be alone in this desolate place. However, as he moves closer he can see that his fellow hitch-hiker is a young woman, and as she notices Gabriel moving towards her, the alarm in her eyes is unmistakable. Her mouth half-opens, as though a cry is being stifled somewhere at the back of her throat, but Gabriel has little choice but to lower his eyes and continue to walk towards her.

The girl points again to the plastic bag that Gabriel is holding on his lap.

'Well, go on then. Have some more food. What's the matter with you?'

Gabriel shakes his head, then he shields his eyes from the light that is spilling in through the cracked windows.

'No, thank you. I am fine.'

He bristles with anger at the way this girl is speaking to him, but he tries hard to control these feelings and to recognise that the girl has been generous for, as promised, she has returned with food. However, he finds her manner irritating, and her appearance, with her dirty, unwashed blonde hair, and her skirt riding up her thigh, is unacceptable.

'You're not hungry any more, is that it?' Now she seems child-like, and almost hurt.

Gabriel puts the bag on the floor and looks at the girl.

'Do you have parents? And please, do they know that you are not at school?'

She laughs and tosses her head as though to indicate the stupidity of the question.

'I already told you, my dad's unemployed and my mum left ages ago. I don't know where she is. Got no idea.'

'But does your father not want you to go to school?'

'He doesn't care, does he? I sometimes work at McDonald's and he likes that because it means if he fancies a Big Mac and fries, he doesn't have to pay for it. He spends nearly all his giro on booze. Why should he care if I go to school or not?'

Gabriel suspects that this line of questioning is annoying her, so he says nothing further. They fall into silence, which she finally breaks by pointing to his leg.

'Is it better now?'

Gabriel taps his leg, as though to reassure himself.

'Yes, it is much better, thank you. I think it will be fine.'

'You got here on a boat, didn't you? One of the cross-Channel ferries.'

'I hurt myself when I jumped into the water.' She shakes her head now.

'It's a wonder you're alive. It's bleeding freezing out there. I wouldn't go in that water if you paid me. Barry, he used to be a lifeboat man. I told him he's mad doing something like that, but he wouldn't listen. He's my old boyfriend. But he dumped me because I suppose he got frightened on account of my being too young. He could have gone to prison, but I didn't care. Anyhow that's all he wanted to do, just start on right away, then get to the pub.' Gabriel continues to listen to her, but she is no longer making any sense. 'What's Africa like? It's not really jungle and animals, is it? I know that much. My dad probably thinks it is, but he's never been anywhere in his life. Claims he once went to Southampton, but that's about it. He says if you live by the water you don't need to go anywhere because all the world comes to you, but that's a load of rubbish. That's just his excuse for being a lazy sod.'

Gabriel has no idea how to participate in this conversation, but he has no desire to embarrass the girl with his silence. And then, as though sensing Gabriel's bewilderment, the girl gets to her feet and announces that she has to go now.

'I can come back later, if you like. You ever had fish and chips? I can bring you some.'

Gabriel looks at the girl standing before him in her school uniform, imagining that she is already a woman. He reminds himself that in his country many girls of her age already have babies and responsibilities, and they do not swear, and they are not abusive about their parents, and they would never sit alone with a man in this way. It is difficult for Gabriel to tell if this girl is typical of all English girls, but although he remains grateful to her for bringing him food, he still does not trust her. She moves quickly to the door.

'I'll see you later then.'

Gabriel watches her walk down the path towards the road, and then her small, overweight body begins to run, as though she is late for an appointment.

Gabriel closes the door. He picks up the plastic bag, and then he looks inside and can see that it contains more bread and cheese. First, he drinks some more of the water, and then he eats quickly and without any concern for decorum. Having finished, Gabriel leans back in the chair and decides that he must follow Bright to London, and that he should leave as soon as possible. And then Gabriel feels somebody pulling his arm, and almost immediately a strange greasy smell wafts over him. Denise speaks loudly.

'Come on, wake up. I've brought you the fish and chips.'

Gabriel opens his eyes and sees Denise looking down at him. She thrusts a warm bundle of paper into his hands, and then she sits and begins to unwrap her own parcel.

'You should be careful, you know, about falling asleep like

that. You never know who might wander in.' She laughs out loud now, clearly amused by her own humour.

Although the smell of this food nauseates him, Gabriel begins to eat.

'Do you like it then?' Gabriel nods and he continues to eat. Then he remembers his manners.

'Thank you.'

'You're welcome.' Denise speaks with her mouth full.

Gabriel stares at the girl and tries to control his anger. 'Do you not eat meals with your father?'

Denise laughs so hard that she begins to cough.

'Are you all right?' Gabriel puts down his food and passes her the water, which she drinks, loudly.

'Some of it went down the wrong way.'

Gabriel does not feel like finishing his food so he wraps it back up in the paper. Denise resumes eating and she continues to speak with her mouth full.

'You haven't told me anything about yourself. You got a wife? And can you sing or dance or do something like that? I mean, I've seen you lot dance, it's like you're sweating away all your problems. Like you're in a trance or something, shaking your head and everything.'

'I cannot sing or dance.' He is about to tell her that he was a soldier, and that soldiers do not sing or dance, but he stops himself for he cannot share this information with a child.

'Well, you got a wife then?'

She is asking him questions that do not concern her, and it troubles him that she cannot see that he is a grown man and she is merely a child. She does not wait for him to answer.

'Me, I don't like families. Especially my dad.'

Gabriel is disquieted by the new tone of melancholy that floods this girl's voice. Denise lowers her eyes, and then she pushes the remains of her fish and chips to one side. Unlike

Gabriel she does not bother to wrap them up. Suddenly she seems distressed, and Gabriel feels moved to rescue her.

'I do not have a family,' says Gabriel. 'They were all killed in the war in my country. But I am here in your country because I wish to be able to take care of my children who are as yet unborn.'

'I don't get it.'

'I am thinking of the future. But God could make it easier for us all if he simply made it possible for my people to march out in peace. Back home many of us continue to suffer.'

She looks up at him.

'I wish they'd kill my dad.'

'You must not talk like that. It is evil to have such thoughts.'

'I'm not evil. He's the one who's evil.' Denise comes over to where Gabriel is sitting and she rolls up the sleeves of her sweater. 'These bruises, you see them?' She points to the bruises on her stubby arms. 'That's where I have to block the punches when he comes home pissed and starts on at me. Every now and then one gets through and I get a black eye or lose another tooth. Nice guy, eh? Which is why my mum left. She got it worse than me.' Gabriel looks at her bruises, and then at her young, outraged face. 'Then Barry, he started with his fists when I didn't do what he wanted. The pair of them are just the same. Anything to get their way. They're sick, all of them. Just sick.' And now the girl begins to shed silent tears, which unsettles Gabriel.

'Please do not disturb yourself like this.'

Gabriel puts his hand on her bare arm.

'Please. You are safe here. This is your safe place. There is no need to cry like this.'

Denise puts her head on Gabriel's shoulder and he can feel her body rising and falling as she continues to sob. He hears a soft pop as her lips separate, and he prepares to listen to her. But whatever it was the girl was going to say, she decides to stifle it inside. Gabriel understands that this house that he and Bright have stumbled across is, for this girl, a place of safety. His anger at her manner, and her way of speaking to him, begins to subside as he realises just how vulnerable she is. He puts his arm around her and holds her. There is something comforting about her young weight on his body, and Gabriel decides to stay in this position until she calms down.

The man on the bunk beneath Gabriel is clearly sick. He hawks and spits blood, and every time he does so he says something which to Gabriel sounds like a prayer. And then he apologises to Gabriel. After being in this cell for an hour, Gabriel is beginning to resign himself to the fact that in all likelihood he will be sent back to Africa. All the money, and the sacrifices of the journey, may have come to this. To be locked up in a prison cell with a sick man who, like himself, is a refugee in England. A man whose life seems also to have run aground. But Gabriel tries to remain strong. He has done nothing wrong. They simply fell asleep, that is all. They slept. In the morning, the girl's father led the police to the house, where he first attacked his daughter, and then began to beat Gabriel with a metal pipe until the police pulled him off.

The procedure at the police station was swift and disrespectful. Gabriel was photographed, fingerprinted, then charged and told that he could make one phone call before being transferred to the local prison. Once there, the day warder told Gabriel that he was lucky, for there was an immigration lawyer in the visiting room seeing somebody else, and that when she had finished she would come along to see him. In the meantime, the warder took Gabriel to a cell which already contained a sick man, and while Gabriel waited for the lawyer, he thought again of the girl and felt his mind beginning to wander. She had ridden to the police station in another car, and Gabriel imagined that she must be frightened. He worried about what she was saying, or what she had already said, but no matter what anybody might say, Gabriel knew that he did not force himself upon the girl. He had done nothing wrong. He was guilty of nothing that would bring shame on his family name. When Gabriel looked up he saw a woman standing silently by the door to his cell. The prison warder pointed.

'That's him. Do you want to talk to him?' Gabriel's eyes met those of a small, masculine woman who tucked a strand of loose hair away from her face and behind an ear. She looked up at the warder and nodded.

'Oi, you!' The warder shouted. 'Down here.'

Gabriel climbed down from the top bunk, and the warder addressed the woman.

'I'll give you five minutes to let him know what's what, then I'll be back. Any trouble, just shout.'

The warder walked off and left Gabriel standing with the woman. She looked over Gabriel's shoulder towards his cell-mate, but she said nothing about this man. She returned her gaze to Gabriel.

'Hi, I'm Katherine. I work for an immigration law firm and we should have a talk.' She waited, but her prospective client said nothing, so she continued. 'Your situation is made all the more complicated by the other charge. You do understand this, don't you?'

Gabriel knew the woman was trying to help, but he wanted her to understand.

'Please, I did nothing bad. The girl was not unhappy.'

Katherine arched her eyebrows. 'The girl is fifteen, Gabriel. The father says you were intimate with her. I'm going to get you a lawyer, and then the official charges will be brought by a Crown Prosecutor and you will have a chance to defend yourself.'

Gabriel clung tightly to the bars of the cell with both hands.

'But I did nothing wrong. You must believe me.'

The woman nodded, and then she pointed.

'That man, does he need some medical attention?'

Gabriel turned to look at his cellmate.

'I think he is suffering.' Having said this, Gabriel turned back to look at the woman. 'Please, I have done nothing wrong. And I cannot go back to my country or they will kill me.'

'Look, give me a day or so and we'll try to get you the best lawyer. Meanwhile, using what information you've already given to the police, I'll start the asylum procedures.' She paused. 'I'd better go now. The warder did this for me as a favour.' She looked again at his cellmate. 'And keep an eye on him. People have a habit of not calling a doctor in these places. Until it's too late, that is.'

Gabriel glanced at his cellmate, who seemed to be attempting to sleep, and then he looked again at Katherine, who smiled and nodded at the same time.

'I'll see you later, then.'

Gabriel watched the woman walk off, and long after she had disappeared from view he continued to stare after her, imagining that it would be from her direction that hope might eventually emerge.

Gabriel looks up and registers the girl's face transforming itself from alarm to outright fear, but he keeps walking through the driving rain. He is tempted to say 'hello', but he is unsure of how she might respond and so he once more lowers his eyes. He decides to stop some fifty yards past the girl, and he turns and peers back down the road. The girl appears to have recovered, for she once again holds her thumb out in the hope of attracting the attention of passing vehicles. But at present there is no traffic, only rain.

Gabriel waits. He holds out his thumb, but he does so

awkwardly as though embarrassed to find himself begging in this manner. And then a car splashes to a halt just beyond the girl, and Gabriel watches as she sprints the few yards and jumps in. The car speeds off and now Gabriel is alone. Once again the wind picks up, and the rain becomes torrential. There is no place to shelter, so Gabriel continues to hold out his thumb in the hope that somebody might take pity on him, but car after car, and lorry after lorry, swish by, their headlights cutting through the driving rain, but none stop for Gabriel. He thinks of Denise, and he wonders if she ever thinks of him. After all, she chose not to speak out against him. Surely she must think of him and wonder what has happened to her friend? Perhaps the honourable thing would be to go back and rescue her from her situation, but he understands that this would not be wise. As he continues to think about Denise, a lorry slows beyond him, its red tail-lights glowing in the darkness, and then it comes to a complete standstill. Gabriel walks tentatively towards the passenger side, his eyes stinging from the slashing rain. When he reaches the lorry, the passenger door swings open and a heavy-set man in a tight T-shirt peers down at Gabriel.

'You getting in, or have you got gills?'

Gabriel doesn't understand, but the man seems friendly enough. He climbs up and is suddenly embarrassed to be dripping water all over the man's seat. The man reaches behind his seat for a musty-smelling towel and he tosses it at Gabriel.

'Don't worry about the wet.' The man begins to pull out into the traffic, and then he starts to laugh. 'Look at the windows. You're steaming the place up.' He takes the towel from Gabriel and rubs the inside of the windows with it, and then he tosses it back at Gabriel. 'What were you doing out there, mate, building an ark?' The man laughs at his own humour and then he points to the radio. 'Do you want music or do you want to talk? You blokes seem to have a routine.'

'Thank you.'

The man looks quizzically at Gabriel and withdraws his hand from the radio controls. He looks again at Gabriel. 'Heading north, I take it?' Gabriel nods.

'Yes, please, north.'

The man registers this information and for a few moments he drives on in silence.

'Now you're not an Afro-Caribbean, are you?'

Gabriel shakes his head and speaks quietly.

'No, I am from Africa.'

'Africa!' exclaims the man, as though it all makes sense now. 'You wanna smoke?'

Again Gabriel shakes his head.

'What's your name, then?'

Gabriel thinks for a moment and then remembers what Katherine told him. 'Solomon,' he says. 'My name is Solomon.'

'Like in the Bible.' Gabriel nods.

'Yes, of course. Something like that.'

III

For a woman of her age she remains in pretty good shape. She was never a beauty, but in her day she was able to turn the odd head. A few men even whistled after her in the street. Not that they were *really* interested, but they noticed her, and then they stopped noticing her, and by the time she and Brian had entered their thirties she was walking down the street to silence. Brian seldom walked anywhere, for he preferred to drive his company car: to work, to the golf club, to his business dinners; Brian seldom bothered to put the car away in the garage. He justified his laziness by banging on about how dangerous the streets were these days, and how you only had to travel a mile or two in any direction to find yourself in the British equivalent of Beirut. He didn't like it when she reminded him of the Chadwicks, who were driving along the avenue at the end of the road and minding their own business when suddenly they were blocked in by two vans. Four men jumped out of the vans and bashed in their windscreen with monkey wrenches and took all their jewellery and money, and so to her way of thinking it didn't seem to matter much where you were these days, for people seemed to feel that they could pretty much do whatever they liked to you. There had even been a story in the local paper about a woman who was badly beaten up by a gang of kids in the park across the way when she tried to stop the young hooligans from mugging her six-year-old daughter for her bike. But because Brian never listened to her when she said that he ought to walk but just be vigilant, and because he used the preponderance of street crime to justify his laziness, Brian began to grow tubby. Their infrequent love-making became, for her, deeply connected with the problem of shifting one's weight. Brian hated her to mention his little potbelly, so she stayed quiet on this subject. Which was generally how they passed through their thirties and forties with each other. By staying quiet.

And then he left her, and the quietness intensified and threatened to overwhelm her until she noticed Mahmood. All things considered, she planned her assault quite well. Nice perfume, translucent nail polish, grey hair unbunned, and the neckline just daring enough to suggest that what lay beneath the horizon might still be worth exploring. And much to her surprise it worked. These days he arrives every Thursday evening at 7 p.m. precisely. Before he comes round she lights a dozen scented candles, and then she turns off the lights. She plumps the cushions, and places a white china bowl of mixed nuts on the glass-topped coffee table. She once tried savouries, but he did not take very well to them. Another time she tried music, but he listened for a while and then told her to turn it off. He did not ask her to turn it off, he ordered her with one hand busily pulling his lobe, as though her choice of Chopin had somehow damaged his oriental ear. These days she does not bother with either savouries or music. At 7 p.m. he knocks twice, and then he rattles the letterbox so that the flap clatters noisily. She has lost count of the number of times she has suggested to him that knocking at the door is sufficient, but he seems to be helplessly addicted to the letterbox. However, as she quickly draws the curtains and then pads her way to the door, she reminds herself that this annoying little habit of his is just another part of their ritual.

Mahmood is tall and striking. To begin with he used to step through the door and bend and kiss her on the forehead before stooping to unlace his shoes. He would place them side by side, like soldiers, in the hallway and then follow her into the candlelit living room. Back then he was slightly apprehensive, and she liked the way his eyes danced nervously around the room without ever alighting on anything. She loved his smell, which was strangely sweet and cloying, but she knew that it did not mask anything unpleasant. Mahmood was scrupulously clean, and she understood that whatever oils or lotions he rubbed into his skin were in all likelihood related to his culture, and she did not mind. In fact, back then she did not mind anything about him. Since Brian had left she had only entertained one other man, a recently widowed partner of Brian's from the bank. However, this man had come to visit wearing a parka, some grubby slacks and trainers, not the suit and tie and the smartly polished shoes that she had been expecting. It was a Sunday afternoon, but there was still no excuse for such ill manners. He demanded a piece of lemon wedge with his tea, and he seemed disappointed that she was only able to offer milk and a tablespoon of honey that she managed to scrape from the bottom of an old jar. He then proceeded to praise his former wife's abilities at knitting tea cosies and bed socks, and he lectured her on the excessive calories in date and walnut cake. She offered him a digestive biscuit instead, but he refused, and then when he went to leave she was forced to momentarily endure the rough wood of his tongue in her mouth.

It was after this visit that she planned her campaign with Mahmood who, at least initially, managed to exude both coyness and interest. These days Mahmood has dispensed with this performance. Mahmood manages to meet her eyes before stepping first on the heel of one foot, then on the heel of the other, and wriggling his way out of his shoes. He still lines them up next to each other, but after such a dismal approach to their removal, this gesture seems almost insulting in its affected formality. She is relieved that he still seems amenable to eating first, for to dispense with the etiquette of the shared meal would be to abandon dignity. However, 'dignity' is a word that Mahmood seems to be increasingly unfamiliar with. These days he eats quickly, often with one hand (always his right hand), and he makes noises that alarm her. Today is no exception. Having finished, he stares at her as she clumsily moves a piece of chicken breast up and onto the back of her fork. He watches closely as she dips the fork into the rice and then dabs the whole construction in a shallow pool of curry sauce before levering it towards her mouth. It is painful, for she understands that he is suppressing laughter.

In bed she knows that she satisfies. He always shudders, but he does so quickly now and only once. These days their bodies separate with indifference and Mahmood is quick to give her his back. Sadly, her lover seems to have bolted down the short slope from attentive to perfunctory without any intervening stages of incremental boredom. One week he took the time to speak with her before, during and, most importantly, after their relations. The following week he was racing through the motions as though he was late for an appointment. Gone were the revealing half-sentences. 'They call us Asians, but that doesn't mean anything, does it?' Or personal titbits that she could take as signs of intimacy. 'When I see my reflection in a mirror I know that I can never go back home.' He used to listen to her when she explained what an electric blanket was, or when she told him what the difference was between a bishop and a priest. When she suggested that he read 'improving' books, he took the trouble to ask her what she meant, and her use of the phrase 'birthday suits' actually made him laugh out loud. They were, of course, in their 'birthday suits' at the time. He kept laughing and repeating the phrase as though unable to comprehend the absurd precision of the imagery, and she laughed along with him. Today she bore his weight and coquettishly wrapped one leg around him as though she wished to pull him deeper. But she did not; it was all show. A gesture to prevent her from feeling as though she was merely an object speared.

She does not blame Mahmood for her present degradation, for she understands the real culprit to be Brian. She silently endured too many years of his conversation in the form of monologues about the virtues of architecturally designed patios and breakfast bars, and the superiority of South African whites over French Chardonnay, conversations in which her opinions were never sought. On other days he would simply seize a seemingly random topic and start to complain. Did she realise that you used to be able to see a specific doctor, but now everywhere's a group practice and you never know who the hell you will be getting? Was she aware of the fact that because of the bloody unions, his bank employees were now only allowed to 'interface' with the public from behind 'anger-proof' glass? She quickly learned that Brian had absolutely no interest in her opinions, but by not answering back she allowed him to look through and beyond her, until he finally convinced himself that she did not exist. When Brian walked away, she too was convinced that he was walking away from nothing, and it hurt. However, at least to begin with, Mahmood did not treat her as though she were invisible.

She stares at his back. To be desired is not unpleasant, and to be mounted and entered suggests desire. In the beginning she toyed with the idea of asking him to find a way to stay over. She wanted him to tell Feroza that he had to visit his brother in Leicester, but somehow she never found the courage to put this proposal before him, and he never suggested it to her of his own accord. One night she did ask Mahmood if the next day they might go to the town museum to see a visiting exhibition of priceless Eastern miniatures, but he looked at her with disbelief writ large across his brown face. With some effort she was able to imagine that his curdled face was rejecting the art and not her company. She smiled. But inwardly she decided that she would never again suggest anything beyond the boundaries of their arrangement. She was not a woman who coped well with rejection. But, if truth be told, Mahmood had not rejected her. He had simply arrived at a place where he no longer felt it necessary to either woo or enchant his fifty-five-year-old mistress.

Strangely enough, she still trusts this lithe man who briefly visits her table on the way to her bed. When he first spoke to her outside the confines of the newsagent's shop, he did so with a candour that she was sure Feroza had never been privileged to hear. He sat in her living room loudly sipping strong tea, and nervously rubbing one blue-socked foot on top of the other. She told him that last week she had been furious at the ill manners of the woman ahead of her in the queue at the shop. The woman had complained that she could smell curry on her copy of *Hello!* magazine, and when poor Mahmood had offered to refund her money, the rude so-and-so had simply stormed out. But they both knew that by itself this incident did not explain her asking him over for tea. She had framed the invitation as an opportunity for social intercourse and cultural exchange in an English home, but as he continued to sip loudly at his tea, her conversation stumbled and she heard herself comment that they had not had much weather of late, and then she fell silent and waited for him to talk. Which, in due course, he seemed eager to do. He told her about his first marriage at the age of twelve in his Punjabi village, and how his family had arranged everything without any concern for his feelings. Mahmood told her that he was traded as though he were a mule, and used as the bargaining tool in a dispute between two families. He told her about his childish attempts at sex with his fourteen-year-old bride, who quickly developed an appetite that a twelve-year-old boy could not satisfy. He admitted that, in an attempt to master his 'woman', he beat her, and he recalled the many times she ran away, and how her own father had once been forced to drag her back by her long black hair, screaming and kicking. The father slapped her face and then, suddenly remembering himself, he begged forgiveness from her husband, a twelve-year-old boy, for this act of transgression. Mahmood rose to his full height and thanked his father-in-law for returning his wife. In his heart Mahmood felt no anger towards his father-in-law; he felt only an embarrassment that his wife had humiliated him for all the village to see. She had made it plain that he could not control her, which by extension suggested that he could not control any woman. His fellow villagers not only sympathised with Mahmood, they despised his wife for her refusal to play the part that had been assigned to her.

Eventually, when he was sixteen, a delegation of men visited Mahmood, and while they were careful to pay him all the respect that his position demanded, they suggested to him that unless he was prepared to beat his wife as though she were a carpet, he should return the woman and shame her. Despite the indignities that he had suffered, Mahmood could not find it within himself to habitually raise his hand to his wife, and he knew that it would be impossible to jettison this woman and keep his honour intact. Therefore, after the departure of the delegation, he made a decision. He had seen the many photographs that the men in England sent back to the village, photographs in which they posed holding a radio, or standing beside a television set, or sometimes just clutching a fistful of five-pound notes. Mahmood made up his mind that he would leave for England and join his older brother in Leicester, where he owned three restaurants. He imagined that there would be no problem finding a well-paid job of some description in Mrs Thatcher's country, and after he had saved some money his ambition was to go to university, hopefully to study law or medicine. Mahmood dreamed of one day returning to his village in triumph as the most important man in the region, and he intended to spit in the face of the woman who had publicly humiliated him.

But she knows that Mahmood runs a modest newsagent's in a small town in the north of England that boasts neither a cathedral nor a university. Mahmood lives in a place where if, on a Saturday afternoon, one happens to turn on the television set as the football results are being read out, towns of unquestionable insignificance will be freely mentioned, but Mahmood's small English town will simply not exist. After ten years working in the kitchens of all three of his brother's restaurants, and rising to a position where he ultimately had sole charge of The Khyber Pass, Mahmood had managed to save enough money so that he could consider starting up a business of his own with his new wife, Feroza. However, Feroza was aware that her husband could no longer stomach the disrespectful confusion of running a restaurant. The sight of fat-bellied Englishmen and their slatterns rolling into The Khyber Pass after the pubs had closed, calling him Ranjit or Baboo or Swamp Boy, and using poppadoms as Frisbees, and demanding lager, and vomiting in his sinks, and threatening him with his own knives and their beery breath, and bellowing for mini-cabs and food that they were too drunk to see had already arrived on the table in front of them, was causing Mahmood to turn prematurely grey. Feroza persuaded Mahmood that the newsagent's business would be better for them both and, having been born and brought up in Leicester, Feroza knew all the intricacies of how to sell the day's news to the English in either tabloid or broadsheet form. She persuaded her husband that they should leave the Midlands and raise their family in a small English town with decent schools and among people who still had some manners. And so Mahmood had fled Leicester, thus incurring his brother's wrath, and only a year ago he had arrived with chubby Feroza to be greeted by the hospitable gloating of those who lived in this town.

Dorothy says very little about her own life, being concerned to make sure that the dominant narrative is male. After all, his story involves passion, betrayal, migration, sacrifice and ultimately triumph. Mahmood is a success. Her story contains the single word, abandonment. Curiously enough, she realises that both stories seem unconcerned with the word 'love', but she keeps this thought to herself. And then one evening, during the second month of their understanding, Mahmood asked her about her life, and specifically about her husband. She blushed which, given the fact that she was lying in bed with Mahmood at the time, suggested that she still carried within her the painful residue of a relationship whose memory she had been trying to shed for the past five years. 'He left me and ran off with a younger woman.' She paused. 'And then I left Birmingham and came back to live here.' She slowly inclined her head away from him, and wondered if a trip to the bathroom, or excusing herself to go and make a cup of tea, might be considered impolite. He said nothing. She imagined Brian parking his car in a succession of country lay-bys and spending the late afternoons wondering just what on earth had happened to his life. And why not, for she was probably at their home with a glass of sherry asking herself the same question. Her teaching career no longer interested her, and although she still derived pleasure from music, it no longer gave her joy. Joy was an emotion which soared on wings, which suggested transcendence, but her life with Brian was firmly anchored. No joy. And then there were Brian's women who, like Brian, she imagined to be overweight. She smirked at the thought of the dreadful collisions that she presumed must pass for sex, with portly Brian no doubt casting himself as a star performer. But it was pathetic really, for she could always tell when he was at it because he stopped wearing a vest. Mahmood said nothing about Brian having run off with a younger woman. She turned to face him and pulled herself up and onto one elbow. 'Are you really interested in my life? I mean there's not much to it, you know.' Mahmood continued to stare at her with his dark eyes.

She began by explaining that, as the eldest, she was expected to set an example. And this she did, much to the annoyance of her younger sister. She worked hard, but she did not regard university to be a viable proposition. However, when she was accepted to read music at Manchester, her shell-shocked parents took her and Sheila out to a restaurant for the first time. Her father was uncomfortable handling the menu, and both girls noticed, but their mother simply laughed nervously and kept looking about herself in the hope that she might see somebody she knew. When the bill came, her father added and re-added it three times, all the while muttering under his breath about forking out money for something that his wife could have whipped up with one hand tied behind her back. He had spent his working life as a draughtsman, reluctantly hovering on the fringes of middle-class respectability, but this close proximity to what he perceived to be 'white-collar smugness' served only to increase the fervour with which he preached 'the value of brass'. Sadly, the celebration dinner at the restaurant merely reminded the girls of the restrictions which had long blighted their young lives, and the evening propelled Sheila one step further along a path that would finally lead her clear away from home.

Dorothy met Brian during her first year at university. A public schoolboy, he had a posh accent and confidence, two things that she knew she could never acquire, no matter how long she searched for them. For three years he protected her as she struggled with her degree in music, while he seemed to breeze through his course in mathematics, which he regarded as an unwelcome distraction from his passion for beer and rugby. As the time drew near for them to be unleashed upon the world, it was clear to their small group of friends that Brian would propose and they would be married, which, within a few weeks of graduation, they were. Brian's parents tried to hide their disappointment, but her mother was delighted, for her ambition had never included a daughter at university, let alone a son-in-law whose family lived in a detached house. Her father, on the other hand, took his kneeling-pad down to the allotment and busied himself there. His youngest daughter had run off and was no longer in touch with home, and his eldest daughter was marrying into a world whose values he despised. Her father saw no reason to pretend, and she saw no reason to beg, and so they kept out of each other's way. The night before the wedding her sister telephoned and wished her good luck, but said that Brian sounded as though he lacked a bit of spark. They had argued, but they did so without passion. She reminded Sheila that the wedding would not be the same without her, and her sister reminded her of the facts that she had recently shared with Dorothy during the university visit. They both fell silent. She decided to conclude the conversation by telling Sheila that after the wedding they would be moving to Birmingham, where Brian was brought up. Sheila laughed.

Long before she went to live there, she had already imagined Birmingham to be a city whose heart was a cold arterial clot of motorways, and whose suburbs were full of windows that displayed washable flowers. Brian was happy, for he had secured a job in a city-centre merchant bank, but soon after their marriage they discovered that they could not have children. They had every test possible, but the doctors claimed that they still did not know what was wrong, which of course meant that they probably did. After years of being prodded and probed they finally did discover the reason for their failure, and their GP was left with the sad task of persuading Brian to accept that the problem was his. However, her compassion quickly soured into anger as she began to hear about his petty affairs at the bank with backroom girls. Straight out of school, these were graceless, slightly dumpy girls still too naïve to be placed in front of the clientele, but who went positively weak at the knees at the thought of being pinned beneath a man who wore a suit and tie to work. She threw herself into her life as a teacher of music at the local secondary-modern school, and having proved her ability to tease tuneful sounds from their discordant souls, she was quickly transferred to the grammar school. This was a place where the parents expected, and where the headmaster expected, although she soon discovered that the pupils were as unfocused as the pupils at the supposedly inferior school. And then Brian's affairs seemed to stop, and she realised that there must be somebody special. She herself had not been totally ignored. There had been staffroom flirtations; the head of physics idly pushing an arm through hers and looking at her in a particular way; and the cricket master forever offering his services as a driver to run her to a concert, or to the supermarket, or to anywhere that took her fancy. Once or twice a month a man would sit next to her on the bus and attempt conversation, but she knew that her days as an object of desire were firmly rooted in the past. She imagined that either pity or curiosity motivated these men, and it never occurred to her that there might be any possibility of her seriously pursuing a liaison beyond the one she endured with Brian.

He left the note on the kitchen table. It simply said, 'Sorry.' At first she did not know what to make of it. She tried to remember the threads of their last argument. There was always an argument in the air, like an unresolved plot line from one of the television soaps whose omnibus editions he liked to watch at the weekends in his socks and sandals. But she could not remember any argument. She put down her bag and went upstairs to get out of her school clothes. Then she taught her private student, and after the hopeless boy had left, she began to prepare dinner. It was only when the light began to fade at 8.30 p.m. that she realised that her inability to locate the source of any argument was far more significant than she was acknowledging. In fact, there was a problem. She called his office, but there was no answer, just the office machine and his dry-toned voice. After a sleepless night in their oversized raft of a bed, everything was clarified. The letter arrived with the morning post. She recognised his handwriting and tore it open. He had gone to Spain with Barbara, whoever Barbara was. He was sorry, but he could not live this life, and it was killing him to pretend. He had to go, but he knew that she would be better off on her own without him. How did he know? she wondered. The selfish pig had walked out on nearly thirty years of marriage and was writing to her as though the only thing that he was guilty of was exchanging the wretched uncertainty of English weather for the calming predictability of blue sky and bright sunshine. She did not dress, nor did she leave the house. She telephoned the school and told them that she needed to take a week's leave of absence because of a family crisis, and the headmaster's secretary answered her in a voice which seemed to be taunting her with secret knowledge of the failure of her marriage. And then, sometime later the same day, having drunk a dozen cups of coffee, a decision was made to sell up and, at fifty years of age, start over again in the nondescript town that she had grown up in. She would leave Brian's Birmingham and go home and find a position among her own.

Mahmood had listened attentively and occasionally raised an eyebrow, but she knew that hers was not a very interesting story. For the past five years she has lived in a neat semi-detached house and earned her daily bread as the music mistress at the grammar school that, soon after her return, abandoned all standards and became the local comprehensive. In the evenings she has become something of a television addict, watching programmes that she acknowledges have no value beyond the killing of dull time. Reality shows and courtroom dramas are her speciality, but once in a while she can enjoy a documentary, particularly if it concerns animals. Meanwhile, in Spain, her former bank-manager husband runs a bed and breakfast (which he insists on calling a 'pension') on the Costa del Sol for 'upmarket' British tourists. Football shirts are not encouraged, and fried breakfasts, not just continental cold plates, are offered. In fact, according to the promotional material that Brian so generously sent to her, fried breakfasts are the speciality of Barbara's house. Apparently, even some of the bigger hotels don't do 'the works', but at Brian and Barbara's 'Casa BeeBee' you can always get a fried breakfast. Having read the brochures, she immediately burned them. For five years she has lived alone, and each passing year she has watched herself age, the increased wrinkling of the skin between her breasts being her secret barometer of decrepitude. Last month the man on the bus asked to see her bus pass and she slapped the two-pound coin down so hard that she hurt her hand. Not turning heads is one thing, not being taken seriously is another thing altogether. And then one morning, as she felt herself finally coming to terms with the futility of years spent mourning a man whom she had never truly loved, she walked into the corner shop for her newspaper and the new owner, a doe-eyed Indian man, handed her a copy of the *Daily Mail* and took her money.

She continues to teach because there is nothing else for her to do. It is too late for a change of career, and there is no other profession that she can imagine herself pursuing. The truth is she lost the passion for teaching music at about the same rate that English schoolchildren appeared to lose the passion for learning. And the piano is not a popular instrument. Was it ever? In the remote hope that she might unearth a singular talent she takes private pupils, but she understands that she is little more than an unwelcome distraction for middle-class children whose parents are determined to provide them with socially acceptable skills. To most pupils she is no different from their ballet teacher or their tennis professional. But, mercifully, she has not lost her love for the music itself. After Brian left she thought about trying to compose. Her few university compositions were praised, and her senior lecturer had written her a note asking her to perhaps consider applying for a scholarship to the Royal College of Music in London. But little did he know that her sail was already hoisted in the direction of Birmingham. These days she practises again, and she tries to tease notes into tuneful shapes. Sometimes she writes down her patterns, but she does not tell this to Mahmood. Occasionally she sees him in his shop wearing a personal stereo, a discordant, tinny whine leaking out from the badly padded headset. She is used to offering herself up to his boredom, but after her disastrous attempt to interest him in Chopin, she now refuses to expose her beloved music to his stone ears.

In the bathroom of the house she lays out towels, a robe, fresh soap and a toothbrush. To start with Mahmood would shuffle heavily into the bathroom and use her 'gifts'. She tried not to allow uncharitable thoughts to enter her head, but she knew that Feroza could not care for him in this way. And back in his native country he could only have dreamed of such luxury. But he no longer bathes. He goes to the bathroom, but he sometimes forgets to shut the door properly and she hears the undignified thunder of urine cascading directly into the water and not against the side of the bowl. And then he flushes and blows his nose at the same time, so that it sounds as though a storm has broken loose in her house. Mahmood comes back and he has another go at her, but it is as though he is trying to knock her through the bed. In the beginning it gave her pleasure to spoil him a little, but these days, Mahmood no longer has time to be spoiled. The presents she buys, the silver pendant, the leather wallet, the address book, are no longer fingered and weighed and then finally held. He simply nods and sometimes he even forgets to take them with him. And so there are no more presents. When he finishes, Mahmood rolls out of bed and steps quickly into his clothes. For some reason he scrunches his white cotton underpants into a ball and pushes them into his trouser pocket. She looks at his smooth, unmarked back as he bends over to pull on his socks.

'Would you like a drink before you go? A cup of tea, or something stronger?'

He turns and looks at her. He smiles with his black eyes, but he says nothing. He is dressed now, and he stands and turns fully to face her. She lies entangled in the sheets and stares up at him, a fish trapped.

'No, thank you,' he says. 'I have to go.'

She notices a slight shrug of his shoulders, and then she watches as he treads silently from the room. He steps into his shoes in the hallway, then she hears the door open and bang to and the letterbox clatter, for he always shuts the door with too much force. After a short period of reflection she struggles clear of the bed linen and pulls on a cotton robe. Then she goes into the sitting room and draws the curtains a little to admit some moonlight, before opening the piano lid as far as it will go.

The following morning she goes into the shop. This is part of her daily routine. A copy of the *Daily Mail* on the way to work. It is his habit to sell it to her in a brusque manner that she knows he has appropriated in order to disguise their affair. However, of late his manner seems to have corroded into indifference. She is trying to learn not to take everything so personally, but she imagines that such anxieties are an integral part of deceit. Today Feroza is sitting on the counter top and in her arms she holds a child. A new-born baby with a head of oily black hair that is already curling wildly into cowlicks and bushy tufts. Mahmood is playing with this child and he does not see her as she walks into the shop. He is showering love and affection upon this child. Her eyes meet those of Feroza, who stares at her with a cold, unblinking gaze. She notices a mocking sneer beginning to buckle Feroza's lips, and then Mahmood turns and sees her. There is no warmth on his face, no glimmer of communal deceit in his eyes, nothing. He simply looks at her and then returns his gaze to the child. 'Give her the paper,' he says without looking up. Feroza picks up the *Daily Mail*. She holds out her hand, and Feroza drops the paper on top of the counter for her to pick up. Feroza is no longer smiling, and the child is revelling in the attention of its father.

During the second period of sixth-form music the pupils stare at her as she stumbles over her words. There are long pauses. She gazes out of the window. Then she turns to face them and laughs. She is conscious of the fact that she is making a fool of herself in front of these children. She tries to convince them of the relative merits of Mozart over his contemporaries. In fact, over all artists of the period. Sacrifice. She rolls the word around on her tongue. Sacrifice. And arrogance. Here she stops. She is brought up quickly against this word. She feels faint and wonders whether she should stop talking and play a few notes on the piano. Demonstrate something for them. Sacrifice is not the problem. Her life with Brian involved surrendering her dignity. Sacrifice. She has known sacrifice all her life. Making chicken curry is sacrifice. Asking him if he has ever been in an English home is sacrifice. Listening to him talking about his years of misery in the restaurant trade in Leicester. Buying a Sunday paper and nattering idly about the weather while others come in and out and cast her baleful glances, now that is sacrifice. They can stare at her if it makes them happy, but she knows about sacrifice. But arrogance is something new. Mozart. Mahmood. Arrogant eyes. Nobody says anything. They simply stare at her. But she is not saying anything. And then she hears the bell and she knows that today she will not have to talk any more about Mozart or about sacrifice. She watches as the pupils scrape back their chairs and stand. They gather up their books and papers, and they look at her as they walk out. They look at her and she looks back at them and grins. They continue to look at her.

She waits, but there is no knocking at the door and no rattling of the letterbox. The lights are dimmed, the candles lit, and the faint odour of Rhogan Josh lingers in the air. She has bought an especially expensive bottle of wine in order to make an effort, even though she knows that Mahmood is not a wine person. The subtleties of the bottle will be lost on him, but nevertheless she has bought the wine. However, there is no knocking at the door. There is no rattling of the letterbox. For the past few days she has gone into the shop and collected her newspaper and he has looked in her direction, but done so without encouraging conversation. But why should he? The shop is generally full and it is not their way to draw attention to themselves. This morning she sat on the top deck of the number forty-two bus and looked down into the back gardens. A woman was throwing a dripping carpet over a thin line that was stretched between two sycamore trees. Behind the woman a wooden shed leaned shoulder to shoulder against an equally unstable garage, and the whole sorry picture was illuminated by a weak pale light which gave the impression that at any moment a storm might break. As the bus passed the park she saw the stone war memorial, and beneath the plaque somebody had spray-painted 'Eat Shit' on the plinth. Again she reprimands herself for her behaviour. She had let herself down in front of her sixth-formers. It was shameful to display such a lack of control, but she knew that they would soon forget her slip-up. It was only one class, and next week she will put everything back on track. And then she smells burning. She hurries to the kitchen and turns down the light under the Rhogan Josh, and then she decides to uncork the wine.

This afternoon she went into the new 'one-stop' shop by the school. There was a new person behind the counter. A young girl, who had that sunken-cheeked, gypsy-like Romanian look about her. It was difficult to tell, but she was not English. That much was clear. She wondered where the girl's parents were, and if they intended to come and help out. In her nose the girl wore a polished silver stud like a small ball bearing, and her black hair was flecked with outgrowths of purple. The child was making a statement, but it was one that was badly in need of interpretation. She chose an expensive bottle of wine and then she pointed to a doll on the top shelf. The foreign girl reached skywards and handed it to her in order that she might inspect it. 'You like?' She ignored the girl and then turned the doll first one way and then the next. She knew that she was going to take it, but she was simply going through the motions. She opened her purse and handed the girl a twenty-pound note, and the girl opened the till and reckoned the change with surprising ease. Then, ignoring her customer's outstretched palm, the girl placed the money on the counter and began to put the doll and the bottle of wine into the same paper bag. She gathered up her change and took the paper bag from the immigrant girl without glancing in her direction or offering any thanks. Once she reached home she took the expensive bottle of wine from the bag and put it in the fridge to chill. The doll she left in the bag and she placed it beside her briefcase. She dimmed the lights and lit the candles. She made Rhogan Josh. And then she readied herself. And waited. But there is no knocking at the door. There is no rattling of the letterbox.

In the morning she stops by the shop for her *Daily Mail*. She closes the door behind her. Feroza is serving a man who seems to be paying a bill. He is squinting at a printout, his glasses pushed up onto his crumpled forehead. She knows that he is questioning Mahmood's arithmetic. Or worse, his honesty. Feroza looks at the man with contempt, and then she glances up at her new customer. The child is asleep in a basket on the counter, which makes her look like a gift that has been delivered and unwrapped. Feroza tosses the *Daily Mail* onto the counter top. She taps the counter with her knuckles and asks, 'Anything else?' The man is absorbed by his puzzled squinting and so she steps around him and approaches the counter where the *Daily Mail* sits between these two women like an unsigned contract.

'I've brought this.' She plunges a hand into the paper bag and produces the blonde-haired doll. 'For your child.'

She offers it as a gift to the wife, who looks first at the doll, and then at her. Feroza's eyes ignite with indignation. The man looks up from the arithmetic, and then the wife spits at the Englishwoman and catches her in the face with her spittle. Feroza moves to spit again, but what spit she has left gets caught on her lower lip and hangs as a stringy testament to her loss of control. She leaves the doll and her *Daily Mail* on the counter top. She turns and exits the shop with the fierce eyes of the wife, and the puzzled eyes of the man, boring into her back. The doorbell tinkles as she opens the door, and the glass rattles as she closes it behind her. Only when she is safely outside does she take the sleeve of her coat and wipe the spittle from her face.

She ought to have known better. She sits in the dusk clutching a mug of cocoa with both hands as though she needs to keep them warm. She can barely remember her day at school, but she is sure that she gave the outward appearance that everything was fine. She can feel her feet perspiring lightly, which they always do when she is racked with any kind of anxiety. At her age she ought to have known better than to patronise a thirty-year-old woman and her child. She had been arrogant enough to presume that she could deceive this woman, who said precious little but whose hooded gaze spoke volumes. Perhaps an apology would make things right, and enable her to close this chapter with some dignity. At present this is all that she desires. Closure with dignity. Nothing more. She telephones him when she imagines that Feroza will have gone to sleep. 'Mahmood,' she whispers, 'it's me. I'm sorry for calling, but I think I need to see you.' There is silence. 'I need to explain about this morning, that's all.' There is a silence that is clearly informed by his exasperation. And then he speaks.

'You must buy your newspaper somewhere else. I do not wish to know you.' He puts down the phone. He does not wish. *He* does not wish. She replaces the telephone on the cradle and holds on to the receiver as though readying herself to make a follow-up call. But there will be no follow-up call. She will draw a hot bath, and then there will be another mug of hot cocoa, and then she will go to her bed, which has unfortunately begun to feel light without a double load. In the morning she will remedy this situation. She will purge her house of all signs of Mahmood, and then she will discover another route to school. One which will neither stir her memory nor trouble her conscience.

It is Monday morning. She sits in the staffroom during a double-free period. Time to do some marking and make a cup of coffee, if she can find a clean cup. The staff have long ago given up the idea of their having individual cups, for invariably somebody would use somebody else's cup and this would lead to a falling out and general bad feeling. This morning she finds a cup that, with a quick rinse, is tolerable. She is also lucky enough to find biscuits that are not stale. And then, as she stirs the UHT milk into the coffee, she looks up and sees him idling by the door.

'Well, come on in. Nobody's going to bite.' He is dressed in the uniform of a relief teacher. His suit is smart, the shoes are well polished, the tie neatly knotted, and the strangely creased shirt is clearly package-fresh. The biggest give-away is the briefcase, which is emaciated and concave as though eager to be nourished with badly written papers. He looks around himself, checking that it really is him that this woman is speaking to. Now he steps into the staffroom and gingerly closes the door behind him.

'Coffee?' she asks. 'I don't recommend the tea.' He nods, then remembering his manners he speaks.

'Yes, please. Just black. No sugar.'

'Just black, no sugar,' she repeats. He sits down and places his briefcase on the floor. She hands him his cup of coffee, then she picks up her own and sits opposite him. 'This is my favourite part of the week. My Monday morning double-free period. I can catch up and get a bit of peace and quiet.' He seems rather alarmed by this confession and puts down his coffee.

'I'm so sorry, I didn't mean to interrupt.' She looks at him, this timid man with greying temples and rather awkwardly knitted hands.

'Perhaps I should introduce myself. Geoff. Geoff Waverley.' He holds out his hand, which she shakes.

'I'm Dorothy Jones.'

'Pleased to meet you, Dorothy.'

He sounds well mannered enough, but she doesn't remember giving him permission to call her Dorothy.

'I hope you don't mind my asking,' she says. 'But would you like to go for a drink after school?' He pauses as though unsure how to respond to this overture, and then he laughs nervously.

'Well, why not?'

'It's all right, I'm quite harmless. And there's a nice pub that nobody goes into, neither sixth-formers nor teachers. That's why it's nice. Your reputation will be safe with me.' He laughs again, the tension flooding out of him in a great volley of high-pitched laughter. She looks at him and smiles. And then, to his evident confusion, she takes a sip of coffee, stands up, and then crosses the staffroom floor and returns to her marking.

Why not? she thinks. It has been a fortnight now since Mahmood put the phone down on her. Apart from the twice-weekly games of tennis with the boring woman who is the head of English, her life has returned to a familiar routine of time spent at the keyboard, assiduous reading, undemanding television programmes and fitful bouts of sleeping. She misses the idea of Mahmood, almost as much as she misses the man himself. Even when he went at her without any intimacy, she felt connected to something that existed beyond the narrow scope of her own predictable world. There was a stimulating confusion in her life which, with the slamming of a phone, has once more become as unsatisfactory as an unopened suitcase on a single bed. These days she finishes her meals, having often done little more than pick idly at the food, and then she stands her knife and fork to attention next to each other and gazes at the floral pattern of the wallpaper. Sometimes she stares out of the window at the people in the streets walking their dogs, stopping at hedges and lamp-posts for their pets to do their business, then quickly yanking at the dog leash and scurrying away from the little parcels that have been deposited. The one bright note in her life is her rediscovery of the joys of walking, although she is always careful to avoid the dog mess. Three miles to school, and three miles back again, all the while positively sucking in great buckets of fresh air. If, as will occasionally transpire, she feels too fatigued to walk back from school, then there is no guilt attached to hopping on a bus and paying the fare. She now notices the frequent stopping, and the tedious waiting at some stops as large numbers of passengers get on and off, but she tries not to let these things annoy her. These days, once they reach her street, she is careful to disembark one stop beyond the corner shop and walk back to her semi.

She watches him as he stands by the bar ordering the drinks. He tries to attract the barman's attention, but he does not realise that the barman has already seen him and will come over after he has finished serving the lady in the wheelchair. Her new friend is too keen to prove himself masterful. She stands and goes to look at the jukebox, which is full of music with which she is unfamiliar. A drink in the pub. Jukebox. She remembers this ritual from the early days with Brian in

Manchester. She looks around the dark, oak-panelled pub, and notices that all the mirrors are filthy and covered in a thick film of dust. The carpet is worn through in places and badly stained, and for some reason the door to the 'Gents' is propped open so that, although she cannot see the actual urinals, she can see a succession of men slowly turning around and zipping themselves up, then wiping their hands on their trousers before ambling back into the gloom of the pub. The place is populated with after-work couples, the men with slightly loosened ties, and the women pulling nervously on cigarettes and speaking with an animation that no doubt eludes them when they are in the office. And then there are the regulars; old men with dun-coloured jackets nursing their solitary pints of beer, and middle-aged women with pinched faces and sugar-sabotaged teeth, who slump in their seats and wait in the dull hope that something approximating to love might once again show itself. As she leaves the jukebox and moves back to their table she decides that there is no reason at all why she should tell him that this is her first time in this pub, which looks as though a jumble sale has exploded in the place. Confession, at this stage, is not going to help the evening to pass.

He places both drinks neatly onto cardboard coasters and, as he does so, she looks up at him with her 'hello' face. He moves his still-emaciated briefcase from the bench and onto a chair, and plops down next to her. Then he takes a large mouthful of a pint of what looks suspiciously like lager and lime, and she picks up her half-pint of Guinness and toasts him. 'Cheers.' She looks at him and wonders if he truly is this nervous, or if this is part of a game that he plays. He looks around himself.

'Nice place, isn't it?' She is out of touch with this kind of conversation.

'And so you teach geography?' she says.

'If I can't see the world, I may as well talk about it.'

'Oh,' she says. 'Why can't you see it?' He laughs now, and for the first time she sees his perfectly spaced white teeth. He is a handsome man, despite the crow's feet that decorate the corners of his eyes.

'Commitments. I've got a wife and child. And they don't pay us like they ought to. Worse if you're just a supply teacher. But you know all this already.' She finds herself nodding slightly.

'I've never done supply, but I can imagine.'

'Well, I don't recommend it, but it does serve a purpose.' She turns around to face him more directly, aware of the fact that as she does so her skirt rides up so that her right knee is exposed. She still has good legs. In fact, they are her best feature. Brian was always jealous of the way that men looked at her legs, and he used to compliment her if she wore a trouser-suit. After he left for Spain she put her two trouser-suits, one blue and one grey, into a black-plastic bin liner and put them out with the rubbish.

After two more pints of beer, and one half-pint of Guinness, it is his idea that they should go for a meal. He suggests La Spiaggia, imagining that she will be familiar with the place. She tells him that she generally does not go out to eat, but that she will be happy to dine with him. Her glass is still half-full, but his pint glass is almost empty and he seems unsure of what to do. She solves the problem for him by suggesting that he go fetch himself a half-pint. She watches as he makes his way to the bar, this time with more confidence, and he appears pleased that the barman pulls his beer without his having to ask. He turns round and smiles at her.

La Spiaggia is a family-owned establishment that looks suspiciously like a chain restaurant, but she imagines that the owners prefer it this way. In this town too much individuality will not be rewarded. He chooses a table by the window and they begin to study their four-page menus, but she reads without absorbing any of the meaning from the words.

'The veal is good,' he says. 'If you eat meat, that is.'

'I'd just like some pasta. That should see me fine.'

He laughs. 'You'll waste away.'

They order, and he chooses a red that he describes as 'special', but to her it seems quite ordinary. Through the window they watch a group of young boys in designer clothes shouting and swearing at each other, and competing for the attention of two girls who walk on ahead, seemingly oblivious to the pandemonium behind them. The spectacle seems to unsettle him and he takes another sip of wine and laughs nervously.

'There seem to be a lot of gangs in the town. Well, hooligans really, but it's their body language more than what they say, I suppose. You start to wonder if they're not carrying knives, or worse.'

'Well,' she begins, 'according to the talk in the staffroom, they're all on hard cider and even harder drugs. We're expected to believe that they're looking to cause trouble, or steal something, simply because they're bored.' She laughs now. 'And so there we have it. I suppose we can't expect the modern kid to find satisfaction by doing "bunny hops" on his or her bike.' She turns towards the window and wonders if she's boring her new friend.

When the food arrives, he orders another bottle of wine. She has only just finished her first glass, but he asks for neither her opinion nor her approval. He starts to eat and he speaks with his mouth full, but at least he makes some attempt to chew before he begins his sentences.

'It's worrying though, isn't it? I mean these days everyone's a victim and nobody's responsible. Do you think it's because there's a lack of discipline and order in schools? Are we to blame?'

Again she laughs. 'You sound like my father. He died a few years ago.'

He stops eating. 'I'm sorry.'

'Don't be sorry. He lived his life, I suppose. It's just that he began to worry about young people. He worried that they no longer had any fear, that it wasn't just how they talked that bothered him, it was what they would do. I suppose he'd have said it was to do with discipline in the home, more than with discipline in the schools. And immigration.'

'Immigration?'

'Well, you know, to some people everything's to do with immigration.'

'But these kids were not black.' He gestures out of the window. 'They were not out to mug anyone.'

'I know.' She lowers her eyes and concentrates on the remains of her plate. 'I know. I agree with you.' She picks up her still-full wine glass by the stem and rolls it in her fingers. 'Your wife and child, they won't be coming here then?'

'Maybe at the end of the year. After the affair with the squash player burns itself out.' He laughs loudly now, throwing back his head. The waiter looks across, but quickly looks away. 'Bit of a cliché really, isn't it? But that's the truth. I'm just giving them space.'

'That's good of you,' she says, taking a sip from her glass.

'I go back to Nottingham at the weekends. To see my daughter, Claire. But I thought it best to get out of town for a while, and this local authority had jobs, so here I am.' He pours a fresh glass of red wine, and he drinks quickly. She watches as he swallows the mouthful that marks the line between coherence and mess. 'I'm staying in lodgings with a landlady. Like I'm a sodding student again.' He laughs and with one hand he loosens his tie. 'Who'd have thought it.'

'Thought what?'

'That I'd come to this.' She looks into his eyes and sees the vulnerability beneath the bluster. 'Thank you, though.'

'For what?'

'For asking me for a drink. I've been dreading the evenings. Leaving my temporary job and going back to my temporary lodgings. Sitting in the living room watching stupid television programmes with Mrs Johnson, and then having to endure the embarrassment of her offering me a cup of Horlicks and a plate of biscuits. It's either put up with her, or go out to the local pub and find somebody to play darts with and bore to death with my life story. So thanks.'

She takes a sip of wine and smiles broadly at him.

'My pleasure.' And then she continues. 'Perhaps we ought to be going now.' He looks at her as though shocked. Then he puts down his glass and reaches across the table and takes her hands in both of his.

'I mean it. I'm really grateful. Thank you.' She lowers her eyes and then gently wriggles her hands out from under his grip. He clears his throat. 'Are you still married to your husband?'

'No, we're divorced.'

'Happily?'

She does not say, no, he washed his hands of me. 'Everything runs its course.'

'Lonely?'

She does not say, I used to be the fancy woman for the Asian man in the corner shop, but he dropped me. 'I'm comfortable with my own company.' She laughs. 'Most of the time.'

As they wait by the bus stop he drapes a protective arm around her shoulders, but she senses that in all probability he is simply trying to maintain his balance. A homeless man, who pulls a filthy sleeping bag after him, crosses the street and looks as though he is walking towards them. She feels her protector grow tense and then, as the tramp ignores them and walks on his way, he releases an audible sigh.

They both look down the street in the direction that they imagine the bus will arrive from. Across the road in the pub car park, some louts, who are all tattoos and bared teeth, are now pushing and shoving each other and making the loud braying noises that suggest they are having a good time. She notices that two among them are brazenly advertising the contents of their bladders in triumphal watery arches, and then to her horror she realises that their performances are competitive. She wonders if any of the young vagabonds are pupils of hers, and then she catches herself and realises that she is ignoring her escort.

'You know, you really don't have to wait for me. The bus won't be long.' He dares to finger her cheek. She hopes that he won't speak, for his words have long since begun to slide, one into the other. And then she hears the sound of the bus rumbling up the hill towards them. He quickly retrieves his hand.

'Ah, your chariot approaches.'

'It's been a lovely evening.' The bus idles before her and then the doors swoosh open accordion-style.

'You saved me from an evening of hell.' He laughs. 'Or you saved somebody from an evening of hell.'

She moves quickly before he can say anything further. Once on board she fishes in her purse for the exact change, and then she takes her ticket. It's a short ride so she sits by the door. As the bus lurches away she turns and sees him still standing by the bus stop. He waves.

The following morning she waits in the staffroom. Everybody arrives in one mad rush. Sally Lomax, the young head of English, flashes her a bright, but clearly manufactured, smile.

'I'll have to bring George and Samantha tonight. But they've got colouring books and crayons, so they should be fine.'

She nods at Sally, who is too busy to register the fact that there has been a response to her statement. As Sally turns away, she can see again just how much the poor woman's body has thickened and run to fat at the waist and hips, which no doubt accounts for her enthusiasm for exercise. Sally gulps down a final mouthful of coffee, then throws the rest in the sink. The cup goes in after the coffee. She is one of those who cannot be bothered to rinse their cup and then turn it up on the draining board. Memos have been posted, but hardly anybody takes the time to read them. She waits in the staffroom until everybody has left, but there is still no sign of Geoff Waverley. It is too late to go into assembly now. The head abhors lateness from pupils. A teacher being late for assembly is an open invitation to a hastily scribbled note of admonishment from Mr Jowett. Instead, she goes straight to her classroom and sits at the piano. A single C establishes a tone. A beginning. But she is too anxious to develop the pattern. Through the window she sees stragglers bolting across the school playground in a pantomime of unpunctuality, their shirt-tails flying in the wind. They will clatter through the door and straight into the clutches of a prefect, but they have forgotten this. Again she hits a single C, and she listens closely to the rise and fall of this one note.

When the bell goes she walks briskly to the computer room. She pulls up the school home page, taps in her password and under 'new staff' she clicks on his name. The screen flickers for a moment, as though dying, and then it bursts to life and all the details are glowing before her eyes. His degree, his previous employment, his wife's name, Claire's full name, her age and their address in Nottingham. The phone number has been omitted, but this will not pose a problem. She pushes the print button and then quickly makes her way past the pupils playing computer games, and those sending lovesick emails. Hers is the first sheet printed at the central terminal and she quickly folds the warm piece of paper into four and tucks it into her bag. One of her fifth-formers, a talented cellist, is staring at her.

'Morning, Miss.'

'Morning, Amanda.' She knows that of all her pupils poor Amanda with the thick ankles will continue to pursue the cello, while others will soon abandon music for more worldly pleasures.

George and Samantha sit at a table by the side of the court. They have been arguing for most of the set, pulling the single colouring book first one way and then the next. Now George throws his crayon at his older sister, who retaliates, marking George across his cheek with an orange gash. Sally comes to the net.

'I'm sorry, but I'll have to see to them.'

She watches as Sally talks firmly to her children. Tennis with Sally has proved to be something of a mixed blessing, for she still has problems with her hips, but she does enjoy the competition. After Brian left she tried golf, but that served only to reinscribe the loneliness. And mistakes had to be viewed purely in the light of individual incompetence. At least with tennis she can win the occasional point off her opponent's mistakes. Like life itself. A distraught-looking Sally wanders back to the net.

'I'm sorry, but I think we should stop now. Maybe five-all is as good a place as any.' She decides to say nothing, but privately wonders what on earth made Sally imagine that a four-year-old and a six-year-old would sit patiently while their mother hit a ball back and forth across a net.

The children seem happier in the cafeteria, pulling joyfully on their straws and slurping Coca-Cola all over their faces and clothes. She drinks an orange juice while Sally sits with a cup of tea and analyses the game.

'You're getting stronger all the time. I think you're a bit of a natural.'

She graciously accepts the younger woman's compliments. However, if it was not for Sally she would not be here. There is nobody else that she knows in the leisure centre, and she has no desire to join up. The woman on the front desk has twice told her that she is losing money doing it this way, and that it would be much cheaper to become a member, but she prefers her temporary arrangement. Sally glances at the two children, who continue to enjoy their newly harmonious, if messy, friendship. Then she looks back at her older companion.

'Tongues are wagging in the staffroom.'

She stares blankly at her, but in a manner that forces Sally to continue.

'It's just that I know you've never been much of a mixer, but these days you seem to keep yourself to yourself. As if you're too grand for everybody, but I know that's not how you really feel. It's just what some people are saying.'

Through the glass, and down on the court below them, she can see two men furiously thrashing a ball back and forth with little concern for finesse. Theirs is a game of brute strength and endurance. She turns to look at Sally. The younger woman's face is calm and etched with concern, but she resents her younger colleague's words. Warning? Admonishment? It matters little. The words are inappropriate and she will not play tennis with this woman again.

Geoff seems slightly less animated than he was at the restaurant. Wine, she thinks. More wine, and she pours him another glass and makes a point of leaving the bottle uncorked. This morning, she slipped a note in Sally's pigeonhole cancelling next week's tennis. She gave no reason. Then she found the hastily scribbled note from Geoff. 'Dinner? Tonight?' She put the note up against the wall and under his double question she scrawled, 'My place, 8 p.m.' Then she wrote down her address, folded the note twice and tucked it into his box. She had hoped for a note from him on the morning after their dinner, but better late than never, she thought. And now, as he sips at his new glass of wine, he finally explains his failure to write.

'Claire hurt herself at school, but my wife made it sound as though the child was going to have a leg amputated. But when I got there we argued, of course. I missed the whole of yesterday, and I didn't get back till one o'clock this morning.'

'I'm sorry.'

He empties his glass in one and pours himself another glass. Again he praises the food, but she knows that there is nothing to praise about tuna casserole. It is nice of him, but not necessary. They move into the living room and he reclines back into the sofa. She takes the armchair and sits opposite him, and then he points to the gilt-framed photograph on top of the piano.

'Your parents?' She nods.

'They were born in this town, and they lived and died here. They're both buried in the local cemetery, side by side.' He sits forward now.

'How do you feel about that?'

About what? she wonders. About parents who had neither the means nor, in the case of her father, the desire to escape their working-class lives? Who never recovered from the shock of their eldest child going off to university in another town? Who resented their youngest child for having the temerity to abandon them and go and seek her fortune in London among the lights? How did she feel? She didn't feel that she owed them anything, but she couldn't deny that she had come running home when her own life had collapsed. She had, in essence, returned to their world, albeit with council houses sold off, Indians controlling the local economy, and new town houses that cost six figures for those who worked in the technology sector. Were her parents to step from their graves and re-enter this world, theirs would no longer be a town that they would recognise. She looks at her guest, and then she returns her gaze to the photograph of her parents. What she cannot tell this man is the degree to which she despises that which has been bequeathed to her. The genetic stain. Cowardice.

It is late. A kiss hangs in the air, but he seems incapable of leaning over and taking it.

'I think I'd better go now, before Mrs Johnson slams and bolts the door on me.' He stands. They have talked about music. They have talked about travel, and about how he loved to ride the trains on Inter-rail both during and after college. Every summer he did this, skipping from Germany to France, from France to Holland and so on, moving around as the mood took him. Geoff Waverley had experienced many adventures on the road, though none, as far as she could tell, of the amorous variety. She hears the words before she has time to sort and arrange them.

'You don't have to go. You're more than welcome to stay here.' Her eyes light upon the clock on the mantelpiece. Again she speaks. 'It's still reasonably early.' He is standing by himself, marooned. She feels uncomfortable leaving him in this position and so she too stands. She faces him, but it is he who reaches out and takes her hand.

'I don't think we should be doing this.'

'Doing what?' she asks.

They lie side by side. She stares at the ceiling, but his

eyes are closed. She lied about her age when he complimented her.

'Fifty,' she said. 'Is that too old?'

He laughed in a manner that let her know that her question was absurd. And then he fell silent and closed his eyes, while she stared at the ceiling. She can feel the surge of guilt begin to course through his stiffening body. She considers putting on some music, or opening another bottle of wine so that they can both have a drink. However, she knows that to leave the bed will break the spell. Sharing his body is one thing. Sharing his thoughts is clearly another thing altogether. And then he rolls over onto his shoulder and he faces her.

'I've got to go.' Her eyes meet his and she nods. 'My head,' he says. 'It's spinning and I'll just keep you awake all night.'

'I understand.' She strokes his face. 'I had a good time. Thank you.' He smiles and then in one movement he rolls away from her and sits on the edge of the bed. She turns her back on him to give him some privacy, and she stares at the blank wall.

The next day she leaves a note for him in his pigeonhole. A simple note, thanking him for coming over to dinner and wondering if he is free this weekend. She reads and rereads the note a dozen times before folding it and putting it into an envelope. The sealed envelope she places between memos and other mail, most of which looks to be of little import. In the staffroom she makes an extra effort to be polite to those she encounters. However, she informs a disappointed Sally that she will not only have to miss next week's game, but tennis will have to be indefinitely postponed because of her private music lessons. Sally has already anticipated this, although she does her best to seem both surprised and disappointed. Clearly Sally wishes to keep things amicable.

'You'll let me know when things change, won't you?'

'Of course,' she says. And so the day begins. It is her heavy teaching day. No free periods, and three classes of beginners. Before the cutbacks there used to be a part-time music teacher to steer the younger classes through recorder lessons and basic music appreciation, but now she has to endure the discordant tones of 'Greensleeves', and tolerate their blank faces as she explains the difference between a concerto and a symphony. Boy groups, they understand. Girl groups, they understand. Rap. Hip-hop. But this generation has finally forced her to accept the possibility that the pleasures of the classical world are in danger of becoming extinct. After her last class she gathers up her books and then finds some extra chores to do in the classroom. In due course, having exhausted all possible tasks, she makes her way along the semi-deserted corridors to the staffroom. She looks first in her box, but there is no note. And then in his, where her note, together with his other mail, has disappeared. She is dumbfounded. She feels the sap of rejection rise in her throat, but not wishing to be discovered lingering by the mail boxes she turns quickly and walks away.

The following afternoon she goes again to her box. He has had the whole of the previous evening to frame his rejection letter, but there is nothing. Only a letter from the union demanding dues, an invitation to apply for cheap travel insurance, and a note from a parent explaining why Jenny Sommerville will be away for the next three weeks. But nothing from Mr Waverley. She is tempted to rifle through his box in an attempt to discover any clue as to his silence, but on reflection she decides to quickly pen him another note and leave it for him to discover. In the staffroom only the two new games teachers linger. She sits at a table and writes quickly, urging her friend to contact her. She feels uncomfortable, but she desires no awkwardness between them. Almost anything else she can tolerate, but not awkwardness. She considers making a plea based on the fact that they work together, but she decides against this. After all, he is a supply teacher and he will soon be leaving. She plays the awkwardness card and leaves it at that. As she gets to her feet Sally bursts into the staffroom. She apologises to the games teachers for keeping them waiting. Clearly she is going to help out, probably with hockey practice. Then Sally sees her former tennis partner.

'Hi, you're here late. Waiting for anyone?' Before she has a chance to shake her head and deny that she is waiting for anybody, Sally laughs and continues. 'Mr Waverley is on a field trip, if that's who you're looking for. Quite like the look of him myself. Half my Shakespeare class have gone with him.' Again she laughs. 'Don't get me wrong. I'm not complaining.' The games teachers are becoming impatient and they hover by the door. 'Look, I've got to rush. See you.'

Sally leaves the door open as she disappears down the corridor. She waits until Sally is out of sight and then she steps outside and puts the note into Geoff Waverley's box. She does not bother to close the staffroom door.

At ten o'clock that night the doorbell rings. She goes to the door and sees his dishevelled person standing before her. His hair is rumpled and he looks as though he has not slept for days. She wonders if he is angry with her for leaving a second note, but as she scrutinises his face she can see that he is more tired than angry.

'Can I come in?'

She steps to one side.

'Of course. What happened?' She pours a glass of red wine and sets it before him at the table. He takes a mouthful and then looks up at her.

'Do you have any food?' She makes him some pasta while he in turn pours himself a second and then a third glass from the bottle. He eats quickly and then pushes the plate away. 'Thank you.' She pours herself a half-glass.

'Do you want to talk?'

He looks at her.

'My wife. I'm not sure if it's going to work.'

'You mean the reconciliation?'

'I went there yesterday. And then again today after the field trip.' He reaches over and makes contact with her hand. 'Can I stay here? Just for tonight, I mean.' She nods. 'On the sofa. I don't think we can do that again, not if I'm still trying to go back with her.' Again she nods.

'I'll make you up a bed.'

As she puts a fresh pillowcase on the pillow she looks over at him. He is exhausted and he sits with his left elbow on the table top, his face cupped into his left palm and his tired eyes closed. As much as she wants to go to him and slip an arm around his shoulders, she knows that she cannot. This is his misery. By respecting this she hopes that she will, of course, make herself necessary.

The next day, after school, she pours herself a cup of tea and then she calls his wife, Vivian. Her voice is young, and thin; a blonde voice full of good cheer mixed with bemusement. 'Who am I speaking to?'

'I am a colleague of your husband's and I'm slightly worried about his behaviour.' There is silence on the other end of the telephone, and for a moment it is difficult to determine what this silence means. She continues. 'Mrs Waverley?'

'Ms. Ford.' The voice fizzes with indignation. His wife continues. 'What exactly do you want?' She draws a deep breath.

'I suppose I just want to let you know that your husband's behaviour is causing many of us some concern. He seems to be upset all of the time.'

'And what is it that you want me to do?'

'I'm not sure. I just thought you might like to know.'

'And so now you've told me.' The silence lingers in the air

for a few moments, then she hears the click and the irritable burr of an open line. Ms Vivian Ford has hung up on her. For a few moments she holds the telephone in her hand. She strikes a pose, as though performing before an audience, and then she runs a hand carefully back through her grey hair and gently replaces the telephone on the receiver. Dignity has been restored.

He waits until most people have left the staffroom before speaking to her. The few who remain can see that this is an encounter that is fraught with tension.

'Don't you have some explaining to do?'

She looks surprised, as though not sure what he is talking about. She deliberately keeps her voice lower than his. This will be her tactic. Whatever he says, she will reply in a whisper.

'I thought I was helping. You seemed so helpless the other night, and I was worried.' She sees the anger flare on his face, and she worries now, for she has no desire to have a public confrontation. He stares at her. She is aware that others are watching them and there is a sense of relief when he utters his one word, 'Outside', as though he were a schoolboy inviting her into the playground for a fight. They go into an empty classroom. Religious studies, judging by the writing on the blackboard. The names of the prophets are listed, somewhat strangely, in alphabetical order.

'Are you listening to me?' he asks. She turns back to face him.

'You know,' she begins, 'I really don't need your anger or your hostility. You come to me when you're in trouble and you need help, and I stay up all night worrying about you, trying to find a way to help you. If I made a mistake, I'm sorry. But I want to help. That's all.'

'So you call my wife? And where did you get the number?' She laughs now.

'For heaven's sake, Geoff. These days you don't need to be

a detective to find things out.' He stares at her with a malevolence that she knows she has elicited. But he shouldn't have slept with her if he couldn't face the consequences. Maybe his past escapades have involved having a quick roll with whoever happened to take his fancy, but if this is what he's bargaining for, then he's made a terrible mistake.

'You have no right to call my wife, and you have no right to enter my life in this way. Have you any idea how much damage you've caused?' She realises that at the present time there is nothing that she can do or say to defuse his anger. However, she will continue to be there for him. He will need to come and see her, and she will help him to understand that although he has begun this relationship by being led by blind desire, it doesn't mean that he'll end up being trapped. She's not that kind of woman, and after all he will need somebody to take to La Spiaggia. He will need somebody to guide him. A firm hand. This will be her role. Although tempted to smile, she understands that such a gesture will be misinterpreted, so there will be no smile. Suddenly she is conscious of her blank expression, so she turns back to the blackboard and wonders just why the prophets are listed in alphabetical order.

'Are you listening?' She nods, but without turning her head. 'You and I are finished. I want you out of my life.' She waits until she hears him storm purposefully out of the classroom, and only now does she turn around. The truth is, there is something comforting about hearing that they are finished, implying as it does that they were actually started.

Her letter is short and to the point. She reminds him that abandonment is a state that is not alien to man. That throughout the ages people have voluntarily or involuntarily left behind people in their lives and gone on to higher and better things. There is nothing unusual about this. She stops short of rehearsing her own story with Brian, but it is all implied. She is making a plea for him to see himself in a bigger context and move on. She does not say who he should move on to, but again this is implied. She reads the letter through, correcting the odd ambiguity in the shaping of her letters and making sure that it is absolutely legible. Then she reads the letter through for grammar, and once she is satisfied she folds it neatly and tucks it into an envelope. She stands and walks to the door, where she unhooks her coat and steps into her walking shoes. His lodgings are easy to find, for on their first 'date' he had described them as a big corner house on Manor Farm Road overlooking the park. There is only one big corner house, and it has the look of a place that takes boarders, for the front garden has been dug up and replaced with gravel. Guests can park off the street behind the hedge. She stands by the gateway and realises that she will have to be stealthy, for the house is ablaze with lights.

She walks back by a different route, aware that she is simply killing time. At this time of night the streets are relatively empty, and even pleasant to walk through, but at 10.30 p.m. there will be a sudden rush of people from the twin-cinema complex, some making their way home, but most dashing to the city-centre pubs for a final drink. Of course, these new pubs with their security staff, and sawdust on the floor and loud thumping music bear no resemblance to what she recognises as a pub, but mercifully she is under no obligation to enter such hovels. At 11 p.m., when the places finally close, the unwashed rabble will slouch out into the streets, full of drink and spoiling for trouble, but she will be safely tucked up in bed. However, at the moment everything is quiet; the lull before the storm. And then she sees him. In the window of La Spiaggia with a woman. She stands across the road and looks at them, sitting at the table right next to the one that they had sat at. She should have brought the letter here. Delivered it to him personally, in front of this woman. She steps back into shadow in order to gather her thoughts, then her mind is clear and she knows what to do. She steps out and crosses towards them. When she is halfway across the road, he looks up and stares directly at her. The woman follows his eyes and turns and looks out of the window. The woman sees her, then looks quickly across at her date, then back at her. He looks angry, and moves as though he is going to get to his feet, but he remains seated as she walks by with her head held high. She is going home. She just happened to be passing La Spiaggia. Nothing planned or premeditated. This is a genuine coincidence. She just happened to be passing by. She continues to walk on her way and she wonders how Geoff Waverley will explain this to his friend. In fact, the more she thinks about it, the more she realises that this could not have turned out much better for her.

She is telephoned before she leaves for school.

'I'm afraid I need to speak to you on a matter of some urgency.' She waits for Mr Jowett to go on. 'This morning, after assembly, in my office.' He pauses and clears his throat. 'I'm sorry for disturbing you so early, but as I'm sure you understand, I would not do so unless it was important.' She finishes her cup of tea and dresses slowly, as though for a funeral. Why would he do something like this? It's between the two of them, and it doesn't concern anybody else. It's nobody else's business. She draws the curtains and can see that it is a grey, overcast morning, the type of day that will refuse to change its character. Across the street she sees that the paper boy is doing wheelies on his bike and it occurs to her that she could always have the *Daily Mail* delivered. She misses her morning paper, and there's really no reason why she should have to go without. Especially if the paper boy stops messing about and can actually be bothered to stuff some of the papers in his bag through people's letterboxes.

When she gets to school Miss Arthurton, Mr Jowett's tall angular secretary, ushers her into the head's office and pulls in the door behind her. Trapped. The deputy-head, Miss Mitchell, is seated to one side of Mr Jowett's desk. It is an awkward place to sit, for she has no place to rest her papers, which she balances uncomfortably in her lap. However, she knows that this suits Miss Mitchell, for she's the type of career woman who likes to cross and recross her legs in the hope that she might accidentally reveal a bit of stocking top.

'Please.' Mr Jowett gestures to the single chair in front of the desk. She sits and looks at him in his smug little cardigan and corduroy jacket, with not a button under pressure. 'I'll get straight to the point, although I suspect that you know what this is about.' He waits for her to reply, but she says nothing. 'Very well. I arrived at school this morning to discover Mr Waverley outside my office. I'm afraid he has lodged some very serious complaints at your doorstep and they will have to be fully investigated. Luckily we have a local-authority code of behaviour and Miss Mitchell here has brought a copy of the guidelines.' Miss Mitchell fishes through the pile of papers in her lap and hands her a flimsy document. 'Now what two consenting adults do outside of this school is, quite frankly, none of my business. Mr Waverley informs me that you two have had a full relationship, but this is not the point. At issue here is harassment, which is preventing a fellow member of staff from doing his job.'

Miss Mitchell coughs. And then she speaks.

'The charges are that you have repeatedly left Mr Waverley notes in his box. That you called his wife and, on behalf of all teachers at this school, expressed concern over his mental and physical health. That you have visited his lodgings and left him abusive mail. And that just last night while he was having dinner with his sister, you stood outside the restaurant window and stared at them both. All of these transgressions have contributed to a climate in which Mr Waverley feels he can no longer carry out his work here, and he has asked Mr Jowett to relieve him of his duties.' Miss Mitchell's speech is over and she leans back in her chair. But then she remembers one other thing. 'If you have anything to say, I think that now would probably be the time to say it.'

She looks at this woman, then at the benevolent, avuncular figure of Raymond Jowett. Do they seriously believe that a fifty-five-year-old divorcee can terrorise a forty-year-old grown man? She begins to laugh. Mr Jowett sighs.

'I'm afraid this is no laughing matter. These days there are laws and guidelines that protect the individual's right to peaceful co-existence with colleagues in the workplace. Unless you categorically tell me that you did not leave inappropriate messages either at his home or in his pigeonhole; that you did not call Mr Waverley's wife; that you did not stalk him last night, then I'm afraid I will have to suspend you from your duties for two weeks while we take statements from all parties concerned, including colleagues of yours with whom you work closely. I'm afraid it's the law.' She shakes her head in disbelief.

'Are you serious? This has to be a joke.' But nobody is laughing. Miss Mitchell stands up. She turns to her superior.

'Mr Jowett, if I may.' Mr Jowett nods surreptitiously, but with sadness. Miss Mitchell turns to face her. 'You have a copy of the code. Either myself, or somebody from the district office, will be in touch regarding your interview. This should take place in the next ten days or so. As of now, as the head says, you should consider yourself on a two-week leave with full pay. This will, of course, be kept strictly confidential.'

She looks from the upright Miss Mitchell to Mr Jowett,

but he merely nods in helpless agreement. She gets to her feet.

In the evening she calls her sister in London. Sheila is surprised to hear from her, and she knows immediately that something is the matter.

'Nothing,' she says. 'I just thought that I'd come and see you, if that's all right.' There is a short pause. She knows that Sheila is trying to decide whether it is best to have the discussion now, or save it until they are together, for she knows that her impatient sister does not like to be lied to.

'What time are you arriving?'

'I haven't checked on the buses yet, but I'll call you from the station tomorrow.' Again there is a short pause, and then Sheila remembers her manners.

'Good. It's been too long.'

'Yes, it has.' After she has spoken with Sheila she pours herself a glass of white wine. Then she sits at the piano, her fingers resting lightly on the keys, but she cannot summon the energy to disrupt the silence. Instead she stares at the score, and sees small anecdotes and exclamation points of advice that over the years she has scratched in the margins. It would appear that back then she was afraid of nothing, for difficult passages are circled in a manner which suggests that one should be aware of the upcoming problem but tackle it nonetheless. But this evening she cannot find it within herself to do anything other than lightly brush the keys with the tips of her fingers.

She wakes early the next morning. The sky is still dark, but she knows that the day will soon arrive. She sits in bed and brushes her hair with idle strokes, transforming her grey locks into a flowing tail. Then, once she sees the first rays of dawn, she gets up and showers and then dresses herself with quiet anxiety coursing through her veins. She has made no preparations. There is no booked seat, no bag standing by the door. She has not cleaned the house, or cancelled the milk. Nothing. It is all very unlike her and it serves to remind her of how unsure she is about what she is doing. She locks the door and steps out into the street as daylight begins to brighten the sky. As she walks to the bus stop she notices that the bold circular disc of the moon is still visible, which leads her to wonder whether night has lingered too long or morning arrived too soon. Once she reaches the main bus station she buys a return ticket on the first coach to London, and then she calls Sheila and tells her what time she will be arriving. Sheila is still asleep, she can hear it in her voice, but her sister tries to pretend otherwise. She buys a copy of the *Daily Mail*, plus a couple of women's magazines, and then she boards the coach and finds a seat behind the driver and close to the front. There are still twenty minutes to go before the scheduled departure time, but her efforts to settle in are undermined by the driver's conversation with a young man who stands by the door to the bus clutching his bicycle. He wants to put the bike in the luggage space underneath the coach, but the driver is pointing out to him that unless the bike folds up flat, then this cannot happen. Soon the young man is shouting at the driver, then cursing him in foul language. The driver looks at the abusive youngster, who could be his son, with a look of sad bemusement etched on his face. The young man continues to jab his finger in the driver's direction and bellow at the top of his lungs. She looks away, ashamed and puzzled. It is one thing to be frustrated by rules, but it is another thing to flout authority in such a vulgar manner. These are not happy times for anybody.

About halfway to London they stop at a motorway service station. She has been sleeping, and as she opens her eyes she finds herself peering out at the bleak scene of unappetising fast-food places, an RAC stand, rows of unused telephones and neon-lit petrol pumps. Most choose to leave the coach, but she decides to stay on board. It is only a fifteen-minute stop, and if she needs the bathroom then there's one on the coach. The man across the aisle begins to make a performance out of loudly munching an apple, and then salting a hard-boiled egg and taking a bite, before switching back to the apple. She looks away in dismay, and then thinks of Sheila, who could never live up to her big sister's exam results. In fact, she fell comfortably beneath them and eventually took off for London where she found work as a secretary in a law firm. Within six months, she had met Roger who, having finished his time as a trainee in music and arts at the BBC, was now dipping his toes into the world of documentary film-making. Whenever she and Brian would travel to London from Birmingham, either to attend a play or a concert, or on one of Brian's business trips, they would generally take Sheila and Roger out for a meal. Then, as Roger's career began to flourish, the young couple moved into a flat of their own in Maida Vale that was in the middle of a bland neighbourhood of crushing respectability whose tedious streets neither gained nor changed character. It all seemed so unlike Sheila, but she thought it best to say nothing to her sister. On a few occasions, Sheila and Roger had them round and insisted on cooking for them, although Brian usually objected to this as he claimed that vegetarian food made him sick. However, never once did Sheila mention marriage, or, more puzzlingly, children. When she got the letter from her sister announcing her split with Roger (who was by now winning awards for his documentary films) and informing her that Sheila was now setting up home with a Maria Kingston 'across the river', she was shocked. After twenty-five years with a man, her sister was only now discovering that she wanted to be with a woman? Brian smirked, and then began to laugh. He claimed that he had always had his suspicions.

With this move came a career change for Sheila, who finally left the legal world and became a full-time employee of the local Labour Party. Two years after the letter, Dorothy met her sister's friend Maria for the first and only time at their mother's funeral. Their father was both too ill and too grief-stricken to notice that Sheila had brought her 'girlfriend' to the funeral, but if it wasn't for Brian's stern words she would definitely have said something to her younger sister. As it was, everybody managed to be civil to everybody else, and then, within a year, her father died, but Sheila and Maria did not bother with this funeral. Roger sent flowers, but Brian removed the card and tore it into pieces, claiming that he'd never liked Roger's holier-than-thou attitude. And then Brian left her, and she left Birmingham and moved back home. As the coach thundered its way towards London she calculated that it was now over six years since she had last seen Sheila at her mother's funeral. The odd Christmas card maintained the illusion of some kind of intimacy, but in reality all that bound them together was blood and the increasingly distant memories of a past that they shared. However, right now, on this coach to London, this was enough.

There was no sign of Maria Kingston. Sheila, however, was clearly visible behind the barriers. She had become thin, emaciated even, but her lopsided grin remained intact. As the coach swooped in an unnecessarily flamboyant semi-circle, she looked at her sister, who as yet did not seem to realise that of the many coaches pulling in and out of Victoria Station, this was the one that she was waiting for. She scrutinised Sheila, then realised that it was not so much that she looked older; the point was her sister appeared to be calmer and more centred. The thin, middle-aged lady with the long coat bore little resemblance to the fiery young woman who loved to tease

Brian over dinner, but when a subject close to her own heart came up, hers were always the first eyes to ignite. Everything always had to be extreme with Sheila. Yes, I will do this. No, I won't do that. No flexibility. But after nearly six years, and even before she has spoken with her sister, she can see that Sheila is radiating a new calm. And, if truth be told, this is what she has come to London for. She has travelled south in search of calmness.

Sheila's house has a sloppy bohemian feel to it that suggests a letting go. She looks around. Her sister has changed not only in appearance, but also in aesthetic taste. With Roger it was stripped pine, and furniture with hard angles and clean lines. The new Sheila appears to embrace hand-woven fabrics, prints, glass jars full of organic pastas, and cats. She wonders what her sister would make of her own ordered existence, but realises that it would, undoubtedly, remind her of their parents, and therefore bring forth little more than contempt. Sheila pours the water onto the two tea bags and then she puts the kettle back onto the stove. She pushes a pile of newspapers to one side, and as she does so she plonks the two mugs down on the table top.

'Herbal tea only. I'm afraid I'm a bit purist these days.' She smiles at her younger sister, but the sadness in Sheila's eyes is clearly visible. She takes the mug of tea and warms her hands on it. 'Rosehip,' says Sheila. 'It's all I have at the moment. I'm sorry if it's not to your taste.'

'It's fine,' she says. 'Just fine.'

'Maybe after you finish the tea we can go for a walk around the garden. Or we could take the tea with us. I bought this place for next to nothing with Maria.' She puts down her cup and looks at Sheila.

'Isn't it a bad area, Brixton? I mean, you hear so much on the news about problems.' Sheila laughs.

'The news? If you believed everything you heard on the news you'd never go anywhere in London. There are places all over this city where middle-class people take a five-minute ride in a mini-cab to the tube station because the silly buggers are afraid of being mugged. But I suppose you can always hide if you've got money. It's no different down here than anywhere else. And besides, it was the only place we could afford.' Sheila pauses and takes a sip of her tea. 'Anyhow, I hope you get to see Maria. I think she'll be back in the next day or so.'

She tries to look pleased, but she knows that it is not going to be possible for her to have this, or any other kind, of conversation unless she says something to her sister.

'Sheila,' she says. 'The wig.' Sheila laughs.

'Lung cancer. That's what you get for years of smoking roll-ups, isn't it?'

She pushes her mug of tea to one side and reaches over and takes her younger sister's bony hands in between her own.

'Sheila. What's going on?'

Her sister lowers her eyes and her shoulders begin to shake, at first slowly, then with a juddering rhythm that passes through her whole body.

'Not now, Dorothy. Later, perhaps, but not now.'

She lies in bed and stares at the bright-blue wallpaper, which seems to be in stark contrast to the rest of the house, and she listens to the wind whipping around the roof and rattling the window panes. Stubborn Sheila who, having endured her sister's silent wrath at bringing her girlfriend to their mother's funeral, simply refused to attend the funeral of their father. As a result Dorothy stood by the grave, along with her father's distraught drinking friends, and a large turnout of neighbours, thinking the whole while of Sheila safe in London, insulated from the hurt and confusion of the ceremony. And then it started to rain, huge drops of fat water, each drop a shower in its own right. Sheila had tucked herself safely away in London and left her big sister to grieve alone in a muddy cemetery in the north of England. And now, crisp between two tightly folded sheets, her sister has again discarded her. Left her to discover for herself facts that should have been shared. But rather than feel angry towards Sheila, she stares at the wallpaper and tries to understand. She wonders if there is not some element of revenge to her sister's behaviour. Sheila was already fifteen when Dorothy left for Manchester University, but perhaps she ought to have written more, or come home more often, not immediately buried her aspirations beneath those of Brian. Through the open window she can see the dark sky, and it surprises her that in London stars can be so bright. And then she understands that she owes her sister the sacrifice of her company, and although she has not told Sheila about her own situation back 'home', she knows now that this is where she should be. It is right that she is in London with her younger sister and her crooked wig, and when Maria comes back her companion will simply have to work around the two sisters. This is how it will be in the future.

The elderly doctor appears to be a kindly man, but he is nervous. There is something discomforting about the way he keeps moving around in his chair, and his eyes seem to be focused on a spot a few inches above her head. When the nurse announced that Sheila had arrived with her sister, he asked if he might speak with the sister alone. Sheila seemed unconcerned and simply went off for more tests.

'I think,' he continues, 'that as the next of kin, so to speak, I have to be blunt with you.' She looks at this man, who appears to be still fascinated by whatever it is that is hovering over her head. 'Your sister's cancer is inoperable. I have asked her to stop working. To keep working will only accelerate her deterioration.' He lowers his eyes, as though curious to see how she is taking this news. She stares directly at him, so he once more looks to the ceiling. 'Will you be staying with her for long?'

'I'm not sure. She has a friend, Maria, who should be back soon. Maybe until then.' She is not about to disclose her own resolutions to the doctor.

'I see.' He waits a beat. Then he once again lowers his eyes to meet her own. 'It's never easy for a patient to come to terms with this situation, but your sister possesses a tranquillity which is in many ways quite remarkable.' The doctor seems worried now, as though wondering if he ought to explain exactly what he means. But she does not require any explication from this doctor. She has seen it for herself. The only thing that puzzles her is whether this tranquillity was there before the illness, or if the illness has brought this on. 'Is there anything that you need to ask me?' The word 'need' seems a little strange to her, but she simply shakes her head. 'There are,' he says 'various agencies who specialise in counselling of one sort or another. The nurse can give you their numbers if you're interested.' She is momentarily puzzled and wonders if he means counselling for her or for Sheila, but she decides not to trouble this man any further.

'Thank you,' she says. He gets to his feet.

'Your sister shouldn't be too long now.' He hands her a card that he takes from a tray on his desk. 'Please call me if there's anything at all that's worrying you. This will not be an easy time for her, and I can see how much of a shock this has been for you.'

In the evening she sits at the back of the hall at the local Labour Party meeting. Resting on the chair next to her is a plastic shopping bag full of files and papers that Sheila has asked her to return to her employers, along with a letter of resignation. After this morning's tests they walked around her sister's garden, and Sheila pointed out all the plants that she and Maria had planted, and she occasionally stopped to pluck off a brown leaf, or break back a weed or a stray branch. Then they sat at the small wooden picnic table, with its two neatly arranged benches, and Sheila confessed to her sister that she was extremely tired. She admitted that her job as the secretary of the local Labour Party was simply too much, and then she rolled her eyes and declared that Tony Blair's revolution would just have to do without her. At least for now. She laughed at Sheila's comment and agreed to take back the necessary files that evening.

Derek is just as Sheila has described him. A tall man who carries himself awkwardly, and who possesses a face that positively oozes nervous concern. He winds up the meeting, fields some gently pitched enquiries, and then strolls towards her at the back of the hall. She stands up to greet him, and he extends his hand.

'I'm happy to meet you,' he says, welcoming her with a smile that she imagines he bought somewhere. 'But I'm sorry to hear about Sheila's resignation. She'll be sorely missed.' She picks up the shopping bag.

'Sheila asked me to bring these for you. She wanted you to have them straight away.'

'Well, it's typical of her to be so thoughtful.' She stares at this man, who seems somewhat unnerved by this encounter.

'Do you have somebody lined up to take her job?'

He laughs nervously. 'Well, I'm only the local chair. And mine's a voluntary position. Sheila's job will have to be decided on by the whole committee, including our MP, but as it's the only full-time job we have there's bound to be plenty of competition.' Then he stops, as though suddenly aware of what he has just said. 'Would you be interested in the job?' He is clearly embarrassed that this has not already occurred to him. She smiles.

'Thank you, but I already have a job.' This poor nervous man.

'Of course.' He laughs skittishly. 'Well,' he says, 'we usually go to the pub for a tipple and to thrash things around somewhat. You know, set the world to rights.' He glances towards a small knot of people who are waiting for him by the door. 'Would you like to join us?'

'No, but thanks very much. I've got to get back.'

'Of course,' he says, 'I understand.' They stare at each other and then he once again holds out his hand, which she shakes. 'Please convey our warmest wishes to Sheila for a speedy recovery.'

'I will,' she says, and she watches as he turns to leave. 'Don't forget the papers.' He stops and laughs. She hands him the shopping bag, which he cradles in his arms like a child.

'How stupid of me.'

The following evening the sisters go to the local cinema to see a film by a friend of Roger's. Sheila is adamant that she and Brian met the director one night at dinner. Sheila is also convinced that Roger has always been jealous of his friend's successful move into features, while Roger has been stuck, albeit at the high end, in television documentary. But she does not remember this man, nor does she remember Roger's jealousy. As she watches the film, her mind wanders. It must be nearly forty years since she last sat with her sister in the dark. No doubt her parents had bullied her into taking Sheila to some cartoon or other, but the rediscovery of something as simple as a trip to the cinema with Sheila fills her with a cautious joy. After all, so much between them continues to remain unspoken. Sheila, for all her new-found serenity, still appears to be unreceptive to intimacy, and the hours between meals are stitched together in silence. There has been no sharing of photographs, or affable tumbling down the paths of old memories. Her sister appears to be grateful for her presence, but she remains hermetically sealed.

She looks across at Sheila. She wants to tell her about how, after she left to go off with Maria, Roger had called her and suggested that the next time she came to London they should meet for a drink. And how she manufactured an excuse to Brian about a concert at Wigmore Hall, and met Roger in a club in Soho that lay behind a single unmarked door. Once she was buzzed inside, and had climbed the seemingly endless steps, she entered a smoky room that appeared to be full of over-confident men. Roger waved to her from the bar and immediately pressed a drink upon her and told her that he was heartbroken to be 'dumped' by Sheila, but as the evening progressed it was unclear what purpose she served, other than to provide him with an audience for his self-pity. Corrosion was the order of the evening: Roger soon began to refer to Maria as 'the lesbian bitch'; the Labour Party became 'the fucking reds'; and Sheila was castigated as 'self-righteous and jealous of my success'. She listened until it was time to take the last train back. Sadly, she would have to mark school papers on the train, and she was already worried that she might have drunk too much wine. As she stood to leave, Roger offered to walk her back downstairs to the door. He had spotted some friends from the world of commercial film standing at the other end of the bar, and so he was staying. She thanked him, but told him that she would let herself out, which she did, and on the train back to Birmingham she didn't know whether to feel pity for Roger or for herself. And now, sitting here in the dark, watching Roger's friend's dreadful film, all she wants to do is reach over and take her sister's hand and tell her about that evening, to share with her how she feels about this betrayal, but Sheila appears to be moored in a peaceful place. She sits with her sister, tears beginning to form in her eyes, and waits. And then eventually the credits begin to roll, and she quickly wipes her eyes, and as the house lights come up, her sister gives her that lopsided grin of hers.

The telephone rings twice and then she picks it up. The man's voice is pleasant, but he speaks with a strangely detached authority. She confirms her name, but as she does so she wonders how this man knows who she is. She has not given anybody Sheila's telephone number.

'I'm calling you from St Thomas's Hospital.' Immediately she knows that something is wrong, for this is not Sheila's hospital. 'I'm a police officer. Your sister has been the victim of a mugging attack, but she's fine. We're bringing her home by car and we just want to make sure that you'll be there to receive her.'

'Can I speak to her?'

The officer laughs slightly, as though mocking her concern. 'Believe me, she's fine. She's actually already in the car. We won't be long.'

She puts down the telephone and feels as though she could scream with frustration. This morning Sheila had insisted in her usual cold manner that she would go to the hospital by herself, and not wishing to cause any argument she had simply let her sister have her own way. She takes a deep breath and then decides that there's little else that she can do except put on the kettle and wait for the police to bring her sister home.

Sheila has a huge piece of white gauze on her forehead that is held in place by two broad strips of Elastoplast.

'It's just where I hit my head when I fell.' Sheila sips at her cup of hot water. 'And the bloody wig came off, lot of use that is. They put in some stitches.'

'Some stitches?'

'About a dozen, they said. I don't remember. But I'm all right.'

'What did he take?' Sheila shrugs her shoulders.

'My bag, but there wasn't much in it. A credit card, some ID, bits and pieces.'

'Shouldn't we stop the card?'

'The nurse at the hospital did that for me.' She stands and pours herself another cup of tea, then sits again, this time next to Sheila.

'Has this ever happened before?'

'Christ, this is London, not Afghanistan. It was just a mugging. I didn't resist, and I got away, okay?'

'But you saw him, right?'

Sheila laughs now. 'Oh, I saw him all right. Strapping bastard, and cocky with it.'

'But you'd recognise him?'

'Not really, they all look the same.' She pauses. 'Of course I'd recognise him.'

'That's not what I meant.' Sheila takes another sip of her hot water.

'Look, I was a little shaken up. I admit it. And I don't much like the sight of blood, especially my own. But I'm all right.' Sheila arches her eyebrows. 'And, I'm glad you're here. Thank you.'

In the afternoon, it is a plain-clothes officer who takes a seat in the living room. He is older than the man who brought Sheila back from the hospital, and he seems more business-like. Either he joined the force late, after a false start in another career, or he is simply not very good at his job and promotion has passed him by. He flips open a pad, jams the head of the ballpoint against his leg so that the nib pops out, and then he looks up at the two sisters who sit on the sofa before him.

'Right then, we've already got the description from the other officer, but is there anything that you'd like to add.' Sheila shakes her head. 'Clothes? Distinguishing facial marks? Voice? What did he sound like? London accent? Jamaican? Anything will help.' Again Sheila shakes her head. The officer sighs.

'He did speak, didn't he? There must be something that you can remember.' Sheila looks across at the officer.

'I don't want to press charges. It doesn't matter.' The policeman seems surprised, but he responds as though he has heard this line before.

'You mean, if you'll excuse my language, you want to leave the bastard on the street so he can do this to somebody else? Except maybe the next person won't be as lucky as you were.' Sheila is adamant.

'I don't want to press charges, and that's the end of it, okay?' Dorothy looks at Sheila in surprise. The officer senses the futility of the situation.

'Is there some reason why you don't want to prosecute this man? He knocked you to the ground, he took your bag and left you bleeding. Do you think you owe him something? Or do you know him, is that it?'

'I don't know him. I've never seen him before in my life, but what's going to happen to him when you lot get hold of him? Accidentally fall over and bang his head in the cell, will he? Or by some mysterious process will his belt find its way around his neck? I know what happens to young blacks in police cells. You just can't wait, can you?' The officer snaps his pad shut and gets to his feet.

'You know, if that's what you think, then maybe you deserve to have these people loose on the streets.'

'These people?' There is a note of triumph in Sheila's voice, but the policeman is unperturbed.

'Criminals.' He spits the word out. 'Crackheads who'll dump you down a rubbish chute, or pour petrol through your door, if you look at them wrong. That's who I mean. Violent bastards who don't respect the law, and whose only ambition in life is to score some draw and stab people up.'

Sheila laughs. 'But you know how to teach them to respect the law, don't you?'

The officer and Sheila stare at each other. Then the policeman reaches into his pocket and pulls out a card. He drops it on the coffee table, and then he turns to face Dorothy. She stands.

'If your sister comes to her senses, that's where you can find me. Otherwise, enjoy the rest of your day. I'll let myself out.'

She hears the door slam and she sits again, this time in the chair opposite Sheila. She looks at her sister, who stares blankly at the wall. She can see that Sheila is tired and wants to go to bed, and she has not got the heart to argue with her.

Her sister sleeps right through until the morning. She is sitting at the kitchen table when the phone rings and she grabs it, keen that it should not wake Sheila. She recognises Mr Jowett's voice.

'Ah, I didn't expect you to answer the phone.'

'Mr Jowett.'

'Well, Miss Jones, thoughtful of you to leave your sister's number, for as it turns out things have moved ahead rather quickly. We've tentatively scheduled a preliminary hearing for you tomorrow. Would this be convenient for you?'

'A hearing?'

'It's just a formality, but it's much better if you're here in person to account for yourself.' She pauses before answering.

'You mean defend myself?'

'I'm merely informing you of the process.' Now it is his turn to pause. He sighs deeply, and then he continues. 'Please, Dorothy, there's really no need for this to become confrontational, now is there?' She wants no more of this discussion.

'What time tomorrow?'

'Two p.m.'

'I'll be there.' Before Mr Jowett has a chance to say anything further she puts down the receiver. And then she looks up and sees Sheila in her nightdress, standing in the doorway to the kitchen. 'I've got to go back. That was the headmaster.' Sheila moves towards her and sits at the table.

'Holiday over, then?'

'I'll be back. I just have to sort something out.' She stands and runs water into the kettle, and then she puts it on the stove. Sheila yawns and leans back in her chair. Her sister slowly pushes her hands in the air.

'I'll be fine. I might volunteer at the communal gardens.'

'Is that a good idea?'

'Of course it's a good idea. I can't just lie around here all day.'

'Tea or water?'

'Water, please.'

'Any idea when Maria is coming back from Brighton?'

'What's that got to do with anything?' Sheila glares at her. Then she sighs. 'Look, I don't know what's going on with her. We've not been getting on too well.'

'Nice timing.'

'I don't expect her to stop her life just because I've got cancer.'

'Isn't she supposed to want to be here for you?'

'She's supposed to do whatever she wants to do.'

'Water or tea?'

'I said water, not tea. What's the matter with you?'

She looks at Sheila, who lowers her eyes.

'I'm sorry, I didn't sleep very well. I kept seeing his bloody face.'

'Whose face?'

'Tony Blair's, who do you think? The mugger's of course. I just can't get it out of my head.'

'Are you sure you don't want to press charges?'

'Come on, what's the bloody point?'

She pours the hot water, and then she reaches for a herbal tea bag. And then she remembers. She hands Sheila her hot water, but she places the tea bag on the side. Sheila can make up her own mind. She leaves her sister to contemplate, and she goes upstairs to pack her bag.

She sits in Mr Jowett's office, but is somewhat surprised to find that only he is present. Miss Arthurton shuts the door gingerly, careful to make no noise whatsoever. She leaves them alone. And now Mr Jowett speaks. He places both hands on the desk in front of him, and she wonders if he is aware of the fact that he is striking an awkward, even vaguely ridiculous, pose.

'First of all, I want to thank you for coming all the way back here from London. As it turns out we don't really have a procedure that is adequate to cover the full nature of Mr Waverley's complaints. I did take the matter up with the local education authority, but I'm afraid we now find ourselves at a bit of an impasse.' She stares at him.

'An impasse? I don't follow you, Mr Jowett.'

'No, of course not.' He clasps his hands and then brings them both up to his chin. 'Well, there is a bit of a problem. You see it looks as though we'll be offering Mr Waverley a full-time position among us. His family situation seems to have resolved itself, and we are in dire need of a geography teacher.' He pauses to allow her to speak, but she says nothing. 'I think it might be best if you were to leave, don't you? Mr Waverley is prepared to let bygones be bygones, and I think I can offer you a decent early retirement package. There will be no question of censure, of course. You're simply doing what so many of your colleagues are doing these days and taking advantage of this new window on life. I believe they call it the third age.' She looks at Mr Jowett, who she is sure never dared imagine that he would ever ascend to such professional heights. To be a history master was probably the full extent of his ambitions, but good fortune has enabled him to exercise an unimagined authority. She stands.

'Thank you, Mr Jowett.' He looks somewhat panicked.

'Well, will you be taking up our offer?'

'I shall let you know.' She turns and begins to walk out before Mr Jowett can uncouple himself from his desk. There is no point closing his door behind her. The mousy-haired Miss Arthurton, who looks up from her desk, will see to that. But only after she has brought Mr Jowett a nice cup of tea.

She looks through the window of the bus at the people in the streets below. Her town feels small after London. She had thought this as she rode home in the taxi from the bus station. She literally dropped her bags in the hallway, nudged the mail to one side with the outside of her shoe, and then dashed back out and into the taxi whose meter continued to tick. She had asked the driver to wait so that she would not be late for her appointment with what she imagined would be a panel of stern-faced interrogators. She smiles at her folly and gazes down at the mid-afternoon trickle of shoppers. And then she sees the newly daubed signs on the sloping slate roofs, signs that are meant to be read from the upper deck. In tall white letters somebody has painted GOD IS GOOD, and on the neighbouring roof, CHRIST DIED FOR OUR SINS. If her mother had had her way, such sentiments would have meant something to her but, with some regret in her heart, she has to acknowledge that her father's opinions in these matters enjoy total dominion. This being the case, she looks at the defaced roofs and finds it surprising that the council doesn't have rules and regulations against this type of graffiti.

When the bus reaches her stop she gets to her feet and

moves quickly down the stairs to the lower deck, and then she steps down and onto the pavement. It is as though she has no control over her decision. She walks straight to the shop and as she opens the door she hears the familiar tinkle of the doorbell. He is alone. Mahmood seems neither shocked nor angry. In fact, he seems curiously shy.

'I just thought I'd come by and say hello. But I'll go if you want me to. It's just that I may be away for some time and, well, it just seems silly.' Mahmood puts down the pile of magazines that he is holding.

'You seem very tired. Have you been sleeping?'

'I'm going away, Mahmood. My sister is not very well, and I've got to help her.' Mahmood seems puzzled.

'But I did not think the two of you got along.'

'Well, we didn't. But things change, and there you have it. And how have you been?' He now looks somewhat dejected.

'Oh, so and so.' As he says this he shakes his head from side to side so that it wobbles as though it might, at any minute, fall off.

'Listen, I'm sorry about the awkwardness with Feroza. I won't come back again, but I just wanted to let you know. About my sister, that is.'

'You can come back in whenever you like. I can control my wife. I am the man of this house. But since the child she is crazy. I cannot allow my wife to smoke and drink. The English they have spoiled her so that she is like them, and happy to sit around and play with the child and expect the wage cheque or the dole cheque.' She looks at Mahmood, and cannot remember having seen him so agitated. But she has often thought that the child in him was put down far too early. 'I have been thinking that I should take my chance and drive a mini-cab rather than suffer all this newsagent business by myself. In fact, this England is crazy. I go in the streets and after all these years in this country they tell me, "Your mother fucks dogs." Why does my mother fuck dogs? They do not know my mother. In my home there is problems. Out on the street there is problems.' Mahmood stops and looks at her. 'I am sorry, but today is not a good day. It is a very bad day.'

'I am sorry, Mahmood.' She takes a step towards him. 'Things will pick up.'

'You, of all people, must not be sorry. You understand Mahmood.' She looks at her friend and finds herself wishing that she had not come into his shop. Not on this bad day.

'I should go now, Mahmood.' She wants to pamper him, innocently. She wants to feel the warmth of his skin. However, she knows that this would be unwise. She smiles weakly, and then she quickly turns and leaves Mahmood's shop.

At home she puts the letters, all of them, into a metal pail. She walks to the back door and pulls it open. The door sticks. It has always stuck, but without a man to help she has had to learn to tolerate the door. For a moment she wonders if she should rummage through the letters in case there is one from Geoff Waverley. A permanent job? Does the man have any idea of what he is doing? She thinks not. She strikes the match against the large household box, and then she drops the lighted stick into the pail. She watches as the flames begin to dance now. The smoke will attract some attention, but most of her neighbours will be at work. It will burn quickly. There is no need to unpack, of course. There is no need to even telephone Sheila. In the morning she will place flowers on the graves of her parents, and then take the bus to London. Once there she will telephone Mr Jowett and accept his offer. Early retirement. And nothing to fill her life with, apart from Sheila. But this is a new blessing. A purpose, and a chance to repair history. She feels fortunate. As though life is now finally beginning. And almost everybody seems happy with her.

When she reaches Brixton she discovers the house to be in darkness. She places her bag on the kitchen table and shouts for Sheila, but her sister does not respond. She goes upstairs and turns on the lights, and then she moves along the hallway to her sister's bedroom and pushes gently at the door. Her sister is lying in bed, and the room is illuminated by a single lighted candle that burns on top of the chest of drawers. Sheila's discarded wig lies on the laundry basket like an unloved pet. She tries not to make any noise as she spies on Sheila, who looks both peaceful and exhausted, although it's apparent that life is slowly leaking out of her. She wonders about the wisdom of having a candle burning in this fashion, but she does not want to blow it out in case her sister has some special reason for the candle being lit. So she closes the door and leaves Sheila at rest. Downstairs she puts on the kettle and makes herself a cup of tea. Then she hears a light knocking at the door and she rushes to open it before the person can knock again. She recognises Derek from the Labour Party meeting, but he is looking at her in a strange fashion, and his eyes are slightly watery, as though he has been crying.

'Sheila told me you'd be back today. I called earlier. I was wondering if we might go out for a drink?' She looks at this man in astonishment.

'A drink?'

'I mean so we can talk privately.' She thinks for a moment, and then she opens the door a little wider.

'Sheila's asleep. If you want to talk privately, then we can do so here.' He hesitates for a moment, and then he realises that he has to make a decision.

'All right then. If you're sure that this is fine by you.' She stands back to let him pass, and then she shuts the door behind him. He takes a seat at the kitchen table and she crosses the room and takes a cup from the cupboard over the sink.

'Tea?' He nods.

'Yes, please. Nothing in it.' She quickly makes the tea, places it before him, and then she sits opposite him. She picks up her bag and removes it from the table.

'Now then, is there something the matter?' Derek takes a sip of his tea and looks directly at her.

'I suppose there's no easy way to say this, but it's to do with Maria.'

'She's not coming back, is she?'

'Well, it's not that straightforward. Maria is outside in the car.' She opens her mouth to speak, but before she can ask any questions he continues. 'Maria and I are, well, I suppose the easiest way of putting it is, an item.' She stares at Derek.

'You mean Maria has left Sheila for you?' He nods. 'And does Sheila know this?'

'No, of course not, but I didn't want to keep you in the dark.'

'I see, but you don't mind keeping Sheila in the dark, is that it?'

'Well, that's just the point. We're both worried about what effect it will have on Sheila's health if she finds out.'

'So you want it to be our little secret?'

Derek says nothing. He paws his mug of tea as though he is about to drink it, but then he gently pushes it away.

'I'm sorry, I'd better go.'

'Yes, you'd better. Especially if she's outside in the car. We wouldn't want her to get lonely, would we?'

Derek stands. 'I can see you're upset and I don't blame you. But these things happen.'

She laughs. 'I won't dignify that with a response.'

She and Derek stare at each other, but she decides to say nothing more, not wanting the responsibility of further curdling this man's already inadequate sense of himself. Derek lowers his shameful eyes and turns to leave, and she follows him to the door. He waits before opening it, and then he turns to face her.

'For what it's worth, Maria is devastated by this situation.'

'You mean the Maria who is sitting outside in the car, right now?'

Derek opens the door and she closes it behind him without bothering to glance out into the street. She begins to wash the cups and the teapot, and having done so she puts everything back into the cupboard and then she sits in a spotless kitchen. The moonlight is streaming in through the kitchen window and again she remembers her father's funeral, and Sheila's wilful absence, but as the years have passed by she has found it increasingly difficult to blame her sister for her absence. After all, her sister's pain is connected to her own guilt with a bond that neither of them can untie, and all that she now hopes for is the belated opportunity to repair the damage that has been wrought between them. Perhaps Sheila could move back north, and maybe buy a place by the seaside. They might walk together on the beach, and occasionally contemplate taking trips together. They might even go abroad. These are pleasant thoughts that will help her to survive another night in London in her sister's lonely home. She turns off the kitchen light and then slowly climbs the stairs. Before going to her own room she checks on Sheila, but her sister is still sleeping peacefully. This time she decides to go in and blow out the candle.

The first policeman, the one in uniform, fingers the pencil with increasing frustration. He stares at her, and although he sympathises with her situation there is precious little that he can do. He has said this a number of times, and his body language makes this abundantly clear. And then the senior officer arrives, the one without a uniform, and he sits down beside her. He fails to reintroduce himself, but it is clear that he has been briefed on the situation.

'I'm sorry, but if your sister doesn't wish to press charges, then there's nothing that we can do. I mean, we're pretty sure we know who he is.'

The officer pushes a piece of paper in front of her. She sees his sour face, and beneath it all his vital statistics. Details of his date of birth, height, weight, colour of eyes, everything. His address, phone number, it all seems so straightforward.

'I know it's difficult to believe, but we just haven't got a case without your sister's co-operation.'

She stares at the officer, but there is effectively nothing further to be said. They both know that Sheila won't change her mind. When Dorothy left the house this morning her sister was still in bed. Sheila had asked for a cup of hot water, and before she went to fetch it she relit her sister's candle. All thoughts of the assault seemed to have fled from her mind. In fact, it was difficult for her to know what, if anything, Sheila was thinking about. The officer scrapes back his chair and gets to his feet.

'I'm sorry, love, but unless you can talk some sense into her, we've got to move on. It's not as if we're short of work round here.'

She sits on the upper deck of the bus, and to the left-hand side, so that she can keep an eye out for Imran's Southern Fried Chicken. The uniformed policeman had told her that it would be the stop after this, and he had warned her to be careful. He'd laughed, 'Don't wear your Rolex', but wishing to maintain some loyalty to Sheila she'd said nothing in reply. The bus is full of schoolchildren whom she knows should be at school, but who seem determined to make as much noise as possible. Her natural reflex as a teacher is to shout at them and demand that they calm down, but she has to remind herself that soon she will no longer be a teacher. That part of her life will presently be over. And even if she were still a teacher, these are London kids and highly unlikely to take any notice of a little old lady who should be downstairs anyhow. And then she sees Imran's Southern Fried Chicken and her hand reaches up to the bell. As she steps from the bus the estate unfolds before her like a dark shadow, a vast landscape of council flats, barking dogs and worn-out grass. Filth is strewn everywhere, and a group of kids are playing what seems to be an organised game of football using a tin can instead of a ball. She walks past Bojangles, which she can see is a former Catholic church that has now become the estate disco, and then she passes the cracked and peeling outdoor swimming pool, which looks as though it has never seen any water.

Pretoria Drive leads to Pretoria Mansions, and she climbs the stinking urine-stained circular staircase to the third floor. Once there, she walks along the balcony and knocks at the door. He answers with a child, a half-caste girl whom she guesses to be about three, clutching one leg. 'Yeah, what do you want?' He seems neither puzzled nor concerned as to why this woman has knocked at his door. No doubt he imagines her to be a social worker or a probation officer.

'I've come about my sister,' she says.

'What about your sister? I don't know who your sister is.'

'You attacked and robbed her.' He reaches down and encourages the girl to go back into the flat. Then he steps out onto the third-floor balcony, forcing her to move back. He pulls the door behind him, then slowly, and very deliberately, he looks her up and down.

'You got a parachute?' She says nothing. 'Cos you're gonna fucking need one if you come round here talking like that.'

'You can keep the money, I just want her things back, that's all.' He looks her up and down again.

'You know, you've got some front, but you can just fuck off. If I ever set eyes on you again you're gonna get hurt, am I making myself clear?' She stares at him and wonders what possible nobility Sheila sees in such savages. He was making himself perfectly clear, standing there sweating his filth and spewing his words. Two steps removed from the jungle.

A week after Dorothy came back from Pretoria Mansions, Sheila died. The elderly doctor came to the house twice during the final day, but he said very little. What could he say? Sheila had refused the services of a nurse, and had made it clear that she would not be going near a hospital. There was always a candle burning in her room now, day and night. Redcurrant was her favourite scent, and its pungency permeated the whole house. Conscious almost to the last moment, Sheila lay back, her bald head supported by two pillows, and she stared at her sister. Her skeletal body could no longer summon the energy to maintain conversations, but there was nothing more to be said. At one point Derek telephoned. She took the call downstairs, but having listened to him express his regrets and then wonder if it might be all right for him and Maria to visit, she hung up. She went back upstairs, but Sheila did not ask her who had just called. Sheila never asked anything. Sheila trusted her. An hour later her sister died. She sat with her for a few minutes, and then she blew out the candle and left Sheila in the dark. Downstairs she was momentarily startled by a low gurgling sound that came from the fridge, but she soon regained her wits. She thought of her mum, who always told her eldest child not to search for God in a time of distress because that's when he's out of sight and busily taking care of you. 'Wait till you've dried your eyes, love, then go looking for him. He'll have more time then.' But her eldest child had never looked for God, and now it was too late.

She made a cup of tea and then sat down at the table and settled herself. To go back upstairs was out of the question, and so she had little choice now but to wait patiently in the hope that she might soon be released from the night that lay ahead. If only she had her piano to hand, for the patterns of music that she had been trying to stitch together in her mind for so long, they all made sense now. But not just music, for there was also a choral accompaniment of voices. Sitting at her sister's table she could feel this powerful surge of music coursing through her body. For a moment she panicked and wondered if she should transcribe the patterns, but she immediately calmed down. She would not forget. The music had been a long time coming, and its disparate pieces were now secured by grief. They would never again become unstitched.

Dorothy sits before Mr Jowett. During the past month she has suffered the misery of organising her sister's affairs. Maria and Derek showed up at the brief cremation ceremony, along with others whom she had never met, but who she presumed had some affiliation with the Labour Party. Roger was conspicuous by his absence, but he sent flowers. The day after the cremation she put Sheila's house on the market, and she found an unwed professional couple who were not in a chain. They didn't seem to mind that she intended to leave the curtains and the kitchen blinds, but she got a company to clear the rest of the house. It almost broke her heart to see the huge patches that suddenly glared from the walls where furniture had once stood or pictures had been hung. And then Dorothy fled London and returned home, where she discovered that all her utility bills were red, that the streets were claustrophobically small and narrow, and that everything was so much bleaker in the North. She also discovered that she was truly by herself. The terms of her early retirement package had arrived in the mail. She required a signature from Mr Jowett, and so an appointment was made with Miss Arthurton. And now she sits opposite Mr Jowett and listens as he idly asks her what her plans might be, given the fact that she has all this time on her hands. As he speaks he hurriedly signs the papers, in triplicate. Might she be travelling abroad? As he asks this question he leans back, and she listens to the sickening creak of his chair. She says nothing and waits for him to hand her the papers. His good humour offends her, but this will be the last time that she will have to see Mr Jowett, so she steels herself for the rest of the ordeal. It does not last long. He hands back the papers, but he still seems keen for a conversation to develop. She takes the papers and climbs to her feet. He extends a hand, which she shakes without enthusiasm, and then she turns and leaves, without closing the door behind her.

Instead of walking out of the school she strays in the direction of the staffroom. She stands outside the door, but decides against entering. After all, it is mid-period and it is unlikely that there will be anybody in there. So she walks from one classroom to the next, peering in through the windows and then quickly moving on before anybody can see her. And then she comes to his classroom and she sees him standing at the head of the class with his back to the door. Some of the pupils see her staring in at them. Slowly he turns to face her. He manages to maintain his composure. He throws her a little raised eyebrow of acknowledgement, but this is all. She does not move and now all the pupils are looking at her. He is uncomfortable. Has he found somebody else's shoulder to cry on? Or has his wife left her squash player and decided to come and live in this town too? What, she wonders, has happened to his life? She feels sorry for him. Helpless man. As he finally gives up the dance of concentration and begins to move towards the door, she turns and walks away from his classroom. She hears the door open behind her, but nobody calls her name and she does not hear the sound of feet pounding down the corridor behind her. She walks out of the school in silence, with Geoff Waverley's eyes on her back.

She sits in her bungalow at the top of the hill in this village that is five miles outside her home town. She counts the weeks. Eight. Two months have passed. It is a new beginning, in a place in which nobody knows her. She saw a drawing of Stoneleigh in the local paper and she bought her bungalow over the phone. Somehow, the phrase 'a new development' sounded comforting. Selling her house was surprisingly easy, largely because she was determined to accept the first offer that was made. In the end it was a decent offer and the buyer, a young Asian doctor, was ready to move in immediately. When she eventually took the bus out to Stoneleigh she was not disappointed. The bungalow was neat, with all mod cons, and it was exactly what she had imagined. They have just finished off the houses in the other cul-de-sac, but the area remains something of a muddy field. Still, she is happy. She looks out of her window and sees the man next door who's washing his car. He keeps it neatly outside his house as though it's a prized possession. Aside from this man, there is nobody else in sight on this bleak afternoon. Just this lonely man who washes his car with a concentration that suggests that a difficult life is informing the circular motion of his right hand. His every movement would appear to be an attempt to erase a past that he no longer wishes to be reminded of. She looks at him and she understands.

IV

Mr and Mrs Anderson stand with me in the rain. The three of us together, and the priest. Sheltering under the trees there are two men who will eventually cover the coffin with dirt. Their two shovels stand straight, exposed to the rain, with their heads buried deep in the soil. I remain brave, and my eyes are dry. This is what my friend would have wished. The priest closes his Bible, and Mum takes a handkerchief from her bag and she blows her nose. A memorable chapter has reached a conclusion. Mr Anderson hands me the keys to Mike's car, but he does not say anything. Mum reaches up and touches my face with her fingertips. I was much caressed by this family, and my attachment and gratitude to them are very great. She is a small thin woman, but this gesture feels strong. Mum holds me in her spell. And then she places the palms of her cold hands against my cheeks and pulls my head down towards her. She kisses me at the point where my wet hair meets my wet skin. And then she releases me.

'Come along, Muriel.' Mr Anderson is eager to escape the rain and he extends his protective arm around Mum's shoulders. He replaces his shapeless cap on his head and he looks closely at me. I can see that Mr Anderson is engaged in a struggle to control his many emotions. He is a very alert and active man, but at this time he is weak.

'Take care, lad. You mind yourself.'

The priest and I watch Mr and Mrs Anderson walk across the muddy grass towards the concrete path. Once they reach the path Mr Anderson takes his arm from around Mum's shoulder and he guides her arm through his own. He pushes his hands deep into the pockets of his blue raincoat and they walk carefully towards Mr Anderson's van. The priest clasps my shoulder, zips his Bible into a plastic pouch, and then he moves quickly in the direction of the church. Understanding the priest's departure to be a signal, the two men beneath the trees throw down their cigarette stubs, pick up their shovels and wearily approach the graveside. They wipe the rain from their eyes. I take a step back, but I am not yet ready to leave Mike. In the distance I witness the illumination of the headlights. An indicator light begins to blink, and then Mr Anderson's van passes out of sight. Soon Mr and Mrs Anderson will be in Scotland and they will be able to participate in what Mum keeps calling 'the rest of their lives'. I feel joy for my benefactors, and I hope that peace, prosperity and happiness will attend them for the remainder of their days.

This morning I officially started my job on the estate and, as is the case with most of the good fortune that has been visited upon me, I have Mr and Mrs Anderson to thank for the blessing of this appointment. But now they have departed and I am on my own, standing by Mike's grave with his car keys in my hand. It is appropriate that rain is falling from the skies, and that I do not possess an umbrella. The disappointing conditions remind me of when I first encountered Mike, standing in the rain, wondering if anybody was going to pay me the compliment of rescuing this stranger. I told my saviour that my name was Solomon and that I was not from the Caribbean, and he nodded and began to enjoy some laughter. Mike did not appear to be like the other English people that I had encountered, but I did not say anything to him about this fortuitous fact. I simply allowed Mike to talk and I listened. Whenever he asked me a question I was always polite and careful about the manner in which I responded. I told him that I was from Africa. That I had come to England by myself. That I had been residing here in England for some weeks. I told him that I did not possess a trade or a job, and Mike listened to me. I did not tell him that I was a soldier. That I had killed many men in battle. I did not tell him that I used to be known as Hawk. Mike shared with me the news that Ireland was his mother country, and that when he first arrived in England he too was not in possession of a trade, but now he drives lorries a very great distance. But only in England. What Mike desired was to experience the extremely long driving jobs that might take him all over Europe, and he lived in the hope that he might one day realise his dream. I looked out of the window and allowed Mike to concentrate on his driving skills. The rain was pouring down out of the black English sky. So he too came from another country? This was difficult for me to understand. At home it was relatively simple to distinguish a man of a different tribe or region, but among these people I was lost. Mike resumed his conversation, and I continued to listen, but my lack of knowledge of the ways of the English caused me to be fearful. I worried about my book, for when I last examined it some pages were disfigured with black mould. I understood that the book was probably once again wet and I imagined that the mould may well have returned, but this time with more vigour. I closed my eyes and trapped my fear inside myself. This was an inappropriate time for me to inspect my belongings.

After many minutes of darkness, Mike began to slow down his lorry. I opened my eyes and watched him turn off the wet road and into an area that was brightly lit in the manner of a small city. I stared at the lights, and at the great number of cars and lorries that were parked in this city. Mike turned off the engine of his vehicle and then he looked at me.

'Fancy a quick bite?' Mike did not wait for me to reply. Immediately he opened the door and fled into the rain, leaving me little choice but to do the same. I ran after him and towards a building where we found shelter. I told Mike that I did not possess money for food or drink, but he slapped me on the back and announced that he would take care of everything and that I should go and sit among the English people. For a moment I did not go anywhere. I stared at him, for I remained frightened. What was this man going to do to me? What did he want? Mike looked puzzled, and then he pointed.

'It's all right, Solomon. You can go and sit. I'll get the stuff.'

I sat at a filthy plastic table and watched as Mike picked up a tray and joined a long line of exhausted men. Those seated at neighbouring tables stared at me with great fascination, and even though I looked away I could feel the weight of their eyes. I prepared myself. Should there be trouble then I would fight, and I wondered if perhaps Mike would join me. He was a large man, although somewhat overweight, but he would make a strong ally.

The food made my stomach turn and I was convinced that I was going to embarrass myself. Mike appeared to have an infinite capacity for food, and in order that I should not make him feel uncomfortable I made a great effort. I took another bite of the hamburger, but this food was not suited to my stomach.

'Do you eat meat? I should have asked you.' Mike now seemed worried that he might bear some responsibility for my discomfort, but I assured him that I accepted meat and I took yet another bite of the hamburger. I looked out of the window and could see that a great deal of traffic continued to flow in and out of this small city, and I listened to Mike drinking his mug of tea. He was enjoying loud mouthfuls and then blowing on the tea to cool it down. My head was hurting, and I knew that I could neither finish the hamburger nor take the tea. Perhaps Mike sensed this too, for he was now quiet. I decided to excuse myself and visit the toilet. This would give Mike the chance to leave me, if this was what he wished to do.

In the toilet I was sick, but once I had emptied my stomach I felt much improved. At the sink I discovered that the water supply was both hot and cold, and it appeared to me that there was no end to this supply of both hot and cold water. I washed out my mouth and then I looked at myself in the mirror. A tired man's face stared back at me. This was not the face of a thirty-year-old man. England had changed me, but was this not the very reason that I had come to England? I desired change. When I returned to the plastic table, I discovered that Mike had taken my tea.

'I hope you don't mind, but it didn't look like you wanted it.'

I did not mind at all, and I also understood that Mike had taken the tea to spare me the indignity of having to waste the drink. He appeared to be worried, but I reassured him that I was happy for him to satisfy himself.

We restarted our journey and to my shame I was immediately conquered by sleep. When I opened my eyes the rains had ceased and the first rays of dawn were visible to the east of the busy road. I rubbed my eyes with the back of my hand and looked quickly all about myself.

'Have a good sleep?' Mike started to laugh now. 'Looks like you've been through the wars. You were out like a light.'

I apologised to him for my rudeness, but this only caused him once again to laugh. And then he asked me if I knew where I wished to be set down, but I had not yet thought of a place.

'Do you have anywhere to stay? Anybody that you're supposed to meet?'

I felt momentarily ashamed, so I simply shook my head.

'Well, we'll soon be near my lodgings. I can probably get you a bed for a day or so, then after that you can think about getting yourself sorted.'

I thanked him, and then I tried to imagine what he must be thinking of me. I was a grown man without a roof to cover my head, and I was travelling aimlessly and without a clear destination in my mind. This was shameful, for I was not a man who was used to being dependent upon other people. This pitiful situation made me feel quite miserable.

Mike stopped his lorry outside the final house on a quiet street that was lined with tall trees. The day was just beginning and I observed neatly dressed English children making their way to school. I was worried, for there was no reason why Mike's comrades should accept this stranger into their lives. Mike knew nothing about me, and it appeared to me incorrect that he should be working so hard for this African. I followed him out of the lorry and down the short path of broken stones towards the large house. He did not reach into his pocket for a key, or knock on the door, he simply opened it. And then he shouted out, 'Hello!' and he bent down to unlace his boots. I too began to unlace my useless shoes, but I was ashamed at their odorous condition. The necessary habit of decency was a part of my father's teachings, and before England I was accustomed to many purifications and washings. To enter another man's house in my unwashed state was to present myself as a poor ambassador for my people.

'Anybody at home?' Mike bellowed his question and it hurt my ears.

I walked with him down the carpeted corridor and into a kitchen where an elderly man was seated at a wooden table reading a newspaper. Before him there was a half-finished bowl of cereal. Standing by the sink, both hands fully submerged in soapy water, there was a small woman.

'I've brought a friend. He seems a bit down on his luck and I thought we might help him. Mum, Dad, this is Solomon.'

They both looked at me, and the woman smiled. The man pointed with his head towards a seat at the table.

'Well, sit down. We'll get you some breakfast, then find you somewhere to put your stuff.' The man returned to reading his newspaper. It was a very large newspaper, and I noticed that he seemed to be experiencing some difficulty folding the paper into a proper shape. Curiously enough, this problem was occupying him more than the strangeness of a foreign person having crossed his threshold.

I sat down and looked around, and then almost immediately the woman placed a bowl of cereal before me and encouraged me to eat. My stomach received the cereal with joy, and as I ate Mike also took more food. And then the man put down his newspaper and climbed to his feet and announced that he must leave for work. Soon after this man's sudden departure, Mike yawned and announced that he was in need of slumber. He squeezed my shoulder, then disappeared, leaving just the woman and myself in the kitchen. As the woman continued to wash dishes, she posed many questions about me, and where I was from, and what I desired to do with myself now that I was in England. Although my natural instinct was to trust nobody, there was something about this small elderly woman that made me feel safe. And so I told her about the pain of leaving my country, and the uncomfortable journey to England, and the difficulties of travelling on the boat. I told her that my greatest problem with England was that sometimes the weather was very cool, but now that I was in England I possessed a great desire to learn. To be educated. I told her that at home things are very, very bad. That the war has left people afraid, and they have nothing, and nobody wishes to remain there, but in England there is peace. In my country there is no peace, and the many griefs of the people do not appear to be wearing away. I told her nothing of Felix, or Amma, or my Uncle Joshua, or Bright; I told her nothing of how my heart bled at these partings; I told her nothing of the temptation of the poor girl, who was one of the most abandoned of her species, and who presented the opportunity to debase myself and simply gratify a passion of nature; I told her nothing of Said, or prison, where I was never condemned to make recompense, for I was innocent of any crime; I told her nothing of Katherine, who had helped me to overcome some of the fear that arose from my ignorance of the ways of English people. I told her nothing of Hawk. I told her nothing of Gabriel. I told her my name was Solomon and that I needed to acquire papers so that I could work and remain in England. I told her that I had no other country. The woman wiped her hands on a towel, and then she prepared a pot of tea. She sat down next to me, and for some moments she lost herself in contemplation. When she returned to my company she poured two cups of tea.

'You'll have to be processed, Solomon, and it will have to be done properly. Dad and I have never done this, but we know people who can help. In the meantime you can stay here. I think you're eligible for vouchers.'

I told her that I had no money, but she laughed and told me that the vouchers were a form of money. She informed me that there was a method whereby a person might exchange them for food or other supplies. Incredibly enough, this did not mark the conclusion of her glad tidings. She told me that a local council would pay for my board and lodgings, and that it was possible that her husband might assist me, should I decide to search for some manner of unofficial work. I looked at the woman and attempted to fathom her motives. Would she and her husband receive some special reward? If so, then I would not begrudge them their bounty, for my sole desire was to be safe in England. If these were bad people, then I would undoubtedly discover my fate at some later stage, but at this moment I was too overcome with fatigue to think any further, and the woman could see this. She stood up.

'There's a spare room next to Mike's. It's not very big, but you can take it.'

The room was small, but very comfortable. However, I could not sleep without suffering bad dreams in which my own mother and father appeared before me with stern faces, warning me of unfortunate events that were sure to blight my life should I choose to remain among these people. I begged my parents to share with me their knowledge of these ill tidings, but whenever they appeared to be about to bless me with an answer, I would wake from my slumber shaking with consternation. I would look around the strange room and once more have to make the attempt to understand where I was, and remember by what means I had arrived there, and only after I calmed down was I able to re-embrace sleep. But sadly, I would once again find myself tossing and turning, for it appeared that my dreams were permanently cursed with the accusatory faces of my parents, who were clearly racked with anxiety over the plight of their 'lost' Gabriel. When the woman came into the room and took my arm, I quickly sprang to my defence. However, I was immediately sorry for I could see that I had alarmed her. She held a cup in her hand, which she set down on the bedside table.

'I've brought you this cup of strong coffee.' She paused and turned to look at me. 'And it'll soon be time for your dinner.

Dad'll be home any minute, and Mike's already awake.' She pointed to a towel that was neatly folded and draped over the armchair near the door. 'I've put a towel over there for you, and the bathroom's out the door to the right. Take your time, no rush.'

I watched her leave the room. Somewhere, in the distance, I could hear music, and then it was replaced by the sound of bells, and then I heard a man's voice reading the news. It was all very confusing. I reached over and enjoyed a mouthful of the strong coffee.

The house in which I live is at the far end of the street, and it is smaller than the other houses. In fact, Mr Anderson said that it was originally a storage hut, but once they decided that it was necessary for somebody to live on the estate, they quickly adapted the house so that it blended in with the others. Mr Anderson moved my belongings in yesterday, but there were few items to transport. They hardly occupied the rear seat of his car, and they were mainly clothes and books that I had managed to acquire. However, now that I am parking my own car, or what used to be Mike's car, outside the house, I feel as though I am truly arriving here for the first time. Strange, because I have been working in this village for many months, helping with the carpentry and installing plumbing. I am familiar with this village, and this area, but now it is to be my home. I am to be the night-watchman, and my job will be to watch over these people.

Inside the bungalow there is little furniture. I do not need much, but what I need Mr and Mrs Anderson have given to me. They purchased new pieces for their home in Scotland, and so the bed, the table and four chairs, and the armchair are gifts from my guardian angels. The developers have made sure that I have a fridge and a cooker. I do not have a television set, but I can survive without this luxury. I have a radio and that is enough for me. I sit in the armchair and I think about Mike's funeral, and wonder how it is that a man who was so friendly can reach the end of his life with so few colleagues to mourn his passing. But this question would not have troubled Mike, for he never concerned himself with what other people thought of him. Or at least, that is what Mike always told me. ('You can't be controlling what others think.') I stand and look out of my window at the cloudy skies. It is still bright, and it is therefore too early for me to take my torch and patrol the area. To begin my job. There will be plenty of time for this at a later hour. Now that it has stopped raining I decide to go for a walk in my new village.

At the bottom of the hill I cross over the road. I see the pub, but I have no desire to once again enter into one of these places, so I follow the pathway beside the water. It was Mr Anderson who encouraged me to take daily exercise, confessing to me that it was the secret to his own good health at his advanced stage of life. He advised me that 'Every day you must take some time by yourself and walk', and so I have tried to follow his guidance. These walks by myself have helped to change my mood for the better. When I first arrived at Mr and Mrs Anderson's, I could not sleep, but I now sleep through almost every night like a peaceful child. I discover this water to be a most harmonious place, and it gives me pleasure to notice how the trees bend over the path so that the ground is striped with thin fingers of sunlight. But I know this vision cannot last for much longer, for although it is the English summer, the wind is already combing through the trees and cruelly stripping them of their leaves. In England the weather is difficult, and every day I watch the sun struggling to reach the roof of the sky. It is very sad, but at least today there is a little sunlight. It is my great ambition to once again feel the comfort of the sun on my skin.

Up ahead I see a group of four boys walking towards me. For a moment I consider turning about-face, but I do not wish to turn my back on them for I know they do not desire to use me well. It is better that I can see them. After all, I recognise them. They are strangely almost hairless, with egg-shaped heads and blue tattoos on their bare arms. They all wear polished boots, which suggests a uniform of some kind, but the rest of their clothes are ill-matched. Sometimes they have visited the estate, and other workmen have been forced to chase them away. I have noticed how they look upon my person, and I know that they have anger towards me. They are blocking my way and laughing. In order to pass by I will have to walk within inches of the water, but this is dangerous and I do not trust them. I stop and politely ask them to 'excuse me', but they continue to stare at me.

'What's the matter?'

I do not answer their leader's question, and as if to punish me they decide to offer abuse in my direction. I turn and begin to retrace my steps, for I know that should I stand my ground, or attempt to sway this spiteful rabble with entreaties, my efforts will prove useless. But they follow me, and spit at my back, and they laugh. I continue to walk at the same deliberate pace, knowing that if one among them should attempt to bruise me, then the situation will become very unpleasant. They do not know who I am. I am the son of an elder, a man who decided disputes and punished crimes. I am a man who travelled a very considerable distance south and then returned to the bosom of my doomed family, always moving at night, and eating berries and drinking water from streams. I am a man who has survived, and I would rather die like a free man than suffer my blood to be drawn like a slave's.

When we reach the pub they turn into the garden and release me. I continue to walk back to the road, and then up the hill to my bungalow. It is becoming dark, and it will soon be time for me to take my torch and go out among these people and attempt to protect them. At the top of the hill I pass the girl who, while I worked on the construction site, always seemed to be staring in my direction. She lives with her mother at the other end of the street to my bungalow. Whenever I see this girl, I have noticed how she looks at me. I am sensitive to the weight of her gaze. The girl reminds me of Denise, and like Denise she too lacks the modesty that I would expect in somebody of her tender years. I walk past the girl and resist the urge to turn and see if she is watching me. I keep walking in the hope that she will soon disappear from my life. I have been fooled already and I do not wish to be fooled again. Once I am inside my house, I stand in the living room and study the street. There is a lamp-post outside my window which bestows light in such a way that it is possible for me to see out, but if I stand back and in shadow I do not think that it is possible for anybody to see in. There are also plastic window blinds, which give me further protection. This pleases me, for although I welcome the opportunity to look out at them, I do not wish these people to be able to look in at me.

Mum embraced the challenge of making my status in England a legal one. Each morning Mr Anderson departed for work, and he left Mum to wrestle with the difficult problem of my situation. Mum informed me that Mr Anderson was the manager of a company that builds houses and small factory units, so he would often have to leave at five o'clock in the morning in order that he might assess progress and decide what tasks were to be accomplished on that particular day. Should he find himself working close by, then there was a possibility that he would consider returning for his breakfast and to read the newspaper, and then he would return again to his work. However, Mike did not live his life in this manner. Once Mike had departed for his work I might not see him again for many days, for he often drove his lorry great distances. Mike told me that he had once been married, and that he was the father of a teenage son to whom he sometimes wrote short but loving letters. He attempted to see his son once or twice a year, depending upon where his driving jobs might take him, but he described himself as 'cured of marriage'. He liked to laugh when he said this. 'Been there, done it', and then he would once again burst out laughing. He had long ago discovered that to ask any personal questions of his new African friend meant that he was likely to be greeted with silence. The situation with Mum was very different, for she seemed to regard it as her duty to question me, but I learned to be tolerant of her habit and I hoped that she did not take offence at my sometimes evasive answers.

At first, while Mike was driving and Mr Anderson was at work, I would help Mum around the house. I enjoyed accompanying her to the shops, and I quickly grew to understand the buses and the money. Soon I was watching the television programmes, and to my eyes England was becoming less of a mystery. It no longer surprised me when I heard women using foul and abusive language in the streets, and Mum took the time to explain why she always put butter on her fingers before taking off her rings. However, it did continue to confuse me why so many of the English newspapers displayed little more than pictures of women in their underwear. However, I felt that this was not a subject I could share with Mum, so I attempted to banish this confusion from my mind. My only real regret was the lack of anybody from my own country with whom I might talk. My language was drying up in my mouth, and sometimes, when nobody was around, I would place my language on my tongue and speak some words so that I could be sure that I was still in possession of it. Every week Mum gave me an allowance, and she would always ask me if I needed paper and envelope and stamps to write to my family, but I would look at her and thank her, but say, 'No.' I would never say anything more to her than this.

Mum must have secretly said something to Mr Anderson, for very early one morning I heard a knock on my door. I glanced at the window and could see that it was still dark. I assumed that the knocking must be the work of Mike, and that he must have fallen into some kind of trouble, so I whispered, 'Yes.' However, when the door opened it was Mr Anderson, and he was holding a cup of coffee in one hand. He set down the coffee on the bedside table and ordered me to prepare myself, for I would be coming to work with him this very morning. I was surprised because Mum had told me that while the officials processed my application it might be difficult for me to work properly. However, I did not question Mr Anderson, and I soon dressed myself and moments later I was sitting beside my benefactor in his van. He said very little as we made our way through the cold dark streets, but once we reached his work he introduced me to a Greek man who he said would show me how everything was done. By the end of the day I had learned something about bricklaying and carpentry. By the end of the week I had also gained experience with plumbing and electricity, and although my hands suffered very much during this initial engagement, I felt as though I might one day have enough knowledge that I might build a house by myself. At the end of the week Mum gave me an allowance, but it was a little greater than was common and I understood that these were my 'wages'. I also understood that Mr Anderson was trying to provide me with a trade, although the rudeness of the other men caused me to occasionally suffer from periods of great misery.

After some months of working on the building site, Mr Anderson began to teach me to drive. Whenever Mike was available he would relieve Mr Anderson and assume this responsibility of providing me with driving skills, thus enabling my mentor to sit by the hearth occasionally and enjoy his evening pipe in peace. Mike was always disappointed when, after his 'lesson', it did not excite my curiosity to go with him inside the pub. I did not tell him that my first experience of such a place had left me without any desire to repeat the experience, for I did not wish to cause offence. He said that I would like 'his' pub because it contained bright mirrors and brass work, and it was a happy place, but I tried to explain. First, I told Mike that I did not drink, but he said that I was free to choose a Coca-Cola. I then told Mike that I was fearful of being among a forest of tongues, but he chose not to believe me. Soon Mike ceased his many invitations for me to accompany him to the pub, and after our lesson he would deposit me at Mr and Mrs Anderson's residence and then venture out by himself. None of us would see Mike for the rest of the night, but I would often hear him staggering about before he finally collapsed in a heap on his bed, or sometimes on the floor. Should I encounter Mike the following day he would always laugh and apologise for any noise that he might have made while 'bladdered'. Mike was a lonely man who, I believed, must miss his family. I imagined that his drinking was the reason that he was not together with them, but I never questioned him on this most private of subjects. However, it did, on many occasions, occur to me that I never saw Mike drink when he had to drive his lorry. I soon came to understand that the lorry might well be saving his life, for I knew that this drinking could not be beneficial to his health.

The morning after the people painted the words on the wall of Mr and Mrs Anderson's house, I sat at the breakfast table with Mum, who kept glancing anxiously out of the window. Mr Anderson had a hard brush and a plastic bucket of water, and he was scrubbing ferociously with a look on his face that I found frightening. Mum seemed nervous and she would not stop talking.

'I'll let this pot of tea mash, but meanwhile another round of toast?'

'No, thank you. I am full already.'

Mum could never disguise her disappointment when I politely refused her food. Mike was away driving, and this only made things worse, for it provided her with the opportunity to once again remind me that Mike would always eat everything that she put in front of him. In twenty years of accommodating people, I knew that we were her only two long-term lodgers. Everybody else came and went: businessmen relocating and who were in need of temporary accommodation while looking for a home for their families; executives at conferences; working-men between contracts; or specialists who were required to operate a piece of machinery, or advise on a contract, before returning to the South. Mr Anderson was able to assist Mum with her business by occasionally providing lodgers with whom he had professional dealings, but Mum told me that her reputation, and being on the council list, ensured that she was never idle. Mum also told me that Mike and I were like the sons that she had never had, but I never encouraged her to develop this thought beyond this one comment.

When Mr Anderson re-entered his home, he put the bucket and brush down in the corner of the kitchen by the door, dropped an empty dog-food can in the rubbish bin, and then he walked quietly to the sink to wash his hands.

'They had the paint in the dog-food can.'

'Cup of tea, love?' Mum got up from the table and went to the cupboard to get another cup.

'That'd be grand.' Mr Anderson looked over at me as he dried his hands on the dishcloth. 'You doing all right, Solomon?'

I nodded.

'Good.' He came and sat at the table, and Mum placed the cup of tea in front of her husband. 'Good.'

Mum now went to the fridge and took out the bacon. Every time she opened the fridge door my heart would leap. I had still not accustomed myself to the fact that inside the door there was milk, fruit, bread and eggs. Everything was free and Mum kept insisting that I should take whatever I wanted. Mr and Mrs Anderson appeared to enjoy life in the manner of rich people, but I had learned enough to understand that in England they were ordinary people, and many families were blessed with the good fortune to live as they did.

After Mr Anderson finished his breakfast we went together to his van to begin the journey to the building site. There was frost on the inside of the glass and I wiped it with the sleeve of my jacket. On this particular morning, without announcing his intention, Mr Anderson took a different route, and he turned off the road and parked his van in the car park of a country pub. I looked around, but I had little understanding of where we were located, and then I looked across at Mr Anderson, who was staring away from me and out of the window, as though preparing himself for something that would be difficult. I noticed the cold winter sun finally break through the clouds, and then I saw a reflection of myself in the glass of the car. In this country, I thought, my skin is turning to ash and inside my head is cold like ice. Mum said summer would soon come, but for me it could not come quickly enough. And then Mr Anderson turned to look at me, and he caught me gazing at my own reflection in the glass.

'Solomon, the first line of defence is prejudice. Once you get past that, there'll always be a little corner where you can live and be who or what you want to be. But you've got to get past that first line, and things are not getting any easier. There's an awful lot of you, and the system's already creaking to breaking point. I mean, things are particularly bad if you want to get into one of our hospitals. People are upset.' He looked closely at me now, as though trying to read my thoughts. 'You do understand what I'm trying to say to you, don't you, Solomon?'

I nodded, although I was unsure of what exactly Mr Anderson was trying to say.

'You see, Solomon, it's just that this isn't a very big island and we don't have that much room. People think that other countries should take you first because we've done our bit.' He paused and looked away. 'I'm sorry, Solomon, but some folk think these things. That you just want an easy living, or that you have too many children. They think that you don't really want to work. It's in their heads and it makes them mad.'

'Who put it there?'

Mr Anderson turned to look at me, and I could see that he was surprised that I had asked this question. And then his face softened.

'I don't know, Solomon. I really don't know.'

We sat together in the car park for many more minutes, but neither of us said anything further, nor did we make eye contact. Mr Anderson was clearly unsettled by what had happened to his house and he did not know what to do. I now understood that explaining these things to me was a way of explaining them to himself, but the puzzled look on Mr Anderson's face suggested that he remained troubled by many questions.

Two days later, Mike returned from a long trip. I sat in my room and I could hear him talking with Mr and Mrs Anderson. Their voices were low, and I assumed that they were whispering to prevent me from hearing whatever words they were exchanging. In my heart I felt that they were speaking of me, but I could not be sure. And then Mike knocked on my door, and I encouraged him to enter and he sat on the edge of my bed.

'How's it going, Solomon?'

I smiled, but I said nothing. For a moment all I could hear was the creaking of the bed, and I worried that perhaps Mike had lost his nerve. But then he coughed.

'Look, Mum told me what happened, but you've got to understand that some people bring things on themselves, you know. I mean, these days particularly the Indian types.' Mike stopped and sighed, and then he looked at me. 'I'm an old traditionalist, Solomon. I want fish and chips, not curry and chips. I'm not prejudiced, but we'll soon be living in a foreign country unless somebody puts an end to all this immigration. These Indians, they still make their women trail after them, and they have their mosques and temples, and their butcher shops where they kill animals in the basement and do whatever they do with the blood. I mean, they're peasants. They come from the countryside and most of them have never seen a flush toilet or a light switch. It's too much for them. And for us. There ought to be some training or they should go back. It's these kinds of people that cause others to have bad attitudes and to do things like they've done to Mum's wall. I'm not saying they're right, because they're not. But I drive around a lot, and I see how people feel, more than what the old folks does. It's everywhere.' Mike stopped talking and he stared at me, but with a worried look on his face. 'You see, you're in a different situation, Solomon. You're escaping oppression and that's different. We've got procedures for that. I mean, you're working. You're no scrounger. But they don't know that, and so that's what happens.' Mike paused. 'You do know what I'm saying, don't you, Solomon?' I looked at Mike and nodded. I knew what he was saying. I understood him.

When my papers finally came through, and the letter arrived informing me that I could legally stay in Britain, Mum insisted that they take me out to a local fish restaurant to celebrate. Mike was away and so it was just the three of us, but I could sense that Mr Anderson was not altogether comfortable. He looked blankly at the menu and then he eventually told Mum to order for him. Mum could not have been happier and, although she tried not to show it, she was proud of me and regarded my 'legal' status as her own personal triumph. I had never before seen her take any alcohol, but with this meal she drank a glass of red wine. Mr Anderson waited until he had finished his food before he turned to me and asked what I thought I might do now that I had, as he put it, 'choice'. I did not know. Nearly one whole year had passed since Mike had brought me to their home, and in that time I had acquired many building skills. I was blessed to be in England, but this life bore no relationship to the one I had known in my own country, and as a consequence I felt as though my new family knew only one small part of me. In truth, only one half of me was alive and functioning. I had tried to talk to the few West Indian people I saw standing on the streets outside Sonja's Caribbean Takeaway with their dreadlocks and their cans of beer, but they were not friendly and they would often look the other way or shout at me and behave like drunken people. And I had long ago learned that there was little point in attempting conversation with the Indians or Pakistanis, for they were worse than some of the English people. I sat in the fish restaurant and looked at Mr and Mrs Anderson and told them that I did not know what I would do now that I had 'choice'. Become less lonely? That was all I hoped for. But then it suddenly occurred to me what Mr Anderson might be suggesting, and I felt stupid. Now that I was legal, they wanted me to leave their home and find somewhere else to live. Their task was complete. Perhaps they had discovered another person to live with them? I could not be sure, but I felt as though Mr and Mrs Anderson were letting me go, and so I decided that as soon as I could find a respectful moment I would share with my benefactors the news that it was time for Solomon to move on and that sadly I would now have to leave their blessed home.

I have been here for a month and the villagers are becoming familiar with me. Each evening they see me with my torch, and some among them even speak to me. They rarely say more than 'Evening', but this is enough. It is a beginning. And then this morning I received a letter. I do not usually receive letters. I am looking at it now, on the table in front of me. It is a letter from somebody who is not my friend, but they have signed their name as though I ought to know who they are. The words are ugly and I am unsure what I have done to offend this person, but after the unfortunate incident at Mr Anderson's house, and after listening to Mike, I know that this type of person exists. Some of these people worked for Mr Anderson on the building site, and the boys I met down by the water, they suffer from this mental condition. Unfortunately, the letter loudly proclaims that such people reside in my immediate vicinity. I hold the letter and then turn it over in my hands. I am not afraid of this communication, but it is difficult for me to know what to do. To discard the offending article would probably be the wise decision, but I wish to keep it although I am not sure why. Perhaps to show that I am not afraid. This seems to me to be a fine reason, and so I replace the letter on the table and decide that I will look at it every day. I am not afraid.

As I drive past the bus stop, I see her. I often see her standing by herself at the bus stop. She lives in the house next to me, but she is a private woman. She is very beautiful for her years. A decent woman, who I feel could help the younger women of this country learn how to groom themselves properly. She carries her head high as though she is proud of who she is, and I admire her dignity. Sometimes I secretly watch her from my living room as she sits and stares out of her window. She appears lonely. Mike saved me from the rain like a Good Samaritan, and although it is not truly raining, for only a helpless drizzle wets my windscreen, I feel that it is my duty to stop at the bus stop and rescue this woman. I continue to drive away from the bus stop, but resolve that the next time that I see this woman, I will stop for her. Sadly, I have to confess I have made this promise in the past and I have failed to find the courage to honour it. But I now know that whatever the price I will rescue this woman.

I spend one hour in the town, choosing my shopping for the week. I am happy, for the weather is now becoming very pleasant. In this country, summer comes in the night. A man can go to bed in winter, and when he wakes up nature is once again singing and his skin is warm. I think of this miracle and I am happy. However, for most of my hour in town I am thinking of a plan that will enable me to meet this woman. The truth is, I need to meet more village people. The letter said that these people do not want me in their village, but they do not know me. Perhaps it is my responsibility to get to know them? If I am to make my new life in this village, then it is possible that I have to do more than just sit alone inside my bungalow, or go for the occasional drive in my car.

But, after the unpleasantness by the water, I do not like to walk abroad during the day. At night I am obliged to go out, for it is my job, but when I travel at night with a torch it is a different matter, for I imagine that I command respect. I am official.

When I return to the village, I park my car outside the small medical centre at the bottom of the hill. Mr Anderson informed me that such places are always in need of drivers. He said this to me when he gave me the news that Mike's car would soon be mine. 'It could be a godsend for getting to know people.' Only now do I fully understand his words. The waiting room is empty, but I can see the young nurse sitting behind her desk, for the door to her office is wide open. She looks up and puts down her pen.

'Can I help you, love?'

I do not know if I should enter, or if I should wait and talk to her from where I am standing. I decide to take a few steps forward and risk entering into her office. She points to a seat, and I am relieved that I appear not to have caused her any offence.

'Sit down, if you like. It's the end of the day and I doubt if I'll be seeing anybody else.'

I look at this dark-haired woman and realise that she probably imagines me to be a patient.

'I have come to volunteer my services. As a driver.'

'Oh, good. We can always use drivers. I take it you've got your own vehicle, have you?'

I point outside, although it occurs to me that from where the young woman is sitting she cannot see my car. 'Yes, I have my own car.'

'I see. Good.' She is happy now and she pushes a pad and a pen across the desk. 'You just write down your name and phone number. What we do is whenever a patient needs a lift into town, then we get them to give you a call to see if you're free.'

I begin to write down my details. As I do so, she continues to talk.

'That way you're not bothered by having to chase people up. And don't be afraid to say "no" if you're busy. You're a volunteer, not a taxi driver. They have to understand that you've got your own life to be getting on with.'

I push the pad and pen back in her direction and I stand. I hold out my hand for her to shake, but hers is a limp handshake.

I sit in the dark with my hands embracing a cup of coffee. I feel safe in my bungalow. The letter is still here, but I feel safe. First, I will complete this cup of coffee and then I will begin my patrol. I venture out with my torch in the early evening, just when the sky begins to darken. Later, when the sky is black, I will go out for a second time. Usually this is around midnight, after people have returned home from their drinking and when the village is becoming peaceful for the night. The moonlight catches the photograph of Mike that sits on my mantelpiece. If he were alive today, Mike would have an alternative to the pub, or staying in with Mr and Mrs Anderson. He could always come here and keep me company. We could talk about Mike's experiences growing up in Ireland, and how his father begged him not to fight against the English, and how he first came to England on the Holyhead ferry, and how he found himself trapped into marriage against his will. My friend repeated these stories many times, but I liked to hear the sound of his voice. And, of course, listening to the sound of my friend's voice meant that I did not have to answer any questions about myself. I look at Mike's friendly grin and I feel sadness beginning to flood my body.

The phone call in the middle of the night roused me from

a deep sleep. And then I heard Mum scream, and then I listened to Mr Anderson trying to calm Mum down, but I dared not rise from my bed. It was Mr Anderson who knocked on the door and who came in and sat down on the solitary chair. With a heavy heart, Mr Anderson conveyed to me the news that Mike had been involved in a road accident and that he would no longer be among us. My body felt cold, and I looked away from Mr Anderson. Of all the people to die in a road accident, Mike seemed the least likely. Mike was an extremely fine master of roadsmanship. And for this tragedy to occur during his first European trip was too cruel. Mike had been very excited about taking his lorry to Germany and 'going into Europe'. I could also see that Mr and Mrs Anderson were very happy, and not only for Mike. After forty years, Mr Anderson was leaving the contracting business and they were both retiring to run a small hotel in Scotland, which was the part of the world where Mum had originated. And now that I was 'legal', Mr Anderson had secured for me a position as a night-watchman. He had spared me the anxiety of having to invent a reason why I would be leaving their home. And then the difficult phone call in the middle of the night robbed us of our great joy, and for days afterwards my dreams became unpleasant.

I remembered walking north, to the left of the sun's rising. It was not possible for me to remain loyal to the cleared paths, and so my secret journey took many weeks. Eventually I reached my family's house, but soon afterwards the blood-thirsty government troops arrived. My father pushed his only son into a cupboard and begged me to remain quiet, no matter what happened. He stumbled over his words and his breath was ripe with the stench of alcohol. 'Gabriel, if one man must survive, it must be you.' There was no time for me to argue, and to do so would have been disrespectful. As the government troops kicked at the door to our family house, I entered the cupboard and my sad father closed the leaves of wood in my face. I watched without fear. I watched with ice in my heart. I remembered my mother lying on a floor in my now far-off country with blood pouring from her wounds. I remembered my father and my sisters being shot like animals. My dreams contained my history. Night and day I tried not to think of these things any more. I tried not to think of these people any more. I wanted to set these people free so that they might become people in another man's story. I wanted to stop dreaming of them at night, or thinking about them in the day, but after Mike's death I was very disturbed and I could escape neither myself, nor my country, nor my family. For three full days and three full nights before the funeral I was a miserable man. A coward. But I could not return to my country, for there was nothing for me to return to. I possessed no family. Each time I opened my eyes I heard Mum crying. I was a coward who had trained himself to forget. I accepted from people. From Mr and Mrs Anderson. I was no longer 'Hawk'. I was no longer my mother's Gabriel. It was Solomon who learned of Mike's death. It was Solomon who was lying in a warm bed in a strange room among these kind people. It was Solomon. I was Solomon.

The funeral was difficult, for not only did I bid farewell to Mike, I was also forced to sever my links with Mr and Mrs Anderson. After Mr Anderson presented me with the keys to Mike's car, he handed me a piece of folded paper with their new address and telephone number in Scotland. He did not instruct me to make sure that I visited. He was simply setting me free. To visit or not visit would be my decision. This was Mr Anderson's way. Mum was too distraught to say anything, and even the prospect of a return to her beloved Scotland could not raise her spirits. As the sky wept, she also wept.

After they left I walked back to their house feeling the weight of Mike's car keys in my pocket. Mike was a good driver, and I later learned that the accident had not been his fault. A car had lost control and crossed the centre of the road. Mike had swerved to avoid the car and turned his lorry over. All of this happened in Kent, so Mike never did leave the country. Before the funeral, Mr Anderson gave me a framed photograph of Mike. That same night, I placed the photograph of Mike on the mantelpiece of my new bungalow. I put Mike's car keys next to the photograph. Mike was in general mild, affable, generous, benevolent and just; he was to me a friend. Thank you, Mike, I said. I looked around. You have given Solomon a new home. In England.

The man next to me will not speak with me. He is an elderly man and his body exudes an unfortunate odour. He does not know how to take care of himself. We drive on in silence and I concentrate upon the traffic. I ignore him. I have no desire to torment conversation out of this reluctant man. I have bought gloves, for occasionally the steering wheel is cold. It is also my hope that the gloves will make the whole business seem more professional. But the man continues to stare resentfully out of the window and he refuses to meet my eyes. I park in the hospital car park, and as he leaves my car he slams the door. He offers no thanks. He says nothing. Yesterday I visited the nurse and informed her that not one person had telephoned me. She appeared somewhat embarrassed, and then she told me that if I came this morning at ten o'clock, then a Mr Simons would be ready for me to transport him to the hospital. She confided that this man did not possess a telephone, as though this was something that Mr Simons ought to be ashamed of. I lingered for a moment, for I wondered if there was something further that she wished to say to me. But the truth was there was something that I wished to say to her.

'The lady next door to me. I do not know her name.' I saw the puzzled crease on the nurse's brow, and so I described the lady's appearance. The nurse continued to appear confused, and so I shared with her the lady's address.

'Oh, I know who you mean.' She paused. 'You know, I think she actually likes the bus.'

I could not think of anything else to say to this woman.

I look at the gleaming new hospital building. In my country if a man goes to the hospital, then he must bring his own blankets and bandages, and some money to persuade the doctor to attend to him. I understand that in England they do things in a different manner. I run my tongue across my teeth, but they do not feel clean. I miss being able to use a chewing stick, for the toothbrush and toothpaste are a strange invention and they leave an unpleasant feeling in my mouth. When I see Mr Simons walking towards me, I steal a look at the clock on the dashboard and can see that only ten minutes have passed. Mr Simons is holding a white paper bag, and I assume that he must have collected some medicine. I lean over and push open the door for him and he gets in. As I drive off he looks across at me.

'Going straight back, right?'

'I will take you back.'

He grunts, as though he wishes to let me know that indeed this is what he desires. None of the letters are signed 'Mr Simons', although I can imagine that this man feels the same as my letter-writers. There are now seven letters, including the one with the razor blades. Last night somebody introduced dog mess through my letterbox. They must have employed a small shovel, for it lay curled in a neat pile. When I awoke this morning, the sight of it caused my stomach to move and

I rushed to the bathroom. These people are unwell, for decent people do not conduct themselves in this way. Writing to me with their filth is one thing, but this is savage. They regard me as their enemy, this much I understand, but their behaviour is unclean. But truly, none of this is the fault of Mr Simons.

I leave Mr Simons at the bottom of the hill and drive slowly in the direction of my home. At the top of the hill I pass the girl, who hurries by as though she is late for the bus. I look at her in the rear-view mirror, but she chooses not to turn around. My car is dusty, and I decide that tomorrow I will bathe it. I turn the key in the door and immediately I can smell the detergent that I used to scrub the doormat this morning. I used the whole bottle. I close the door behind me and a part of me is relieved to find neither more dog mess nor another letter. I can see her sitting in the window. She is at home. Why Mr Simons and not this woman? I would appreciate somebody to talk with and this is a respectable woman. This is a woman to whom I might tell my story. If I do not share my story, then I have only this one year to my life. I am a one-year-old man who walks with heavy steps. I am a man burdened with hidden history. I look in the mirror and straighten my shirt collar and then I adjust my tie. I leave my bungalow and walk across the neatly trimmed grass towards her house. I knock on her door. She is a respectable woman and perhaps the nurse is wrong. Perhaps this woman does not love the bus. Perhaps her love for the bus is merely temporary. I knock again.

V

These flowers, they all have a personality, or so it said in a magazine that I once read. Or maybe I heard it on the radio. I can't remember. It was a long time ago. But I definitely remember that flowers are all supposed to have distinct personalities. I suppose the red ones are angry, and the yellow ones are girls, and the blue ones are boys. I like looking at them, out here in the garden. The nurse puts a chair under the tree for me, but it's not a very nice chair. It's wooden, with a straight back, like she's punishing me by making me sit in it. I've no idea what I've done wrong that would make her give me such a horrible chair. Mind you, at least she's sitting in one that's just the same. It's not as if she's put me in this chair and then gone and got a nice comfy one for herself. Her name's quite long, and I don't seem to be able to twist my tongue far enough to pronounce it properly. So I don't bother, but she doesn't seem to mind. She's about my age, so she probably understands. I just call her nurse. I've noticed that she doesn't like to sit too close to me. She likes to give me my space, which is, I suppose, how she'd like to think about it. And so she's sitting where she always sits, about twenty yards away in some shade by the ornamental pond, with a book in her hand. Some days it's a book, other days it's a magazine, and once she even brought some knitting. But today it's a book, although I know she's not really reading it. I suppose she'd get the sack if all she did was plonk us in the garden and then get lost in a good book. She's supposed to watch over us and make sure we're all right, but I can see that she has to strike a fine balance. On the one hand she wants us to be free to be ourselves, but on the other hand she doesn't want to neglect us. If truth be told, she can't really win either way.

Today I've made a decision to not say anything to anybody, and I can see how uncomfortable this is making her feel, but it's not really my problem, is it? I'm interested in flowers and she's not, and that's about all there is to it. I didn't ask her to sit with me, so if she wants to go that's fine. But at least it's a nice day and we can sit outside. For the past two days it's been teeming down and it's been really depressing being stuck inside in the recreation room with the television on, and half-finished jigsaw puzzles everywhere, and people milling about and trying to behave like they're normal. She doesn't know how lucky she is to be sitting outdoors in the garden, with her clunky shoes and that silly tight blouse. My feet tend to perspire when I get anxious, but today they are drip-dry. I'm happy here in the sun with my flowers, and sitting under my overdressed tree that's keen to hide its brittle bones. Winter will be the undoing of it, but as it's still autumn my tree is allowed to flaunt herself. The nurse has no idea that I'm happy. She sneezes, then discreetly blows her nose into a proper handkerchief. I think she's got allergies. However, one thing that I can say about her is she's clean, and around these parts such things count.

I have to give it to them on the cleanliness front in this place. Every day they scrub the showers and the bath tubs, they empty the wastepaper bins, and then they mop and polish the tiles on the floor so that you can almost see your face in them. I can set my watch by the appearance of the two young women, with their long, stringy-haired mops and plastic buckets. Ten o'clock, every day on the dot. First they sweep, then mop, then give it all a good waxed buffing. If cleanliness is next to godliness, then we're living pretty close to heaven in this home. Except at night. We're not allowed anything like scissors or a razor or tweezers, even. I'm not used to going to bed untrimmed and unpresentable. But it's not allowed, so that's that. And then they come in every hour with their torches, shining them in my face to make sure I've not done anything to myself. They try to be quiet, but I always hear them. The breath patrol, listening to make sure that we've not slipped over into the next world during the night. I expect that would mess up their bookkeeping. And then in the morning, just like in the real world, I put on my day face. Actually, most of them don't bother with this part, which is partly why they're in here in the first place. They just shuffle around looking miserable, as though death has tried to talk to them in the night. Well, it also tries with me sometimes, but you're not forced to listen. There's nothing that says you have to pay attention.

I won't meet the eyes of the nurse. I prefer the flowers, but I know that she wants to talk. She can't take any more silence. I'm being difficult with her, but I suppose it's not her fault, none of it is. I look at the poor woman sitting in the uncomfortable chair, and I realise that there's nothing to be lost by being nice to her, and so I smile at her and then watch her closely as she smiles back in my direction. It occurs to me that there's nothing much wrong with my exotic nurse that a slash of red lipstick and some make-up couldn't fix. And then I wonder, perhaps she *does* have an interest in flowers? Perhaps we can talk about them, and this would give us something in common. And I could share with her my only fear in this regard, which is to do with how secretive they are, for flowers grow so slowly that you never quite know what they're going to turn into. There's no talking to them about this, for they're quite cunning. The nurse puts her book face down so she'll know what page she's on, and then she walks out of the shade towards me. She continues to smile. The nurse is trying too hard to be happy. She asks me a question, but I say nothing in reply. I simply look at my nurse. I've no desire to keep her here against her will. If she wants to leave, then she's free to do so. Really.

Dr Williams has come to visit me. They have a tendency to call him when things are difficult, but it must be very annoying for him because it's not as if he doesn't have anything else to do. He's a very busy man. He's looking at some papers and occasionally glancing up at me, but that's about it. He isn't saying anything. I hear my stomach rumble. I'm hungry, but I hate the dinners because everything in this place is so childish. First, we all have to gather in the dining room, which is also the place where you have to meet for announcements and group activities such as jewellery-making, modelling clay, and art. Sometimes they don't even bother to clear up the activities things, and they just shove them to one side of the room. Then three orderlies roll metal trolleys of food into the room and you pick up a tray, then squeeze into a space on a bench and plonk the tray on the table top. There are two tables, with long benches on either side. We have to sit and eat off the trays, looking at each other and deciding whether or not we have anything to say to the person opposite who's watching us gulp our food. There is a colour television set in this room, but during dinner half the residents want it on and half want it off. Eventually the nurses made a decision to keep it off, but when dinner's over they turn it on whether anybody's watching or not. At least until midnight, when it has to be shut down for good. That's their idea of how to do things.

Dr Williams stops looking at his papers and he glances up

at me, then back to the papers, and now he looks at me again. He pushes the papers away and brings his elbows up and onto the table. ('So, Dorothy, tell me how things are?') I stare at him, but it's difficult to know where to begin. I feel as though I'm wasting his time, but I've got to say something. I think about telling him that there's a room near here where some of them play table tennis. I pass this games room on the way to my own room, but it's far too bright to go into it. They have those long neon lights hanging from the ceiling. There's always a nurse in there, just sitting and watching in case things get a little out of hand. But hardly anyone plays table tennis, except two young girls who look so sedated that it's a wonder they can lift the bats. They're thin, and they must have that eating disease. If you ask me it's a bit of a waste of time having the nurse there. She could be far better deployed in some other part of this place. Or answering the question, where are all the men? There are a couple of men who shuffle around with their trousers half-hanging off, and a younger man who dresses nicely, apart from some stains on his blue polo-neck jumper. They look like food stains. I suppose men drink their problems away in the pub. Or hit people. Maybe Dr Williams knows why there are so few men in this place. I think about asking him, but instead I begin to laugh at the absurdity of it all.

He says nothing, and he looks at me as though whatever it is that he's going to say will be difficult for us both. ('You don't appear to be getting any better, Dorothy.') But he doesn't understand, there are good days and there are bad days. I thought today was a good day, but apparently today was a bad day, which is why they called him out. But I *am* happy. However, I just don't have the time for this. I'm sorry, but this is a waste of my time. ('Don't you want to return home?') I mean, it's not that I'm not grateful for everything that these people have done for me, but there are things to be done. When I look back at my life, only now do I realise that I've thrown away hundreds of days thinking that I could always reclaim them. But, sadly, I now know that this is not the case. There are things to be done. Solomon must have some family. I mean, how would you like it if your son or brother went abroad and you never heard from him again? They'll be living in pain for ever, unless I go and help them. They'll want to know that the three murderers are locked up in prison, and that apparently Carla and her mother decided that it was best to leave Weston and settle somewhere in the Midlands. Telling them all the facts is the decent thing to do. It's compassionate. It gives them a chance to heal. ('You'll still have to be monitored, but these days there are many care-in-the-community programmes.') But it hasn't sunk in with this man, has it? I look at him, but I don't want to argue. In the past I've felt let down by him, but as time's gone by I've grown to understand my specialist, probably better than he thinks. He stands up and I look at him, all neat and tidy. Now that he takes care of himself he reminds me of Solomon. He didn't used to, but being over forty I can see that he's finally made the decision to fight back. ('Get some sleep, Dorothy. I'll stop by and see you later in the week.') He's not a bad man. When he goes I know what will happen. I understand the routine. They'll take me back to my room and give me tablets with some hot milk in the hope that I'll sleep properly. But I won't sleep.

I don't like visitors. Last night, after Dr Williams left, they decided to skip the tablets and the hot milk and they put me to sleep with a needle. Now the nurse tells me that I have another visitor, but she won't tell me who it is. I'm still in bed, ensnared in a single twist of cotton sheeting. I slept, perhaps too much. Because of this they make a special exception and offer to help me get myself right. I sit up in bed while the nurse tries to make me look respectable. I remind her that these days I prefer to wear my hair up in a bun, and so she helps me with this. I no longer have to use make-up to cover up the bumps and bruises from where the gypsy woman hit me, for it's all mended. I'm as ready as I'm going to be, and then I see him. An older, even tubbier, Brian, clutching a bunch of red flowers. His shoes are unpolished. I thought he'd have a bit tucked away by now, but apparently not. He doesn't know what to do, whether to come to the bed and lean over and kiss me, or remain standing or what. The nurse eventually leads him in the direction of the plastic chair by the side of the bed, and he takes a seat. And then he begins to talk, as if he's frightened to stop talking. The nurse sits on a chair by the door and buries herself in her book. He tells me that his wife, Barbara, has left him and that he's back in Birmingham and running a bed and breakfast. He tells me that computer technology has overtaken him so he couldn't get back into banking, but he doesn't mind. He's quite happy. It turned out that Spain wasn't everything he'd hoped it would be. I can see him looking at me as he continues to jabber on like a crazy man. He's shocked, that much is clear. And I don't blame him. I suppose somebody must have called him out of the blue and told him that his ex-wife was convalescing in a home, and he probably thought it's nothing to do with me any more, and he's right. But he came anyway. I look at shabby Brian, and I try to turn him back into that slim, impressive posh boy that I met at university, but he no longer fits. However, I'm sure that I don't fit with whatever it was that he saw when he first met me at university. What were we thinking of? I'm sure that love has never stirred any kind of disorder in poor Brian's lumpish heart. I look away, but I can feel his eyes upon me, as though he feels sorry for me, but it's pathetic. I feel sorry for him.

He clears his throat and so I turn back ready to hear whatever else he's got to say for himself. He should have shaved. There's nothing more unattractive than stubble on a man who's gone grey. It really brings it home to you that they're at that stage where they can't look after themselves. That's something that's just around the corner for both Mahmood and a certain Mr Geoff Waverley. Brian smiles at me. It's long been over with him. He's well past his sell-by date. I can't help it, but I have to laugh. The nurse looks over at me, but I make eye contact with her so she knows that everything is fine. Reluctantly she returns to her book. He reaches out an arm towards me as though he wants to touch me. No fear! I pull back, and I can see it in his eyes. He doesn't understand. Why don't I want his grubby hand on me? Why am I laughing? I stop laughing. He's got to go now. I mean, this is embarrassing. I stare at him, which clearly makes him even more uncomfortable. He forces a smile, but he has no idea how unappealing this is. The nurse puts down her book, and I notice her fold over the corner of the page to mark her spot before she closes it shut. I hate it when people do this. They could easily get a bookmark, or a piece of paper or something. Why damage the book in this way? It shows no respect for the book. I want to tell all of this to her. Perhaps I will, but not now. ('Dorothy.') I turn and look at him. He's still smiling. He only said my name to get my attention. Flowers don't speak. That's one of the things I like about them. You can sit quietly with them and they don't have to have your attention. ('Dorothy.') Again he stops. If he thinks I'm going to help him out, then he's very much mistaken. I've nothing to say to him, especially if he wants to sound like a broken record. Dad always used to say that in the end it didn't matter what somebody had in terms of money or qualifications. What mattered was manners, and how you respected other people. I mean, after all, without manners we're no better than animals. In fact, I saw a television programme once about gorillas. It seems to me that some animals have got far better manners than us, and that's a fact. He should go now. I shouldn't have to tell him this, or make a fuss in any way, but he's leaving me no choice. I'm here because my nerves are bad and they've collapsed. I'll admit it. I'm not ashamed to admit it because this kind of thing happens to a lot of people, including many famous people. And they recover, so it's not as if there's something unusual about it, or there's no cure for it. It's fine, and it will soon just go away and I can get back to normal. That's what I'm doing. Convalescing. I let Sheila down. I know this now. I was a coward. But right now I just need to be protected, the doctor told me this. I need to feel as though somebody is looking after me until I get my strength back. And sometimes I can't cope with everything. I'll admit that too. But I'm not stupid, so why is this man treating me like a fool and repeating my name? He should go now. I don't like visitors and I don't want any more. Why don't they ever listen? I see the book slide from her lap, and I watch her start to run towards me. And now she's holding her hand over my mouth telling me to be quiet. I begin to struggle because I don't like the way she's holding me. I can hear her shouting for help. She's telling Brian to go and he stands up and begins to back away. As he back-pedals I tumble out of the bed. The nurse is on top of me now. I can see the flowers that Brian brought for me. The red ones are the angry ones. I know that now. They are the only ones that I can see. I can see this man's feet in his ugly unpolished shoes. He's walking backwards, and I can see red flowers.

I like to lie on my bed and stare at the ceiling. Particularly at night. Of course, days in this place never really begin. There's no routine. There's nothing that you have to do, except take your tablets and your hot milk and behave. A piano would help. Especially now that the years of discord between the keys has been resolved, and I'm once more able to make them speak easily to each other. I'm lucky because the patterns of music that Sheila helped me to discover remain firmly stitched together, as I knew they would. But there's no piano. There's no routine. The unit, as they like to call it when they're being official, is supposed to be a place that's different from out there. A retreat. Somewhere where you can lick your wounds and gather some strength before going back to the world. A place where you can learn to remember, and therefore understand your life. But what use is that now? They say they're protecting us. In here, time doesn't matter. At night they allow me to leave the curtains open and I watch the shadows of the trees making strange shapes against my wall. I know that this is not Weston. Or Stoneleigh. There is no viaduct in the distance. My heart remains a desert, but I tried. I had a feeling that Solomon understood me. This is not my home, and until they accept this, then I will be as purposefully silent as a bird in flight. Sometime before dawn, as light begins to bleed slowly through the night sky, I will ease myself out of this bed and proceed to put on my day face.